All
Fall
Down

Center Point
Large Print

Also by Jennifer Weiner and available from Center Point Large Print:

Fly Away Home
Then Came You
Next Best Thing

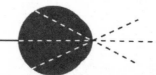

**This Large Print Book carries the
Seal of Approval of N.A.V.H.**

All Fall Down

JENNIFER WEINER

CENTER POINT LARGE PRINT
THORNDIKE, MAINE

This Center Point Large Print edition is published
in the year 2014 by arrangement with Atria Books,
a division of Simon & Schuster, Inc.

The text of this Large Print edition is unabridged.
In other aspects, this book may vary from the original edition.
Printed in the United States of America on permanent paper.
Set in 16-point Times New Roman type.

ISBN: 978-1-62899-100-0

Library of Congress Cataloging-in-Publication Data

Weiner, Jennifer.
All fall down / Jennifer Weiner.
pages ; cm
Summary: "The story of a woman's slide into addiction and struggle to
find her way back up again"—Provided by publisher.
ISBN 978-1-62899-100-0 (library binding : alk. paper)
1. Women drug addicts—Rehabilitation—Fiction.
    2. Self-realization in women—Fiction. 3. Large type books.
    4. Domestic fiction. I. Title.
PS3573.E3935A78 2014b
813´.6—dc23
                                                    2014019453

For my readers . . .
who have come with me this far

Vera said: "Why do you feel you have to turn everything into a story?" So I told her why:

Because if I tell the story, I control the version.

Because if I tell the story, I can make you laugh, and I would rather have you laugh at me than feel sorry for me.

Because if I tell the story, it doesn't hurt as much.

Because if I tell the story, I can get on with it.

—FROM *HEARTBURN* BY NORA EPHRON

PART ONE

Down the Rabbit Hole

One

Do you generally use alcohol or drugs more than once a week?

I hesitated with my hand over the page. I'd picked up the magazine to read the "How to Dress Right for Your Shape" story advertised on the cover, but it had opened to a quiz that asked "Has Your Drinking or Drug Use Become a Problem?" and something had made me stop. Maybe it was the black-and-white photograph of a woman in profile, bending sadly over her wineglass, or maybe the statistic beside it that said that prescription painkiller overdose was now the leading cause of accidental death of women in America, surpassing even car crashes. I had a pen in my hand—I'd been using it to fill out the stack of forms for Eloise's five-year-old well-child checkup—and, almost without thinking, I made an X in the box for "Yes."

I crossed my legs and looked around Dr. McCarthy's waiting area, suddenly worried that someone had seen what I'd written. Of course, no one was paying any attention to my little corner of the couch. Sleet ticked at the panes of the oversized windows; a radiator clunked in the corner. The lamplit room, on the third floor of an office building at the corner of Ninth and

Chestnut, with a volunteer in a striped pinny at a knee-high table reading *Amelia Bedelia* to kids sitting in miniature chairs, felt cozy, a respite from the miserable winter weather. Three years ago my husband, Dave, my daughter, and I had moved out of Center City and into a house in Haverford that I refused to call a McMansion, even though that's exactly what it was, but I loved Ellie's pediatrician so much that I'd never even tried to find a suburban replacement. So here we were, more than half a year late for Ellie's checkup, in the office where I'd been taking her since she was just a week old. We'd parked in the lot on Ninth Street and trekked through the February slush to get here, Ellie stepping delicately over the piles of crusted, dirty snow and the ankle-deep, icy puddles at the corners, complaining that her feet were getting wet and her socks were getting splashy. I'd lured her on with the promise of a treat at Federal Donuts when her checkup was over.

Ellie tugged at my sleeve. "How much longer?"

"Honey, I really can't say. The doctors need to take care of the sick kids first, and you, Miss Lucky, are not sick."

She stuck out her lower lip in a cartoonish pout. "It isn't FAIR. We made an APPOINTMENT."

"True. But remember when you had that bad sore throat? Dr. McCarthy saw you right away. Even before the kids who had appointments."

She narrowed her eyes and nibbled at her lip before dropping her voice to a stage whisper that was slightly more hushed than your average yell. "I am having an idea. Maybe we could tell the nurse lady that I have a sore throat now!"

I shook my head. "Nah, we don't lie. Bad karma."

Ellie considered this. "I hate karmel." She smoothed her skirt and wandered off toward the toy basket. I recrossed my legs and checked out the crowd.

The room was predictably full. There were first-time mothers from Queen Village and Society Hill, who wore their babies wrapped in yards of organic cotton hand-dyed and woven by indigenous Peruvian craftswomen who were paid a living wage. The moms from the Section 8 housing pushed secondhand strollers and fed their infants from plastic bottles, as opposed to ostentatiously breast-feeding or slipping the baby a few ounces of organic formula in a BPA-free bottle with a silicone-free nipple hidden under a prettily patterned, adorably named nursing cover-up (I'd worn one called the Hooter Hider).

On the days when you use drugs or alcohol, do you usually have three drinks/doses or more?

Define "dose." One Percocet, from the bottle I got after I had my wisdom teeth pulled? Two Vicodin, prescribed for a herniated disc I suffered in a step class at the gym? I'd never taken more than two of anything, except the day after my father had been diagnosed with Alzheimer's and my mother had set up a temporary fortress in our guest room. Could three pills count as a single dose? I decided not to answer.

Do you use drugs or alcohol to "unwind" or "relax"?

Hello. That's what they're there for. And was that so bad, really? How many times had I heard my husband say "I need to go for a run," or my best friend, Janet, say "I need a glass of wine"? What I did was no different. It was, actually, better. A run was time-consuming and sweaty and hard on the joints, and wine could stain.

"Mommy?"

"Hang on, sweetie," I said, as my iPhone rang in my purse. "Just one minute."

"You ALWAYS say that. You ALWAYS say just one minute and it ALWAYS takes you for HOURS."

"Shh," I whispered, before hurrying toward the door, where I could keep an eye on her while I talked. "Hi, Sarah."

"Allison," said Sarah, in the gruff, all-business tone that surprised people, given her petite frame, sleek black bob, and freckled button nose. "Did the fact-checker call?"

"Not today." The *Wall Street Journal* was in the midst of its every-six-months rediscovery that women were online. They were doing a piece on women who blog, and Ladiesroom.com, the website that I wrote for and Sarah ran, was to be featured. I was alternately giddy at the thought of how the publicity would raise Ladiesroom's profile and nauseous at the notion of my picture in print.

"She just read my quotes back to me," said Sarah. "They sounded great. I've really got a good feeling about this!"

"Me too," I lied. I was optimistic about the piece . . . at least some of the time.

"Mom-MEE."

My daughter was standing about six inches from my face, brown eyes brimming, lower lip quivering. "Gotta go," I told Sarah. "We're at the doctor's."

"Oh, God. Is everything okay?"

"As okay as it ever is!" I said, striving to inject good cheer into my tone before I slipped the phone back into my purse. Sarah, technically my boss, was twenty-seven and childless. She knew I was a mother—that was, after all, why she'd hired me, to give readers live, from-the-trenches reports on married-with-children life. But I tried to be a model employee, always available to talk through edits or help brainstorm a headline, even if Ellie was with me. I also tried to be a model mother, making Ellie feel like she was the center of my universe, that I was entirely present for her, even when I was on the phone, debating, say, the use of "strident" versus "emphatic," or arguing about

15

which picture of Hillary Clinton to use to illustrate another will-she-or-won't-she-run story. It was a lot of juggling and quick switching and keeping my smile in place. "Sorry, honey. What do you need?"

"I'm FIRSTY," she said, in the same tone of voice an old-school Broadway actress might use to announce her imminent demise.

I pointed at the water fountain on the other side of the room. "Look, there's a water fountain!"

"But that is where the SICK kids are." A tear rolled down my daughter's pillowy cheek.

"Ellie. Don't be such a drama queen. Just go get a drink. You'll be fine."

"Can I check what is in your purse?" she wheedled. Before I could answer, she'd plunged both hands into my bag and deftly removed my bottle of Vitaminwater.

"Ellie, that's—" Before I got the word "Mommy's" out of my mouth, she'd twisted off the cap and started gulping.

Our eyes met. Mine were undoubtedly beseeching, hers sparkled with mischief and satisfaction. I considered my options. I could punish her, tell her no screens and no *SpongeBob* tonight, then endure—and force everyone else in the room to endure—the inevitable screaming meltdown. I could ignore what she'd done, reinforcing the notion that bad behavior got her exactly what she wanted. I could take her outside and talk to her there, but then the receptionist would, of course, call us when we were in the hall, which meant I'd get the pleasure of a tantrum on top of another half-hour wait.

"We will discuss this in the car. Do you understand me?" I maintained the steady eye contact that the latest parenting book I'd read had recommended, my body language and tone letting her know that I was in charge, and hoped the other mothers weren't taking in this scene and laughing. Ellie took another defiant swig, then let a mouthful of zero-calorie lemon-flavored drink dribble back into the bottle, which she handed back to me.

"Ellie! Backwash!"

She giggled. "Here, Mommy, you can have the rest," she said, and skipped across the waiting room with my iPhone flashing in her hand. Lately she'd become addicted to a game called Style Queen, the object of which was to earn points to purchase accessories and makeup for a cartoon avatar who was all long hair and high heels. The more accessories you won for your avatar—shoes, hats, scarves, a makeup kit—the more levels of the game you could access. With each level, Ellie had explained to me, with many heaved sighs and eye rolls, you could get a new boyfriend.

"What about jobs?" I had asked. "Does Style Queen work? To get money for all that makeup, and her skirts and everything?"

17

Ellie frowned, then raised her chubby thumb and two fingers. "She can be an actress or a model or a singer." Before I could ask follow-up questions, or try to use this as a teachable moment in which I would emphasize the importance of education and hard work and remind her that the way you looked was never ever the most important thing about you, my daughter had dashed off, leaving me to contemplate how we'd gone from *The Feminine Mystique* and *Free to Be . . . You and Me* to this in just one generation.

The magazine was still open to the quiz on the couch beside me. I grabbed it, bending my head to avoid the scrutiny of the übermommy two seats down whose adorable newborn was cradled against her body in a pristine Moby Wrap; the one who was not wearing linty black leggings from Target and whose eyebrows had enjoyed the recent attention of tweezers.

Do you sometimes take more than the amount prescribed? Yes. Not always, but sometimes. I'd take one pill and then, ten or fifteen or twenty minutes later, if I wasn't feeling the lift, the slow unwinding of the tight girdle of muscles around my neck and shoulders I'd expected, I'd take another.

Have you gotten intoxicated on alcohol or drugs more than two times in the past year? (You're intoxicated if you use so much that you can't function safely or normally or if other people think that you can't function safely or normally.)

This was a tricky one. With painkillers, you did not slur or get sloppy. Your child would not come home from school and find Mommy passed out in a puddle of her own vomit (or anyone else's). A couple of Vicodin and I could function just fine. The worst things that had happened were the few times Dave had accused me of being out of it. "Are you okay?" he'd ask, squinting at my face like we'd just met, or apologizing for being so boring that I couldn't muster five minutes of attention to hear about his day as a City Hall reporter at the *Philadelphia Examiner.* Never mind that his anecdotes tended to be long and specific and depend on the listener's deep interest in the inner workings of Philadelphia's government. Some days, I had that interest. Other days, all I wanted was peace, quiet, and an episode of *Love It or List It.* But I'd been occasionally bored and disinterested even before my use of Vicodin and Percocet had ramped up, over the past two years, from a once-in-a-while thing to a few-days-a-week thing to a more-days-than-not thing. It wasn't as if one single catastrophe had turned me into a daily pill popper as much as the accumulated stress of a mostly successful, extremely busy life. Ellie had been born, then I'd quit my job, then we'd moved to the suburbs, leaving my neighborhood and friends behind, and then my dad had been diagnosed. Not one thing, but dozens of them, piling up against one another until the pills became less a luxury than a necessity for getting myself through the day and falling asleep at night.

I checked "No" as Ellie skipped back over. "Mommy, is it almost our turn? This is taking for HOURS."

I reached into my purse. "You can watch *Les Miz*," I said. She handed me the phone and had the iPad out of my hands before I could blink.

"That's so cute," said the mother who'd just joined me on the couch. "She watches musicals? God, my two, if it's not animated, forget it."

I let myself bask in the all-too-rare praise: Ellie's passion for Broadway musicals was one of the things I loved best about her, because I loved musicals, too. When she was little, and tormented by colic and eczema, and she hardly ever slept, I would drive around in my little blue Honda, with Ellie strapped into her car seat and cast recordings from *Guys and Dolls* and *Rent* and *West Side Story* and *Urinetown* playing. "Ocher!" she'd yelled from the backseat when she was about two years old. "I WANT THE OCHER!" It had taken me ten minutes to figure out that she was trying to say "overture," and I'd told the story for years. *Isn't she funny. Isn't she precocious. Isn't she sweet,* people would say . . . until Ellie turned four, then five, and she was funny and precocious and sweet but also increasingly temperamental, as moody as a diva with killer PMS. *Sensitive* was what Dr. McCarthy told us.

Extremely sensitive, said Dr. Singh, the therapist we'd taken her to visit after her preschool teacher reported that Ellie spent recess sitting in a corner of the playground with her fingers plugged into her ears, clearly pained by the shouts and clatter of her classmates. "Too loud!" she'd protest, wincing as we got close to a playground. "Too messy!" she'd whine when I'd try to lure her outdoors, into a game of catch or hide-and-seek, or ply her with finger paints and fresh pads of paper. Movies "made too much noise," sunshine was "too bright," foods that were not apples, string cheese, or plain white bread, toasted and buttered and minus its crust, were rejected for "tasting angry," and glue and glitter gave her "itchy fingers." For Eloise Larson Weiss, the world was a painful, scary, sticky place where the volume was always turned up to eleven. Dave and I had read all the books, from *The Highly Sensitive Child* to *Raising Your Spirited Child.* We'd learned about how to avoid overstimulation, how to help Ellie through transitions, how to talk to her teachers about making accommodations for her. We'd done our best to reframe our thinking, to recognize that Ellie was suffering and not just making trouble, but it was hard. Instead of remembering that Ellie was wired differently than other kids, that she cried and threw tantrums because she was uncomfortable or anxious or stressed, I sometimes found myself thinking of her as just bratty, or going out of her way to be difficult.

The woman beside me nodded at her son, who seemed to be about eight. He had a Band-Aid on his forehead, and he was making loud rumbling noises as he hunched over a handheld video game. "A little girl would have been so nice. I've got to bribe Braden to get him in the tub."

"Oh, that's not just a boy thing. Ellie won't go near a tub unless it's got one of those bath bombs. Which are eight bucks a pop."

The woman pursed her lips. I felt my face heat up. Eight-dollar bath bombs were an indulgence for a grown-up. For a five-year-old, they were ridiculous, especially given that our mortgage payments in Haverford were so much higher than they'd been in Philadelphia, and that instead of a raise last year, Dave and everyone else at the *Examiner* had gotten a two-week unpaid furlough. When we'd filed our taxes the year before, we'd both been surprised—and, in Dave's case, morti-fied—to learn that I was earning more with my blog than he was as a reporter. This, of course, had not been part of our plan. Dave was supposed to be the successful one . . . and, up until recently, he had been.

Three years ago, Dave had written a series about inner-city poverty, about kids who got their only balanced meals at school and parents who found it less expensive to stay at home, on welfare, than to look for work; about social services stretched too thin and heroic teachers and volunteers trying to turn kids' lives around. The series had won prizes and the attention of a few literary agents, one of whom had gotten him a book deal and a hefty advance. Dave had taken the chunk of money he'd received when he'd signed the contract and driven off to Haverford, a town he'd fallen in love with when the newspaper's food critic had taken him there one night for dinner. Haverford was lovely, with leafy trees and manicured lawns. The schools were excellent, the commute was reasonable, and it all fit into my husband's vision of what our lives would one day be.

Unfortunately, Dave didn't discuss this vision with me until one giddy afternoon when he'd hired a Realtor, found a house, and made an offer. Then, and only then, did he usher me to the car and drive me out past the airport, off the highway, and into the center of town. The sun had been setting, gilding the trees and rooftops, and the crisp autumnal air was full of the sounds of children playing a rowdy game of tag. When he pulled up in front of a Colonial-style house with a for sale sign on the lawn, I could hear the voices of children playing in the cul-de-sac, and smell barbecuing steaks. "You'll love it," he'd said, racing me through the kitchen (gleaming, all stainless steel appliances, granite countertops, and tile floors), past the mudroom and the powder room, up the stairs to the master bedroom. There we had kissed and kissed until the Realtor cleared his throat twice, then knocked on the door and told us we needed to respond to the seller's offer within the hour.

"Yes?" Dave asked. His eyes were shining; his whole face was lit up. I'd never seen him so boyish, or so happy, and it would have been heartless to tell him anything except what he wanted to hear.

"Yes."

I hadn't thought it through. There wasn't time. I didn't realize that I was signing up not just for a new house and a new town but, really, for an entirely new life, one where, with Dave's encouragement, I'd be home with a baby instead of joining him on the train every morning, heading into the city to work. Dave wanted me to be more like his own mother, who'd gladly given up her career as a lawyer when the first of her three boys was born, swapping briefs and depositions for carpools and class-mom duties. He wanted a traditional stay-at-home mother, a wife who'd do the shopping and the cooking, who'd be available to sign for packages and pick up the dry cleaning and, generally, make his life not only possible but easy. The problem was, he'd never told me what he wanted, which meant I never got to think about whether it was what I wanted, too.

Maybe it would have worked if the world hadn't decided it had no great use for newspapers . . . or if the blog I wrote as a hobby hadn't become a job, turning our financial arrangement on its head, so that I became the primary breadwinner and Dave's salary ended up going for extras like private school and vacations and summer camp. Maybe our lives would have gone more smoothly if I hadn't found the house so big, so daunting, if it didn't carry, at least to my nose, the whiff of bad luck. "The sellers are very motivated," our agent told me, and Dave and I quickly figured out why: the husband, a political consultant, had been arrested for embezzling campaign contributions, which he used to fund his gambling habit . . . and, *Examiner* readers eventually learned, his mistress.

Dave and I had both grown up in decent-sized places in the suburbs, but the Haverford house had rooms upon rooms, some of which seemed to have no discernible function. There was a kitchen, and then beside it a smaller, second kitchen, with a sink and a granite island, that the Realtor ID'd as a butler's pantry. "We don't have a butler," I told Dave. "And if we did, I wouldn't give him his own pantry!" The main kitchen was big enough to eat in, with a dining room adjoining it, plus a living room, a den, and a home office with floor-to-ceiling bookshelves. Upstairs there were no fewer than five bedrooms and five full bathrooms. There was the master suite, and something called a "princess suite" that came with its own dressing room. The basement was partially finished, with space for a home gym, and out back a screened-in porch overlooked the gentle slope of the lawn.

"Can we afford this?" I'd asked. It turned out, between Dave's advance and the embezzler's desperation, that we could. We could buy it, but we couldn't fill it. Every piece of furniture we owned, including the folding card table I'd used as a desk and the futon from Dave's college dorm, barely filled a quarter of the space, and it all looked wrong. The table that had fit perfectly in our Philadelphia row house was dwarfed by the soaring ceilings and spaciousness of the Haverford dining room. The love seat where we'd snuggled in Center City became dollhouse-sized in the burbs. Our queen-sized bed looked like a crouton floating in a giant bowl of soup in the master bedroom, and our combined wardrobes barely filled a third of the shelves and hanging space in the spacious walk-in closet.

Overwhelmed, out of a job, and with a baby to care for, I'd wander the rooms, making lists of what we needed. I'd buy stacks of magazines, clip pictures, or browse Pinterest, making boards of sofas I loved, dining-room tables I thought could work, pretty wallpaper, and gorgeous rugs. I would go to the paint store and come home with strips of colors; I'd download computer programs that let me move furniture around imaginary rooms. But when it came time to actually buy something—the dining-room table we obviously needed, beds for the empty guest rooms, towels to stock the shelves in the guest bathrooms—I would go into vapor lock. I'd never considered myself indecisive or suffered from fear of commitment, but somehow the thought *That bed you are buying will be your bed for the rest of your life* would make me hang up the phone or close the laptop before I could even get the first digits of my card number out.

Four months after Dave had signed his advance, another book came out, this one based on a series that had run in one of the New York City papers, about a homeless little girl and the constellation of grown-ups—parents, teachers, caseworkers, politicians—who touched her life. The series had gotten over a million clicks, but the book failed to attract more than a thousand readers its first month on sale. Dave's publisher had gotten nervous—if a book about the poor in New York City didn't sell, what were the prospects for a book about the poor in Philadelphia? They'd exercised their option to kill the contract. Dave didn't have to give back the money they'd paid him on signing, but there would be no more cash forthcoming. His agent had tried but had been unable to get another publisher to pick up the project. Poverty just wasn't sexy. Not with so many readers struggling to manage their own finances and hang on to their own jobs.

Dave's agent had encouraged him to capitalize on the momentum and come up with another idea—"They all love your voice!" she'd said—but, so far, Dave was holding on to the notion that he could find a way to get paid for the writing he'd already done, instead of having to start all over again. So he'd stayed at the paper, and when Sarah had approached me about publishing my blog on her website, saying yes was the obvious choice. Once I started working, I had no more time to fuss with furniture. Just finding clean clothes in the morning and something for us all to eat at night was challenge enough. So the house stayed empty, unfinished, with wires sticking out from walls because I hadn't picked lighting fixtures, and three empty bedrooms with their walls painted an unassuming beige. In the absence of dressers and armoires, we kept our clothes in laundry baskets and Tupperware bins, and, in addition to the couch and the love seat, there were folding canvas camp chairs in the living room, a temporary measure that had now lasted more than two years—about as long as Dave's bad mood.

I remembered the sulk that had followed the *Examiner*'s edict that every story run online with a button next to the byline so that readers could "Like" the reporter on Facebook.

"It's not even asking them to like the stories," he'd complained. "It's asking them to like me." He hadn't even smiled when I'd said, "Well, I like you," and embraced him, sliding my hands from his shoulder blades down to the small of his back, then cupping his bottom and kissing his cheek. Ellie was engrossed in an episode of *Yo Gabba Gabba!*; the chicken had another thirty minutes in the oven. "Want to take a shower?" I'd whispered. Two years ago, he'd have had my clothes off and the water on in under a minute. That night, he'd just sighed and asked, "Do you have any idea how degrading it is to be treated like a product?"

It wasn't as though I couldn't sympathize. I'd worked at the *Examiner* myself, as a web designer, before Ellie was born. I believed in newspapers' mission, the importance of their role as a watchdog, holding the powerful accountable, comforting the afflicted and afflicting the comfortable. But it wasn't my fault that newspapers in general and the *Examiner* in particular were failing. I hadn't changed the world so that everything was available online immediately if not sooner, and not even our grandparents waited for the morning paper to tell them what was what. I hadn't rearranged things so that "if it bleeds, it leads" had become almost quaint. These days, the *Examiner*'s home page featured photographs of the Hot Singles Mingle party that desperate editors had thrown, or of the Critical Mass Naked Nine, where participants had biked, nude, down ten miles of Broad Street (coverage of that event, with the pictures artfully blurred, had become the most-read story of the year, easily topping coverage both of the election and of the corrupt city councilman who'd been arrested for tax fraud after a six-hour standoff that ended after he'd climbed to the top of City Hall and threatened to jump unless he was provided with a plane, a million dollars in unmarked bills, and two dozen cannoli from Potito's). "A 'Like' button is not the end of the world," I'd said, after it became clear that a sexy shower was not in my future. Then I'd gone back to my iPad, and he'd gone back to watching the game . . . except when I looked up I found him scowling at me as if I'd just tossed my device at his head.

"What?" I asked, startled.

"Nothing," he said. Then he jumped up from the sofa, rolled his shoulders, shook out his arms, and cracked a few knuckles, loudly, like he was getting ready to enter a boxing ring. "It's nothing."

I'd tried to talk to him about what was wrong, hoping he'd realize that, as the one who'd gotten us into this mess—or at least this big house, this big life, with the snooty private-school parents and the shocking property-tax bills—he had an obligation to help figure out how we were going to make it work. Over breakfast the week after the "Like" button rant, while Ellie dawdled at the sink, washing and rewashing her hands until every trace of syrup was gone, I'd quietly suggested couples therapy, telling him that lots of my friends were going (lie, but I did know at least one couple who had gone), and adding that the combined stress of a new town, a sensitive child, and a wife who'd gone from working twenty hours a week to what was supposed to be forty but was closer to sixty would put any couple on edge. His lip had curled. "You think I'm crazy?"

"Of course you're not crazy," I'd whispered back. "But it's been crazy for both of us, and I just think . . ."

He got up from the table and stood there for a moment in his blue nylon running shorts and a T-shirt from a 10K he'd completed last fall. Dave was tall, broad-shouldered, and slim-hipped, with thick black hair, deep-set brown eyes, and a receding hairline he disguised by wearing baseball caps whenever he could. When we'd first started dating we would walk holding hands, and I'd try to catch glimpses of the two of us reflected in windows or bus-shelter glass, knowing how good we looked together. Dave was quiet, brooding, with a kind of stillness that made me want nothing more than to hear him laugh, and a goofy sense of humor you'd never guess he had just by looking at him. *Still waters run deep,* I'd thought. Later, I learned that silence did not necessarily guarantee depth. If you interrupted my husband in the middle of one of his quiet times, asked him what he was thinking about, and got him to tell you, some of the time the answer would concern the latest scandal at City Hall, or his attempts to confirm rumors about a congressional aide who'd forged his boss's signature. Other times, the answer would involve his ongoing attempt to rank his five favorite 76ers.

Still, there was no one I wanted to be with more than Dave. He knew me better than anyone, knew what kind of movies I liked, my favorite dishes at my favorite restaurants, how my mood could instantly be improved by the presence of a Le Bus brownie or a rerun of *Face/Off* on cable. Dave would talk me into jogging, knowing how good I'd feel when I was done, or he'd take Ellie out for doughnuts on a Saturday morning, letting me sleep until ten after a late night working.

He could be considerate, loving, and sweet. The morning I suggested therapy, he was none of those things. He went stalking down to the basement without a word of farewell. A minute later, the treadmill whirred to life. Dave was training for his first marathon, a goal I'd encouraged before I realized that the long runs each weekend meant I wouldn't see him for four or five hours at a time on a Saturday or Sunday, and would have the pleasure of Ellie all to myself. While the treadmill churned away in the basement, I got to my feet, sighing, as the weight of the day settled around my shoulders.

"Ellie," I said. Ellie was still standing at the sink, dreamily rubbing liquid soap into her hands. "You need to clear your plate and your glass."

"But they're too HEAVY! And the plate is all STICKY! And maybe it will DROP!" she complained, still in her Ariel nightgown, dragging her bare feet along the terra-cotta tiled floor until finally I snapped, "Ellie, just give me the plate and stop making such a production!"

Inevitably, she'd started to cry, dashing upstairs to her room, leaving soapy handprints along the banister. I loaded the dishwasher, wiped down the counters, and swept the kitchen floor. I put the milk and juice and butter back in the fridge and the flour and sugar back in the pantry. Then, before I went to Ellie to apologize and tell her that we should both try to use our inside voices, I'd taken a pill, my second Vicodin since I'd gotten up. The day had stretched endlessly before me—weepy daughter, angry husband, piles of laundry, messy bedroom, a blog post to write, and probably dozens of angry commenters lined up to tell me I was a no-talent hack and a fat, stupid whore. *I need this,* I thought, letting the bitterness dissolve on my tongue. It had been, I remembered, not even nine a.m.

Have you ever felt like you should cut down on your drinking or drug use?

Feeling suddenly queasy, I lifted my head and looked around the waiting room again to see if anyone had noticed that I was taking this quiz seriously. Did I think about cutting down? Sure. Sometimes. More and more often I had the nagging feeling that things were getting out of control. Then I'd think, *Oh, please.* I had prescriptions for everything I took (and if Doctor A didn't know what Doctor B was giving me, well, that wasn't necessarily a problem—if it was, pharmacies would be set up to flag it, right?). The pills helped me manage everything I needed to manage.

Have other people criticized your drinking or drug use, or been annoyed by it?

I checked "No," fast and emphatically, trying not to think about how nobody criticized my use because nobody knew about it. Dave knew I had a prescription for Vicodin—he'd been there the night I'd come hobbling home from the gym—but he had no idea how many times I'd gotten that prescription refilled, telling my doctor that I was doing my physical-therapy-prescribed exercises religiously (I wasn't), but that I still needed something for the pain. Dave didn't know how easy it was, if you were a woman with health insurance and an education, a woman who spoke and dressed and presented herself a certain way. Good manners and good grammar, in addition to

34

an MRI that showed bulging discs or an X-ray with impacted molars, could get you pretty much anything you wanted. With refills. Pain was impossible to see, hard to quantify, and I knew the words to use, the gestures to make, how to sit and stand as if every breath was agony. It was my little secret, and I intended to keep it that way.

"Eloise Weiss?" I looked up. A nurse stood in the doorway with Ellie's chart in his hands.

Startled, I half jumped to my feet, and felt my back give a warning twinge, as if to remind me how I'd gotten into this mess. I wanted a pill. I'd had only one, that morning, six hours ago, and I wanted something, a dam against the rising anxiety about whether my marriage was foundering and if I was a good parent and when I'd find the time to finish the blog post that was due at six o'clock. I wanted to feel good, centered and calm and happy, able to appreciate what I had—my sunny kitchen, with orchids blooming on the windowsill; Ellie's bedroom, for which I'd finally found the perfect pink chandelier. I wanted to slip into my medicated bubble, where I was safe, where I was happy, where nothing could hurt me. *As soon as this is over,* I told myself, and imagined sitting behind the wheel once the doctor had let us go and swallowing a white oval-shaped pill while Ellie fussed with her seat belt. With that picture firmly in mind, I reached out my hand for my daughter.

"No shots," she said, her lower lip already starting to tremble.

"I don't think so."

"No SHOTS! You SAID! You PROMISED!" Heads turned in judgment, mothers probably thinking, *Thank God mine's not like that.* Ellie crossed her arms over her chest and stood there, forty-three pounds of fury in a flowered Hanna Andersson dress, matching socks and cardigan, and zip-up leopard-print high-top sneakers. Her fine brown hair hung in braided pigtails, tied with purple elastic bands, and she had a stretchy flowered headband wrapped, hippie-style, around her forehead.

The nurse gave me a smile that was both sympathetic and weary, as I half walked, half dragged my daughter off to the scales and blood-pressure cuffs. Eloise whined and balked and winced as she was weighed and measured. The nurse took her blood pressure and temperature. Then the two of us were left to wait in an exam room. "Put this on," the nurse said, handing Ellie a cotton gown. Ellie pinched the gown between two fingertips. "It will ITCH," she said, and started to cry.

"Come on," I said, taking the gown, with its rough texture and offending tags, in my hand. "I bet if you just get your dress off, you'll be okay."

Still sniffling, Ellie bent gracefully at the waist—she'd gotten her ease in the physical world from her father, who ran and ice-skated and, unlike me, did not inhabit a universe where the furniture seemed to reposition itself just so I could trip over or bang into it. I watched as she eased each zipper on her high-tops down, slid her foot out of her right shoe, pulled off her pink sock, and laid it carefully on top of the sneaker. Off came the left shoe. Off came the left sock. I sat down in the plastic chair as Ellie moved on to her cardigan. I had never mistreated her while under the influence. I'd never yelled (well, not scary-yelling), or been rough, or told her that she needed to put on her goddamn clothes this century, because we couldn't be late for school again, because I couldn't sit through another lecture about Your Responsibilities to Stonefield: A Learning Community (calling it just a "school," I supposed, would have failed to justify its outrageous tuition). It was the opposite. The pills calmed me down. They gave me a sense of peace. When I swallowed them, I felt like I could accomplish anything, whether it was writing a post about the rising costs of fertility treatments or getting my daughter to school on time.

"Mom-MEE." I looked at Ellie. Glory be, she'd gotten all the way down to her Disney Princess underpants. I held open the gown. She made a face. "Just try it," I said. Finally, with the hauteur of a high-fashion model being forced to don polyester, she slipped her arms through the sleeves and permitted me to knot the ties in the back while she pinched the fabric between her fingertips, holding it ostentatiously away from her body, making sure the tag wouldn't touch her. She retrieved my iPad and cued up *Les Miz.* I went back to my quiz. *Have you ever used more than you could afford?* Hardly. My doctors would write me prescriptions. My copay was fifteen dollars a bottle. But it was true that the bottles were no longer lasting as long as they were supposed to, and I spent what was beginning to feel like a lot of time figuring out how many pills I had left and which doctor I hadn't called in a while and whether the pharmacist was looking at me strangely because I was picking up Vicodin two or three times a week.

Have you ever planned not to use that day but done it anyway?

Yes. I had thought about stopping. I had tried, a few times, and managed, for a few days . . . but during the last few not-today days, it was as if my brain and body had disconnected at some critical juncture. I'd be standing in my closet, in my T-shirt or the workout clothes I'd put on in the hope that wearing them would make me more inclined to exercise, thinking *No,* while watching my body from the outside, watching my hands uncap the bottle, watching my fingers select a pill.

Have you ever not been able to stop when you planned to?

"Mommy?" Ellie sat on the examining table, legs crossed, gown spread neatly in her lap. "Are you mad?" she asked. Her lower lip was quivering. She looked like she was on the verge of tears. Then again, Eloise frequently appeared to be on the verge of tears. When she was a baby, a slammed car door or the telephone ringing could jolt her out of her nap and into a full-fledged shrieking meltdown. In her stroller, she'd cringe at street noises; a telephone ringing, a taxi honking. Even the unexpected rustling of tree branches overhead could make her flinch.

"No, honey. Why?"

"Your face looks all scrunchy."

I made myself smile. I held out my arms and, after a moment's hesitation, Ellie hopped off the table and sat on my lap, folding her upper body against mine. I breathed in her little-girl smell— a bit like cotton candy, like graham crackers and library books—and pressed my cheek against her soft hair, thinking that even though she was high-strung and thin-skinned, Ellie was also smart and funny and undeniably lovely, and that I would do whatever I could to maximize her chances of being happy. I wouldn't be like my own mother, a circa 1978 party girl who hadn't realized that the party was over, a woman who'd slapped three coats of quick-drying lacquer over herself at twenty-six—teased hair, cat-eye black liquid liner, a slick, lipglossed pout, and splashes of Giorgio perfume—and gotten so involved in her tennis group, her morning walk buddies, her mah-jongg ladies, her husband and his health that she had little time for, or interest in, her only child. I knew my mother loved me—at least, she said so—but when I was a girl at the dinner table, or out in the driveway, where I'd amuse myself by hitting a tennis ball against the side of the garage, my mother would look up from her inspection of her fingernails or her *People* magazine and gaze at me as if I were a guest at a hotel who should have checked out weeks before and was somehow, inexplicably, still hanging around.

When I was almost eight years old, my parents asked me what I wanted for my birthday. I'd been thinking about it for weeks and I knew exactly how to answer. I wanted my mother, who was usually asleep when I left for school, to take me out to breakfast at Peterman's, the local diner that sat in the center of a traffic circle at the intersection of two busy highways in Cherry Hill. Everyone went there: it was where kids would get ice cream cones after school, where families would go for a dinner of charcoal-grilled burgers for Dad and dry tuna on iceberg lettuce for Mom and a platter of chicken wings, onion rings, and French fries with ranch and honey-mustard dipping sauces for the kids. One of my class-mates, Kelly Goldring, had breakfast there with her mother every Wednesday. "She calls it Girls'

Day," Kelly recounted at a Girl Scout meeting, taking care to roll her eyes to show how dopey she found the weekly breakfasts, but I could tell from her tone, and how she looked when she talked about splitting the Hungry Lady special with her mom and still having home fries left over to take in her lunch, that the breakfasts were just what Mrs. Goldring intended—special. I imagined Kelly and her mom in one of the booths for two. Mrs. Goldring would be in a dress and high heels, with a floppy silk bow tie around her neck, and Kelly, who usually wore jeans and a T-shirt, would wear a skirt that showed off her scabby knees. I pictured the waitress, hip cocked, pad in hand, asking "What can I get you gals?" As I imagined my own trip to the diner, my mother would order a fruit cup, and I'd get eggs and bacon. The eggs would be fluffy, the bacon would be crisp, and my mother, fortified by fruit and strong coffee, would ask about my teacher, my classes, and my Girl Scout troop and actually listen to my answers.

That was what I wanted: not a new bike or an Atari, not cassettes of Sting or Genesis, not *Trixie Belden* books. Just breakfast with my mom; the two of us, in a booth, alone for the forty-five minutes it would take us to eat the breakfast special.

I should have suspected that things wouldn't go the way I'd hoped when my mother came down to the kitchen the morning of my birthday looking wan with one eye made up and mascaraed, and the other pale and untouched. "Come on," she'd said, her Philadelphia accent thicker than normal, her voice raspy. Her hand trembled as she reached for her keys, and she winced when I opened the door to make sure the cab was waiting out front. I rarely saw my mom out of bed before nine, and I never saw her without her makeup completely applied. That morning her face was pale, and she seemed a little shaky, as if the sunshine on her skin was painful and the floor was rolling under-neath her feet.

This, I reasoned, had to do with the Accident, the one my mother had gotten into when I was four years old. I didn't know many details—only that she had been driving, that it had been raining, and that she'd hit a slick patch on the road and actually flipped the car over. She'd spent six weeks away, first in the hospital, having metal pins put into her shoulder, then in a rehab place. She still had scars—a faint slash on her left cheek, surgical incisions on her upper arm. Then there were what my father portentously referred to as "the scars you can't see." My mom had never driven since that night. She would jump at the sound of a slammed door or a car backfiring; she couldn't watch car chases or car crashes in the movies or on TV. A few times a month, she'd skip her tennis game and I'd come home from school to find her up in her bedroom with the lights down low, suffering from a migraine.

The morning of my birthday, my mother slid into the backseat beside me. I could smell Giorgio perfume and toothpaste and, underneath that, the stale smell of sleep.

The cab pulled up in front of the restaurant. My mother reached into the pocket of her jacket and handed me a ten-dollar bill. "That's enough, right?" I stared, openmouthed, at the money. My mom looked puzzled, her penciled-in eyebrows drawn together.

"I thought you'd eat with me," I finally said.

"Oh!" Before she turned her head toward the window, I caught an expression of surprise and, I thought, of shame on her face. "Oh, honey. I'm so sorry. When you said 'I want you to take me to Peterman's,' I thought . . ." She waved one hand as if shooing away the idea that a daughter would want to share a birthday breakfast with her mom. "Since I knew I'd be getting up early, I set up a doubles game." She looked at her watch. "I have to run and get changed . . . Mitzie and Ellen are probably there already."

"Oh, that's okay," I said. Already I could feel tears pricking the backs of my eyelids, burning my throat, but I knew better than to cry. *Don't upset your mother,* my father would say.

"Is ten dollars enough?"

How was I supposed to know? I had no idea . . .

but I nodded anyhow. "Have a good day, then. Happy birthday!" She gave me a kiss and a cheery little wave before I got out of the cab and closed the door gently behind me.

I hadn't braved the restaurant. It wasn't Wednesday, but I could still imagine sitting at the counter and seeing Kelly and her mom in a booth. I didn't even know whether an eight-year-old could be in a restaurant and order by herself—I could read the menu, of course, but I was too shy to talk to a waitress, and shaky about the mechanics of asking for a check and leaving a tip. I went to the bakery counter instead, where I ordered by pointing at the case—two glazed doughnuts, two chocolate, a jelly, and a Boston cream. There was a path through the woods that led from downtown to my school, and in those days a kid—even a girl—could walk through the woods alone, without her parents worrying that she'd get kidnapped or molested. I walked underneath the shade, kicking pine needles and gobbling my breakfast, devouring the doughnuts in huge, breathless mouthfuls, cramming down my sadness, trying to remember what my mom had said—that she loved me—instead of the way she'd made me feel. By Language Arts, I was sick to my stomach, and my mother had to take a cab to come get me. In the nurse's office, still in her tennis whites, she'd been impatient, rolling her eyes as I checked my backpack for my books, but in the backseat of the taxi her pout had vanished, and she looked almost kind.

She had on a tennis skirt and a blue nylon warmup jacket with white stripes. Her legs were tan and her thighs barely spread out as she sat, whereas my legs, in black tights underneath my best red-and-green kilt, were probably blobbed out all over the seat.

"I guess breakfast didn't agree with you," she said. She reached into her tote bag for her thermos and a towel, giving me a sip and then gently wiping my forehead, then my mouth.

In Ellie's doctor's office, I sighed, remembering how special I'd felt that my mother had shared her special blue thermos, how I'd never have dreamed of grabbing it out of her bag, let alone backwashing, when Ellie's doctor came striding into the room.

"Hello, Miss Eloise!" Dr. McCarthy wore a blue linen shirt that matched his eyes, white pants, and a pressed white doctor's coat with his name stitched on it in blue. Ellie sprang out of my arms and stood, trembling, at the doorway, poised for escape. I gathered her up and set her onto the crinkly white paper on the table, ignoring my back's protests. The doctor, with a closely trimmed white goatee and a stethoscope looped rakishly around his neck, walked over to the table and gravely offered Ellie his hand.

"Eloise," he said. "How is the Plaza?"

She giggled, pressing one hand against her mouth to protect her single loose tooth. Now that she had a handsome man's attention, she was all sweetness and cheer as she sat on the edge of the examination table, legs crossed, poised enough to be on *Meet the Press*. "We went for tea for my birthday."

"Did you now?" While they chatted about her birthday tea, the white gloves she'd worn, the turtle she had, of course, named Skipperdee, and how her computer game was "very sophisti-cating," he maneuvered deftly through the exam, peering into her eyes and ears, listening to her chest and lungs, checking her reflexes.

"So, Miss Ellie," he said. "Anything bothering you?"

She tapped her forefinger against her lips. "Hmm."

"Any trouble sleeping? Or using the bath-room?"

She shook her head.

"How about food? Are you getting lots of good, healthy stuff?"

She brightened. "I like cucumber sandwiches!"

"Who doesn't like a good cucumber sand-wich?" He turned to me, beaming. "She's perfect, Allison. I vote you keep her." Then he lowered his voice and took my arm. "Let's talk outside for just a minute."

My heart stuttered. Had he seen the quiz I'd

been working on? Had I done, or said, something to give myself away?

I handed Ellie the iPad and walked out into the hallway as a young woman, one of the medical students who assisted in the office, stepped in to keep an eye on the patient. "Do you like Broadway musicals?" I heard my daughter ask, as Dr. McCarthy steered me toward the window at the end of the hallway.

"I just wanted to hear how you were doing. Any questions? Any concerns?"

I tried to keep from making too much noise as I exhaled the breath I'd been holding. Maybe I'd picked Dr. McCarthy for shallow reasons—he was the first pediatrician we'd met with who hadn't called me "Mom"—but he'd turned out to be a perfect choice. He listened when I talked, he never rushed me out of his office or dismissed any of my ridiculous new-parent questions as silly, and he provided a necessary balance between me, who was prone to panic, and Dave, who was the kind of guy who'd wrap duct tape around a broken leg and call it a job.

Dr. McCarthy put Ellie's folder down on top of the radiator. "How's the eczema?"

"We're still using the cream, and we're seeing Dr. Howard again next month." Skin conditions, I'd learned, were one of the treats that went along with the sensitive child—that, and food allergies.

"And is school okay?" He paged through Ellie's

47

chart. "How was the adjustment from preschool to kindergarten?"

I grimaced, remembering the first day of school and Ellie clinging to my leg, weeping as if I were sending her into exile instead of a six-hour day at the highly regarded (and very expensive) Stonefield: A Learning Community. (In my head, I carried out an invisible rebellion by thinking of it as just the Stonefield School.) "She had a rough few weeks to start with. She's doing fine now . . ." "Fine" was, perhaps, an exaggeration, but at least Ellie wasn't weeping and doing her barnacle leg-lock at every drop-off. "She's reading, which is great."

He looked at her chart again. "How about the bad dreams?"

"They've gotten better. She still doesn't like loud noises." Or movies in theaters, or any place—like the paint-your-own-pottery shop or the library at storytime—where more than two or three people might be talking at once. I sighed. "It's like she feels everything more than other kids."

"And maybe she does," he replied. "Like I said, though, most kids do grow out of it. By the time she's ten she'll be begging you for drum lessons."

"It's so hard," I said. Then I shut my mouth. I hated how I sounded when I complained about Ellie, knowing that there were women who wanted to get pregnant and couldn't, that there were children in the world with real, serious problems that went far beyond reacting badly to loud noises and the occasional rash. There were single mothers, women with far less money and far fewer resources than I had. Who was I, with my big house and my great job, to complain about anything?

Dr. McCarthy put his hand on my forearm and looked at me with such kindness that I found myself, absurdly, almost crying.

"So tell me. What are you doing to take care of yourself?"

I thought for a split second about lying, giving him some story about actually attending yoga classes instead of just paying for them, or how I was taking Pilates, when, in fact, all I had was a gift certificate from two birthdays ago languishing in my dresser drawer. Instead I said, "Nothing, really. There just isn't time."

He adjusted his stethoscope. "You've got to make time. It's important. You know how they tell you on planes, in case of an emergency, the adults should put their oxygen masks on first? You're not going to be any good to anyone if you're not taking care of yourself." His blue eyes, behind his glasses, looked so gentle, and his posture was relaxed, as if he had nowhere to go and nothing more pressing to do than stand there all afternoon and listen to my silly first-world problems. "Do you want to talk to someone?" I

49

didn't answer. I didn't want to talk to someone. I wanted to talk to him. I wanted to go to his office—it was small but cozy, with cluttered bookshelves, and a desk stacked high with charts, and a comfortably worn leather couch against the wall. He'd offer me a seat and a cup of tea, and ask me what was wrong, what was really wrong, and I would tell him: about Dave, about Ellie, about my dad, about my mom. About the pills. I'd tuck myself under a blanket and take a nap while the volunteers kept Ellie amused in the waiting room and Dr. McCarthy came up with a plan for how to fix me.

Instead, I swallowed hard. "I'm okay," I said, in a slightly hoarse voice, and I gave him a smile, the same one I'd given my mother on my way out of the taxi on my eighth birthday.

"Are you sure? I know how hard this part can be. Even if you can find twenty minutes a day to go for a walk, or just sit quietly . . ."

Twenty minutes. It didn't sound like much. Not until I started thinking about work, and how time-consuming writing five blog posts a week turned out to be, and how on top of my paying job I'd volunteered to redesign the website for Stonefield's annual silent auction. There were the mortgage payments, which still felt like an astonishing sum to part with each month, and the *Examiner*, where it was rumored there'd be another round of layoffs soon. There was the laundry that never got folded, the workouts that went undone, the organic vegetables that would rot and liquefy in the fridge because, after eight hours at my desk and another two hours of being screamed at by my daughter because she couldn't find the one specific teddy bear she wanted among the half-dozen teddy bears she owned, I couldn't handle finding a recipe and preparing a meal and washing the dishes when I was done. We lived on grab-and-heat meals from Wegmans, Chinese takeout, frozen pizzas, and, if I was feeling particularly guilty on a Sunday afternoon, some kind of casserole, for which I'd double the recipe and freeze a batch.

Dr. McCarthy tucked Ellie's folder under his arm and looked down at the magazine in my hand. "Are you reading one of those 'How to Be Better in Bed' things?" he asked. I gave a weak smile and closed the magazine so he couldn't see what I was really reading. This was craziness. I didn't have a problem. I couldn't.

He glanced over my head, at the clock on the wall. From behind the exam-room door, I could hear Ellie and the medical student singing "Castle on a Cloud." "Nobody shouts or talks too loud . . . Not in my castle on a cloud."

I gave him another smile. He gave my arm a final squeeze. "Take care of yourself," he said, and then he was gone.

I pushed the magazine into the depths of my

purse. I got Ellie into her clothes, smoothing out the seam of her socks, buttoning her dress, re-braiding her hair. I held her hand when we crossed the street, paid for parking, and then, before I drove southwest to Federal Donuts for the hot chocolate I'd promised my daughter, I reached for the Altoids tin in my purse.

No, I thought, and remembered the quiz. *Have you ever planned not to use that day but done it anyway?* What excuse did I have for taking pills?

Maybe my mother had been cold and inattentive . . . but it had been the 1970s, before "parent" became a verb, when mothers routinely stuck their toddlers in playpens while they mixed themselves a martini or lit a Virginia Slim. So I had a big house in the burbs. Wasn't that what every woman was supposed to want? I had a job I was good at, a job I liked, even if it felt sometimes like the stress was unbearable; I had a lovely daughter, and, really, was being a little sensitive such a big deal? I was fine, I thought. Everything was fine. But even as I was thinking it, my fingers were opening the little box, locating the chalky white oval, and delivering it, like Communion, to the waiting space beneath my tongue. I heard the pill cracking between my teeth as I chewed, winced as the familiar bitterness flooded my mouth, and imagined as I started the car that I could feel the chemical sweetness untying my knotted muscles, slowing my heartbeat, silencing the endless monkey-chatter of my mind, letting my lungs expand enough for a deep breath.

At the corner of Sixth and Chestnut, I saw a woman on the sidewalk. Her face was red. Her feet bulged out of laceless sneakers, and there was a paper cup in her hands. Puckered lips worked against toothless gums. Her hands were dirty and swollen, her body wrapped in layers of sweaters and topped with a stained down coat. Behind her stood a shopping cart filled with trash bags. A little dog was perched on the top-most bag, curled up in a threadbare blue sweater.

Ellie slowly read each word of her sign out loud. " 'Homeless. Need help. God bless.' Mommy, what is 'homeless'?"

"It means she doesn't have a place to live." I was glad Dave wasn't in the car. I could imagine his response: *It means she doesn't want to work to take care of herself, and thinks it's someone else's job to pay for what she needs.* I'd known my husband was more conservative than I was when I married him, but, in the ten years since, it seemed like he'd decided that anything that went wrong in his life or anyone else's was the liberals' fault.

Ellie considered this. "Maybe she could live in our guest room."

I bit back my immediate reply, which was, *No, honey, your daddy lives there.* That had been true for at least the past six weeks. Maybe longer. I didn't want to think about it. Instead I said, "She probably needs a special kind of help, not just a place to stay."

"What kind of help?"

Blessedly, the light turned green. I pulled into traffic and drove to the doughnut shop, feeling the glow of the narcotic envelop me and hold me tight. Leaving the shop, I caught a glimpse of myself in the window, and compared what I saw—a white woman of medium height, in a tan camel-hair trench coat, new-this-season walnut leather riding boots, straightened hair lying smoothly over her shoulders—with the woman on the corner. *A little makeup,* I thought, in the expansive, embracing manner I tended to think in when I had a pill or two in me, *and I could even be pretty.* And even if I wasn't, I thought, as I drove us back home, as Ellie sang along to Carly Rae Jepsen and the city where I'd been so happy slipped away in my rearview mirror, I was a world away from the woman we'd seen. That woman—she was what addiction looked like. Not me. Not me.

Two

My alarm cheeped at six-fifteen. Without opening my eyes, I crab-walked my hand across the bed-side table, located my throbbing phone, and swiped it into silence. Then I held still, flat on my back, listening to Ellie snore beside me as I fought the same mental battle I fought every morning: Exercise or sleep?

I should exercise, I told myself. The day after Ellie's doctor's appointment the fact-checker had called me and said the story about Ladiesroom would show up today on the *Wall Street Journal*'s website, and would be in the printed paper tomorrow. I'd told Dave it was coming, but we'd barely discussed it. I didn't want him to think I was bragging, or that I was drawing a distinction between us—Dave, who wrote stories, and me, who had somehow become one of the written-about. Dave hadn't noticed my nerves, how I'd picked at my dinner and been awake most of the night, worrying that the picture would be terrible and that the world, and everyone I knew in it, would wake up and bear witness to precisely how many chins I actually had.

Lying underneath the down comforter, I touched my hips, feeling the spread, then moved my hands up to the jiggly flesh of my belly. My waistline had been the only thing that kept me from resembling a teapot in profile, but, unfortunately, it had never really reappeared in the months, then years, after Ellie's birth. I'd always told myself that I'd get around to losing the baby weight when things calmed down, but that had never happened, and the baby was now almost six.

I could see Ellie's eyes moving underneath her

lavender eyelids, and then Dave, with his pillow in his hands, dressed in pajamas that he wore buttoned to his chin, creeping into the room. Quickly, I shut my eyes so he'd think I was still asleep and we wouldn't have to talk. It had been like this for longer than I liked to think about— every night he'd sleep in the guest room, and every morning he'd come tiptoeing back to the marital bed, the reverse of a teenage boy sneaking out through his beloved's window. The idea was that when Ellie woke up and came to greet us, she'd see a happy couple, not two people who communicated mostly through texts about picking up milk and putting out the recycling. The good news was, Ellie generally showed up in the middle of the night, half-asleep and not in a position to notice anything.

Dave settled himself on the far side of the bed, arranging his pillows just so. I turned on my side, remembering how it had been when we'd first moved in together, how his first act after waking would be to spoon me, his chest tight against my back, his legs cupping mine, how he'd scratch his deliciously stubbled cheeks against the back of my neck and whisper that it couldn't be morning, it was still early, we didn't have to move, not yet. These days, he was more likely to open his eyes and fling himself, facedown, to the carpet for a quick set of planks and push-ups before his run.

I opened my eyes and considered the clothes I'd

left folded on the dresser: Lululemon yoga pants and an Athleta tank top in a pretty shade of pink, with my sneakers and a running bra and a pristine pair of white ankle socks beside them. All good, except I'd laid out the shoes and the clothes on Sunday night, and it was now Thursday morning, and all I'd done with the cute outfit was admire it from the safe remove of my bed.

Five more minutes, I decided, then reached for my cell phone, scanning my e-mail. As usual, Sarah had been up for hours. "Pos col?" she'd asked—Sarah-ese for "possible column"—in a message sent an hour earlier that linked to the Twitter feed of a prominent comic-book creator. When asked how to write strong female characters, he'd answered, "Be sure not to give them weenies." "So transwomen are out?" one of his followers had shot back, touching off a lengthy debate about biology and genitals and who qualified as female. Among her "pos col" contenders, Sarah had also included an update on the trial of the celebrity chef being sued by her (male) assistant for sexual harassment, and a profile of the showrunner of an Emmy Award–winning soap opera.

I considered clicking over to the *Journal,* but decided to wait. The story probably wasn't up yet. I'd get in a workout—maybe thirty minutes on the treadmill, instead of the forty-five I'd been shooting for, but still, better than nothing—and then, with endorphins pumping through my body, giving me a lovely post-exercise high, I'd read the story. And look at the picture. If it was terrible, I'd use it as motivation. I'd print it out, tape it to the refrigerator and to the treadmill. It would be my "Before" shot. All the moms in the carpool lane would tell me how fantastic I looked, how together I had it, after three months, or six months, or however long it took me to lose twenty pounds and maybe get some Botox.

Eloise muttered in her sleep, then rolled over and opened her eyes.

"Good morning, beautiful," I said.

She yawned, eyelashes fluttering, arms stretching over her head. "Mommy, there's somefing I need to tell you."

"What's that?" Maybe I wasn't objective, but Ellie was a gorgeous child. She had light-brown hair that curled in glossy ringlets, big brown eyes that tipped up at the corners and gave her a playful, secretive look, and the kind of porcelain skin that is the exclusive property of infants and children. A perfectly symmetrical spray of freckles ornamented her nose, her lips were naturally pink and curved into a Cupid's bow, and she already showed signs of inheriting my husband's lanky, long-limbed frame.

My daughter was delicious in the morning, I thought, as she nuzzled up next to me, and I kissed her cheek.

"What is it, sweetie?" I whispered.

"I peed in the bed," Ellie whispered back.

"Oh, Christ." Dave rolled himself onto the floor and leapt to his feet, with his hair sticking up in tufts on his head and the head of his penis wagging through the slit of his pajama bottoms as he examined himself for dampness.

"Dave!" I hissed, and jerked my chin toward the offending area. He tucked himself into his pajamas and stalked off toward the bathroom, while I pushed myself out of bed (twenty minutes on the treadmill? I'd still have time for that, right?) and yanked back the duvet. Ellie lay in a slowly widening stain. Her nightgown was soaked. So were the sheets underneath it, and probably the bed underneath that. I'd been meaning to find a waterproof mattress cover, but, like most of my well-intentioned domestic chores, it had been postponed and postponed again and eventually forgotten.

"Oh, God," I breathed.

"I'm SORRY!" Ellie wailed, and began to cry.

"It's okay, baby. Don't worry. These things happen." *About once a week,* I thought. "Ugh," I groaned before I could stop myself. I knew you weren't supposed to embarrass kids for having accidents. I'd read a million child-care books when I was pregnant, which was a good thing, because I barely had a spare ten seconds to read my horoscope now that I had a child, and I knew that shaming them over bodily functions was a bad idea, but seriously?

I scooped her into my arms, ignoring the clammy wetness and the smell. I wished that I'd kept her in overnight diapers, but Ellie would lift her nose and say, "Those are for BABIES," every time I'd offered. "Honey, can you strip the bed?" I called, just as I heard the sound of the shower turning on. *Of course,* I thought. Because letting me wash her off in our bathroom would make it too easy, and helping with the mess would have been too kind. I carried her down the hall.

"NO! NO SHOWER! DON'T WANNA!"

"Ellie," I said, looking her in the eye, "we have to get you clean."

"USE WIPIES!"

Wipies were not going to cut it, I thought as I unstuck her nightgown from her belly and tugged it off over her head, then peeled off her underwear and left them in a crumpled heap on the bathroom floor. Ellie looked at them and started to cry harder. "Princess Jasmine is ALL WET!"

"It's okay, sweetie. We'll put her in the washing machine, and she'll be good as new."

Ellie was unconsoled. "I PEED ON PRINCESS JASMINE!" she sobbed. Never mind that she'd also probably soaked our mattress. Our expensive, less-than-a-year-old, pillowtop mattress.

I cannot take this. The thought rose in my

head. It was instantly chased by a second thought. *I know what would make it better.*

"Stay right here, honey," I said, and trotted back to the bedroom. I yanked back the top sheet, the fitted sheet, and the mattress pad. Sure enough, the mattress was soaked . . . and, before I knew it, the bottle was in my hands. *Take one pill every four to six hours as needed for pain.* I popped the lid, shook one pill into my hand, debated for a moment, then added a second, noticing as I did that the bottle was getting light. I'd taken one at five o'clock the night before, after Ellie had thrown a fit because the TiVo had deleted her favorite episode of *Team Umizoomi*, and then another one at midnight, when I couldn't fall asleep.

In the bathroom, I scooped a mouthful of water from the sink and swallowed. Immediately, even before the pills were down my throat, I felt a sense of calm come over me, a certainty that I could handle this crisis and whatever others emerged before seven a.m. *All will be well,* the pills sang as they descended. *All will be well, and all will be well, and all manner of things will be well.*

"Here we go," I said to Ellie. I pulled off my own evening finery—an XXL T-shirt from Franklin & Marshall College and a pair of cotton Hanes Her Way boy shorts, which I'd bought because they covered more real estate than briefs or bikinis. Maybe I could count this as a workout, I thought as I lifted my shrieking daughter and stepped under the spray.

"Too hot! TOO HOT!" Ellie flailed her arms. One fist clipped me underneath my eye. I yelped, then gripped her arms tightly.

"Hold still," I said. With one hand, I kept her immobilized. With the other, I reached for the Princess body wash, wishing I'd added a third pill, wondering if I would have a chance to see the article before I had to take Ellie to school.

Dave stuck his head into the bathroom. "Did you pick up the dry cleaning?" he yelled over the drumming of the water. I could picture his face, the tightness around his mouth, the expression of disappointment he'd have in place even before I disappointed him.

"Oh, shit."

Ellie blinked at me through the water. "Mommy, that's a bad word."

"Mommy knows." I raised my voice. "Honey, I'm sorry."

He didn't sigh or complain, even though I knew he wanted to do both. "I guess I'll get it. Do you want me to pick you up for tonight?" he asked, in a tone of exaggerated patience and goodwill.

"What's tonight?" The second the words were out of my mouth, I remembered what "tonight" was—Dave's birthday dinner. I'd made reservations at his favorite restaurant, invited two other couples, picked out and picked up the wine, and ordered the fancy heart monitor he'd asked for, and wrapped it myself.

"It's Daddy's birthday," Ellie said pertly.

"I know that, honey." I raised my voice so Dave could hear. "I'm sorry. Senior moment." I was six months older than Dave. In better, pre-baby times, we'd joked about it. He'd call me his "old lady," or install a flashlight app on my phone so I could read the menu in dimly lit restaurants. Lately, though, the jokes had taken on an unpleasant edge. "I can meet you at Cochon."

"Fine." He didn't exactly slam the bathroom door, but he wasn't particularly gentle when he closed it, either. I sighed, flipped open the body wash—pink and sparkly, with a cloying scent somewhere between apple blossom and air freshener—and squirted a handful into my palm. I washed Ellie's hair and body, trying to ignore her kicks and shrieks of "THAT HURTS!" and "IT TICKLES!" and "NOW YOU GOT IT IN MY EYES!" and then washed myself off. I bundled her into a towel, wrapped another towel around my midsection, then scooped her sodden clothes and the soaked bath mat off the floor and tossed them toward the washing machine on my way to Ellie's bedroom.

I gave Ellie a fresh pair of panties and dumped detergent into the machine. When I turned around, Ellie was still naked, her belly sticking out adorably, frowning at the panties.

"These are not Princess Jasmine."

"I know, honey. They're . . ." I squinted at the underwear. "Meredith? From *Brave*?"

"Not Mere-DITH, Meri-DA."

"Right. Her."

"Meridas are for Fridays!"

"Well, you're going to have to wear Merida today. Or else you can try . . ." I pawed through the laundry basket, producing a pair with a grinning cartoon monkey on the back. "Who is this? Paul Frank?"

"I HATE Paul Frank. Only BOYS like Paul Frank."

"Ellie. We're late. Pick one."

She chewed her thumbnail thoughtfully, before extending her index finger at the first pair. "Eenie . . . meenie . . . miney . . . moe."

"We don't have time for this."

"Catch . . . a . . . tiger . . . by . . . the . . . toe."

"Ellie." I bent down so I could look her in the eye. "I didn't want to tell you this, because I didn't want to scare you, but the truth is, there is actually a very dangerous monster living in your closet, and he only eats girls without underpants."

She smiled indulgently. "You are FIBBING."

"Maybe I am," I said, tightening my towel, "and maybe I'm not. But if I were you, I'd put on my underwear."

Back in my bedroom, the wet sheets and comforter were still on the floor. Sighing, I picked them up, ran them to the laundry room, and tried to pull up the *Journal* on my phone. It was seven o'clock, which gave me thirty minutes to get myself and Ellie dressed, fed, and out the door, and no time at all for a workout. I pulled on my panties and a bra, a pair of leggings, and a dress that was basically an oversized long-sleeved gray tee shirt, and went back to Ellie's room.

She stared at me, gimlet-eyed, hip cocked, a bored supermodel in a pair of panties with a monkey on the butt. I took the requisite three dresses out of her closet, holding their hangers as I made each one speak. "Hi, Ellie," I said in my squeaky pretending-to-be-a-dress voice as I wiggled one of the choices in front of her. "I am beautiful purple!"

"Well, I have a tutu!" I squeaked next, shoving the second dress in front of the first one.

"But I am the favorite!" I said, in the persona of dress number three, a yellow-and-orange tie-dyed number that I'd picked up at a craft fair in Vermont, where Dave and I had gone for Columbus Day weekend two Octobers ago. We'd run a race together—well, Dave had run the 10K, and I'd started off the 5K at an ambitious trot, which had slowed to a stroll, the better to enjoy the foliage and the smell of smoke in the air. When no one was looking. I'd tucked ten dollars into my running bra, and when I was sure I was the last person in the race I'd stopped at a stand

and bought a cider doughnut. We'd spent the night in a gorgeous old inn, and slept in a four-poster bed set so far off the floor that there was a miniature set of stairs on each side. Dinner had been in a restaurant built in a former gristmill, at a table overlooking a stream—roast duck in a dark cherry sauce, a bottle of red wine so rich and smooth that even I, who enjoyed things like piña coladas, knew it was something special. There'd been cream puffs with chocolate sauce and glasses of port for dessert. The innkeepers had lit a fire in the fireplace in our bedroom, and left out a box of chocolates and a bottle of Champagne. I remember climbing into that high bed, and Dave saying, "Let's do it like we're Pilgrims."

"What's that mean?"

He gathered me into his arms, kissed my forehead, then each cheek, then my lips, slowly and lingeringly. "You lie there and don't make any noise, like you're just trying to endure it."

"So, the usual."

"Oh, you," he said, flashing his white teeth in a grin, sliding his hand up the white lace-trimmed nightgown that I'd bought for the occasion. We made love, and then slept for fourteen hours, our longest stretch since Ellie had joined us, and then we ordered room-service waffles and sausage for breakfast, and made love again. We spent the rest of the day walking around the quaint little town, holding hands, buying maple candies and painted wooden birdhouse.

This had been before the *Examiner*'s first lay-offs, before everyone who'd been eligible for the buyout had been persuaded—or, in some cases, strongly encouraged—to take the money and go. Now, instead of three reporters covering City Hall, there was just one, just Dave. Instead of leaving the house at nine, he left at eight, then seven-thirty, and I rarely saw him home before eight o'clock at night. On weekends he'd be either hunched over his computer or pounding out miles around Kelly Drive. When we were first married, we'd had sex three or four times a week. Post-baby, that dwindled to three or four times a month . . . and that was a good month. Sometimes it felt as if I'd gone to the hospital, given birth, then lifted my head five years later to find that my husband and I were barely speaking, and that sex with him was at the very end of a very long to-do list, instead of something that I actively wanted and missed.

Part of me thought this was normal. Certainly I'd read and overheard plenty about post-baby bed death. I knew that the passion of the early years didn't last over the length of the union, but lately I'd started to wonder: If we weren't talking, what was he not telling me? And who might he be talking to? The truth was, I wasn't sure I wanted to know the answers, or his secrets, any more than I wanted him to know mine.

"Mommy? Oh, Mommmm-eeee." Ellie was wiggling her fingers in front of my face, then trying hard and, so far, without success, to snap them.

"Sorry," I said.

She pointed at the dresses. "Make them fight!"

"Pick me!" I squeaked, shaking one of the dresses so it looked like it was having a seizure. "No, me!" Using both of my hands and skills that would have impressed a puppeteer, I maneuvered the dresses, making them wrestle and punch. Finally, Ellie pointed at the tie-dyed dress. "I will wear she to school this morning, and she"—an imperious nod toward the purple one—"when I get home for my snack."

"In your face! IN YOUR FACE!" I chanted, making the winning dress taunt the other two as the losers hung their hanger heads. I found red tights and located one of Ellie's favored lace-up leopard-print high-top sneakers under her bed, and the other one in the bathroom. "Wait here," I said, and trotted into the bedroom for my shoes. It was 7:18. I pulled my wet hair away from my face and secured it with a plastic clip, grabbed my phone, and clicked on the link that read—ugh— LETTING IT ALL HANG OUT, IN CYBERSPACE: A NEW GENERATION OF WOMEN WRITERS SHARE (AND SHARE) ON THE INTERNET.

Typical, I thought, and shook my head. It was an old reporter's trick—call your subject and say,

"I'm so interested in what you do!" Of course, "interested in" could mean anything from "impressed with" to "disgusted by." Judging from that headline, I strongly suspected the latter.

"Breakfast!" I called. Ellie slouched down the stairs in slow motion, like she was dragging herself through reduced Nutella. I grabbed a box of Whole Foods' pricy, organic version of Honey Nut Cheerios from the pantry, and scooped coffee into the filter. The phone began to buzz against my breast.

"Hello?"

"Did you just call?" Janet asked.

"Nope. I must have boob-dialed you."

"I feel so special," she said. "Did you see the story?"

"Just the headline."

"Well, the article's adorable, and the picture looks great."

"Really?" Part of me felt relieved. Another part knew that Janet would tell me I looked cute even if the picture made me look like a manatee in a dress.

"Yeah, it's . . . CONOR, PUT THAT DOWN!" I winced, poured water into the coffeemaker, and shook cereal into Ellie's preferred Disney Princess bowl.

Ellie pouted. "I WANT FROOT LOOPS!"

Of course she did. Needless to say, I'd never fed her a Froot Loop in my life—all of her food was low in fat, high in fiber, hormone-free, made with whole grains and without high-fructose corn syrup, with, of course, its name correctly spelled. Dave's mother, the Indomitable Doreen, had hosted her for a weekend, during which Ellie had discovered the wonders of highly processed sugary breakfast treats. "I only gave it to her once!" Doreen had told me, her voice laced with indignation, even though I'd asked in my least confrontational tone and hastened to reassure her that it was no big deal. Clearly, once had been enough.

"I'll send you the link!" Janet said. I slid the coffeepot out from underneath the filter and replaced it with my aluminum travel mug. "Let me know if you need me to—DYLAN, WHERE'S YOUR JACKET?"

"I'll see you tonight," I said. Janet had three kids, five-year-old twins Dylan and Conor and a nine-going-on-nineteen-year-old daughter named Maya, whose pretty face seemed frozen in a sneer and who already regarded her mother as a hopeless embarrassment. Janet and I had met in the Haverford Reserve park when Ellie was two and I was still attempting (when we could still afford for me to attempt) the life of a nonworking stay-at-home mom. I'd gone to the park to kill the half hour between Little People's Music and Tumblin' Tots. Janet was standing in front of a bench with her hands over her eyes, a short,

70

medium-sized woman with light-brown hair in a ponytail, Dansko clogs, and a gorgeous belted white cashmere coat that I correctly identified as a relic of her life as a career lady (no mother of small children would ever buy anything white). "Okay, ready?" she'd called.

Her boys nodded. They were dressed identically, in blue jeans and red-and-blue-striped shirts. Over a glass of wine, the first time we met for drinks, Janet told me that the boys shared a single wardrobe. After her third glass, she confided that she was convinced she'd mixed them up on the way home from the hospital, and that the boy she and Barry were calling Dylan was actually Conor, and vice versa.

"One . . . two . . . three . . ." she began. The boys had dashed away and hid as Janet counted slowly to twenty. When they were gone, she'd looked around, sat down on the bench, and picked up her latte and an issue of *The New Yorker.* I watched for a minute, waiting until she'd turned a page. Then I cleared my throat.

"Um . . . aren't you going to look for them?"

"Well, sure. Eventually." She closed her magazine and looked at me. She had a heart-shaped face, olive skin, and a friendly expression. She wasn't beautiful—her eyes were a little too close together, her nose too big for her face—but she had a welcoming look, the kind of expression that invited conversation. She smiled as she watched me finish daubing Ellie's cheeks with sunscreen, then start swabbing the bench with a sterilizing wipe.

"Your first?" Janet asked.

"However did you guess?" My stroller was parked in front of me. Hanging from the handlebars were recycled-plastic tote bags filled with fruits and vegetables that I would cook and cut up for the nutritious lunch Ellie would eat two bites of, then push around her plate. Tubes of sunscreen and Purell were tucked into the stroller's mesh pocket, along with BPA-free containers of snacks and juice, and a copy of *The Happiest Toddler on the Block*—which I already suspected my daughter would never be—stuck out from the top of my pink-and-green paisley silk Petunia Pickle Bottom diaper bag.

"All that effort," Janet said, and shook her head. "I did all of that with my first. Sunscreen, hand sanitizer, organic everything, baby playgroup . . ."

I nodded. Ellie and I were enrolled in a playgroup that met at the JCC one afternoon each week. Eight moms sat in a circle, complaining, while our kids splashed in the sink, and played with clay and blocks, and dumped oats and eggs and honey into a bowl, which they'd stir with eight plastic spoons while singing "Do You Know the Muffin Man"—or "Do You Know the Muffin Lady," because God forbid the program send the message that girls could not be perfectly adequate and professionally compensated makers of tasty baked treats. For this fun, we paid a hundred bucks a session. What did moms who lacked the cash do? Suffer silently? Watch soap operas? Drink?

"Tumbling class?" Janet asked.

"Check." Ellie and I attended once a week.

"Music Together?" She was smiling, a wide, slightly lopsided grin. I liked her for her teeth—a little too big, crooked on the bottom. Most of the women I met in the various groups and lessons and Teeny Yogini classes had blindingly white veneers or teeth that had been bleached an irradiated white so bright it was almost blue. My theory was that, having given up high-powered jobs to become mothers in their thirties, they now divided all the time and energy that would have gone to their careers between their children and their appearance. I'd gotten the first part of the mandate, quitting my job at the *Examiner* at Dave's urging and making sure that Ellie's every waking hour was full of enriching activities, her meals were wholesome, and her screen time was restricted, and reading to her for one half hour for every ten minutes I let her play on my iPad.

As for my looks, I kept up with my hair color, mostly because I'd started turning gray when I was thirty. However, my closet was not filled with the flattering, expensive, classic garments that the other mommies at Mommy and Me wore.

Nor did I have the requisite taut and flab-free body to carry those pricy ensembles. I was always meaning to go to Pilates or CrossFit or Baby Boot Camp, so I could quit slopping around in Old Navy yoga pants or one of the super-forgiving sweater dresses I'd found on clearance at Ann Taylor to go with the inevitable Dansko clogs, the clumsy, clown-sized footwear of the hard-charging stay-at-home suburban mom.

"Since I'm coming clean, we also do Art Experience," I confessed.

"What a cutie," she said, bending down to inspect Ellie, who gave her a sunny grin, the kind of smile she'd never give me. "I'll bet she's never had high-fructose corn syrup in her life."

"Actually . . ." I'd never told anyone this—not Dave, not any of the mothers at the JCC or on the PhillyParent message board, not even my own mother, who wouldn't have understood why it was a big deal—but something about Janet invited confidence. I lowered my voice and looked around, feeling like a con on the prison yard. "I gave her a McNugget."

Janet gave me a look of exaggerated horror, with one hand—unmanicured nails, major diamond ring—pressed to her lips. "You did not."

"I did!" I felt giddy, like I'd finally found someone who thought mommy culture was just as crazy as I did. "On a plane trip! She wouldn't stop screaming in the terminal, so I bought a

Happy Meal." I paused, then thought, *What the hell?* "She had fries, too."

"Whatever it takes, that's my motto," said Janet. "Flying with kids is the worst. When we went to visit my in-laws in San Diego last Christmas, I bought my oldest an iPad, and brought mine and my husband's so I wouldn't have to listen to them fight about who got to watch what three iPads. My husband thought I was crazy. Of course, he got upgraded to first class. I told him he could either give me his seat or suck it up."

"So did he suck?"

"He sucked," she confirmed. "Like he was going to give up the big seat to come back and run the zoo. Thank God I had half a Vicodin left over from when I had my wisdom teeth out."

"Mmm." On that beautiful, long-ago morning, I hadn't had any painkillers since my post-C-section Percocet had run out, but I remembered loving the way they'd made me happy, loose-limbed, and relaxed. A kindred spirit, I thought, looking at Janet—someone with my sarcastic sense of humor and my by-any-means-necessary tactics for getting kids to behave.

That had been three years ago, and now Janet and I talked or texted every day and saw each other at least twice a week. We'd pile the kids in her SUV and go to one of the indoor play spaces or museums. In the summer, we'd take the kids to the rooftop pool in the high-rise in Bryn Mawr

75

where her parents had a condo. In the winter, we'd go to the Cherry Hill JCC, and sometimes meet my parents at a pizza parlor for dinner. Eloise adored Maya, who was happy to have a miniature acolyte follow her around and worshipfully repeat everything she said, and I was happy that Ellie had a big-girl friend, even if it meant that sometimes she'd come home singing "I'm Sexy and I Know It," or tell me seriously that "nobody listens to Justin Bieber anymore." She and the boys mostly ignored one another, which was fine with me. If Ellie had favored one over the other it would have meant I'd finally have to figure out how to tell them apart.

Back in the kitchen, I stowed my phone, picked up my mug of coffee, and grabbed Ellie's lunchbox from the counter. The instant I felt its weight—or, rather, its lack of weight—in my hand, I realized I'd forgotten to pack her lunch the night before. "Crap," I muttered, and then looked at Ellie, who was busy taking her shoes off. "Ellie, don't you dare!" I yanked the refrigerator door open, grabbed a squeezable yogurt, a juice box, a cheese stick, a handful of grapes, and a takeout container of white rice from when we'd ordered in Chinese food that weekend. I'd probably get a sweetly worded e-mail from her teachers reminding me that Stonefield had gone green and the Parent-Teacher Collective had agreed that parents should do their best to pack lunches that would create as little waste as possible, but whatever. At least she didn't have any tree-nut products. For that, your kid could be suspended.

It was 7:41. "Honey, come on." Sighing, in just socks, Ellie began a slow lope toward the door. I grabbed her jacket, then saw that her hair was still wet, already matted around her neck. Steeling myself, I set down the mug and the lunchbox, sprinted back upstairs, and grabbed the detangling spray, a wide-tooth comb, and a Hello Kitty headband.

Ellie saw me coming and reacted the way a death-row prisoner might to an armed guard on the day of her execution. "Nooooo!" she shrieked, and ducked underneath the table.

"Ellie," I said, keeping my voice reasonable, "I can't let you go to school like that."

"But it HURTS!"

"I'll do it as fast as I can."

"But that will hurt MORE!"

"Ellie, I need you to come out of there." Nothing. "I'm going to count to three, and if you're not in your chair by the time I say 'three' . . ." I lowered my voice, even though Dave was gone. "No *Bachelor* on Monday." Obviously, I knew that a cheesy reality dating show was not ideal viewing for a kindergartner. But the show was my guilty pleasure, and Dave usually worked late on Mondays, so rather than wrestle Ellie into bed and have her sneak into my bedroom half a dozen times with requests for glasses of water and additional spritzes of "monster spray" (Febreze, after I'd scraped the label off the container), thus risking an interruption of the most dramatic rose ceremony ever, I let her watch with me.

Moaning like a gut-shot prisoner, she dragged herself out from under the table and slowly climbed up into her chair. I squirted the strawberry-scented detangling spray, then took a deep breath and, as gently as I could, tugged the comb from her crown to the nape of her neck.

"Ow! OWWWW! STOBBIT!"

"Hold still," I said, through gritted teeth, as Ellie squirmed and wailed and accused me of trying to kill her. "Ellie, you need to hold still."

"But it HUUUUURTS!" she said. Tears were streaming down her face, soaking her collar. "STOBBIT! It is PAINFUL! You are MURDER-ING ME!"

"Ellie, if you'd stop screaming and hold still it wouldn't hurt that much!" Sweating, breathing hard, I pulled the comb through her hair. *Good enough,* I decided, and used the headband to push the ringlets out of her eyes. Then I scooped her up under my arm; snatched up her jacket; half set, half tossed her into her car seat; and, finally, got her to school.

Three

My cell phone was ringing as I pulled into the driveway. "Did you see it?" Sarah asked.

"Just the headline," I told her. I'd been late again. Mrs. Dale, the take-no-shit teacher who was on drop-off duty that morning, had given me a tight-lipped smile as I'd made excuses over Ellie's still-damp head.

"It's mostly great. Seventy-five percent positive."

My skin went cold; my heart contracted. "And the other twenty-five?" I asked, trying to keep my voice light.

"Oh, you know." She lowered her voice until she sounded like Sam the Eagle of *The Muppet Show* fame. " 'Some in journalism question the proliferation of female-centric websites, and whether the issues they cover—such as sex, dating, and the politics of marriage and motherhood—and the way that they cover them, with a particular off-brand, breezy sense of humor, are doing feminism any favors.' "

" 'Some in journalism,' " I repeated. "Did he quote anyone?"

Sarah gave her gruff bark of a laugh. "Ha. Good one. As far as I'm concerned, 'some in journalism' are his girlfriend, his mom, and a pissed-off intern who couldn't cut it at Ladiesroom."

I flipped open my laptop, saw that the battery had died because I'd failed to plug it in the night before, and then started hunting the living room for Dave's. I knew that Sarah was probably right. I'd been in journalism long enough to know that anonymous quotes usually came from disgruntled underlings too chicken to sign their names to their critiques. But I was the one who'd written about—how did the *Journal* put it?—"the politics of marriage and motherhood," and whatever the piece said was sure to sting.

I had started on the marriage-and-motherhood beat by accident with a post on my personal read-only-by-my-friends blog called "Fifty Shades of Meh." I'd written it after buying *Fifty Shades of Grey* to spice up what Dave and I half-jokingly called our "grown-up time," and had written a meditation on how the sex wasn't the sexiest part of the book. "Dear publishers: I will tell you why every woman with a ring on her finger and a car seat in her SUV is devouring this book like the candy she won't let herself eat," I had written. "It's not the fantasy of an impossibly handsome guy who can give you an orgasm just by stroking your nipples. It is, instead, the fantasy of a guy who can give you everything. Hapless, clueless, barely able to remain upright without assistance, Ana Steele is that unlikeliest of creatures, a college student who doesn't have an e-mail address, a computer, or a clue. Turns out she doesn't need any of those things. Here is dominant Christian Grey, and he'll give her that computer, plus an iPad, a Beamer, a job, and an identity, sexual and otherwise. No more worrying about what to wear—Christian buys her clothes. No more stress about how to be in the bedroom —Christian makes those decisions. For women who do too much—which includes, dear publishers, pretty much all the women who have enough disposable income to buy your books— this is the ultimate fantasy: not a man who will make you come, but a man who will make agency unneces-sary, a man who will choose your adventure for you."

I'd put the post up at noon. By dinnertime, it had been linked to, retweeted, and read more than anything else I'd ever written. The next morning, an e-mail from someone named Sarah Lai arrived. She was launching a new website and wanted to talk to me about being a regular contributor. "I write about sex," she told me. "Don't be alarmed when you Google me." So I'd Googled her and read her posts on pony play and next-generation vibrators on my way to New York City.

I'd walked into the Greek restaurant in Midtown where we'd decided to meet for lunch expecting a leather-clad vixen, a kitten with a whip, in teetering stripper heels and a latex bodysuit. Sarah Lai looked like a schoolgirl, in a white button-down shirt with a round collar tucked into a pleated gray skirt. Black tights and conservative flat black boots completed her ensemble. "I know, I know," she'd said, laughing, when I told her she wasn't what I expected. "What can I say? The quiet ones surprise you." She set down the wedge of pita she was using to scoop hummus into her mouth and said, "So how'd you know your husband was The One?"

I looked at her, surprised. I'd figured she'd want to know how I got started with my blog, where I found my inspiration, which writers I admired, what other blogs I read. What I saw on her face, underneath the tough-girl pose of a cynic in the city, was unguarded curiosity . . . and hope. She was twenty-six, maybe old enough to have a serious boyfriend of her own, and wonder, as I had at her age, whether he was a keeper or just a guy who'd keep her happy through the holidays.

"On our first date, I wasn't even sure I wanted to see him again," I told her, picturing Dave across the table at the Chinatown restaurant where we'd walked after work. "He was handsome, but really serious. He scared me a little. I thought he was a lot smarter than I was—I still think that, sometimes—and he was, you know, completely focused on his work." We'd talked about his current project, about the mayoral candidate he admired and the three others running for the office he thought were stupid or corrupt, and then he'd told me the story that had won my heart forever, his dream of the Me So Shopping Center.

"The what?" Sarah's expression was rapt, her eyes wide. She'd done everything but pull out a notebook to take notes.

"You're probably too young to remember the movie *Full Metal Jacket*, but there's a scene where this Vietnamese prostitute says, 'Me so horny'? It was the title of a rap song." I was convinced Sarah had no idea what I was talking about, but she nodded anyhow. "Dave's big idea was to have a bunch of shops. Like, Me So Horny would be the town brothel, and Me So Hungry would be the diner, and there'd be a psychiatrist's office called Me So Sad, and a clothing shop . . ."

"Me So Naked?" Sarah guessed.

"It was either that or Me So Cold. And the doctor's office, Me So Sick, and the cleaning service, Me So Messy." I was laughing as I remembered the increasingly silly ideas we'd come up with, how I'd contrived to touch Dave's hand and wrist as I'd laughed. "And that was it. He was already losing his hair, and I could see that sometimes he'd bore me, but I thought, we'll always have Me So. He'll always make me laugh."

Sarah nodded. I had the sense of clearing some invisible hurdle, passing a quiz I hadn't known I'd taken. Sarah had moved to New York from Ohio, had gotten a job in a coffee shop and given herself a year to make it as a writer. When we met, she'd started making a decent amount of money from the ads on her blog. Her dream was to start a bigger, more comprehensive, less sex-centric site. "Fashion, food, magazines, marriage, children, all that," she'd rattled off, before giving the waiter our order—moussaka, grilled lamb, stuffed grape leaves, and more warm pita. "I'll write about sex, of course, but I'll need someone to cover marriage and motherhood." Throughout the lunch we discussed design and ad buys, ideas, headlines, and titles. By the time dessert arrived, Sarah suggested I give the column a shot and try to write a few blog posts.

"Are you sure you don't want someone with more experience?" I'd asked. I'd never thought of myself as a writer. Dave was the writer; I was a graphics-and-images girl. But we could certainly use the extra money. And the truth was that staying at home with a baby—now a toddler—did not fulfill me the way working at the paper once had. With work, there was a sense of completion. You'd start to lay out a page, or create graphics, or embed just the right video clip in an article about the city's failing schools, and eventually, after editing and feedback and sometimes starting over again, you'd be done. With motherhood and marriage there was no finish line, no hour or day or year when you got to say you were through. Life just went on and on, endless and formless, with no performance evaluation, no raises or feedback or two weeks' vacation. I thought that maybe working for money again could give me back that sense of satisfaction I'd once gotten from a job well done . . . or even just done.

"How is this website going to be different from the women's websites that are already out there?" I had asked. Sarah, who'd clearly been waiting for that question, launched into her answer, about tone and content and reader engagement. I nibbled a stuffed grape leaf and thought about how lucky I was—how without my even trying, a solution for my worries had landed, like a gift-wrapped box dropped out of a window, right in my lap.

Ladiesroom.com had launched six weeks after my interview, finding its niche in the online world —and its advertisers—faster than either of us could have expected. Four months after its launch, the site was acquired by Foley Media, a bigger company looking to expand its brand. I was working harder than I had at the *Examiner*, pulling my first all-nighters since college, powering through the next day on espresso and a twenty-minute nap, engaging each day with the people who commented on my posts. And now the *Wall Street Journal* had decided we were, in a sense, newsworthy.

"Call me when you've read it," Sarah said. I made some kind of affirmative noise and then turned on Dave's laptop and found the story. I scrolled through their recap of our success, the quotes that captured Sarah's and my funny banter, and the claims from critics who questioned our experience and asked whether our motives were self-promotional. Beneath the words living out loud, I found my photograph. "Oh, God," I groaned. I'd worn a pink jersey dress and nude heels, and Sarah and I had posed on Sarah's desk, in front of her floor-to-ceiling windows that overlooked Bryant Park. When the shot had been set up, I'd thought we looked nice. Seeing the picture now, all I could think was Before and After. Way, Way Before and After. Worst of all, the caption underneath read "sexy mamas: Mom-bloggers Allison Weiss and Sarah Lai at play in Manhattan." Never mind that I hardly looked sexy, and Sarah wasn't a mom.

Ah, well. At least we looked reasonably pro-fessional. The photographer, who'd clearly been expecting the online version of *Girls Gone Wild*, had been disappointed to find ladies in business clothes, one of whom was almost forty, with nary a tattoo in sight (Sarah had a few—"just not," as she put it, "where the judge can see them"). He had not-so-subtly pushed me toward the edge or the back of the shots, while trying to get Sarah to bend over her desk, or to stand with her hands on her knees and wave her bottom in front of her laptop—"so it's, you know, sex and the Internet." When she refused, and also politely turned down his offer to shoot her posing with a whip, he'd asked us to have an edible-body-paint fight (thanks but no thanks). Finally, he asked if we would at least stand side by side. "And can you kind of touch each other?"

We'd declined but agreed to play catch with the Egg, a vibrator designed to look like a retro kitchen timer that Sarah had reviewed in her monthly sex-toy roundup.

I turned away from the laptop and slipped my finger into my bag, found my tin, put the pills I knew I'd be needing—two Percocet, courtesy of my dentist, who was still prescribing them for the wisdom teeth he'd taken out six months ago—underneath my tongue. Then I called Sarah.

"It's great!" I said. I'd meant to sound cheery, but I thought I sounded closer to hysterical.

"I told you it was NBD," Sarah answered. I took a deep breath.

"I guess I'm just worried about what Dave's going to think."

"Ah." Sarah's boyfriend, an architect ten years her senior, was unswervingly supportive and, as far as I knew, completely unthreatened by a girlfriend who wrote about threesomes and bestiality for a living.

"But it'll be fine," I reassured her. "Hey, I should get going on my post. Call you later?" We hung up and I scrolled, idly, to the bottom of the *Journal*'s story, where twenty-three comments had already appeared.

I clicked, and began to read. *LOL the one in the pink looks like Jabba the Hutt. No wonder she needs sex toys!* "But I'm not the sex-toy writer," I said, as if my computer could hear me. I shook my head and kept reading. *I'd hit that . . .* the second commenter had written, followed by three blank lines that I scrolled past to read, *. . . with a brick, so I could get to the hot one.* The third left behind the topic of my looks to consider my credentials. *This is why the terrorists hate us,* added commenter number four.

I closed my eyes. I told myself it did not matter what a bunch of strangers who, clearly, could hardly read and who would never meet me had to say. I told myself that it was ridiculous to get upset by comments on the Internet . . . It wasn't as if the people could reach through the screen to actually hurt me. It wasn't as if I was real to them; I was a name, a picture, a thing: Feminism, or Women Today. I told myself that I looked just fine and that the people who'd written those hateful things were probably idiots who played video games in their parents' basement, putting down their joysticks only long enough to spew a little hate online and then masturbate bitterly.

Dave's computer gave a soft chime, the same noise my laptop made when an e-mail arrived. Reflexively, I toggled to the e-mail screen and double-tapped the link that would let me read the incoming missive. Which turned out to be for

Dave, from one LMcintyre@phila.gov. *Happy birthday!*

Okay, I thought. Totally benign. Except that when another e-mail arrived, I clicked it open again, almost without thinking. This one was from Dave, asking, *We still on for lunch?*

Absolutely, wrote back L. McIntyre. I ran through lists of male names that began with "L." Larry. Luke. Lawton. Lonnie. Then I scrolled to the next line. *I wouldn't miss it!*

Hmm. Possibly still innocuous. Dave's reply, *See you soon,* was also perfectly proper. But, in addition to his usual e-mail signature—*David Weiss, Reporter*—he'd used an emoji, a winking yellow smiley face, the kind that subliterate fourteen-year-old girls would text to their crushes, the kind Dave and I rolled our eyes at and had vowed to never use. "We're word people," Dave had said, and even though I was more of a picture person myself, I'd agreed with him that these silly symbols were the height of the ridiculous, turning adult conversations into puppet shows and ruining the English language. Except, if I could believe what I was seeing, here was my husband, using emojis, with someone named L. McIntyre.

Don't do it, a voice in my brain mourned. The computer chimed again, and here was L's reply, another smiley-face emoji, only hers had lipstick and long eyelashes.

"Oh, you have got to be kidding me!" I cried.

First things first. I pulled my hair into a ponytail and literally rolled up my sleeves. I'd never acquired the ninja-level Googling skills that *Examiner* reporters took for granted, but I didn't need them. A quick search revealed that L. McIntyre was Lindsay McIntyre, and she was an assistant United States attorney, and she had gone to UPenn and law school at Temple and she looked—I would ask Janet to confirm this—like a younger, paler, mousier version of me. We both had shoulder-length hair, and similar features, only my face was rounder and her complexion was lighter. But there was a definite resemblance. Except she was single. And young.

It was just after ten o'clock in the morning, but it felt like my wet-the-bed wake-up call had happened to a different person, possibly a century ago. I was considering another pill but decided that I didn't have the luxury. No matter what was going on with my husband, I had work to do.

I sat in front of the laptop. I opened a new window and typed a single word: *Exposed.* The word seemed to expand and contract, throbbing like an infected tooth at the top of the page. *I think my husband is having an affair,* I wrote, then, as if typing them might make it real, I erased the words, then wrapped my arms around my shoulders, sitting in front of the computer and rocking. I thought about calling Sarah and asking for a sick day, but I knew that, today of all days, with traffic probably at an all-time high, there was no way I could afford to go dark.

I squeezed my eyes shut, hearing the percussion of my fingers coming down harder than they had to on the keys as I typed: *Hey, commenters, I'm sorry. I'm sorry my disgusting, blobbity body (which is, after all, no bigger than the average American woman's, but who's counting) offends you. I'm sorry I was foolish enough to pose for a photograph, and let that photograph appear in the world, instead of hiding behind an avatar of an actress or insisting on being air-brushed into acceptability. I'm sorry my mere existence has forced you to actually consider the reality of a woman who is neither a model nor an actress and does not feel compelled to starve herself, or binge and purge, or spend hours engaged in rigorous workouts so that she scrapes into "acceptable" territory and can thus be seen in public.*

I'm sorry I'm not skinny. I'm sorry I haven't had my fat sucked, my face plumped, my nose bobbed, my skin peeled, and my brows plucked. I'm sorry that I forced you into the unwelcome realization that MOST WOMEN DO NOT LOOK LIKE THE WOMEN YOU SEE ON TV. I'm sorry that even the women you see on TV don't look like the women you see on TV, because they've been lit and made up, strapped into Spanx and posed just so.

I'm sorry that, evidently, you are living with

91

terrorists who have the ability to force you to read stories you're not interested in reading. That must be terrible! I, personally, can click or flip away from something that doesn't hold my attention, or interest me, or line up with a worldview that I want affirmed. Whereas you, poor, unfortunate soul, are required to read every loathsome syllable written by some uncredentialed house-wife. How sad your life must be!

They'll never print this, I decided. So I saved it, logged off, and then sat there, my heart beating too hard, wishing I was somewhere else, or someone else.

I told myself I wouldn't look at Dave's e-mail again, and I didn't. I also told myself I wouldn't read any more comments on the *Journal* story, but of course I found myself refreshing obsessively, watching the tally grow higher, feeling each insult and cruel remark burn itself into my brain. *FEMINAZZI,* read one. Angry and a shitty speller. Excellent. I wondered whether Dave had seen the piece, whether he was reading the comments, how he might feel, watching the world consider his wife and find her wanting.

Just before noon, my phone buzzed, flashing my mother's number. Since the day she'd called me and said, "Daddy got lost on the way to the JCC this morning," we'd talked every day, even if most of those "talks" consisted of my mother sobbing softly while I sat there and squirmed.

I picked up the phone. "Hi, Mom."

"Are you okay?" she asked. For a crazy instant, I thought that somehow she knew about L. McIntyre and that she was calling to comfort me. Which was, of course, insane on two fronts: my mother had no idea what was going on in my private life, and if she did, she wouldn't have any idea of how to help, and she wouldn't even try.

"Am I okay with what? Did something happen?" Did I sound awful? I must, I decided, if every caller's first question was whether or not I was all right.

"Oh, no. But I saw the story."

"Don't read the comments," I said. As soon as the words were out of my mouth, I realized that if she hadn't already, my telling her not to look was a guarantee that she would.

"It's been quite a morning," said my mother. "Sharon Young picked me up for yoga, and she had the story up on her phone." She paused. I braced myself.

"Slow news day," I murmured.

"I told her that probably not many people read it. I told her that Dave's the real writer, and you just do it for fun."

"For shits and giggles," I said.

"What?"

"You're right. I only do it for fun," I said, marveling, as I often did, at my mother's passive-aggressive genius, the way she could minimize and dismiss any of my achievements, all under the guise of doing it for my own good.

Having dispensed with the subject of her problematically opinionated daughter, my mom moved on to a new one. "Daddy has an appointment at the urologist's tomorrow."

By "Daddy," she meant her husband, my father, not her own . . . and I thought the visit was next week. Had I gotten it wrong, maybe entering the date incorrectly after taking a few too many pills?

My mom lowered her voice. "He had an accident this morning, so I called to see if they could fit him in."

I cringed, feeling ashamed for my father and sorry for my mom, that she now had to see her husband, the man she'd loved and lived with for almost forty years, shamefaced, with sodden PJ's clinging to his skinny legs. "There's a lot of that going around," I said.

"What?"

"Nothing."

My mother started to cry. "I'm sorry," she said, the way she always apologized for her tears. "It's just so hard to watch this happening to him."

"I know, Mom." It was horrible for me, too, seeing the slackness of his mouth, the eyes that had once missed nothing swimming, befuddled, behind his bifocals.

"He was so embarrassed," said my mother. "It was just awful."

"I can imagine," I said, knowing that as hard a time as Eloise had given me, coaxing a seventy-year-old man in the grip of early Alzheimer's out of his clothes and into the shower would be exponentially more difficult, especially for my five-foot, ninety-five-pound mother.

"I need you to take him to the doctor's."

"When's the appointment?"

"Nine." She sniffled. Her Philadelphia accent stretched the syllable into *noine.* "That was the earliest they could see him."

"Okay," I said. "I'll make it work."

My mother hung up. Without remembering reaching for it, I found a pill bottle in my hand and two more pills in my mouth. Crunching and swallowing, I waited for the familiar, comforting sweetness to suffuse me, that sunny, elevating sensation that everything would be all right, but it was slow in arriving. My heart was still pounding, and my head was starting to ache along with it, and I was so overwhelmed and so unhappy that I wanted to hurl my phone against the wall. *My husband is cheating. Or at least he's flirting. My father is dying. My mother is falling apart. And I'm not sure what to do about any of it.*

Instead of throwing the phone, I punched in one of my speed-dial numbers. The receptionist at my primary-care physician's office put me through to Dr. Andi.

"The famous Allison Weiss!" she said. "I was

95

drinking my smoothie this morning, and there you were!"

"There I was," I repeated, in a dull, leaden voice.

"Ooh, you don't sound good." It was one of the many things I liked about Dr. Hollings—she could take one look or one listen and know something was up. "Back go out again?"

My life, I thought. *My life went out.* "You got it. This morning. I crawled up to bed and I've been here ever since. I took a Vicodin, but, honestly, it's not doing much, and I can't stay in bed all day. I've got a million things to do, and it's Dave's birthday dinner tonight."

"Well, God forbid you miss that!"

"I know, right?"

There was a pause. Maybe she was pulling my chart, or checking something in a book. "Okay, let's see. We called in a refill, what, three weeks ago? I don't normally recommend doing this because of the acetaminophen—it's not great for your liver—but if you're really struggling, you can double down on the Vicodin."

"I tried that," I confessed. "I know I wasn't supposed to, but . . ." I let her hear the quaver in my voice, the one that had nothing to do with my discs and everything to do with L. McIntyre, my dad, and the article. "I'm really not doing so well here."

She clicked her tongue against the roof of her mouth, thinking. "Okay. I can call you in a scrip for OxyContin. It's a lot stronger, so be careful with it until you see how you react. I don't want you driving . . ."

"No worries. I can take a cab tonight."

"Good. Check in with me in a few days. Feel better!"

"Thanks," I said.

An hour later, the pharmacy had my prescription ready. I zipped through the drive-in window to pick it up and tucked the paper bag into my purse, but at the first traffic light I hit I found myself opening first the bag, then the bottle inside it.

The OxyContin pills were tiny, smaller than Altoids, and bright turquoise. "Take one every four to six hours for pain." *Pain,* I thought, and crunched down on one, wincing at the bitterness, then swallowed a second.

By the time I got home, I was finally beginning to feel some relief. I floated up the stairs and drifted into the bathroom for a proper shower, not one with Princess Bath Soap. As I lathered my hair I sang "I'm Gonna Wash That Man Right Outa My Hair" under my breath. Why had it taken me so long to find OxyContin? It was lovely. Blissful. Heaven.

L. McIntyre. Maybe she was just a work friend who'd become more like a work wife. I felt the knot between my shoulder blades loosen incrementally as I thought of those words. I knew what a work wife was. I'd been one myself, back when

I was at the *Examiner*. My work husband's name was Eric Stengel. He was a photographer, and very discreetly gay, my friend and ally, my partner-in-crime and my lunch buddy. We talked about everything—MTV series, the spin classes that were just popping up in Philadelphia, the mysteries of men's hearts, our shared obsession with the movie *Almost Famous*. We never saw each other outside of the newsroom hours, but every Monday morning I'd pick up cappuccinos for both of us and a single muffin to split, and we'd spend our first hour of the workweek at his desk, debriefing each other about our weekends. We had lunch together at Viet Nam at least once a week. In warm weather, we'd buy fruit salads from the vending truck on Callowhill, and sit outside and talk about Liev Schreiber and Jake Gyllenhaal and the mysterious appeal of Ryan Gosling (Eric got him; I didn't). I was there to talk Eric out of having his name legally changed to Edward ("It has nothing to do with *Twilight*; it's just that Eric's such a nerd name," he'd said). He'd been there to convince me that Dave wasn't cheating after I'd found an inscribed book of Pablo Neruda poetry, dated two weeks after we'd started seeing each other, under Dave's bed. "He's not going to marry someone who reads Neruda," Eric had told me. "Cummings, maybe. Auden, Larkin, those guys, I could see it. But Neruda? Nuh-uh."

"He's so mysterious," I'd moaned—back then,

when I thought I had things to complain about. "How am I supposed to know if he's cheating?"

Eric had lifted one finger. "Is he working late?"

I shook my head. Some nights, he was even home before I was.

Eric continued the questions. Was Dave finding excuses to go out, alone, on the weekends? Had he joined a new gym, started wearing a new cologne, bought himself a new wardrobe or a new car? No, and no, and no again.

"Finally," Eric had said, performing a fingertip drumroll on his desk, "are you two still making the beast with two backs?"

I'd giggled and said, "All the time." It had been true, then . . . and it was true now that at least one of us wanted an active sex life. At least once a week I'd get into bed and feel my husband's hand brush the side of my breast, or my thigh, marital shorthand for *You wanna?* The trouble was, I didn't. Ever. At the end of a day, especially after I'd taken a pill or three to deal with the emotional obstacle course of getting Ellie to bed, the absolute only thing I wanted to do was curl on my side with my cheek against the soft white pillowcase, close my eyes, and let sleep take me. Sex felt like an invasion. Things weren't as bad as they had been the first few months after Ellie was born, when Dave's touch had actively revolted me, when, more than once, I'd shuddered in dismay if he tried for a kiss, but they hadn't improved all that much. I hadn't worried about it, either. Judging from the women's magazines I read, and the stories I'd hear on the playground or in the school pickup lane, our story wasn't especially original. When we'd first started dating, and during the first year and a half of our marriage, we'd done it in the bed, in the shower, on the kitchen table, and, a few times late at night, in various corners of the newsroom. By the time I left the paper, there was one editor's desk I couldn't look at without blushing. Dave had a great body. Better than that, he had an amazing imagination, and the two of us would pretend all kinds of crazy stuff. He'd be a reclusive dot-com genius who'd made ten million dollars at nineteen but had never slept with a woman, and I'd be the high-priced hooker he hired to teach him about women. He'd be the quarterback for the Eagles, and I'd be the rookie sportswriter he invited up to his apartment for an in-depth interview. He'd be a BMW salesman, and I'd be a woman who'd do anything to get a break on the price of the new sedan.

The last time we'd attempted any role-playing had been months ago. It had not gone well. "How about we're both virgins, and we've just gotten married in an arranged marriage, and it's our first night together?" he'd suggested, one leg slung over both of mine, his erection growing against my thigh.

I'd stifled a yawn. I wasn't bored, just tired. "Were there elephants at our wedding?"

"Boy, you really weren't paying much attention," Dave said.

Focus, I told myself. Maybe I wasn't a hundred percent into it, but for the sake of the greater good, I could, as they said, take one for the team. "Okay. You're Ramesh, and I'm Surya. What's your job?"

"I'm a chemical engineer."

"What, you don't own a Dunkin' Donuts?"

He'd propped himself up on his elbow, glaring at me. "Jeez, Allie."

"I was kidding!" I said, thinking, sadly, that there was a time, not long ago, when I wouldn't have had to explain that it was a joke.

"Fine." He flopped onto his back, removing his leg from mine. His erection was wilting. I placed one hand gently on his chest, on top of his T-shirt. "Can I touch you?" I whispered, in character as an inexperienced bride.

"Yes," he whispered back. Slowly, I began stroking his pectoral muscles, feeling his nipples getting stiff against my palm. I tweaked one gently, hearing him suck in his breath. "Just like mine!" I said, delighted. "Will you kiss me?" I whispered.

He nibbled at my neck, nipped at my earlobe, pressed his lips gently against mine. I shut my eyes, lost in the sensation of his tongue dipping into my mouth, gently prodding my own tongue, as one hand slid up the leg of my pajamas. "Actually," he breathed in my ear, "I lied. I have been with a woman before."

I drew back, feigning shock. "When was this?"

In the darkness, he looked ashamed. "Well. You know I'm an engineer. But I also play the sitar in my uncle's restaurant on the Lower East Side on Saturday nights. And you know how ladies love musicians."

"So you didn't save yourself for me?" On behalf of the imaginary Surya, I was feeling legitimately angry. "Where did you take your groupie?"

"We did it . . ." He stifled a yawn. "In the back of my uncle's minivan."

"You couldn't even spring for a hotel room?" Unbelievable. Why did Dave have to be cheap, even in fantasies?

He flopped on his back. "You know what? Let's forget it."

And that had been the end of that. The truth was, in the past year, I could count the times we'd had sex on two hands . . . and I'd probably have fingers left over.

Tonight, I promised. It was, after all, his birthday. I would force all thoughts of L. McIntyre and the jerks from the comments out of my head. I would pull on my flimsiest, most tight-fitting T-shirt, and the drawstring bottoms Dave liked best. I'd light candles by the side of the bed; I'd sing "Happy Birthday to You" Marilyn Monroe style; I would do all the things he liked, just the way he liked them, and we would come back to each other and be a team, a partnership, again.

Four

I spent almost an hour in a pilled-up haze, styling my hair, applying my makeup, squeezing myself into a dress with a built-in belt that made it seem like I still had a shape. Even the five minutes it took me to wrestle myself into my Spanx weren't so terrible.

"Oh, you look beautiful!" our sitter, Katrina, said as I came down the stairs, while Eloise narrowed her eyes. I was carrying my pair of Jimmy Choos, one of the few surviving relics from my single-lady days, in one hand.

"When will you be BACK?"

"Not too late. It's a school night."

"Why aren't you taking me?" Her lower lip quivered. "I want to go out to dinner!"

"No, you don't. This place only has fish," I lied. Ellie's face crumpled. "I'll bring you a dessert," I promised . . . and then, before her pique could swell into a full-blown tantrum, I brushed a kiss on her forehead and trotted out to the car, feeling a pang of guilt at my broken promise about not driving. Dave would drive us home, I told myself . . . and, at this point, sad to say, I had enough of a tolerance that even the new medication didn't seem to be hitting me too hard. It was just making me feel unguardedly wonderful, like life was a delicious lark, full of possibilities, all of them good. So what if a few online meanies had jerky things to say about me? Tonight was my husband's birthday. We would celebrate with our friends, share a delicious meal, fall asleep in each other's arms, and wake up in the morning once more, one hundred percent, a couple.

Cochon was a tiny BYOB in our old neighborhood, one of our longtime favorites. With its black-and-white-checked floors, café tables, and framed Art Deco posters on pumpkin-colored walls, it looked Parisian . . . or as Parisian as you could get in Philadelphia. As I pulled my Prius to the curb, I saw David waiting inside by the hostess stand with his phone pressed to his ear. My heart started hammering. I wondered if he was chatting with L. McIntyre, and made myself promise that I wouldn't bring anything up until we were alone and, preferably, after I'd spoken to Janet. No dropping the bomb, and no drinking, I told myself sternly as I struggled to parallel park, a skill I'd lost almost entirely since our move to the burbs.

As I backed into the curb for the second time, I watched Dave through the window. He turned his back to end his call and put the phone back in his pocket. While he walked outside, I extricated myself from the driver's seat. It took a little while, given that my undergarments made it hard for me to breathe and my gorgeous shoes were half a size smaller than what I usually wore now. *Damn clogs,* I thought.

"Happy birthday," I said once I reached him, and handed off the bag containing six bottles of wine to the hostess.

Dave's hands were in his pockets, his stylish canvas messenger bag—the one I'd had made for his last birthday—was slung over his shoulder, and his jaw was already bluish, even though he'd shaved that morning. In his best blue suit, he was so handsome, I thought, feeling a wave of nostalgia, and sadness. I knew all of his quirks and failings, his hairy hands and short, stubby fingers, his toes oddly shaped, the nails so thick he needed special clippers to cut them. I knew the sound he made when he ground his teeth, deep in sleep; how he'd sometimes skim the first paragraphs of a story or chapters of a book and then claim he'd read it; the name of the boy at his high school who'd stolen his backpack and thrown it into the girls' locker room; and how he cried every time he read *The World According to Garp*. I knew him so well, and I loved him so much. Why had I pushed him away that last time in bed, and the time before that, and the time before that? What woman wouldn't want him? What was wrong with me?

Dave, meanwhile, was looking me over carefully. "Did you get the party started early?" he asked. He took one hand out of his pocket and rubbed it against his cheek, checking to see if he was due for a shave. "You look a little loopy."

"I'm fine," I said, and did my best not to teeter in my heels. A little loopy, I thought, was better than looking like my heart was breaking. I grabbed his arm, which he hadn't offered, and let him walk me the few steps to the empty table, trying to act casual as I brought my head close to his shoulder and inhaled, hoping I wouldn't smell unfamiliar perfume. The new pills made my body feel loose and springy, warmed from the inside, but I didn't think there was a chemical yet invented that could have quelled my insecurity, or convinced me, in that moment, that my husband loved me still.

A waiter, touchingly young, in a crisp white shirt, black pants, and an apron that looped behind his neck and fell to his ankles, pulled out my chair. "Something to drink?"

"Let's open the white," said Dave, before I could announce, virtuously, that I would just have water. Before I knew it, there was a glass in my hand. "Mmm," I hummed, taking a sip, enjoying the wine's tart bite. Show him you love him, I thought, and tried to give the birthday boy a seductive look, lowering my eyebrows and pouting my lips.

Dave frowned at me. "Are you sure you're okay?"

"I'm fine. Why?"

"Because you look like you're half asleep."

So much for seduction. Dave got to his feet as Janet and Barry came through the door, followed by Dan and Marie. I adored Janet's husband, who was round and bearded, a professor in Penn's history department, smart about pop culture and FDR's legacy, and madly in love with his wife. He and Dave weren't really friends—they tolerated each other because Janet and I and the kids spent so much time together, but they didn't have much in common. Still, they gave each other a manly hug and back slap, and Barry's "Happy birthday, buddy" sounded perfectly sincere.

"My man," said Dan, thumping Dave between his shoulders hard enough to dislocate something. "How'd this happen? How'd we get so goddamned old?" As much as I liked Barry, I disliked Dan. Dan managed a consortium of parking garages that stretched from Center City to the Northeast and did what I thought was extortionate business, charging someone (me, for example) eighteen dollars for half an hour's worth of time spent at Twentieth and Chestnut so she (I) could run into the Shake Shack for a cheese-burger and a milk-shake. He and Dave had been fraternity brothers at Rutgers, and Dan was the kind of guy I could picture sitting on his frat house's balcony, watching girls as they walked along the quad and holding up cards rating them from one to ten; the kind of guy who took it as a personal affront when a woman larger than his all-but-anorexic wife had the nerve to show herself in public.

Said wife, Marie, gave Dave a peck on the cheek and mustered a weak smile for me. Marie was the kind of lady the Dans of the world ended up with: eight years younger than her husband, slim of hip and large of bosom. The hair that fell halfway down her back was thickened by extensions, human hair glued to her own locks, then double-processed until it was a streaky blonde. "Two thousand dollars," she'd once told me, raking her bony fingers through her tresses, "but it's worth it, don't you think?" Marie worked as an interior designer, although in my head, the word "work" came with air quotes. She had a degree in theater and had built sets for student and community-theater productions before she'd landed Dan. Now she spent her time redecorating her girlfriends' beach houses. She'd drive down the Atlantic City Expressway to Ventnor or Margate or Avalon with her Mercedes SUV stuffed full of swatch books, fabrics and trims and fringes, squares of wallpaper and samples of paint. Marie had offered to give me a consultation about our place after we'd bought it, and I'd been putting her off as gracefully as I could, knowing that eventually, for the sake of Dave and Dan's friendship, Marie and her swatches would be a regular fixture in my life, and that I, too, would end up with shelves full of objets d'art, at least one statement mirror, one red-painted wall, and prints that had been chosen because they matched the furniture.

"Should we open up the Beaujolais?" asked Barry, who'd helped me choose the wine. Dan had another glass of white. Marie pulled a Skinnygirl margarita packet out of her purse and gave it to the waiter. "Did you get a lot of feedback from the story?" asked Janet, after our waitress distributed menus and ran down the specials.

I eased my feet out of my shoes, wondering where to start as I recalled some of the choicest comments—*Fat load* and *Feminazzi* and *This is why alpha men marry women from other countries.* "I need another drink," I announced. I said it without thinking about it, and certainly without thinking about the quiz I'd taken in the doctor's office, or the pills I'd been downing all day. Nobody looked shocked. In fact, nobody seemed to hear me.

"I thought the story came out great," said Barry. I glanced to my left, where Dave was sitting, and wondered if he'd heard. If he knew about the story, he hadn't said anything to me yet.

"The comments were a real treat." As if by magic, my wineglass was full again. I lifted it and sipped.

"Oh, God, do not tell me you actually read the comments!" Janet cried. "Please. How many times have I told you? You lose brain cells every time you read one."

"I know," I said, nibbling at an olive. Certainly I did know how bad online comments were—I'd read enough of them, in stories about celebrities and politicians. But why me? Who was I hurting? Why even bother going after me?

"Seems like it's been good for business," Barry offered. "Your post today got a ton of hits."

I managed a faint smile. I'd written a new version of my apology—*sorry for offending you, sorry for the nerve of showing up unairbrushed, unretouched, looking like your mom or your sister or maybe even you.*

"You read it?" I was touched.

"I read everything Janet tells me to read." He leaned across the table to brush a kiss on Janet's cheek.

"As if," she said, coloring prettily. Janet had confided once that Barry believed she was seriously out of his league, all because the guy she'd dated before him had been a professional athlete. "Never mind that he was a benchwarmer for the Eagles who got cut after three games, and that we only went out once," Janet said. That single date had been enough to convince Barry that Janet was a prize above rubies. He treated her with a kind of reverence that might have been funny, if he hadn't taken it so seriously. Janet never drove the car when they were together, never pumped gas, never lifted anything heavier than a five-pound bag of flour, and Barry never questioned her spending—on pricy shoes, on designer handbags, on a cleaning lady who came five days a week, meaning that the only house-work Janet was responsible for was hand-washing her own bras, a task she refused to entrust to anyone else.

"He loves me more than I love him," she'd told me one morning while our kids splashed in her parents' pool and we ate the bagels we'd bought, still warm, on South Street.

"Really?" I'd asked.

"I think, in every couple, there's one who loves the other one more. In our case it's Barry." She looked at me from behind her fashionably gigantic sunglasses. "How about Allison and Dave? What's the history?"

I hadn't answered right away. Dave and I had met when we were both in our late twenties. He'd been newly hired at the *Examiner*, where I'd worked since I'd graduated from Franklin & Marshall with a degree in graphic design. I'd always loved drawing and painting. When I was a teenager, every artist I discovered became my favorite for a few days or weeks or months. I fell in love with Monet's dreamy pastel gardens, Modigliani's attenuated lines, the muscular swirls of van Gogh's stars, the way a Kandinsky or a Klimt could echo inside me like a piece of music or the taste of something delicious.

I loved looking at art. I loved painting. But I'd been realistic about the world and my own talents, and susceptible to my father's influence. "It's good to have a skill you can depend on," he'd told me during one drive into the city, where I was taking a figure study class at Moore College. My parents supported my dreams, but only up to a point. They'd paid for classes, for paints and canvas; they'd attended all my student shows and even sent me to art camp for two summers, where I had a chance to blow glass and try printmaking and animation, but they let me know, explicitly and in more subtle ways, that most artists couldn't make a living at art, and that they had no intention of supporting me once I was an adult.

Graphic design was a way to indulge my love of color and proportion, my desire to make something beautiful, or at least functional, to see a project through from start to finish, and still have a more or less guaranteed paycheck.

So I'd gone to Franklin & Marshall and studied art and art history, supplementing my courses in drawing and sculpture with summer courses in video and layout and graphic design. The *Examiner* had come to a recruiting session on campus; I'd dropped off my résumé, then gone to the city for an interview, then gotten hired, at a salary that was higher than anything I had the right to expect. At twenty-two, with an apartment in Old City, I'd been the pretty young thing, with a wardrobe from H&M and the French Connection and a few good pieces from Saks, a gym membership, a freezer full of Lean Cuisine, and a panini press that I used to make eggs in the morning and sandwiches at night.

After almost six years on the job, I'd met Dave. He had graduated summa from Rutgers and started his career at a small paper in a New York City suburb in New Jersey, where he'd covered five local school districts. After his second year there, he'd exposed how a school superintendent and the head of the school board were colluding to raise the superintendent's salary. By his third year, he'd won a statewide prize for his stories about how the Democratic Party was paying homeless men and women to fill out absentee ballots. Then, at the *Examiner*, I'd been tapped to design graphics for his series about the mayor's race, fitting together the text elements with pictures and, online, with video.

"Hey, thanks," he'd said, bending over in front of my oversized screen as I'd shown him my first draft. "That's really great." Unlike most of the other, dressed-down reporters, he wore a crisp, ironed shirt and a tie. He smelled good, when I was close enough to notice, and I'd already appreciated his slender-hipped, broad-shouldered body and imagined myself folded against the solidity of his chest. He'd smiled at me—white teeth, beard-shadowed cheeks. "Can I buy you a snack item?" He'd walked me out into the hall to the vending machine, where I'd selected a bag of pretzels and he'd bought himself a bottled water, and we sat in the empty stairwell, exchanging first names, then work histories. The conversation flowed naturally into an invitation to meet at a bar the next night. Drinks became dinner at Percy Street Barbecue, where we sat over plates of ribs and Mason jars of spiked lemonade, talking about our parents, our schools, which bones we'd broken (his leg, my wrist), and our shared love of Dire Straits and Warren Zevon. We'd both been startled when our waiter had cruised by our table to announce that it was last call. We'd talked from six o'clock that night until two in the morning.

Within a week, we were a couple. I imagined he'd only get more successful as time went by. Neither of us believed that newspapers were going anywhere or that, eventually, my funny, dashed-off blog posts would be more valuable than his ability to wrest a great (or damning) quote out of a politician or a criminal, to write fast on dead-line, to think of witty headlines and slyly funny photo captions, or to bide his time for months, filing Freedom of Information Act requests, gathering documents, hunting down sources, doing the kind of reporting the *Examiner* ended up not being able to afford anymore. He would be the breadwinner, I would be the homemaker . . . only now, as I looked at him, with his eyes the same shade as Ellie's and the circles that had been underneath them since her birth, I marveled at how everything had changed, and wondered if our marriage could survive it.

"Ma'am?" I blinked. The waitress stared down at me, pen and pad in hand. Somehow, my wine-glass was empty. I'd had an oyster—Dan had ordered two dozen of them—and a single slice of bread, but nothing else.

"Oh . . . um . . ." I fumbled for my menu, doing the quickstep between what I wanted (scalloped potatoes and slow-roasted pork shoulder) and what I should allow myself (steamed asparagus, grilled salmon). I settled on the stuffed pork chop.

"Very good," she said, and vanished. I turned back to Janet, who was gossiping with Dave and Barry about whether the pretty twenty-four-year-old pre-K teacher with the tattoos we could sometimes glimpse under the sleeves of her vintage blouses had actually worn nipple rings to Parents' Night.

The food arrived. I used my heavy steak knife to slice into the glistening meat. A puddle of juice pooled underneath the pork chop. I squeezed my eyes shut and made myself nibble a tiny sliver.

"Not hungry?" Janet asked. She'd ordered the

pork shoulder dish with a lot of garlic—per its name, Cochon was heavy on the pig—and the smell was making me queasy.

"I think I already drank my calories," I said. The truth was, I hadn't been hungry much lately, a strange situation for a girl who'd always loved her food. Nothing looked good, and the effort of purchasing groceries, preparing a meal, setting the table, and washing the dishes seemed monumental. I'd heat up organic chicken nuggets for Eloise and keep the freezer stocked with Trader Joe's heat-and-eat meals that Dave could prepare on the nights I was stuck at my computer, writing or editing or interacting with Ladiesroom's readers. For myself, I'd grab a yogurt or a bowl of cereal. The irony of the Internet comments was that I was thinner now than I'd been in years, but I didn't look good, and I knew it. My complexion had taken on a grayish undertone; my flesh— even if there wasn't as much as usual—seemed to sag and hang.

Janet touched my arm. I looked up, startled. We were good friends, but neither of us was the touchy-feely type. "Are you okay?" she asked quietly.

I bent my head. "I'm scared," I said quietly.

"Of what?" Janet asked, looking worried. "What's wrong?"

"Hey, honey, can we get that Pinot down here?" Dan asked. I reached out and managed only to knock the bottle onto the floor. There were gasps, a flurry of fast motion, Skinny Marie thrusting herself away from the spill like it was toxic. A waiter and a waitress hurried over with rags. "I'm sorry," I whispered. Nobody appeared to hear me. "Oh, this'll never come out of silk," Marie was fretting, and Janet was asking, "Could you bring us some club soda, please?" and Barry was patting Marie's back, saying "No big deal," and, from the other side of the table, Dave was looking at me with his eyes narrowed and his lips compressed.

"It was an accident," I said. My voice came out too loud, almost a shout.

"It's okay." Dave sounded cool. "It happens." Which, of course, was what we said to Ellie when she wet the bed.

Eventually, the tablecloth got changed and the worst of the damage was mopped up. Marie had returned from the ladies' room, where she'd fled with a carafe of club soda and an offended look on her face, and I'd apologized half a dozen times, my face hot as a griddle, wilting underneath my husband's disapproval. I'd just tried to restart the conversation, asking Janet and Barry about the twins' hockey season, a topic guaranteed to take up at least ten minutes of their time, when I heard Marie's high-pitched voice from the opposite side of the table.

"Did you all hear about that Everleigh Connor?"

she asked. I looked up to see Dave pouring the last bit of the last bottle of red into his glass. Everleigh Connor was a reality-TV star who'd launched her career on one of those shows about the private lives of rich people—she'd been the teenage daughter of one of the face-lifted fortysomething moms who were the ostensible stars of the show. Then she'd appeared in a sex tape—she put out some statement about how the tape was a private memento she and her boyfriend had made that had been stolen from a safe in her house, but it was obvious that the tape had been made with a hired porn star, not a boyfriend, and that she, her mother, and their PR firm had managed every step of its release. From there, Everleigh had gotten and dumped a boyfriend in the NFL, landed a small role on a network drama, and had most recently become the Las Vegas bride of an eighteen-year-old pop star.

"What happened?" I asked . . . Did my voice sound the tiniest bit slurry?

Marie smiled. "You didn't hear? OMG. It's all over Twitter!"

"What?" There. It was impossible to slur on words of one syllable. To reward myself for sounding coherent, I had another sip of wine.

"She's pregnant," said Dave, directly to me.

"They're saying that she basically forced Alex to put a ring on it," said Barry.

Janet rolled her eyes. "My husband the twelve-

118

year-old girl. 'Put a ring on it,' Bar? Really?"

I looked down the table at my husband. He looked back at me, his eyes meeting mine, one eyebrow lifted, like he was daring me to say something.

I felt as if I'd been slapped, having him give me that look, when I wasn't the one sending dozens of chatty, flirty e-mails to someone who was not my spouse. I raised my chin, suddenly furious . . . and sober. Or at least it felt that way. "Honey, you should tell everyone about your big story. The one about the casino." For months, Dave had been tracking down rumors about which consortium would be the next to put a casino in Philadelphia, about where they'd buy, what they'd build, which neighborhood could brace for the boom and the nuisance of dozens of buses loaded with slot-machine-playing, quarter-toting retirees and well-lubricated frat boys rolling through its streets each day.

"Seriously, Dave-O, give me a tip," said Dan. "We build a parking lot in the right place, we're golden."

"Dave's got all the best sources," I said, my tongue loose and reckless. "Who's that woman in the mayor's office you're always talking with? Lindy someone?"

From across the table I thought I saw my husband flinch, and saw hurt in his hooded eyes.

"She's a wonderful source, isn't she?" I asked.

"What's the word . . . 'forthcoming'? Is that it? You're the word guy, right?" Janet was looking worried. Barry was, too. I got myself away from the table in a series of small steps: pushing my palms against the edge, unlocking my knees, levering myself upright, making my way carefully around my chair, squinting through the dimly lit restaurant past groups of laughing, red-faced men with empty bottles lining their tables, until I found the bathroom, a spacious stall for just one, thank God. I locked the door and, without turning on the lights, sat on the toilet and rested my cheek against the cool stainless steel of the toilet-paper dispenser, feeling stunned and empty and furious.

There was a gentle tap at the door. "Allie?" Janet said, her voice a whisper. "Are you okay?"

"I'm fine," I told her. "Just a little too much wine. I'll be right out." My heart was thudding; my temples were pounding. My purse was in my hands. My hands were in my purse. My new little blue friends were in their bottle. I shook one of them out into my palm, craving the comfort they would give me, the easing-toward-sleep feeling that would take away the scalding hurt, the shame of the way Dave had looked at me.

Nobody knew this—not Janet, not my parents, not anyone—but after Dave and I had been dating for a little over a year, my period, typically regular, had failed to arrive. I was on the pill, and I'd always remembered to take it, but I knew, from my tender breasts to the way I woke up nauseated by the smell of coffee, what had happened. I'd freaked out and gone to Dave in a panic, watching his face turn pale and his lips tighten until they were almost invisible as I'd laid out the options: I could have the baby and place it for adoption. I could have the baby and raise it myself. Or we could get married.

By then, we'd been seeing each other exclusively for months. The Pablo Neruda girl was gone—or, at least, I'd never seen evidence of another female in his apartment, or on his phone (which I had guiltily checked once). We'd been saying "I love you" and talking, casually, about which neighborhoods we liked, whether we preferred condos in the new high-rises in Washington Square West or a row house in Society Hill or Bella Vista. There had been no explicit promises, we were spending three or four nights a week at my place but not yet living together, we had not plighted our troth nor promised our future, and I would never have tried to trick Dave, or trap him by getting knocked up accidentally on purpose. Still, I'd been confident that, in light of the reality of our situation, he would do the thing he'd been planning on doing, albeit on a somewhat expedited schedule.

Instead of looking happy, though, Dave had pinched the bridge of his nose between finger and thumb and looked everywhere but at me after I'd laid out the news.

"You wouldn't get an abortion?" he had asked. We were in my walk-up apartment on Arch Street, Dave on my denim-covered couch, me in the armchair I'd inherited from my mother and had slipcovered in a pricy French toile I'd found on Fabric Row. My cute little living room, perfect for two, was in no way big enough for three. Even the thought of dragging a stroller up three flights of stairs left me exhausted. My eat-in kitchen would be just a kitchen if I had to add a high chair; my bathroom had a luxurious shower, with extra showerheads poking out of the walls, but no bathtub. It was all entirely unsuitable for a baby.

"I don't know," I said slowly. I was certainly pro-choice in my beliefs—I'd gotten my well-woman checkups and my contraception at Planned Parenthood since I was an undergraduate, and I'd been supporting them with regular, if modest, donations since I'd gotten my job—but in my mind, it was a baby, Dave's and mine, and I could no more consider aborting it than I could hurting myself, or hurting him.

The silence stretched out until I heard Dave give a slow sigh. "Well, then," he said, "let's get hitched." It was not, needless to say, the proposal of my dreams . . . but Dave was the man of my dreams, and, surely, the life we would build together would be the stuff I had dreamed about, the life I had always wanted, a partnership with a man I adored and admired. I flung my arms around his neck and kissed him and said, "Yes."

Four weeks later, with a hastily purchased one-karat princess-cut diamond ring on my finger and the memory of the Indomitable Doreen's stiff smile and my mother's insulting exuberance at our meet-the-parents-slash-engagement party still crisp and bright in my mind, I'd gone to my obstetrician and learned, during the ultrasound, that there was an egg sac, but no heartbeat. No baby. My body, it seemed, had ended the pregnancy before it really started. He gave me four pills; I went home and took them, then endured the worst cramps and bleeding of my life while Dave fetched me hot-water bottles and shots of brandy. Half-drunk, with my fifth industrial-strength sanitary napkin stuck into my high-waisted cotton briefs, I'd said, "We don't have to go through with it now, if you don't want to. I won't hold you to anything. You're free."

"Don't be crazy," Dave had said. He'd been so tender as he helped me into the shower. He washed my hair, soaped my body with my favorite vanilla-scented body wash, and then smoothed lotion on my arms and legs before bundling me into a warm towel, putting me into my pajamas, and tucking me into bed. I'd hung my future on that night. Whenever I'd had doubts, whenever he seemed quiet, or moody, or distant, I remembered the smell of vanilla and brandy, and how gentle he'd been, how kind, how he hadn't considered, even for a minute, the possibility that he could be rid of me.

"Allison?" Janet's voice was worried. "Tell me you're okay or I'm going to get a manager and have them unlock the door."

"I'm fine. I'm okay," I rasped. *I'm fine,* I told myself, even as a voice inside whispered, softly but firmly, that I was a world away from fine, that I was not okay at all.

Five

I splashed water on my face, freshened my lipstick, and crammed my feet back into my shoes. With Janet's help, I found the waiters, gave them instructions, and led the crowd in "Happy Birthday" after the cake I'd ordered from Isgro's, with buttercream icing and a flaming crown of candles, was brought to the table. I clapped when Dave blew out all the candles, without letting myself wonder what he might have wished for, and used my fork to push bits of cake and frosting around my plate. I laughed at the jokes, raised my glass in a toast, and discreetly managed the payment of the check. I kissed Dan and Marie goodbye, let Barry hug me, and whispered, "I'm okay. I promise," after Janet pulled me into a hug and said, "You know I'm here if you want to talk about anything."

The ride home was silent, as if we'd both tacitly agreed not to fight until we were back at the house. I paid Katrina, Dave drove to her dorm, and I crept past Ellie's bedroom and into my own, shucking off my dress and my painful under-garments, then pulling on a T-shirt that dated back to the 1990s and was where sexy went to die. I had planned on feigning sleep by the time Dave returned from the drop-off, but he turned on the lights and waited at the door until I sat up.

"Happy birthday," I said, blinking at him. In my dreams I'd been in the bathtub, with Dave kneeling beside me, rubbing a warm washcloth against my shoulders, telling me that he loved me.

"What was that about?" he demanded.

I could have been coy, asking what he was talking about. Instead, I said, "Why don't you tell me?"

He stared in my direction, hands jammed in the pockets of his suit pants, jaw jutting.

"Come on," I sighed. "L. McIntyre? Lindsay? Linds? The one you e-mail with all day long?"

I watched as one of his hands went to his cheek and started rubbing. When he finally managed to speak, his voice was strangled. "It's not like that."

"Oh? Then what's it like?"

"We talk," he said, sounding indignant. Some-how, I didn't think he was lying. I knew how he looked when he lied, how he'd rock from his heels to his toes, how his voice would rise. There was no shifting and no squeaking. Just Dave, looking wretched. "She's a friend."

I didn't reply, or let my face show my relief.

"This hasn't been easy for me." Dave's eyes were wide, his face arranged in his little-boy-wants-a-cookie expression, the one that usually made me feel sympathetic.

"Which part?" I asked, hearing the edge in my voice.

"Living here," Dave said.

"What do you mean?" I was honestly bewildered. "You were the one who wanted to move. You were the one who complained all the time about us being in a starter house, and how you didn't want to raise Ellie in the city." I would have been happy to stay. I loved our little house, with its spiral staircase, the fireplace in the kitchen that contractors had uncovered when they'd installed our new dishwasher, the French doors that opened onto a narrow brick walkway, and a niche that was the perfect size for a grill and a hanging basket of impatiens that I'd set on the ground when we cooked.

Without a word, Dave turned, walked into the bathroom, and shut the door. I could hear water running, could picture him squeezing more toothpaste than he needed from the center of the tube, then leaving the tube uncapped and spit and toothpaste drips inside the sink, because buying the toothpaste and cleaning the sink were my jobs. That was the deal we'd made, the terms we'd both agreed on, before everything had changed.

Not fair, I thought, and was suddenly so angry that I jumped out of bed and knocked—pounded—on the door. "Do you think I'm happy like this? Doing everything?" I asked. "I'm the one who's paying the mortgage. I'm the one who takes care of Ellie. I'm the one who's in charge of her schedule, and our social life, and keeping the house clean and making sure the car gets inspected. Don't you think I get tired? That maybe I'd like someone to talk to? Someone to take me to lunch?"

His voice came through the door, maddeningly calm. "You seem to be doing just fine by yourself."

My fingers curled into fists. "So, what? I should complain more, so you know that I'm unhappy? Well, consider this an official update: I'm unhappy."

"Keep your voice down," Dave hissed as he opened the door. In his white T-shirt and boxer shorts, with his hair combed away from his forehead, exposing the growing wings of skin on his temples, he had a narrow, aquiline appeal, and I knew that if we were to split, it would take him approximately ten minutes to replace me. "You just don't seem very interested in hearing from me."

"I'm just . . . I'm overwhelmed. It's all too much. I need you to help me." I meant to sound sincere, but I thought I'd only managed sullen. Reaching out, I let my fingertips brush his forearm, feeling the soft hair, the warm skin, remembering that I used to spend hours dreaming of when he would touch me again, happy week-ends when we barely got out of bed, delighting in each other's bodies.

"I'm busy, too." He went to the bed, pulled off a blanket and two pillows, and stood, facing me, with the bedding bundled in his arms. "I'm basically doing the work of three people now. And blogging and answering e-mail, and doing those goddamn live chats." He rubbed at his cheek again. "I'll help you as much as I can, but full-time is full-time."

"I can't keep doing all of this," I said. There were tears on my cheeks. I scrubbed them away. "I can't. There's my work, my dad, my mom, and everything with Ellie, and the house, and it's all just too much, Dave."

He tilted his head, skewering me with his gaze. "Just a thought here, but do you think maybe the pills are part of the problem?"

My breath froze in my throat. My hands turned to ice. I couldn't move. Had he guessed the extent of it, how many pills I was taking, how many different doctors were prescribing how many different things, and how I'd come to depend on medication to get through my days? "What are you talking about?" I asked.

He looked at me for a long moment. I felt myself cringing, wondering what he'd say . . . but instead of confronting me with what he knew or what he'd guessed, he said, "I need to get some sleep."

"David . . ." He turned toward the door. I followed him into the guest room, reaching for him and not quite touching his shirt. "I'm sor—," I started to say, then stopped when I realized that I didn't know what I was apologizing for. Was I sorry that I wasn't the one he wanted to talk to, to share his life with? Was I sorry I was taking so many pills, or just sorry that I'd gotten caught?

"Do you think we should go to counseling?" I asked, hating how timid I sounded. "Maybe we just need to sit down with someone and figure it all out."

He shrugged, pulling back the covers on the guest-room bed. There was a phone charger plugged into the wall and a stack of *Sports Illustrated* and *ESPN: The Magazine* on the floor beside the bed, where I'd meant to put a table. He had more or less moved in here, and somehow I'd let it happen.

"Look, I'm sorry if I seem a little spacey, but things have been so stressful," I said. "Did you see what people were saying about me in the comments on that story?" I tried to sound like I was joking, like it didn't really bother me. "Jesus, who's reading the paper these days? A bunch of sixteen-year-old virgins stockpiling guns in their parents' basements?" I wanted to tell him how much the comments hurt me, and how much I wanted him to need me, to want me in his life, the way my own parents had not. I wanted to tell him why I needed the pills, and maybe even ask him for help . . . because, honestly, it was starting to scare me, how many of them I took, and how I couldn't imagine getting through a day without them.

"What an encouraging thought," he said. "Given that newspaper readers are my employers."

I pressed my lips together. I wanted to cry. I wanted to scream. I wanted to take pills until I couldn't feel anything anymore. I wanted to hate him, wanted to be angry enough to throw something heavy and sharp at his face, but I wasn't. Maybe because I loved him . . . or maybe it wasn't love so much as knowledge, or time, something weedy and unlovely and impossible to kill; the cockroach of emotions, a feeling that could survive even nuclear war. We had spent the past ten years of our lives together, and now every place I went, every song I heard, all of my familiar phrases and jokes, Ellie's bedtime ritual (three kisses on her forehead and a quick spritz of monster spray), all of it I'd seen or heard or experienced or created with my husband. At our favorite restaurants I knew what he'd order, and then what I'd convince him to order by saying *I just want a few bites,* after which I would end up devouring it. I knew which pump he'd pull up to at the gas station, which glaze he liked on the chicken at Federal Donuts, and how he'd always forget his mother's birthday and have to spend a hundred dollars on flowers at the last minute unless I reminded him to get her a gift. I was myself, but, I realized as I looked at his silhouette, I was also half of a marriage. How could I live a life where the person who'd built and experienced and created it alongside me, the person who'd seen me in a hundred different moods, at my highest, at my lowest, in the middle of a C-section with my uterus laid out on my belly, was gone?

With stiff jerks of his arms, Dave pulled the decorative pillows off the guest-room bed and tossed them on the floor. "I'm going to sleep," he announced.

"Wait," I said. He didn't answer, just lay on the bed, on his side, knees drawn up toward his chest, hands folded. He might as well have donned a sandwich board reading CLOSED. "Dave." He didn't answer. I stood there, wringing my hands, and then I stepped back out into the hallway and closed the door. After the miscarriage, he was the one who'd handled the business of telling both sets of parents that there would still be a wedding but there wouldn't be a baby. I'd never asked what he'd said, and all he told me was, "There's nothing for you to worry about. Just concentrate on getting better." He'd never made me feel like

I'd trapped him, and, if his parents had decided I was a gold digger and told him this was his chance to slip free of the handcuffs and make a better choice, he'd never let me hear about it.

I walked back to the master bedroom, remembering when Ellie was six weeks old and barely sleeping two hours at a time and Dave had found, on his own, a little cottage at Bethany Beach. "Maybe the sound of the water will calm her down," he'd said, and I'd been so frayed, so exhausted, shuffling through my days like a zombie in need of a shower, that I'd agreed, thinking that anything had to be better than the nights of screams we'd endured. Dave had packed for all three of us, considerately choosing only my most comfortable leggings and sweatpants, nothing with an actual waistband or buttons or zippers, because my scar was still tender and my actual waist was still buried under rolls of water weight and pregnancy bloat. He'd picked out onesies and tiny cotton pants for Ellie, as well as the dye-and-scent-free detergent we washed her stuff in; he'd packed my breast pump and bottles and nipples and pacifiers, rattles and board books and burp cloths and diaper cream and the dozens of items, big and small, that the baby required. He had loaded up the little Honda, slotting the Pack 'n Play and the suitcases, the bassinet and the jogging stroller into the trunk as if expertly engineering a game of Tetris.

In the cottage, a pair of sunwashed rooms plus a galley kitchen, he'd instructed me to nap on the daybed on the porch while Ellie, who'd fallen asleep after a hundred miles of wailing, slept in her car seat beside me, and he made the beds and set up the Pack 'n Play. He'd held the baby while I swam. The cottage was on the bay, and there was a little island, just a clump of trees and shrubs and wild blackberries, maybe a quarter of a mile out. I'd done the crawl all the way there, then breaststroked back, feeling my heart beating hard, the muscles of my chest and shoulders working, and then I'd flipped on my back and let the salt water buoy me and the waves rock me. "Don't worry, I've got her," he said after I'd rinsed off in the outdoor shower and had nursed Ellie on the porch. He clipped her into the jogging stroller and trotted off to town, returning an hour later with cartons full of shrimp and fries, clams and coleslaw—a feast, exactly what I was craving. "I've got her," he said again that night, and I'd collapsed onto the crisp sheets just after seven, falling almost instantly into the deepest sleep I could remember.

When I woke up to the rosy glow of the sunrise, it was just after five in the morning. Ellie had slept through the night—there she was, blinking calmly from the center of the bed, where Dave had put her. He was on her other side in his familiar position, curled up with his knees pulled toward his chest, in his T-shirt and his boxers, dark hair sticking up in unruly cowlicks, breathing deeply, not quite snoring as he slept. I could hear the sound of the waves through the window, and of Ellie smacking her lips while she wiggled her fingers in the air and stared as if they were the best movie she'd ever seen. *Now we are three,* I thought. That thought filled me with such unalloyed delight that it took my breath away. This was what it meant to be a family; all three of us, so close. This was what I'd worked for and wanted since I was a little girl.

Now my husband was taking some other woman to lunch. He thought that I was spacey. No, actually, he thought I was a junkie. Worse, he was discontented with his life, our life, in a way I couldn't understand and, thus, couldn't fix. Had we ever really been that happy, I wondered, remembering that morning at the beach, or had I still been taking the post-C-section Percocet?

The bottle of OxyContin was still in my purse, but there were Vicodin on the bedside table. I crunched two pills between my teeth and lay back on the pillow, remembering to set the alarm on my phone so that I could wake up at six the next morning, when the life I'd always wanted would start all over again.

Six

"Allison?"

"Yes, Mom?" I called toward the car's speakers as I steered, one-handed, into the parking lot of BouncyTime, where the birthday party for a classmate of Ellie's named (I was almost positive) Jayden was starting in ten minutes. It was a miserable April day, gray-skied and windy, with a dispirited rain slopping down.

"Are you almost here?" she asked in a quivering voice.

Dave sat next to me, stiff and silent as one of those inflatable man-shaped balloons that drivers in California buy so they can use the high-occupancy-vehicle lanes. It had been several weeks since his birthday dinner, but we hadn't talked about anything more substantive than whether we were running out of milk or if I'd remembered to make the car insurance payment. I took my pills, he, presumably, found comfort in conversation with L. McIntyre, and we tried to be polite to each other, especially in front of our daughter. Said daughter was in the backseat, chatting with her friend Hank.

"If you are going to put something in your nose," I heard Ellie announce, "it should not be a Barbie shoe."

"Okay," Hank snuffled. Hank was a pale and narrow-faced little boy with a ring of whitish crust around his eyes and mouth. He was going on six, the same as my daughter, but thanks to his allergies to eggs, wheat, dairy, shellfish, and pet dander, he was the size of a three-year-old and he sniffled nonstop.

How did Ellie even know what a Barbie doll was? I wondered as I maneuvered into a parking spot between a Jaguar and a minivan. I wasn't sure, but I bet that I had Dave's mother, the Indomitable Doreen, to thank. Doreen scoffed at my "notions," as she called them, about organic food, gender-neutral toys, and limiting Eloise's TV time. Doreen was tall, broad-shouldered, and slim, with the same fair complexion that her sons had inherited and the same cropped dark hair, although I suspected she dyed it. Doreen had raised three boys and had been waiting for years to have a girl child to dote upon. Whenever Doreen got my daughter alone, she'd let her gorge on ice cream and candy. They would stay up all night in Doreen's silk-sheeted king-sized bed, playing Casino and watching *Gilligan's Island* and God only knew what else. "Lighten up," Doreen would tell me, sometimes with a good-natured (but still painful) sock on the shoulder, when I politely reminded her that Ellie did better when she kept to her bedtime schedule, or mentioned that Dave and I gave her an allowance for doing her chores, and that when she slipped our daughter twenty bucks it tended to undermine our authority. "Calm down, or you're going to make yourself crazy!"

I knew that my mother-in-law meant well. She'd never talked about whether she'd missed the job she gave up once her sons were born, but I wondered if she had, and if she saw how I had struggled, first as a full-time stay-at-home mother and now as a stay-at-home mom with a part-time (inching ever closer to full-time) job. I could have asked, but the truth was, things hadn't been great between us since I learned that she'd read my birth plan out loud to her book club. In retrospect, the plan might have been a little excessive—it was eight pages long and spelled out everything from the music I wanted to how I didn't want any external interventions, including an epidural, and had gone on, at length, about the necessity for a "peaceful birthing environment"—but that did not mean I wanted the six members of Words and Wine laughing at me over copies of Sue Monk Kidd's latest.

In the backseat, Ellie was regaling Hank with the story of the dead squirrel she'd seen at the corner of South Street during one of our visits to the city. "Its middle was all crumpled, and there was BLOOD on its BOTTOM," she said, as Hank mouth-breathed in horror.

"Hey, El, I'm not sure that's appropriate," I said.

Ellie paused, gnawing at her lower lip. Then she turned to Hank and said, in such a perfect lady-at-a-cocktail-party tone that both Dave and I smiled, "And what are your plans for the weekend?"

I put the car in park and waited until Hank said, "I don't know."

" 'Plans for the weekend' just means what you are going to do," Ellie explained. "Like, you could say, 'Watch *Sam & Cat*,' or maybe 'Put all your nail polishes into teams.' "

"I don't have nail polishes," Hank said wistfully.

The phone rang again. I ignored it, thinking that at least, unlike my mother, Doreen didn't need instructions for the most basic tasks—calling the oil company to have the tank refilled, remembering to change the car's windshield wipers instead of just, as she'd once done, buying a new car. If my father had still been himself, I would have asked how he dealt with her, even though I suspected the answer probably involved sex.

If I'd had time I would have helped more, but in the six weeks since the *Journal* story had run, traffic to Ladiesroom.com had increased by more than two hundred percent, and Sarah had started hinting that I should think about writing not just five times a week but every day. I'd also gotten a few queries from other outlets—some websites, two in-print magazines, and a cable TV shout-show—asking if I'd want to write or blog or dispense online or on-the-air commentary. So far,

I'd turned them all down, but I suspected that if Sarah learned about the offers she'd encourage me to take them, knowing it would only help build Ladiesroom's brand.

Ideally, Dave would have taken over Ellie duties a few nights a week, and maybe even spared an hour each week for counseling, but Dave, bless his heart, had declined both of those requests and instead signed up for another marathon. I'd tried not to read too deeply into the symbolism, about how he'd be spending hours each week literally running away from his wife and his daughter, and I'd assiduously avoided Googling L. McIntyre's name to see if she, too, would be participating in the race, thus avoiding the need to imagine the two of them logging training runs along the Schuylkill, trotting side by side along the tree-canopied paths of the Wissahickon. Instead of complaining, I'd bumped my housekeeper up to two days a week, hired a backup sitter who could work nights and weekends, and enrolled Ellie in after-school activities every day but Thursday—tumbling, swimming, Clay Club, even a class on "iPad mastery." It was heartbreaking, but the more she was out of the house, the more smoothly things ran inside of it. She'd even found a new best friend. Hank did most of the same activities she did—his mom was a urologist who worked full-time. Ellie had all but adopted Hank, who was even more sensitive and high-strung than she was, and appointed herself as his unofficial advisor and life coach.

"If you need to go to the potty, just ask me," I heard her saying as she unhitched herself from her booster seat, then reached over to help Hank with his buckles. "I've been to probably a billion parties here before."

I helped Ellie out of the car, handed Dave the birthday boy's gift, and then stood with him in the parking lot, feeling as if we'd been shoved onstage without a script. Normally, we would have kissed before I drove away—just a little peck, a quick brush, enough for me to get a whiff of his scent, which I still found intoxicating, and then we'd separate. Instead, Dave gave me a half wave and a "See ya" before shepherding the kids through the front doors. Part of me wanted to run after him and hug him, taking strength from even an instant of physical connection. Another part of me felt like giving him the finger. Since the birthday-night fight, Dave had barely touched me, and he'd continued to spend his nights in the guest bedroom. I imagined him under the covers, curled on his side with that goddamned BlackBerry pressed against his ear, talking to his work wife, L. McIntyre, while his real wife was alone in bed down the hall, staring up into the darkness, sometimes crying, until the narcotics allowed her to fall asleep.

I sat behind the wheel as the doors closed

behind Dave and Hank and Ellie, feeling hollow underneath the euphoria the pills guaranteed. At least I still had that—a guaranteed pick-me-up at the start of the day; a comfort at the end. With a pill or two (or three, or four) coursing through my bloodstream, I felt calm, energetic, in control, as if I could manage work and being a good mother and a good daughter, keeping the house running and the refrigerator stocked and even performing the occasional stint as a chaperone during a Stonefield trip to the Art Museum.

The bad news was that Dr. Andi was being far stingier with the Oxy handouts than she'd been with the Vicodin. "You want to be careful with this stuff," she'd said the first time I called for a refill. "It's seriously addictive."

"Oh, I will be," I promised. I could keep that promise easily because, during one of my daily rounds of the gossip websites that I wasted too much time on, I'd come across a story I at first assumed had to be fake. "Introducing Penny Lane: the Top Secret Website Where You Can Buy Any Drug You Want." *No way,* I'd thought, but the story at least made the site sound legitimate as it described a kind of Amazon.com for illegal substances. You had to use anonymizing software to get to the site, and use encryption to register. Once you'd cleared those hurdles, you could, allegedly, order anything you wanted—anything from pot to Viagra to painkillers to heroin. You'd send the vendors your real name and address—encrypted, of course—and payment via a new kind of online-only currency, and the vendors would send you the goods.

I figured it had to be a scam . . . but what did I have to lose? Other than some money. And my freedom, I assumed, if you could be jailed for trying to buy prescription drugs on the Internet, but that was a risk I decided I was willing to take. I spent about ten seconds wondering if anyone would recognize my name, then decided that the overlap between illegal drug dealers and Ladiesroom.com readers was probably tiny. Downloading the software took less than a minute; learning how to use it took maybe five minutes more. The hard part was figuring out how to trade dollars for the e-coins the site used instead of cash. It took me the better part of another week to register the bank account I'd established for my own personal use, an account at a different bank from the one Dave and I used. I'd then had to register with yet another website to send my e-currency to my account at Penny Lane. Once I'd picked a screen name ("HarleyQueen," a play on the name of one of the sexy lady villains in *Batman*) and loaded a thousand dollars' worth of cash into my account, I started wandering through the virtual aisles, amazed at what was for sale. Hallucinogens. Amphetamines. Dissociatives, whatever they were. Viagra and Cialis, Ecstasy and Special K and crystal meth. I'd clicked on "Opiods," and there was everything—your Percocet, your Vicodin, your Tylenol with codeine. With my mouth open in disbelief, I put twenty OxyContin pills into my cart, then browsed around, pricing Vicodin from India and wondering, again, whether this could possibly be legitimate.

I figured that I'd be sent fakes, if the vendors bothered sending anything at all. Then the first delivery arrived. The pills were in a tiny plastic bag that had been encased in a layer of bubble wrap and folded and tucked into an Altoids tin. They looked exactly like the ones I'd been prescribed and, according to Pillfinder.com, they appeared to be exactly what I'd paid for. Cautiously, I slipped one underneath my tongue, waiting for the familiar bitterness. It arrived right on schedule, but, still, I was seized with dread. What if it was a clever fake? What if I'd taken poison? What if Ellie came home and found me convulsing on the kitchen floor? But ten minutes later I was dreamy-eyed and practically floating around the kitchen. Since then, my use had ramped up slightly (or maybe "considerably" would be more accurate) . . . but if I could get as many pills as I wanted whenever I wanted them, if I could afford my vices, and if the whole trans-action felt as risky as ordering a bra from Victoria's Secret, what did it matter?

At a stoplight, I punched in my mother's number.

"Daddy just woke up," she said. "He thinks he needs to get dressed to go to the airport. I've been telling him and telling him . . ."

"Okay, Mom."

". . . but he won't listen. I didn't get any sleep last night. He kept shaking me, or turning on his phone and shining it in my eyes. At three a.m. he started packing his suitcase . . ."

"I'm ten minutes away," I said, mentally canceling the pit stop I'd planned at Starbucks (or, if I was being honest, at McDonald's). I'd spent so much time trying to coax a few bites of cereal into Eloise's mouth that I hadn't had time for my own breakfast. I deserved a hash brown. Hash brown, singular, I told myself, and definitely no sausage biscuit.

"Ronnie!" I could hear my dad yelling. "Where's the cab?"

"Put him on the phone with me," I told her, figuring it couldn't hurt.

A minute later, my father was growling "Who's this?" into my ear.

"Daddy, it's Allison. Mom says you need a ride?" I hadn't been sure whether it was a good idea to play along with someone suffering from early-stage Alzheimer's or dementia—which my mother, God love her, pronounced *dee-men-she-ah*—but Dad's doctor said it was all right to indulge him up to a point. "A therapeutic lie" was what he'd called it. Translation: whatever worked.

"Allison," said my father. I held my breath. Last Saturday, when I'd sent Eloise to Hank's house for a playdate and invited my parents over for brunch, he'd known who I was, but sometimes he thought I was his sister and called me Joyce. I knew that the day was coming when he wouldn't know me at all, but I prayed it hadn't come yet, not so much for my sake, but for my mother's.

My parents had met when my mom was eighteen-year-old Ronnie Feldman, with an adorable pout and soft brown eyes, a cute little figure and shiny black hair, and my dad was twenty-eight, a college graduate who'd served for two years as an information officer in the army, stationed in Korea, and was finishing up his MBA at Penn. She'd been a CIT at the summer camp he'd attended, and he was back for a ten-year reunion. She was still in high school, still riding her ten-speed with a wire basket embellished with plastic flowers between the handlebars and buying her clothes in the children's department. Little Ronnie, who'd dotted the "i" of her name with a heart, who'd never lived on her own, never paid a bill, and never held a job outside of being a not-quite counselor at Camp Wah-Na-Wee-Naw in the Poconos; Little Ronnie with her tanned legs and pert chin and the ponytail she tied in red-and-white ribbons—camp colors, of course— had married him two summers later, going straight from her parents' house to the apartment my dad had rented, where she played house until I came along and it stopped being a game. There had always been a man to take care of her, first her own father, then mine. My mother never had any reasons to master the fundamentals of adulthood—balancing a checkbook, registering a car, buying a house. My dad had taken care of everything. Pretty Little Head, or PLH, was what Dave and I called my mom in happier times, when we'd still had a private language of jokes with each other, as in "Don't worry your pretty little head about a thing."

"Are you all packed?" my father asked.

So he thought I was coming on this imaginary trip. "All packed and ready to go."

"I'm proud of you," he said, his voice thick, the way it got after he'd had the second of his two pre-dinner martinis. "I hope you'll have fun in college. Blow off some steam! Put down the paints and go to some parties! Meet some nice boys! College isn't just for book learning, you know."

So he thought he was taking me to college. At a red light, I took a deep breath, remembering that trip, how we'd stopped for milkshakes and he'd given me a pained and heartbreakingly sweet speech about how college boys would want certain things, and how, at parties, I shouldn't ever put my drink down lest some knave try to "slip me a mickey," and how I should be careful about what I wore. "I know that's not a very modern thing to say," my dad had told me, and I'd been so embarrassed when he used the phrase "it's just their nature" that I'd spent the next ten minutes hiding in the bathroom.

I stepped on the gas and tried not to think about what it would be like when the time came to drive him to an assisted-living facility, or a nursing home, or whatever he'd end up requiring. No milkshakes; no speeches about how he should avoid the divorcées with hungry eyes; no joking or resigned tenderness about how this was just what happened: little birds left the nest. It was all wrong, I thought, remembering how impressive my dad had looked offering my new roommate his hand, and how he'd helped me make my bed. I cleared my throat so he wouldn't be able to tell that I was crying. "I'm just grabbing some coffee, and then I'll be ready to go."

"Sounds good, princess." He sounded jovial, hearty, so completely himself. I thought, not for the first time, that maybe it would have been better if he'd just died, a thunderclap heart attack, an artery bursting in his brain, a peaceful exit in the middle of the night, in his own bed, after his favorite meal, with my mom beside him. We'd have mourned, then moved on. This was a slow-motion catastrophe, death by a thousand cuts.

"Why don't you watch CNBC?" I said, forcing

cheeriness into my voice. "Check your stocks. Let Mom take a shower. I'll be there as soon as I can." His love of CNBC was one of the things he'd retained, even as he slipped further and further down the rabbit hole. In my parents' house, the television in the den was always on, at a volume just slightly less than deafening, tuned to the financial news so my dad could keep an eye on his portfolio, which was, in fact, being managed by his former protégé, a man named Don Ettlinger, who worked in Center City and who remembered me from when I was a girl.

"Okay, then. I'll see you when I see you." There was a thumping sound as he set the phone down—sometimes he'd get confused, then angry, when he went to hang up the phone and discovered that cell phones had no cradles, just chargers. I clenched my hands on the steering wheel. When I was fourteen, after my complexion had calmed down and the rest of my features had caught up with my nose, a boy asked me out to a movie. His mother drove us there. We spent the next two hours palm to sticky palm, eyes on the screen, each, undoubtedly, waiting for the other to make a move. My father picked us up and drove us home. In the kitchen, where my mother had left a plate of cookies, he'd looked sternly down at all five feet three inches of Marc Schwartzbaum. "You two are behaving yourself, correct?" he asked, in a voice that seemed deeper than usual, and Marc, gulping, had bobbed a nervous nod.

"Excellent," Dad said. "Because I'll be watching." With that, according to the plan I'd begged my parents to approve, Marc and I went down to our finished basement, where there was a wide-screen TV, a Ping-Pong table, and an air hockey game where the puck glowed in the dark, requiring that the lights be turned off. I'd flicked the switches and plugged in the machine, and after a few minutes, Marc and I had retired to the couch for what I even then recognized was inept and unsatisfying fumbling when, suddenly, my father's voice came booming out of the ceiling, sounding, for all the world, like God. "I'LL BE WATCHING," he intoned. Marc, shrieking like a girl, sprang into the air, hit his back on the arm of the couch, and tumbled to the floor in a groaning, tumescent heap. I started laughing, and every time I came close to collecting myself to the point where I'd be able to comfort my paramour, I'd hear my dad's voice again, coming through the house-wide speaker system he'd installed last year so my mother could hear James Taylor and Simon & Garfunkel wherever she went. "I'LL BE WATCHING." Marc had never asked me out again. I didn't mind. It had been worth it.

In the driveway of the modern four-bedroom house in Cherry Hill where I'd grown up—a model of late-eighties chic, all angled hardwood and glass—I sat for a moment, taking deep breaths. I pictured a deserted beach, with white sand and lace-edged waves lapping at the shore. That was good. Then I slipped my hand into my purse and curled my fingers around the Altoids tin that contained ten magical blue pills. That was even better. I put one in my mouth and stepped out of the car.

The instant my feet touched the driveway the front door popped open. My mom opened her mouth, undoubtedly prepared to launch into her catalog of woe, and then shut it, slowly, as she considered my outfit. "You know," she said, "in my day you'd have to put on your face to even open your front door to get the paper."

"Aren't I lucky that times have changed," I said lightly, wishing I'd taken two pills. I looked down at myself: black leggings, a gray-and-black wool tunic that could have benefitted from a trip to the dry cleaner's, black patent-leather clogs. No makeup, true, and my hair was in an untidy bun, but it at least had been recently washed. My mother, meanwhile, had lost her bounce, the ponytailed girlishness that had kept my father in thrall for all those years. Her skin, normally tanned and glowing, had a crepey, wrinkled pallor, suggesting that she'd been spending most of her waking hours indoors. The polish on her fingernails was chipped, and her ring, a rock the size of a marble that my father had purchased (at her insistence, I suspected) for their thirtieth anniversary, hung loosely from her finger. She was, as always, tiny. Never in her life had she topped a hundred pounds—"except," she liked to say, in a just-short-of-accusatory tone, "when I was pregnant with you." She had on the same Four Seasons bathrobe she'd been wearing last Saturday, only there was a stain I hoped was ketchup on one sleeve, and a smear of something yellow on the lapel. Her trembling hands were pressed together—my mother's hands had shaken for as long as I could remember. I think I'd been told it was related somehow to the Accident. When I hugged her, I breathed in her familiar scent, something fruity and sweet with top notes of Giorgio and Listerine. Her tiny feet were bare, with chipped coral polish on the toenails and purple veins circling her ankles. In the morning sun, I could see the outline of her skull through her thinning hair.

"Sidney!" she yelled, over the sound of financial news. "I'M GOING TO TAKE A SHOWER!"

My father called back something I couldn't hear. My mother walked up the stairs, head bent, moving slowly, as if every step hurt. I draped my coat over a chair at the breakfast bar. I guessed Brenda, the last cleaning lady the agency sent, hadn't worked out any better than Maria, or Dot, or Phyllis, or whoever had preceded Phyllis. When my dad had gotten his diagnosis, I'd offered

151

to pay for a cleaning lady–slash–helper to come five days a week. But Blanca, who'd worked for my parents forever, coming every Tuesday and Thursday to wash the floors, vacuum the carpets, run a load of laundry, and wipe down the countertops with bleach, had other families to tend to and couldn't quit on them. I'd found an agency and explained what I needed—someone to do the housework, to help with the laundry, to take my mother to the grocery store and the dry cleaner's and to run whatever other errands she might have, someone with a decent personality and a driver's license. The agency had sent over an entire football team's worth of women, but my mom had a complaint about each one of them. Maria the First had insisted on being paid in cash, not by check, and my mother refused to "make a special trip to the bank, just for her." The second Maria drove a Dodge that was missing one of its front hubcaps. Exit Maria the Second. "There's no way," my mother had sniffed, "that I'm driving around in that . . . vehicle." Dot had either refused to iron the sheets or done it badly. Phyllis, my mom claimed, had stolen a pair of Judith Leiber earrings right out of her jewelry box. (My suspicion was that if I looked hard enough, I'd find those earrings somewhere—my mother was a notorious loser of things, from keys to credit cards to jewelry—but it was easier to call the agency again than to have the fight.)

That morning, the kitchen table was covered with salad-bar take-out containers, a glass with an orange juice puddle coagulating at the bottom, a collection of prescription bottles, and crumpled sections of the newspaper. I started to straighten the mess, then gave up and went to the den to find my father.

He was sitting on the couch in a crisp white shirt with monogrammed cuffs, suspenders, and pin-striped navy pants. His suit jacket, still on its hanger, was waiting on the doorknob. I swallowed hard. He looked just the way he had the morning he'd driven me to Lancaster for college, the way he'd looked every morning of my girlhood, when he'd slipped into my bedroom, smelling of Old Spice and the grapefruit he ate for breakfast. "With your shield or on it," he would say, which is what Spartan fathers would say to their sons before sending them off to war.

Maybe he'd have been a little gentler, more inclined to treat me like a little girl instead of a son or a successor, if I'd looked more like my mom . . . but I'd inherited my face and figure from my dad's mother, Grandma Sadie, who was tall, especially for a woman back then, and busty. I'd learned to modulate my voice (Grandma Sadie's honk could silence an entire supermarket), and, after an embarrassingly minor amount of begging, I'd gotten my nose done the summer between high school and college. (My father had said, "You look fine!" My mom had asked if I wanted to get a breast reduction, too.)

My mother was Sadie's opposite, tiny and soft-voiced and sweet. Unlike my grandma, who drove the car and signed the checks and made all of her household's big decisions, my mother was utterly dependent on my dad. He hired Blanca so she wouldn't have to clean; he hired a car service so she wouldn't have to drive after the Accident. When they entertained more than one other couple, he'd hire a catering company to cook and clean. If it had been possible to pay someone to go through pregnancy and labor for her, so she wouldn't have to suffer even an instant of pain, he would have done that, too.

Until now, she had drifted through life like a queen who had only a few ceremonial duties to discharge. She didn't work, or take care of me or the house. What she did was amuse my dad. She would gossip and dance and play card games and tennis and golf; she'd listen to his stories and laugh at his jokes and use her long, painted finger-nails to scratch at the back of his neck. Her biggest fear, voiced daily, was that she would outlive him and be left all alone in a world she couldn't begin to handle, so it wasn't surprising that she became a world-class hypochondriac by proxy. If my father sniffled, she'd schedule a doctor's appoint-ment to make sure it wasn't pneumonia. If he had indigestion, she'd want him to go to the emergency room to make sure it really was the tomato sauce and not his heart. She'd stand by the front door in the morning, refusing to let him leave until he'd put sunscreen on his hands, face, and bald spot (his own father had died of melanoma), and in the evening she'd bring him a glass of red wine (okayed because of the healthful tannins). Instead of nuts, he'd take his drink with a little green glass dish filled with vitamins, supplements, fish-oil capsules—whatever she'd read about in *Prevention* or *Reader's Digest* that week.

We would have dinner, the two of them would retire to the den, and I'd go to my bedroom and shut the door, doing my homework or listening to music or drawing in my sketchbook.

I wasn't the most popular girl in my school, but I wasn't a total embarrassment either. In high school, I was moderately popular, with a circle of reliable friends and, from the time I was sixteen on, a boyfriend, or at least someone to make out with at the movies. I worked hard on my looks, keeping a food journal all the way through college that recounted everything that went into my mouth and every minute of exercise I'd done. (Recently I'd found stacks of notebooks in my childhood room's desk drawers describing cottage- cheese lunches and apple-and-peanut-butter snacks. Why had I saved them? Had I imagined wanting to reread them someday?)

In the den, my father was bent over, pulling on his white orthopedic walking shoes, the ones that closed with Velcro straps. I turned away, my chest aching. My father had always been fastidious about his clothing. He'd loved his heavy silk ties from Hermès, the navy blue and charcoal gray Hickey Freeman suits he wore to work. Once a year, he and I would make a trip to Boyd's, an old-fashioned clothing store on Chestnut Street in Philadelphia, where the clerks would greet my father by name. I'd sit on a velvet love seat with a cup of hot chocolate and an almond biscotti from the store's café, and watch as my father and Charles, the salesman who always helped him, discussed summer-weight wool and American versus European cuts and whether he was getting a lot of use out of the sports jacket he'd bought the year before. My dad would ask about Charles's sons; Charles would ask me about school and sports and if I had a boyfriend. Then my dad would disappear into the changing room with one suit over his arm and two or three more hanging from a hook on the door, and he'd emerge, with the pants bagging around his ankles, for more discussion with Charles, before turning to me.

"What do you think, Allie-cat? How's the old man look?"

I would narrow my eyes and nibble my cookie. "I like the gray suit the best," I would say. Or, "I bet that navy pinstripe would look nice with the silver tie I got you for Father's Day."

"She's got quite an eye," Charles would say—the same every year.

"She's an artist," my dad would say, his tone managing to convey both pride and skepticism.

Eventually, a tailor would be summoned, and my dad would stand in front of the three-way mirror while the stooped old man with a mouthful of pins and a nub of chalk between his fingers marked and pinned. Then my father would change back into his weekend wear—khakis and leather boat shoes and a collared shirt—and he would take me out to a dim sum lunch. We'd order thin-skinned soup dumplings, filled with rich golden broth and pork studded with ginger, and scallion pancakes, crispy around the edges, meltingly soft in the middle, fluffy white pork buns and cups of jasmine tea, and then we'd walk to the Reading Terminal for a Bassetts ice-cream cone for dessert.

My father got up. Ignoring the gray nylon Windbreaker my mother had left hanging over one of the kitchen chairs—an old man's jacket, if ever there was one—he took his trench coat off the hanger in the closet, put it on, and followed me out the door.

"Remember when we used to go to Boyd's for your suits?" I said as I pulled into the street.

"I'm not brain-dead," he said, staring out his window. "Of course I remember."

"Do you think Charles still works there?" In all the years we'd shopped at Boyd's, Charles, a handsome, bald African-American man who always matched his pocket square to his tie, had never seemed to age.

"I have no idea," said my father. "I haven't needed a new suit just lately, you know."

We rode toward Philadelphia listening to NPR, not talking. My plan was to get him lunch at Honey's Sit 'n Eat, a Jewish soul-food diner where they served waffles and fried chicken and all kinds of sandwiches. "Where's your girl?" asked my father, as we pulled off the highway at South Street. I tried to remember whether he'd called Ellie "your girl" before, or if this was new and meant he'd forgotten her name.

"She's with Dave at a birthday party." Although Dave was never around as much as I'd hoped he would be, when he was with Ellie, he was a wonderful dad. The two of them adored each other, in exactly the way I'd always hoped my dad would adore me. Ellie would slip her little hand sweetly in his, beaming up at him, or pat the pockets of his jacket, searching for treats, when he came home from the *Examiner.* "Hello, princess," he would say, and hoist her in his arms, tossing her once, twice, three times gently up toward the ceiling as she shrieked in delight.

I found a parking spot on the street, fed the meter, and followed my father into the restaurant, where we were seated at a table overlooking South Street: the fancy gym, the fancier pet shop, the moms piloting oversized strollers, hooded and tented against the rain.

"I love the fried chicken. And the brisket's great. Or if you want breakfast, they serve all their egg dishes with potato latkes . . ." I was chattering, I realized, the same way I did with Ellie, trying to keep the conversational ball in the air without any help from my partner.

My father shrugged, then stared down at the menu. Was he depressed? It wouldn't be surprising if that were the case . . . but could he take antidepressants, with the Aricept for his dementia and the other meds he took for his blood pressure? Was there even a point in treating depression in someone who was losing touch with reality?

By the time the waitress had filled us in on the specials and we'd placed our orders—a brisket club sandwich for my father, a grilled cheese with bacon and avocado for me—I was exhausted.

"Tell me the story of the night I was born." Asking someone with memory loss to tell you a story, to remember something on cue, was risky . . . but this was one of my father's favorites, one I'd heard him tell dozens of times, including but not limited to each of my birthdays. Maybe he would talk for a while, and I could sit quietly, catching my breath, maybe sneaking a pill in the ladies' room before we left.

He took a bite of his sandwich, dabbed at his lips, and began the way he always did: "It was a dark and stormy night." I smiled as he went on. "It was three days after your mother's due date. We lived on the fourth floor of an old Victorian at Thirty-Eighth and Clark. I was a starving graduate student, and she was . . ." He paused, his eyes losing focus, his features softening, his face flushed, looking younger than he had in years, more like the father I remembered, as I mouthed the next five words along with him. "Your mother was so pretty." We smiled at each other, then he continued. "When she started having contractions, we weren't worried. First babies can take a while, and we were maybe ten blocks from the hospital. Her bag was packed, and I'd memorized the numbers for two different cab companies. She had one contraction and then, ten minutes later, another one. Then one more five minutes after that, then one two minutes after that . . ." He used his hands as he told the story—how my mother's labor progressed faster than they had expected, how by the time they got down to the street to wait for the cab, rain was lashing the streets and the wind was bending the trees practically in half, and the mayor and the governor were on the radio, telling people to stay inside, to stay home unless they absolutely had to leave. "I was ninety percent sure you were going to be born in the back of a taxicab," my father said.

He got every detail, every nuance of the story right—the way the cab smelled of incense and curry, the driver's unflappable calm, how he'd left my mother's little plaid suitcase on the sidewalk in front of our house in his haste to get my mom in the cab, and how one of the neighbors had retrieved it when the rain stopped, dried each item of clothing, and brought it over the next day.

"Did you want more kids?" I asked him. All these years of wondering, and I'd finally gotten up the nerve to ask. He waited until the waiter had cleared our plates and taken our orders for two cups of coffee and one slice of buttermilk chocolate cake, and patted his lips with his napkin again before saying, "It wasn't meant to be. We had you, and then your mother had her trouble . . ."

"What trouble?" I asked, half my mind on his answer, the other half on my sandwich. He probably meant the Accident. That was the only trouble I'd ever heard about.

He pushed the salt and pepper shakers across the table like chess pieces and did not answer.

"Was I a hard baby?" I asked. Had I been like Ellie, shrieky and picky and inclined toward misery? Again, no answer from Dad. I knew, of course, how overwhelming a baby could be, and I suspected that in addition to feeling like a newborn's demands were more than she could handle, my mother had also felt isolated. It couldn't have been easy, I thought, and pictured

Little Ronnie, her flawless skin suddenly mottled with stretch marks, her beauty sleep disrupted, all alone in the apartment and, eventually, in the big house my father had bought her. Who had she gone to with her questions and concerns? I'd had friends, a pricy lactation consultant, and the leader of the playgroup I attended, who had a degree in early childhood development. I'd had Janet, and my own mom, and even the Indomitable Doreen. My mother had no one. Her own mother had died before I was born, and as a teenage bride and young mother, she hadn't yet formed bonds with the types of women I'd come to know. She had only my father . . . and that might have been lonely.

I pictured her now, back in Cherry Hill. Was she trying to clean up the mess in the kitchen? Was she paging through old photo albums, the way she had the last time I'd spent the day with her, looking at pictures of cousins I couldn't remember and uncles I'd never met? Was she remembering my father, dashing and young and invulnerable, and wishing that she'd been the one to get sick instead of him?

"Excuse me," I said. The bathroom at Honey's had a rustic wooden bench to set a purse or a diaper bag on. The walls were hung with framed magazine ads from the 1920s advertising nerve tonics and hair-restoring creams, and a mirror in a flaking gold frame.

I looked at my reflection. My face looked thinner, and the circles under my eyes seemed to have deepened over the past few weeks. I'd lost a few more pounds—with the pills, I'd found myself occasionally sleeping through meals—but I didn't look fit or healthy, just weary and depleted. Even on my best days, I was no Little Ronnie, with her bright eyes and long, thick hair, the kind of girl a man would want to tuck in his pocket and keep safe forever.

Turning away from the mirror, I reached into my purse. I crunched up two pills, washed them down with a scoop of water from the sink, and walked back to the table. I'd had an idea of how to give my mother some extra time, and make the day go by. "Hey," I said to my father, "do you want to go see Ellie?"

As soon as I walked into BouncyTime, I knew that bringing my dad there had been a mistake. Raucous music boomed from overhead speakers. The singer fought against the roar of the blowers that kept the climbing and bouncing structures inflated. Kids dashed around the room, screaming, racing up the giant slide, hurling inflatable beach balls at one another's heads, or shooting foam missiles out of air cannons. A clutch of mothers stood in a circle, in the Haverford uniform of 7 For All Mankind jeans and a cashmere crewneck, or Lululemon yoga pants and a breathable wicking top in a complementary color. Along the wall, a smaller group of dads had gathered, heads down, tapping away at their screens, looking up occasionally to cries of "Daddy, look at me!" or, more often, "Daddy, take a video!" I found Dave with two other men, one a lawyer, one who ran a dental insurance business.

"Hey," said the lawyer. "It's the Sexy Mama from the *Wall Street Journal*."

"That's me," I said, pasting a look of fake cheer on my face. "Have you guys met my dad?" I let Dave handle the introductions while I looked around for Ellie. She wasn't in the bouncy castle with the girls, or waiting in line for the air cannons with the boys. Eventually I found Hank, sitting glumly on one of the benches with an ice pack clutched to his forehead. He pointed out Ellie huddled against a wall, with her skirt smoothed over her lap, playing with what appeared to be the iPod I'd lost the week before.

I walked over, trying not to look angry. "Ellie, is that my iPod?"

She looked up. "You're not supposedta BE HERE!"

"Well, hello to you, too." I sat down on the floor beside her and held out my hand. "You know the rules. You don't just take other people's things. You need to ask first." She threw the iPod at me. It hit me just above my left eyebrow and fell to the floor.

"Ellie! What was that for?"

"Jade and Summer and Willow all have THEIR OWN iPODS!" She widened her eyes into a look suggesting she could barely bring herself to contemplate such unfairness.

"Ellie, we do not throw things," I said, struggling not to yell. Ellie ignored me.

"And they're the new touch ones, not STUPID TINY BABY ONES like YOU HAVE!"

"We don't throw," I repeated. "And you shouldn't have taken Mommy's things without permission."

Ellie stuck out her lower lip. "I didn't even WANT TO COME to this STUPID BABY PARTY! Why can't everyone just LEAVE ME ALONE!"

I sighed as she started to cry. Maybe—probably—this place was just too bright and noisy for Eloise. As if to confirm my thought, she leaned against me, resting her head on my shoulder. "I'm sorry I taked your thing and threw it at your head."

"It's okay," I told her. "Just next time, ask first."

At the sound of sniffling, I looked up to see Hank. "Will you do the slide?" he asked.

Ellie shook her head. "Too scary," she proclaimed.

"What if we went down together?" I asked. "You could sit on my lap."

Ellie narrowed her eyes, judging the steep angle of the slide, watching the kids zip down, hands raised, mouths open, squealing with glee. Most slid on their own, but a few made the descent seated on parents' laps.

"You want to try it?"

She sighed, as though she was granting me an enormous favor. "Oooh-kay."

"How about you, Hank?"

He shook his head. "I'm allergic to burlap."

But of course. I got to my feet—not half as gracefully as one of the yoga moms would have managed—and held out my hand. Ellie and I were walking toward the line at the back of the slide when Dave intercepted us.

"Hey, Al. You want to check on your dad?"

"What's wrong?" I peered toward the benches where I'd left him, and saw him sitting there, staring into space the same way he stared at CNBC.

"He seems kind of uncomfortable."

I gave him a patient, beatific Mary Poppins kind of smile, and hoped I didn't look drugged. "Ellie and I are going to try the slide. Just sit with him. I'll be there in two minutes."

"I don't wanna," Ellie said as soon as she realized she'd have to climb a ladder built into the back of the slide to get to the top.

"Honey, I'll be right here. Just put your hands like this . . ." I bent down and lifted, putting her feet on the bottom rung and her hands on the one above it. "Now just take a step . . ."

"I don't WANT TO DO THIS. I'm SCARED!"

"Hurry up!" shouted the little boy—Hayden? Holden?—behind us. I scooped Ellie into one arm and hauled us both up the ladder.

"Come on! You'll love it! I used to love slides when I was a little girl!"

"I WILL NOT LOVE SLIDES!" said Ellie, but she let me carry her to the top of the slide. Red-faced, panting, with sweat dribbling down my back, I grabbed a sack, marveling at the lack of progress—in these days of satellite radios and wireless Internet, why were kids still sliding on actual burlap sacks? I hoisted Ellie in my arms and got us in position.

"One . . . two . . . three!"

I kicked off with my heels. I could hear my daughter screaming—from fear or delight, I wasn't sure. Nor was there time to figure it out, because the instant we got to the bottom of the slide, someone grabbed my shoulders and started shaking me.

"What are you doing with my daughter?"

I tried to wriggle away, but my father's hands were clamped down tight, his fingers curling into the flesh of my upper arms. His shirt was untucked, his tie had been yanked askew, and the Velcro closure of one of his shoes had come undone and was flapping.

"How could you be so irresponsible?" he asked.

"Dad. *Dad!* It's me, Allison!"

"You put her down right this minute, Ronnie! Don't you ever, *ever* do that again!"

Oh, God. Eloise was wailing as another mother-child duo came hurtling down the slide and slammed into my back, knocking Ellie out of my arms and onto the floor . . . where, unsurprisingly, she started to scream.

"Ohmygod, I'm so sorry!" said the mother.

"How could you be so irresponsible!" my father was shouting.

"Ellie's mommy is in trou-ble," sang the little boy as I finally managed to wrench myself free. Ellie, weeping, limped dramatically over to Dave. Everyone in the place was staring at us, moms and dads and kids.

"Um, ma'am? Excuse me?" A teenage girl in a BouncyTime T-shirt tapped my shoulder. "You can't stay here. There are other people waiting to use the slide."

"Believe me, I am trying to leave," I told her. I took my father by the elbow and steered him away from the slide and over to the metal bench against the wall.

"Dad," I said, trying to keep my voice low and calm as, beside me, Dave attempted to soothe Ellie. "Listen to me. I'm your daughter. I'm Allison. That was Ellie, your granddaughter, and she's fine . . . that slide was perfectly safe . . ."

"Why was Grandpa YELLING at me?" Ellie wailed. She lifted the hem of her skirt and blotted her tears.

"Ew, gross!" a little boy said. My eyes followed his pointing finger. Oh, God.

"I think your dad had an accident," Dave said. His voice was quiet, but not quiet enough. I figured Ellie would be revolted, but instead she slipped her hand into my father's hand and pulled him toward the door.

"Don't worry, Pop-Pop," she stage-whispered. "Sometimes that happens to me, too."

Ellie and Dave arranged to ride home with Hank's mother. I got my dad back into the car, slipping a towel from the trunk onto his seat, and concentrated on getting him back home as fast as I could.

"Dad, are you okay?" I asked. "Do you need anything?"

He didn't answer . . . he just lifted his chin and turned his face away from me. As soon as we were moving I rolled down my window, holding my breath and hoping he wouldn't notice. When I heard what sounded like a choked sob from the passenger seat, I kept both hands on the wheel and my eyes straight ahead. *Get through this,* I told myself. *Get through this, and there will be happy pills at the end.*

We arrived to find my mother asleep on the couch, curled up in her housecoat with her bare feet tucked around each other, the same way Ellie arranged her feet when she slept. "Do you want me to . . ." I asked my dad, then let my voice trail off and cut my eyes toward the stairs. My father ignored me, pressing his lips together as he made his way past me. I waited until I heard the water running in the bathroom before I let myself collapse at the kitchen table. The room was still a mess, the sink piled with dirty dishes, the counters greasy and streaked, the flowers I'd brought the previous weekend dying in a vase of scummy water. I emptied the vase, loaded the dishwasher, sprayed and wiped down the counters, and took out the trash. I pulled a package of turkey thighs past their expiration date out of the refrigerator, along with a bag of softened zucchini and three dessicated lemons, and threw them all away. I dumped sour milk down the drain, wiped off the refrigerator shelves, and boiled water for a pot of tea, which I placed on a tray with a napkin and a plate of cookies.

I knocked on the bedroom door. "Dad?" No answer. I eased the door open. He was curled on his side, his fist propped underneath his chin, mouth open, sleeping. With his forehead smooth and his eyes closed he looked like a little boy, a boy who'd played until he was exhausted and had fallen asleep on his parents' bed. I set down the tray, then picked up my dad's wet pants using my thumb and forefinger and carried them to the washing machine, which was already full of damp, moldy-smelling clothes. I ran the machine again, adding more detergent. Then I slipped back into my parents' bedroom. Half-empty water glasses, crumpled tissues, and discarded newspapers covered the bedside tables. Dirty clothes were heaped on the floor; magazines and newspapers were stacked in the corners. I stepped over a tangle of ties and a dozen discarded shoes and opened the bathroom door. The room was still steamy from the shower. Wet towels were piled in the tub, and a few more lined the floor. Hot water was pouring into the sink, and my father's razor rested against an uncapped bottle of shaving cream. I turned off the water, capped the cream, and opened the medicine chest. My hands moved expertly over the bottles, fingertips just brushing the tops long enough to distinguish between over-the-counter and prescription stuff. I pulled down propranolol, diltiazem, and various other medica-tions for high blood pressure and diabetes before I got to the good stuff. Vicodin 325/10. "Take as needed for pain." Tramadol. And—bingo—OxyContin. Without pausing, without thinking, I uncapped the bottles and emptied half of each one into my hands.

What are you doing? a part of my brain cried as I crunched three of the pills, then bent down to gather the dirty towels, pick up the soap off the shower floor, pull a wad of hair out of the drain, and sweep discarded Q-tips and Kleenexes into the wastebasket. *You're stealing medicine from your father, your sick father. Have you really sunk so low?*

It appeared that I had. *I need this,* I told myself as I moved through the bedroom, gathering armloads of clothing and piling them into garbage bags, and then loading the bags into the trunk of my car to take home to wash and fold. *I need this.*

PART TWO

All Fall Down

Seven

"Welcome to Eastwood." The woman who met me on the front lawn of the Eastwood Assisted Living Facility had her silver-gray hair in a neat bob, a high, sweet voice, and a cool, brisk handshake. She wore khakis, a sweater, and a nametag with KATHLEEN YOUNG written on it, and she led me through the doors with a bounce in her step, like a former high-school jock who'd stayed on campus to teach phys ed. "Let me show you around!"

Her bubbly, energetic manner only made the handful of residents—a man in a wheelchair by the door, hands shaking as he held up the *Examiner*; a woman in a pink-and-white bathrobe, using a walker to make her slow way toward the art room—look even older and sadder. I tried to picture my father here, my smart, strong, competent father in a bathrobe, requiring the kind of care a place like this could give him. It hurt, but it was a distant kind of pain. The pills let me consider his future without feeling it too deeply. It was almost like watching a movie about someone else's sorrows—*now her father can't remember his granddaughter's name; now he's having temper tantrums; now he's having accidents, and wandering away from home, and crying*—and knowing they were painful without feeling them acutely. Narcotics were like a warm, fuzzy comforter, a layer of defense between me and the world.

"Follow me, please," said Kathleen, bounding down the hallway on the balls of her feet. I grappled with a brief but fierce desire to go sprinting back to my car, to burn rubber out of the parking lot and never see this place again . . . only what good would that do? My mother was unlikely to take this on. Someone had to step up and do what was required.

In the foyer I braced myself for the smell of urine, of industrial cleansers and canned chicken soup that I remembered from my dad's last hospital stay, but Eastwood's green-carpeted corridors smelled pleasantly of cedar and spice. There was a basket of scented pinecones on top of the front desk, behind which two women in headsets were busy typing. Behind them was an oversized whiteboard, the kind I remembered from Ellie's preschool, with sentences left open-ended, so the kids and teachers could fill in the blanks. *Today is MONDAY,* read the top line. *It is APRIL 7th. The weather is . . .* Instead of the word "sunny," someone had affixed a decal of an affably beaming sun. *Our SPECIAL ACTIVITIES are BINGO in the Recreation Parlor, and a TRIP TO THE CAMDEN AQUARIUM.* I felt a tug at my sleeve, and heard a whispered "Help me." I looked down. While Kathleen was deep in conversation with one of the head-setted ladies behind the desk, a tiny, curled shrimp of a woman had wheeled up beside me and grabbed my sleeve.

"What's wrong?" I asked.

The woman gave a very teenager-y eye roll. Fine white hair floated around her pink scalp in an Einsteinian nimbus. Her frail torso was wrapped in an oversized pink cardigan, and she wore pink velour pants and a pair of white knitted slippers beneath it. Her veined hand trembled, but her eyes, behind enormous glasses, were sharp, and I was relieved to see a full set of teeth (or realistic-looking dentures) when she started talking.

"This place is what's wrong," she murmured, speaking out of the side of her mouth, like a prisoner in the yard who didn't want the guards to overhear. "The steak is tough. The pudding's bland. They've been promising me for weeks to order my gluten-free crumpets, and . . ." She lifted her hands in the air, palms up, a mute appeal to the God of gluten-free crumpets. "Also, my kids never visit."

"I'm sorry," I stammered, then squatted, my face close to hers. She extended one of her gnarled paws toward me.

"Lois Lefkowitz. Formerly of sunny Florida, until I broke my hip and my kids moved me back here."

I shook her hand gently. "I'm Allison Weiss." I shot a glance at the counter, making sure the brisk

Ms. Young was still occupied, before I whispered, "Is it really that bad here?"

She patted my hand and shook her head.

"What's not to like?" she asked. "I don't have to cook, I don't have to clean, I don't have to shop, and I don't have to listen to Murray go on about his fantasy football team. I read . . ." She tapped the e-reader in her lap. "With this thing, every book is a large-print book. I go to the museum, I go to the symphony, and the beauty shop's open once a week for a wash and set." She patted her wisps of white hair, then put one gnarled paw on my shoulder. "Mother or father?"

"My dad."

"Memory loss or just can't get around?"

"He's got Alzheimer's."

"Oh, sweetie. I'm sorry." Pat, pat, pat went the wrinkled little hand. It felt surprisingly nice. Both of my grandmothers were long gone—my mother's mother had died of breast cancer before I was born, and my father's mother, Grandma Sadie, had gone to Heaven's screened-in porch when I was in college. I liked to imagine her sometimes, sitting in a rocking chair, listening to the Sox and yelling at my grandfather. "They'll take good care of him here."

My throat felt thick as I swallowed. "You think so?"

"I see things. I watch. They'll make sure he's safe. Do you have children?"

"A little girl."

"Pictures?"

I pulled my phone out of my purse. Ellie, in her favorite maxidress, was my wallpaper. In the picture, she stood on the beach in a broad-brimmed sun hat, with waves foaming at her feet. My new friend peered at the screen, then sighed. "It goes so fast," she told me. "One minute you're putting diaper cream on their tushies, the next thing you know, you're walking them down the aisle. Then they're putting you in a place like this." She sighed again, and I thought I saw the glimmer of moisture on one seamed cheek. "And you sit here and wonder where the time went, and how you never wanted to live long enough that someone should be changing your diapers." Another sigh. "Still. I wouldn't have missed a day of it." She poked at my phone. "You got Candy Crush on here?"

"Oh. No. Sorry."

Kathleen Young was heading toward us, her pleasant smile still in place, but I noticed the creases around her eyes had deepened.

"Mrs. Lefkowitz, you're not scaring away prospectives, are you?"

My new friend gave Ms. Young a sunny smile. "You mean I shouldn't tell them about the rats in the showers?"

"She's kidding," said Ms. Young. Mrs. Lefkowitz gave me another smile of surpassing sweetness.

179

"I hope I'll see you again," she said. "And that pretty little girl!"

"Nice to meet you," I said, and gave her little paw another squeeze.

"Right this way," said Kathleen Young. "This is the Manor," she said, walking at a swift clip past opened doors with nameplates on them. "Our residents who require the most care stay here. This," she said, opening a door, "is a typical double room."

I stepped inside. The room wasn't large, with most of the space taken up by adjustable hospital beds with side rails that could be raised or dropped. There were two oak dressers; two bookcases; two armchairs, one on each side of the room, each upholstered in blue plastic, dyed and patterned to make it look like cloth. The bathroom had all of the stainless steel rails you'd expect, with a metal-and-plastic chair in the oversized walk-in shower cubicle, and grippy mats on the floor. Back in the room, I let my fingertips drift along the armrest of one chair and tried not to wince at the feeling of plastic. Would my dad see the difference between the furniture in his house and this stuff? How could he not? Noticing my expression, Kathleen said, "Of course, our residents are welcome to bring their own furniture. Most do. We find it helps with their sense of dislocation." I nodded, mentally erasing the hospital bed, the cheap bureau and bookcase, and the plasticized armchair, and replacing them with things from my parents' home. Better.

"Are there single rooms available?"

"Of course. They're significantly more expensive . . ."

"That shouldn't be a problem," I said, and watched Kathleen's pupils expand. Years ago my father, in a tacit admission that my mother was equipped to handle precisely nothing that his golden years might entail, had bought himself a life-insurance policy and all kinds of disability and extended-care policies, too. There was money to pay for everything he'd need, and to pay for the help my mother might eventually require, now that my father was unable to arrange her days. "Tell me about the, uh, level of care." I'd done all kinds of research about the questions I was supposed to ask, even if the answers were all on the website. As Kathleen recited statistics about physician's assistants, physicians on call, and nurse-practitioners, LPNs, and nurse's aides, and how it was a goal at Eastwood to encourage as much independence as was feasible and safe, I thought of when I was twelve, and my father had taken me to New York City.

The whole thing was an accident. He'd gotten the tickets for *South Pacific* as my mother's birthday present. For weeks, she'd gone around playing the cast recording, singing "Younger than Springtime," making appointments for a haircut and color, trying on and returning different dresses. I had come home on the Friday afternoon of their proposed trip and found her sick in bed. Some kind of twenty-four-hour bug, I'd thought, remembering the sounds of retching, murmuring behind closed doors, my dad asking if she wanted a doctor and my mother, shrill and weepy, saying she'd be fine, just fine, she just needed to sleep. My father had emerged tight-lipped, visibly unhappy. He'd already paid for the tickets, made plans for dinner, reserved the hotel room. If there'd been time he would have found a way to cancel the whole thing. Instead, he'd mustered up a smile and said, "How'd you like to go to the Big Apple with your dear old dad?"

At twelve, I was not looking good. My breasts and my nose had both sprouted to what would become their adult dimensions, with the rest of my body and my face lagging behind. I had braces, with rubber bands to pull my upper jaw back into alignment with my lower jaw, and my oily skin, in spite of all the Clearasil and the benzoyl-peroxide-soaked scrubbie pads, was routinely spattered with pimples. I was wearing my hair with bangs, figuring the more of my troubled complexion I could hide, the better, and my oversized button-down shirts, paired with pants pegged at the ankles and flowy everywhere else, did nothing to minimize my size. But on that night, due to some miracle of luck and timing, my skin was clear, my hair was behaving, and I looked like a girl any father would be happy to escort to a show.

"Try my silver dress," my mother had croaked from her bed. It was meant to be knee-length. On me, it was a hip-skimming tunic. Paired with plain black leggings and my mom's black leather boots, it made me look almost like a grown-up, sophisticated and smart. She swept my bangs back with one of the wide cotton bands she wore to yoga, then blow-dried and straightened my hair and let me wear a little lipstick, red, which made my skin look olive instead of sallow. "Nice," she whispered with a smile, before turning on her side and falling noisily asleep. My father had been dressed in his newest suit and the tie my mom had gotten him for his birthday. His eyes widened in appreciation as I came down the stairs, with my mother's good black winter coat draped over one arm. "Those boys don't know what they're missing," he'd blurted, and then instantly looked ashamed, but I carried that compliment close, like a jeweled locket, something wonderful and rare. He had held the car door open for me, regaled me with stories of the brain-dead interns from Penn's and Temple's graduate schools who descended on his office every summer, and how one of them had gotten so drunk at the managing partner's Fourth of July party that he'd vomited in the hot tub. Exiting the car, paying the parking-lot attendant, holding his arm out to hail a taxi, or holding a door open and saying "After you," he'd looked so handsome, tall and assured in his camel-hair topcoat, his shoes polished to a high gloss, the Rolex my mother had bought him for his fiftieth birthday gleaming on his wrist. In the theater, he kept one hand lightly between my shoulder blades as he steered us toward our seats, and in the restaurant, the pride in his tone was unmistakable as he introduced me to the maître d' and the waiter, who both seemed to know him, as "my daughter, Allison."

I could remember everything from that night— the look of the theater, lit like a temple in the frosty Manhattan night, the smell of perfume and silk and fur in the air, the rustle of programs as the audience settled into the seats, the plaintive voice of the lead actor, lamenting about how paradise had once nearly been his. I remembered how women's eyes had turned toward my father, the approving looks they gave him, how I'd felt about the way he belonged in their company, tall and smart and successful. I could name everything we'd eaten at the little French bistro on Fifty-Sixth Street, and could conjure up the taste of lobster bisque laced with sherry, profiteroles drizzled in dark chocolate, the single sip each of white wine and red wine and after-dinner port he'd let me have. Half-asleep in the taxi's backseat as it cut through the traffic, humming the overture to myself, I had thought that I would never feel more content, more beloved, more beautiful.

Today is MONDAY, read the sign in the dining room, where tables for four were draped in pink cloths and set at wide intervals, the better to steer wheelchairs around them. On a shelf were dozens of paperbacks by Lee Child, Vince Flynn, Brad Thor. Was there some kind of law that men who wrote military thrillers had to have two-syllable names where the first and the last sounded interchangeable? There were romances for the ladies—your Nora Roberts, your Danielle Steel—and board games in worn boxes, some with their sagging edges reinforced with duct tape, the same games I played with Ellie: Sorry! and Parcheesi and Monopoly and Battleship. *Our next meal will be DINNER,* read the whiteboard at the front of the room. *Tonight we are having CREAM OF MUSHROOM SOUP, LONDON BROIL, MASHED POTATOES, and GREEN BEANS. Oh, Dad,* I mourned, and wondered how my mother would survive, seeing her beloved husband in a place like this.

Kathleen interrupted my reverie, giving me a glossy "Welcome to Eastwood" folder and a big smile. "If you're ready, we can go back to my office. There's some preliminary paperwork you can fill out, and then, once our finance department has had a look, they'll be in touch. Did you bring your father's tax returns?"

185

"I'm sorry," I said. The insides of my eyelids were stinging, and I was already blinking back tears. "I think I'm going to have to take care of that another time."

"Are you all right?" Kathleen's tone was not unsympathetic. She must have seen this dozens, if not hundreds of times—spouses and children who thought they were ready flipping out and running when it came time to sign the forms, to write the checks, to make it real. I managed a nod, and then hurried past the front desk, through the doors, out to the parking lot, and into my car. *One dream in my heart,* I heard in my head, and brushed my sleeve against my cheeks to wipe away the tears. *One love to be living for . . . One love to be living for . . . This nearly was mine.*

Eight

"Allison Weiss?" The girl waiting at the door was tiny, with a nose the size of a pencil eraser and feet so small I bet she had to shop in the children's department. It was May, the weather springtime-perfect. The scents of flowers, cut grass, and freshly turned earth wafted on a warm breeze (I could see a gardener digging the beds adjacent to the parking lot), and the sky outside the television studio was a perfect turquoise, dotted with cotton-ball clouds.

I smiled at the young woman with the warmth and goodwill that only the pure of heart, or the people who've recently swallowed a handful of OxyContin, can muster. "I'm Allison Weiss. Are you Beatrice?" I had gotten the call the night before, from a woman who'd introduced herself as Kim Caster, a producer for *The News on Nine*, the local evening newscast. "Did you hear about that mess in Akron?" she had asked.

"I did." The mess in Akron was the kind of story that had become depressingly familiar since every teenager in America, it seemed, had been issued an iPhone. On a fine spring weekend, a fifteen-year-old girl had gone to a party. She'd gotten drunk. Four different boys, all football teammates, had taken advantage of her. Then, just to add to the fun, they'd posted photographs of their deeds on Instagram and video on YouTube. Within the next twenty-four hours, almost every kid who attended the town's high school saw what had happened. The girl had tried to kill herself after a few of the most lurid shots ended up on her Facebook page. The boys had been arrested . . . but their defenders spread the word that the girl had come dressed provocatively with a vibrator in her purse and had texted her friends that she was looking for action.

"As someone who writes a lot about sex and relationships—and, of course, as a mother yourself—what are your thoughts?"

"I don't think owning a vibrator, or even having one with you, is a standing invitation for guys to do whatever they want," I'd said. "A girl can wear a short skirt and not be asking for it. She can even get drunk and have the right not to be raped. It's never the victim's fault."

"Mmm-hmm . . . uh-huh . . . great . . . great," said the producer. "And what about the argument that it wasn't really a gang rape because some of it involved only digital penetration?"

I'd rolled my eyes. A columnist at no less an institution than the *Washington Post* had made that very point on the op-ed page last week, and the *Examiner* had reprinted his column. In our better days, I might have given Dave some grief about it, but these days Dave and I were barely speaking. It felt as if we were trapped in the world's longest staring contest, neither of us willing to blink and bring up the topic of L. McIntyre, or Dave's ever-lengthening stay in the guest room, or the pills. "There's no 'only' when it comes to rape," I said. "I don't think it matters whether it's a penis or a finger. Anything you don't want inside you shouldn't be there."

The producer had seemed impressed enough with my answers to invite me to come on the air for the channel's Sunday-morning *Newsmakers on Nine* show, where local folks gave their opinions on the issues of the day. I'd spent an hour on my makeup and allotted myself fifteen minutes to just sit quietly and catch my breath after wrestling myself into many layers of compressing undergarments, and now here I was. I'd calibrated my dosage carefully; just two pills, enough to take the edge off, to let me push through the sorrow that threatened to keep me pinned to the bed in despair.

"Follow me, please," said Beatrice, whose hair bounced as she walked. "We'll go right to makeup."

"That bad, huh?"

Beatrice stopped mid-stride and turned and studied me carefully.

"That was a joke! Don't answer!" I said.

"Oh. Okay."

Kids these days, I thought, as Beatrice waved a plastic card at an electronic eye and glass barriers parted.

"Makeup" turned out to be a closet-sized room with two beauty-salon chairs, a mirror that covered one wall, and a table stocked with a department store's worth of pots and tubs and containers of eye shadow and foundation and fake eyelashes arrayed like amputated spiders' legs. One chair was empty. In the other sat a middle-aged white guy with short, sandy hair, bland features, a wedding ring on his left hand, and a class ring with a gaudy red stone on his right. The makeup artist introduced herself as Cindy, handed me a smock, and went back to patting foundation on the man's face.

I sat down in the empty chair. "Hey, that's my brand!" I said to the man, who did not smile. "Hi, I'm Allison Weiss. Are you on the panel, too?"

Without meeting my eyes, he gave a stiff nod. "I am." His small brown eyes were sunk back into the flesh of his oddly rectangular head, like raisins in dough that had risen around them. "You must be the sex worker."

I laughed. I couldn't help it. "Sex worker? Who do you think would hire me?" When the man didn't answer, I realized that he wasn't kidding. "I'm not a sex worker. I'm a blogger." Realizing that might not sound any different to the uninitiated, I said, "I write about marriage and motherhood on a website called Ladiesroom.com." Which, I thought with a sinking heart, also sounded vaguely pornographic. I mustered a smile. "Trust me, I'm about as far from a porn star as you could be."

"We're all set," said the makeup lady, giving the man's nose a final dusting. He stood up and unsnapped his smock, revealing the plain black shirt and white clerical collar underneath. Oops.

"Good God," I said. The makeup lady giggled. The pills did not make me slurry or sloppy, but they did lower my inhibitions. On them, I'd say whatever was on my mind, and think it over later. Usually it wasn't a problem. This might turn out to be an exception. I bit my lip and wondered if it had been a good idea to take anything before leaving for the studio. This, of course, led me to wonder if the shipment I was expecting that day would show up, and whether I had enough to get through the weekend if it didn't. I wondered, as I walked down the hall, who Penny Lane's vendors were, the druggy Oz behind the Internet's green curtain. Were they cancer patients willing to sell their meds and suffer in order to pay off their bills and leave their kids cash? Scummy thieves who robbed cancer patients, then sold their pills for cash? Kids who worked in drugstores, sneaking out five or ten pills at a time, or people getting them from doctors without ethics, or maybe even actual doctors?

Never mind. "Did you do your own makeup?" Cindy asked, cupping my chin in her hand and turning my face first left, then right.

"My friend helped." Janet and Maya had come over that morning, lugging a light-up mirror and bags of makeup. Maya had actually been excited enough to speak directly to her mother while they debated brown versus black eyeliner and whether my brows required additional plucking.

"Not bad," Cindy said.

"Just please don't make me look too slutty," I said, as she began filling in my lashes with a brush dipped in brown powder. "Slutty would not do." With that in mind, I'd worn a pencil skirt and pumps with a not-too-high heel, a fuchsia

191

cardigan with a pale-pink T-shirt underneath, and a single strand of pearls. I was going for "mildly sexy librarian," and I'd already solemnly vowed to refrain from looking at any and all online commentary on my outfit, my figure, or what I had to say.

"Good luck," Dave had told me as I'd gathered my car keys and my purse. He sounded friendlier than he had in weeks, and, almost without thinking, I'd turned my face up toward his for a good-luck kiss. Maybe he'd just intended to brush my lips with his, but I'd stumbled, as a result either of the heels or of the Penny Lane pills, and we'd ended up with his arms around me, the length of my body pressed against his, close enough to feel the heat of him through the cotton and denim, to smell his scent of shampoo and warm, clean skin. I'd opened my mouth and he'd settled one hand at the small of my back, tilting me against him, the better to feel his thickening erection, the other at the base of my neck so he could keep my head in place while he kissed me, lingeringly, thoroughly . . .

"EWWW!"

We sprang apart. I stumbled again—this time, it was definitely the heels—and staggered back-ward, praying that my skirt wouldn't rip. "Ellie, what's wrong?" I'd asked. Ellie, predictably, had started to cry.

"I don't like KISSING. It is DISGUSTING."

"Not when mommies and daddies do it!"

"That," my daughter proclaimed, chin lifted, "is the MOST DISGUSTING OF ALL!"

"Well all righty, then," I'd muttered, as Dave helped me to my feet. I could still barely believe what had happened, and wondered what had prompted it. Had he realized that, deep down, he really loved me . . . or, my mind whispered, had L. turned him down, telling him to go home to his wife unless he was ready to leave her?

"Later," he'd whispered, and I'd sailed out the door, resolved not to think too hard about it, buoyed by this unexpected show of affection, by lust, and by the confidence that only a dose of narcotics could give me. Maybe everything was going to be fine. Maybe I'd go home and we'd make love (in my fantasy, Ellie had been whisked away, possibly by the Indomitable Doreen). Dave would tell me that he loved me, that he'd always loved me, and, more than that, that he was proud of me. He would tell me he was grateful that I'd kept us going during hard times. Then he'd tell me that he'd come up with another book idea, that his agent loved it, that the publisher loved it, that they'd given him another advance even bigger than the first one, and that L. McIntyre had been transferred to Butte, Montana.

"No slutty," said Cindy. Working quickly, she touched up my foundation, patted concealer underneath my eyes, glued a few falsies into my lashes, and ran a flat iron over my hair. "Put on more lipstick and lipgloss right before they start," she said, handing me tubes of both. Beatrice and her clipboard were waiting in the hallway.

"I'll take you to the greenroom. You've got about ten minutes."

"Who else is on this segment?" I asked as we walked.

Her heels clipped briskly against the tiled floor. "Let's see. It's you, Father Ryan of the Christian League of Decency, and, um, a parenting person. She's a child psy . . . psychologist? Psychiatrist?" She frowned at her clipboard as if she were disappointed it wasn't volunteering the answer. "A child something."

"Great. Can I ask you a quick question?" Without giving her time to mull it over, I said, "You guys know I'm not a sex worker, right?" The line between her eyebrows reappeared as Beatrice looked from her clipboard to my face, then down at her clipboard again. "So you're not a sex worker."

I shook my head.

"But you work in the sex industry?"

"No, no I don't. Really, the most accurate thing you could say is that I work for a website that sometimes addresses women's sexuality." *Sarah,* I thought. Sarah was Ladiesroom's go-to sex-positive person, but she wasn't here because this was Philadelphia, and I was the local girl.

She scribbled something on her clipboard. "Got it."

I was unconvinced. But I said, "Okay, great," and followed her pointing finger into another closet-sized room. This was the greenroom—painted, I noticed, an unremarkable beige. It had a conference-style table, a big flat-screen TV set to Channel 9, and a cart with three cans of Diet Coke, a bucket full of water I assumed had once been ice, and a black plastic tray covered in crumbs and two barely ripe strawberries. Father Ryan sat at one end of the table, with his Bible open and his head bent. At the other end sat a tiny, dark-haired woman in a red suit talking into a Bluetooth headset. "Mmm-hmm. That's right. Have Dolly pick up the sushi on her way in. The flowers come at five and the caterers start at six. Right—oh, hang on." She jabbed at her phone with one fingertip. "Hello, this is Dr. Carol Bendinger, how can I help you?"

I took one of the cans of Diet Coke and found a seat. When neither of my fellow panelists acknowledged me, I pulled out a copy of my morning blog post and highlighted the points I wanted to make. *Being sexually active is not an invitation to rapists,* I'd written. True. *The fact that a teenage girl chooses to have sex with someone doesn't mean she's willing to sleep with everyone.* Also true. But rape wasn't sex. Should I be making more of a distinction between a girl using her vibrator with her boyfriend (or girlfriend, I reminded myself) and what the boys at the party had done to her?

I rummaged oh-so-casually in my purse until I found the Altoids tin. Flipping it open, I counted two, four, six, eight, ten pills. I'd taken those two pills less than an hour ago, but I was already starting to feel the familiar anxiety working its way through my body, nibbling at my knees, making them feel as if they were filled with air instead of flesh and blood and bone, and my brain was revving too quickly, flooding with thoughts of Ellie and Dave and Sarah and Ladiesroom and whether I really needed to start writing seven times a week and how I was going to get two hundred plastic eggs filled with school-approved treats before the Celebration of Spring on Monday afternoon. There was the mortgage that needed paying. The roof that needed replacing. The second car we needed to buy, and Ellie's tuition, and summer camp, and had I ever made her a dentist appointment? I couldn't remember.

"Panelists?" Beatrice and her clipboard were back. "We're going to mic you, and then get you seated during the commercial break."

I held still while a big, bearded man with delicate fingers clipped a microphone to my sweater collar and looked me up and down before hanging a small black box with an on/off toggle switch to the back of my skirt's waistband. The Decent

Christian got his clipped to the back of his belt. The parenting expert, evidently a TV veteran, produced her own microphone from her pocket. Then we were led onto the set that I'd seen a thousand times from my own kitchen and living room—the curving desk where the sports guy and the weather girl would banter with the anchorman, a map of Pennsylvania off to one side. The three of us were positioned on a raised platform, in armchairs grouped around a coffee table with a neat stack of books and a vase of flowers on top of it. As soon as the commercial break began, the Sunday anchor, a gorgeous woman named LaDonna Cole, came and took the seat across from us.

"Pretend we're all just sitting around talking," she instructed as a woman with a blow-dryer in a leather holster around her waist sprayed something onto LaDonna's hair and another lady brushed powder onto her cheeks. "Interrupt each other! Jump in if you've got something to say! Keep it lively, 'kay?" She gave us a twinkling smile. I studied her face anxiously. She was wearing a ton of makeup, even though, as far as I could tell, her skin was flawless. Should I be wearing more?

"In three . . . two . . . one." The bearded man behind the camera pointed two fingers toward LaDonna, who flashed her dazzling teeth again. "Good morning. I'm LaDonna Cole. It's the case that's on every paper's front page, and all over social media. It happened in Akron, last Friday night, and almost everyone knows the details. A fifteen-year-old girl goes to a party hosted by an eighteen-year-old classmate, whose parents are away. There's drinking. The girl passes out. Her ex-boyfriend, who's seventeen, tells her friends that he'll take her home. Instead, according to the girl's testimony, he and three of his friends carry her down the street, to one of the friends' basements, and sexually assault her, posting pictures and video of the assault to popular social media sites. And that's where things get complicated." Photographs flashed on the screen behind LaDonna's head to illustrate her talking points—yearbook pictures of the accused, candids from the football field. "The ex-boyfriend, a popular athlete, says that she did, in fact, consent to their activities. He claims he had no idea that his friends were recording them. The other boys also posted pictures of a vibrator the girl allegedly had in her purse. The case has sparked vigorous debate," said LaDonna, angling her body expertly to face a second camera. "Does the young woman have any responsibility for what allegedly happened that night? Is this a case of rape or, as some have said, a case of a girl who woke up with regrets the morning after? We're joined this morning by Father David Ryan of the Christian League of Decency, Dr. Carol Bendinger, child psychologist and author of *Online and On Guard: Keeping Our Kids Safe in a Wired World*, and Allison Weiss, a popular blogger whose column at Ladiesroom.com deals with sexuality, marriage, and motherhood."

Okay, I thought. *Not bad.*

"Father Ryan, let's start with you."

"Of course, what happened last Friday is a tragedy, for all the young people involved—the young woman and the young men," Father Ryan intoned. "None of them will emerge from this unscathed. The young woman's had her reputation ruined, and the young men are now facing the possibility of prison time, and of having to be registered as sex offenders for the rest of their lives."

"And you think that's wrong," LaDonna prompted.

"I think it's a tragedy, and I think that the young woman has to shoulder some of the blame."

"Why is it her fault?" I asked. All three of their heads turned toward me, and, out of the corner of my eye, I caught the camera's motion. "She went to a party and drank. So did the boys. We've got a lot of he-said/she-said about whether she consented to sex. But the pictures aren't ambiguous. The pictures don't lie. And what the pictures show is a group of boys assaulting a girl who is clearly unconscious, a girl who is in no position to say yes or no or anything at all."

"The pictures also show how she was dressed," Father Ryan said smoothly. "You can't go to a party wearing little more than underwear and not realize that you've put yourself in danger."

"So she deserves to be raped for wearing a short skirt, and the boys who did it, and the ones who took pictures of their buddies, they don't deserve to be punished at all?" I was surprised to find how furious I was, how easily I could imagine my own daughter wearing the wrong thing, downing a drink that was stronger than she'd known, letting the wrong guys walk her home. "What kind of fine, upstanding citizens go to a party and take pictures of one of their buddies having sex, and then put those shots online?"

"Those boys were provoked," Father Ryan said.

"So she was asking for it?" I could feel my anger . . . but I could feel it from a distance, from behind the protective, warm bubble of the drugs, the invisible armor that let me be brave.

"It might be a pleasant fantasy to imagine that women can dress any way they want to and nothing bad will happen," said Father Ryan. "But we live in the real world. Teenage boys, teenage boys who've been drinking . . ."

". . . know that stealing is wrong. They know that arson is wrong. Yet these boys managed to get drunk without helping themselves to anyone's wallets or setting the house on fire. It's ridiculous to give them a free pass for sexual misconduct, to think that everything they know about what's right and fair and legal goes out the window because they've had a bunch of beer and they see a girl in a short skirt."

"Let's hear from Dr. Bendinger," said LaDonna. Her widened eyes suggested that she might have gotten a more lively conversation than she'd envisioned.

Dr. Bendinger said the case illustrated how social media raised the stakes of all of our actions; how no matter what you did, it would dwell online, forever.

"And is that fair?" asked LaDonna.

Father Ryan shook his head. "This was a youthful indiscretion," he said.

"This was a rape," I replied.

He shook his head again, looking annoyed, like I was a mosquito who wouldn't quit buzzing. "A young girl goes to a party in a short skirt and a tank top. She gets drunk. She's announcing her intentions to have sex. She's got a vibrator in her purse . . ."

"None of which meant it was okay for four guys to carry her down to the basement and rape her."

"So you don't have a problem with a fifteen-year-old having a vibrator?" asked LaDonna.

"I do not," I said. "I think it's better for a young woman to use a vibrator in a loving, committed, monogamous relationship, or to use it all by herself, in no relationship at all, than for her to participate in hookup culture, where she's there to service a guy, where he gets off and she gets nothing." Was I allowed to say "get off" on TV? Never mind. The pills were lifting me, buoying me, making me feel invincible, effortlessly witty, even cute. "Maybe vibrators are actually keeping girls out of trouble," I said. "Maybe every girl should get one along with her driver's license. A chicken in every pot and a vibrator in every purse!" I said. Father Ryan looked horrified. I, on the other hand, felt great.

"With that, I'm afraid we're out of time," said LaDonna Cole, who looked more than slightly relieved. "Father Ryan, Dr. Bendinger, Ms. Weiss, thank you so much for joining us." When the camera was off, we all shook hands; then, still glowing with triumph, I sailed out of the building and into my car. My phone was buzzing, flashing Sarah's picture on the screen.

"Hi!"

"A chicken in every pot and a vibrator in every purse?" She sounded somewhere between bemused and grossed out. "Dude. You have got to write that and get it up ASAP."

"ASAP," I repeated, and giggled. Oh, but I felt good! And a few more pills—two, maybe even three, why not?—would only make me feel better. I could surf this delicious, happy wave all the way home. I could write my next blog post, make love with my husband and fall asleep in the warmth of his arms, and then I'd get up, go to the grocery store, and buy the ingredients for his favorite coq au vin for dinner. While it was simmering, I'd call Skinny Marie and give her carte blanche and a blank check. My house would finally have furniture. My life would finally be okay.

"Six hundred words. Quick as you can." Then Sarah paused. This was uncharacteristic. Sarah was usually full speed ahead, without as much as an "um" to disrupt the staccato rhythms of her thoughts. "This is kind of awkward, but I need to ask you something."

"Ask away!" I said. Just like that, the delicious wave of joy collapsed underneath me, leaving me splayed on an icy shore. Suddenly I was terrified. *She knows,* I thought. Maybe I'd accidentally typed my work address at Penny Lane, and they'd delivered a package of Percocet or Oxy to the office?

Sarah cleared her throat. Then, before I could beg her to put me out of my agony, she said, "There's some money missing from the petty cash account."

"Oh!" Ladiesroom maintained the account Sarah had mentioned, a few thousand dollars that all writers and editors above a certain level could access if they wanted to, for example, pay for membership to a sex club without using their own credit card or having to wait for the expense reports to wend their way through the accounting department (which had been, we guessed, outsourced to some country where women would work for a dollar an hour).

On Wednesday afternoon, sitting idly at my computer, I'd realized, with an unpleasant jolt, that at my current rate of consumption I would run out of pills by Sunday. Purchasing drugs online was a tedious affair that involved buying Internet currency on one site, then moving those coins to Penny Lane . . . and I saw, as my heartbeat sped up, that the checking account I used to fund my illicit activities was almost empty. I could transfer money in from a household account, or get a cash advance from one of my credit cards, then make a deposit . . . but what if Dave decided to look?

Unable to think of a solution, feeling desperate and trapped, I'd taken a thousand dollars out of the petty cash account, moved it to my personal checking account, and then used it on Penny Lane. I'd planned on replacing the cash first thing Monday, as soon as I got paid, and hoped that nobody would notice.

Except, of course, somebody had.

"Oh my God, I'm so sorry!" I said, apologizing to buy time while I tried to come up with some kind of plausible explanation. "I meant to tell you. What happened was, I got caught short on my property taxes. I had no idea how high they'd be out here—I mean, obviously, I did know, at least at some point, but I must have repressed it. So my accountant called me last Wednesday and was, like, you need to pay this before the end of the workday, so I just moved the money, and I was going to e-mail you about it, and of course I was going to pay it back as soon as I got my paycheck Monday morning, but it must have totally slipped my mind. It was a really stupid thing to do, and I am so, so sorry . . ."

I made myself shut my mouth. In the silence that followed, I imagined the cops showing up, Ellie watching as they snapped on the handcuffs and led me away. Sarah had every right to accuse me of stealing. Petty cash was for work-related expenses, not property taxes. She could turn me in to the cops, or to Ladiesroom's bosses. Worse than that, she could demand to know why I really needed the money. My tale of property-tax woe sounded flimsy even to my own ears.

Instead of asking more questions, though, Sarah said, "Okay. I figured it was probably something like that. It wasn't like you were trying to be sneaky about it . . . I mean, you didn't exactly try to cover your tracks."

I felt like my internal organs were turning to soup, like my bones were caving in. I was shaking all over, sweating at my hairline and underneath my arms, struggling to keep my voice steady as I repeated how sorry I was, how stupid I'd been, how of course I would put the money back immediately if not sooner and how I would never ever ever do anything that dumb again.

"It's okay." Sarah sounded a little stiff. My eyes prickled with tears; my cheeks burned with humiliation. Did Sarah have any idea what was really going on? Had I lost her respect and her trust? "Just get home and get to writing. 'A chicken in every pot and a vibrator in every purse.' I wonder if we can get T-shirts made?"

On that happy note, I apologized some more, then unclenched one sweat-slicked hand from the steering wheel and shoved it into my purse. I didn't have enough pills to calm myself down, to erase what I'd done and make it okay. When I was wound up like this, four or five or even six pills could barely take the edge off. But I had to do something to slow my racing heartbeat, to get rid of the sick, sinking feeling in my gut, the shame that had taken up residence in my bones . . . and this was the only thing I knew. "I'll call you as soon as I'm done writing," I said, and slipped my medicine under my tongue.

I paid close attention to the speed limit and kept a safe distance between my front bumper and the car ahead of me. I'd never been the most mindful of drivers even in my pre-pill era, and a fistful of Oxy did not do much to improve one's concentration. More than once since I'd found Penny Lane, I had pulled out of our driveway with my coffee mug on top of the car or driven away from a gas station with the gas cap still dangling. I put on music, practiced yoga breathing, and tried to tell myself that everything was fine, that I'd dodged the petty-cash bullet, and that, as soon as I finished my blogging, Dave and I could pick up where we'd left off.

That thought should have been enough to keep me occupied. When we first fell in love, we had a fantastic sex life. We were spontaneous, but we would also plan elaborate surprises for each other, scavenger hunts and carefully thought-out gifts and getaways. Even when we didn't have a lot of money, we had always managed to delight each other on special occasions and, sometimes, just on regular Friday nights.

For our first anniversary, I'd done an Alice in Wonderland–style adventure. I had propped a stoppered glass vial filled with Dave's favorite Scotch on the kitchen table, with a card reading DRINK ME and an arrow pointing down the hallway. A trail of roses led to the bedroom. After contemplating and rejecting the idea of lying on the bed naked, except for some cute lace panties with a card reading EAT ME affixed to the waistband, I'd instead left those words on a card with a single chocolate-dipped strawberry beside it. On the flip side of the EAT ME card was another clue, telling Dave to go "where I like to get wet." This led him to the Lombard Swim Club, where we'd splurged on a membership for the summer. The girl behind the desk had given him an *Amazing Race*–style envelope with a hand-made crossword puzzle, which had sent him to the Boathouse Row Bar in the Rittenhouse Hotel, where I'd been waiting with cocktails and a reservation at a restored Victorian bed-and-breakfast in Avalon down on the Jersey Shore, where we would run in a race together the next morning.

Maybe I should plan something like that again, I thought as I swung the car onto our street. True, I hadn't been running much these days, but it wasn't as if I'd been sitting around doing absolutely nothing. (*You run after drugs,* my mind whispered. *You run to the bank. You run to the pharmacy.* I told it to shut up.) A few weeks of training and I'd be able to run at least the better part of a 5K. I'd find a race some-where pretty, not too far away, get Doreen to take Eloise for the night or maybe even the weekend, buy a bottle of good Champagne for when we were through . . .

A blue Lexus was parked in our driveway, with Pennsylvania plates and an Obama bumper sticker. Hmm. I grabbed my purse, got out of my car, and walked in through the garage, hearing the sound of singing coming from the kitchen.

Ellie was standing on a chair, performing what I recognized as her *Legally Blonde* medley. " 'Honey, whatcha crying at? You're not losin' him to that.' "

"A star is born," Dave said to a woman sitting at the table. Ellie was in full Ellie gear, with a tutu around her waist and a tiara on her head, a fake feather boa wrapped around her neck, and my high heels on her feet. Dave was wearing jeans and a Rutgers T-shirt, his hair still wet from the shower. The woman at the table looked as comfortable as if she lived there . . . or as if Dave had called some casting agency and asked for a slightly younger, significantly hotter version of me. Her jeans were crisp, dark, and low-rise, tucked into knee-high leather riding boots. Her fuchsia T-shirt had just enough Lycra for it to hug her torso in a flattering line, with a boatneck showing off her collarbones and pale, freckled skin. Her blonde hair was drawn into a sleek ponytail that looked casual but must have taken at least twenty minutes of fussing and a few different products to achieve, and she wore subtle makeup—light foundation, a little tinted lip-gloss, mascara and pencil to darken her brows and her lashes. L. McIntyre, I presumed.

"Hello," I said, and dropped my purse on the counter. I rested my left hand on Dave's shoulder, wedding and engagement bands on proud display, and extended my right. "I'm Allison."

"Lindsay is a work friend of Daddy's," Ellie explained.

"She came by to drop off some documents," Dave added. I thought I could feel him flushing.

"Wasn't that nice," I said. "Do you live out this way?"

"Old City," L. answered. "I'm Lindsay McIntyre." She had one of those cool, limp handshakes, with no grip at all. I moved her fingers up and down once, then let go.

"Dave, can you come give me a hand for a moment?" My voice was sugar-cookie sweet. His expression was unreadable as he followed me through the kitchen and into the mudroom.

"What is going on here?" I hissed. "You're bringing your girlfriend over for playdates?"

He raked his fingers through his damp hair. "Allison, she isn't my girlfriend. I'm married. You don't get to have girlfriends if you're married."

"Glad we're on the same page with that. So what is she doing in my house?"

"*Your* house?" Dave repeated. Underneath the TV makeup, I felt my cheeks get hot.

"Our house. Why is she in our house, at our kitchen table, singing show tunes with our daughter?"

"She's doing exactly what I said. She was dropping off some information I needed for a story I'm working on. It's part of the election series," he added, his tone suggesting I was supposed to know what that was. Since I didn't, I said, "And she just decided to hang out and do a number?"

"She and Ellie seemed to be getting along."

How nice for you, I wanted to say, *that you can audition my replacement before I'm even gone.* Cut it out, I told myself. Maybe this was com-pletely innocent. Maybe the pills were making me paranoid.

My phone buzzed in my purse. Sarah, terse as ever, was texting me. *ETA?* she'd written. Shit.

"I need to write something. Can you keep Ellie amused for an hour?"

"I actually need to get to the office. I've had her all morning," he said.

While I was goofing off, I thought. Instead, I walked wordlessly into the kitchen, where Ellie was wrapping up her finale.

"I should get going," L. said, after Ellie, who'd moved on to *The Sound of Music,* hit the last notes of "So Long, Farewell." She got to her feet, straightening her shirt and giving her hair a pat. It was astonishing, really. A few subtle changes in features and hair color and she could have been me, ten years ago.

"Can we go to the zoo?" Ellie wheedled after L. and Dave had departed.

"I'm sorry, honey. Mommy has to blog." On the couch, my laptop open, Ellie bribed into com-pliance with a bag of jelly beans and the remote

211

control, I thought of what Lindsay McIntyre had seen when she stopped by. The kitchen, at least, had furniture. There was a cheerful jumble of family pictures on the refrigerator. One wall had been painted with blackboard paint and turned into a calendar, with "Clay Club" and "Daddy's 10K" and "Stonefield Pajama Party" written in colorful chalk. There were apples in a yellow-and-blue ceramic bowl, the orchid that I hadn't managed to kill in a clay pot on the windowsill. You would never see my kitchen and guess how many milligrams of narcotics I required to drag myself through the day. You would never look at my living room and know how much I'd cried reading comments on one of my blog posts, or looking at the online banking site and fretting about the increased frequency with which I was moving money to my secret account or the widening gap between what I put in each month and Dave's contributions. You'd check out the big house with its princess suite, the princess herself, her brown hair for once neatly combed, and imagine that we had a happy life. *Nothing to see here,* you would think. *Everything is fine.*

Nine

In all my years of working at the *Examiner* and then for Ladiesroom, I'd never had anything come close to going viral. When I'd organized the slide show of nude cyclists that ran with the paper's coverage of Philadelphia's annual Naked Critical Mass ride, the pictures had gotten a tremendous number of hits, but that had all been local attention. Nothing I'd done, and certainly nothing I'd said, had ever gained national traction. Maybe it was a slow news week, or maybe it had to do with prudish, hypocritical America's fascination with anything related to women and sex, but by Sunday night the "vibrator in every purse" sound bite was racking up hits on YouTube (I'd smartened up enough to know not to watch the clip or even glance at the comments). On Monday morning, a nationally syndicated conservative radio host spent ten minutes frothing into his microphone, incensed at the notion that the writers and editors of Ladiesroom—"a pack of pornography purveyors," as he put it—wanted the government to equip innocent teenage girls with vibrators. Where he got the idea that we were asking for government money, I wasn't sure, but I welcomed the attention. Every hyperbolic, spittle-flecked "THIS is what liberals WANT!"

harangue got Ladiesroom.com another ten thousand hits. More hits meant more attention, and more money. Money: Our corporate masters offered a generous bonus for pieces that topped fifty thousand views. I stuck the cash directly into my Naughty Account, knowing I'd need drugs to get through the backlash, the inevitable dissection of my looks and politics and sex life, or lack of same. I was planning on cutting back . . . just not now. There was even a bit on *The Daily Show*, with Jon Stewart smirking as he repeated my line: "A chicken in every pot and a vibrator in every purse! Just make sure you don't get them mixed up," he said as the screen behind him showed a picture of a Hitachi Magic Wand in a Dutch oven. My inbox overflowed with e-mailed condemnations and praise, which I quickly gave up trying to answer. A "thank you for reading my work" would suffice, whether the reader was telling me that I was a genius and a hero and an inspiration to girls everywhere, or a fat ugly whore bent on making men obsolete.

I tried to distract myself by writing something new. "A Mother's Guide to the Online World" was the idea I'd been playing with, a series of tips and how-tos for protecting girls on the Internet and in real life. Nothing scared me more than the idea of Ellie as a teenager, among peers who accepted as normal things like girls texting topless shots of themselves to boys they liked, or boys filming sexual activity and then making the video available to their buddies. She was too young for even the most preliminary conversation—only six months ago I'd stumbled through a speech about where babies came from—but I thought if I could come up with a list of what to do and what to say, maybe I'd be prepared for when she was eight or nine or ten or twelve and the conversation was no longer theoretical.

"Mommy, come visit with me!" Ellie would say, banging on my locked bedroom door in the days and weeks after my TV debut.

"Mommy's working right now," I would call back, telepathically begging her babysitter to come upstairs and whisk her away. Katrina, bless her heart, meant well, but she would usually come with some elaborate craft or cooking project that would take a while to arrange, leaving Ellie free to wander the house, or bang on my door, while her sitter laid out pages of origami paper or baked gingerbread for a gingerbread house.

Dave, meanwhile, had gone back to being tight-lipped and silent, his face unreadable and his body rigid as he passed me in the kitchen or the halls. I was afraid to try to grill him about L. McIntyre. I wanted to know the truth . . . but I suspected that the truth would burst my opiated bubble, revealing the unhappy realities that even four or five Oxys couldn't mask—that my marriage was a sham, that my happiness was an illusion, that even though the pieces were in place and everything seemed okay, underneath the veneer of good looks and good manners, the three of us were falling apart.

Or, at least, I was.

Two weekends after my television triumph, the guilt got to me. I woke up early, chewed up sixty milligrams of OxyContin, took a shower, and announced, over a breakfast I'd cooked myself, that I was putting everything on hold and taking Ellie on a girls' day outing.

"Great," Dave said. He even managed to smile. Ten minutes after I'd made my announcement, he had his running shoes in his hand, his high-tech lap-and-pace-counting watch on his wrist, and his body covered in various wicking and cooling fabrics made from recycled bamboo. "Bye," he called, closing the door behind him. Ellie gave me a syrup-sticky smile. "Can we go to my museum? And the Shake Shack? And the zoo? And to sing-along *Sound of Music*?"

"Sing-along *Sound of Music* was a special treat. How about you pick two of the other things?" I said pleasantly. Meanwhile, I was performing a mental inventory of how many little blue Oxys I had left, and how I'd space them out to get me through until noon the next day, when my next batch would come in the mail. *You're taking too many,* a voice in my head scolded. I stacked dishes in the sink, then rinsed them and put them in the dishwasher, and told the voice to shut up. *How much money did you spend last month?* the voice persisted. *Four thousand dollars? Five?* I can afford it, I thought uneasily, shoving aside the memory of the petty cash I'd borrowed, or how worried I was that Dave would take a hard look at our joint checking account. *As long as I stay on top of things, as long as I'm careful, I'll be fine.*

After lengthy deliberations, Ellie decided on the zoo, and burgers for lunch. For two hours, we admired the elephants, held our noses in the monkey house, screamed "Ew!" at the naked mole rats, and sat on a bench eating soft-serve pretzels in the sunshine. I let her have everything she wanted—a pedal through the pond on the swan boats, a pony ride, and a trip on the miniature train that circled the zoo. She got her face painted to look like a leopard (a pink-and-white-spotted leopard) and bought friendship bracelets and a souvenir keychain and widened her eyes in disbelief when, at the Shake Shack, I said she could have both cheese fries and a milkshake, when usually I made her choose one or the other.

The cashier gave Ellie a buzzer—by far, one of the highlights of the Shack. "It'll go off when your food's ready."

"I KNOW it! I KNOW it will!" Using two hands, Ellie carried the buzzer to our table and set it reverently in the center after cleaning the surface with an antibacterial wipe from my purse. "Now, don't freak out," she instructed the buzzer.

"Okay. I won't. I won't freak out," I answered, in character as Wa, which is what we'd named the Shake Shack's buzzers, for the *wah-wah-wah* sound they made.

"Just be CALM, Wa," she said, giggling.

"I'm gonna. I-I'm gonna be calm," I stammered, in Wa's trembling, not-at-all-calm voice.

"Just say, 'Your food is ready,' in a NORMAL voice. Don't LOSE YOUR BUSINESS," Ellie said, her eyes sparkling with mirth.

"I got it. I got it. No freaking out. No losing my business. No . . ." Ellie was already starting to giggle as the buzzer lit up and started to hum. "WA! WA! WA! Yourfoodisready!" I said. "Wa! Wa! WAWAWAI'MFREAKINGOUTHEREWA!"

"Wa, calm down! It's just a burger!" Ellie gave the buzzer an affectionate pat as I continued to narrate its breakdown. An older woman sitting at the counter watched the proceedings. On our way back with our tray, she tapped my shoulder.

"Excuse me. I just want to say how much I'm enjoying watching you and your daughter."

"Oh, thank you!" I said, touched almost to tears.

"So many parents, you see them on their phones, barely looking at their kids. You're giving your daughter memories she'll have forever."

Now I was tearing up, thinking about what the woman would never see—the times I had been on my phone or my laptop or napping when Ellie wanted my company.

"That's really nice of you to say," I said, just as—irony!—my phone rang. I gave the woman an apologetic smile. "Hello? Mom?"

For a minute, all I could hear was the sound of her crying. "He f-f-fell . . . out of bed . . . I tried to pick him up and then he p-p-pushed me . . ."

I sat down in my chair. "Okay, Mom. Take a deep breath. Is Daddy there?"

"He left! He ran away!" Another burst of sobbing. "I tried to stop him, but he pushed me down and he ran out the door. He's got bare feet, or maybe just his slippers. I couldn't s-s-stop him . . ."

"Okay." My head spun. Ellie, for once, was sitting quietly, maybe appreciating the seriousness of the situation, staring at me wide-eyed over the lid of her milkshake. "Do you know where he went?"

"No," she sobbed. "By the time I got to the door he was gone."

"Okay. I think you need to get off the phone with me and call the police."

"What do I say?" she wailed.

"Tell them what you told me. Tell them that Daddy has Alzheimer's, and that he was confused and that he's . . ." Run away from home? Wandered off? Gone for a walk in his bare feet? "Just tell them what happened. I'm in Center

City, I'm going to put Ellie in the car right now. We'll be there as soon as we can." Even as I was talking, I was packing up my purse, handing Ellie a wipe for her face, rummaging for my parking stub and a twenty-dollar bill.

"Good luck," the woman who'd praised my parenting said as I hustled Ellie out the door, across the street, into the car, and, as fast as I could legally manage it, over the Ben Franklin Bridge and into New Jersey.

There were three police cars at my parents' house when I arrived, one in the driveway and another two parked at the curb in front of the house. On my way over, I'd had a two-minute conversation with Dave, telling him what had happened.

"What can I do?" he'd asked, and I'd found myself almost in tears, melting at the kindness in his voice.

"Just sit tight . . . Actually, you know what? Can you call . . ." What was the woman's name? I pulled to the side of the road and rummaged through my wallet until I found the business card I'd tucked in there for this very moment. "Kathleen Young. She's at Eastwood—you know, the assisted-living place out here?"

"Kathleen Young," Dave said, and repeated the phone number after I read it.

"If she's not working on the weekend, ask for whoever's handling intake. I went there a few weeks ago, just to check it out, so they know me, and they'll at least know my dad's name and his situation. If you tell them what's going on, maybe they'll have a bed for him, or they'll be able to find us someplace that does."

"Got it," said Dave. "Call when you can."

I parked on the street behind one of the cruisers, grabbed Ellie, and raced into the house. My mother was on the couch with an officer in uniform on each side of her. My father, in sweatpants, his bare feet grimy and one big toe bleeding, was sitting in an armchair, his face completely blank. He was missing his glasses, and his hair hadn't been combed.

"Oh, Dad," I said. I put Ellie down and half sat, half collapsed on the couch next to his armchair. He didn't move, didn't acknowledge me, just kept staring into the middle of the room as my mother, bracketed by cops, cried into a fistful of tissue. "What happened?" I asked the room. My mother continued to cry. My dad continued to stare. Finally, one of the cops, who introduced himself as Officer Findlay, said that they'd found my father two blocks away from the house, walking toward the elementary school in his bare feet. "He appeared disoriented, but he didn't give us a hard time."

"Climbed right in the backseat and let us take him home," said the second officer. "Your mother was explaining your dad's situation . . ."

"We should call his doctor," I said to my mom. I hoped, foolishly, that she'd say she'd already done so—that she'd done something. Of course she hadn't. She just sat there, mutely, shaking with sobs.

"I'm going to call," I told the police officers.

I got Ellie situated in front of the television set, handing her the remote and watching her eyes widen as if I'd given her a key to the city, and went upstairs to my dad's study to try to reach his physician. Of course an answering service picked up. I left my name and number and a brief version of the story. Then I called Dave.

"They have a bed available," he reported. "But it'll have to be paid out of pocket until you finish giving them your dad's insurance information. They'll need a copy of your parents' tax returns, too. I'm going to e-mail you all that information," Dave said, in his full-on brisk-and-businessy reporter mode. "There's an Emily Gavin you'll be talking to—she's handling intake over the weekend. They e-mailed a packing list that I can forward along . . ." While Dave kept talking, I let my eyes slip shut.

"Do you think . . ." I swallowed hard. Here was the part I hadn't quite figured out, the puzzle piece I'd never managed to snap into place. "Honey, would it be okay if my mom stayed with us for a while?"

I'd expected objection, at least a pained sigh.

But Dave's voice was gentle when he said, "Of course it's fine."

I started to cry. "I love you," I said as the call waiting beeped to let me know that someone from my dad's doctor's practice was calling.

"Love you, too," said Dave.

I sniffled. How long had it been since I'd felt that certainty, that unshakable belief that Dave had my back? And did he know that I had his? Would he come to me in a crisis, or just try to get through it on his own . . . or, worse, would he turn to L. McIntyre, with her understated makeup and sleek ponytail, and ask her to help?

My father's doctor was calling from a movie-theater lobby. "Count yourself lucky that no one got hurt," he said. "Now, clearly, Dad's ready for a higher level of care."

I agreed that Dad was.

"You picked out a place?" He'd given my mother and me a list of possibilities the same day he gave us my father's diagnosis.

"Eastwood has a bed for him."

"Good. They're good people. Don't forget to bring two forms of ID when you go. Pack all his medication—they'll probably let him take his own meds for the first night, then they'll have their doctors call in new scripts for everything, just so they know exactly what he's taking, and when, and how much." I half paid attention as he explained the process of getting my dad situated—what to pack, whom to call—as I tried to figure out how I would actually get my father to Eastwood. Could I leave Ellie with my mother while I drove my father there? What if he got confused, or even violent, or refused to get in my car, or refused to get out of it when he saw where we were? Maybe I'd wait for Dave to make the trip from Philadelphia and have him come along. That would work. I thanked the doctor, got off the phone, closed the study door quietly . . . but before I went downstairs, I detoured into the bathroom that had been mine when I was a girl. The seat was up, the hand towels were askew, and something white—toothpaste, I hoped—was crusted on the cold-water handle at the sink. I ignored it all, shoved my hand deep into my bag, retrieved my Altoids tin, and piled two, then four, then six pills into my mouth.

Ten

Maybe my dad had been belligerent in the morning, but by the time the cops departed, all the fight had gone out of him. He sat quietly in front of the television with a glass of juice and a plate of cheese and crackers while I went upstairs to start packing. "Mom, you want to help?" I asked, pulling a suitcase out of the guest-room closet. There was only silence from downstairs.

No matter. I began emptying the drawers, consulting the packing list Dave had e-mailed. Undershirts and underwear, jeans and khakis, pullover tops ("We find our clients do best in familiar, comfortable clothing without clasps, zippers, buttons, or buckles," the list read). I packed up his phone and its charger, wondering if he'd need it. I added a stack of books, biographies of Winston Churchill and FDR, a copy of *Wolf Hall*, which I knew he'd read and loved. Toothbrush, toothpaste, shaving cream, soap . . . I put in everything I thought he'd need. When I heard Dave arrive, I went downstairs and found my mom next to my father on the couch. I knelt down and took one of her hands between both of mine.

"Dave and I are going to take Daddy to Eastwood. You can wait here with Ellie, and we'll be back as soon as he's settled." I put my arm around her, feeling like someone had just handed me a script, and I was reading the lines and playing the part of the Good Daughter. "Try not to worry. They'll take good care of Daddy. He's going to be safe."

She didn't answer, but I felt her body shaking. After a minute, she bent forward, briefly resting her body against mine. Her lips were pressed together, her tiny hands clenched in fists. She rocked, and rocked, and I heard a faint whistling noise coming from between her pursed lips, a wretched, keening sound.

The side of her face was already swelling—she'd bounced into the dresser when my dad had pushed her that morning. I found an ice pack in the freezer, wrapped it in a dish towel, then pressed it against her cheek, and murmured nonsense: *Don't worry* and *He'll be fine* and even *He's going to a better place.* Dave was the one who got my father into the backseat and the suitcase into the trunk. He drove, and I cried, and my father sat, silently, with his seat belt on and his hands folded neatly in his lap.

Three hours later, he was relatively settled in a double room, with a framed picture of my mom on his nightstand and his favorite afghan draped across the bed and a social worker, whose job was to help him transition through his first few days, introducing him to his temporary room-mate. *Today is SUNDAY,* read a whiteboard on the door. *The next meal is DINNER. We are having ROAST TURKEY, SWEET POTATOES, and SALAD. After dinner, you can watch "SISTER ACT" in the Media Room, or play HEARTS in the Recreation Room. Tomorrow morning is ART THERAPY at nine a.m.*

I looked at the board, then looked away, as Dave, maybe guessing at what I was feeling, took my hand. "It's the right thing to do," he told me, and I nodded, feeling hollow and sad.

Back at my parents' house, Ellie and my mother were where I'd left them, on the sofa, with the

TV switched from CNBC to Nickelodeon and a cheese sandwich, missing two bites, in front of them.

"I made SANDWIDGES," Ellie announced.

"I can tell." The sandwich was decorated with no fewer than six frilly toothpicks, and there was a neat pile of gherkins, Ellie's preferred pickle, beside it.

"Come on, Mom," I said, and took my mother's cool, slack hands. Then I raised my voice, trying for cheer. "Hey, Ellie, guess what? Grandma's going to be visiting with us for a while!"

"Yay!" said Ellie. Wordlessly, soundlessly, my mother got to her feet and climbed the stairs, with Ellie and I trailing behind her. For a minute, she stood in front of the unmade bed, with one pillow still bearing the impression of my dad's head. Then, as I watched, she took the pillow in her arms and hugged it.

"I love him so much," she said. She wasn't crying, and that was scarier, even, than the keening she'd been doing before. Her voice was quiet and matter-of-fact, and she shook off my hand when I tried to touch her shoulder. "You have no idea . . . How will I live without him?"

"You'll still see him," I said, trying to sound encouraging and hold back my own tears. "He needs you." I paused. "I need you," I added, trying not to notice how strange those words sounded. Had I ever told my mother I needed her? Had it ever been true? "And Ellie needs her grand-mother."

We packed a bag for her, with what I guessed was a week's worth of clothes, and loaded another bag with her cosmetics, her blow-dryer and curling iron, the pots and bottles and canisters of sprays and gels and powders she used every day. While I zipped up the bags, I explained to her that Eastwood was convenient to both of us. I told her that I'd visited a number of places (true, if online visits counted) and had settled on this one as the best of the bunch. I described the attractive facilities, the comfortable room, the doctors on staff, and the trips Dad could take. On the drive back to Haverford, she sat in silence with her hands folded in her lap, watching the trees flash past, as if she were a corpse that no one had gotten around to burying yet.

"Why isn't Grandma TALKING?" Ellie demanded from her booster.

Before I could answer, my mother said, "Grandma is sad," in a rusty, tear-clogged voice. I waited for her to elaborate. When she didn't, Ellie said, "Sometimes I am sad, too."

"Everyone gets sad sometimes," I said, and left it at that. I was thinking, of course, of my pills. Instead of lifting me out of the misery of the moment, they had left me there, shaky and wired and miserable, thinking, *If I just take one more* or *Maybe if I took two.* Since I'd gotten the call at the Shake Shack, I had swallowed . . . how many? I didn't want to think about it. I was afraid the number might have entered double digits . . . and even I knew that was way, way too many.

I'll cut back, I promised myself as I swung the car into my driveway. Now that my father was somewhere safe, now that things weren't quite so crazy with work, I could start tapering off. But, as the days went by, as the media furor over the vibrator-in-every-purse remark died down and my dad settled in to the routines of Eastwood, the tapering never began. I would start each day with the best of intentions. Then Ellie would have a tantrum after she realized we'd run out of her preferred breakfast cereal, or I would find my mother slumped at the kitchen table, still in her bathrobe, waiting, along with my five-year-old, to be fed, and I'd have to coax her to eat a few bites, to put on her clothes, to please get in the car because if you don't, we're going to be late for Daddy's appointment with the gerontologist, and I would think, *Tomorrow. I'll start cutting back tomorrow. I just need to get through today.*

When she wasn't at Eastwood visiting my dad, my mom spent her days in the guest room, with the door shut, doing what, I didn't know. When Ellie came home she'd emerge—pale and quiet, but at least upright and clothed—and the two of them would spend the afternoon together. My mom was teaching Ellie to play Hearts, a game she and my father used to play together on the beach. She was also teaching Ellie how to apply makeup—which didn't thrill me, but it wasn't a battle I was going to fight. From my computer, behind the bedroom door, I'd brace myself for shrieks of "NO," and "DON'T WANT TO," and, inevitably, "YOU ARE MURDERING ME WITH THE COMB!" But Ellie rarely complained. After dinner, I'd find them cuddled together in the oversized armchair slipcovered in toile, a relic of my single-girl apartment, flipping through *Vogue*, discussing whether or not a dress's neckline flattered the model who wore it.

One morning, after shuttling yet another thousand dollars from my secret checking account to the account I'd set up at Penny Lane, I started adding up what all the pills had cost me. I stopped when I hit ten thousand dollars, feeling dizzy, feeling terrified. The truth was, I had probably spent much more than that, and I was equally sure that if I tried to stop, cold turkey, I'd get sick. Already I'd noticed that if I went more than four or five hours between doses, I would start sweating. My skin would break out in goose bumps; my stomach would twist with nausea. I'd feel dizzy and weak, panicked and desperate until I had my hands on whatever tin or bottle I was using, until the pills were in my mouth, under my tongue, being crunched into nothingness.

Just for now, I told myself. Just until my parents' house sells, just until I figure out what to do about my mom, just until my father settles in. Another six weeks—two months, tops. Then I'd do it. I'd figure out how many pills I was taking each day, and cut down by a few every day, slowly, gently, until I was back to zero. I'd have a long-postponed confrontation with Dave. I'd ask the questions that scared me the most: *Are you in or are you out? Do you love me? Can we work on this? Is there anything left to save?* Whatever he told me, whatever answers he gave, I would work with them. I would be the woman I knew I could be: good at my job, a good mother to my daughter, a good wife, if Dave still wanted me. Just not right now. For now, I needed the pills.

Eleven

"How's your dad?"

I sighed, taking a seat at Janet's kitchen counter, next to a stack of catalogs and what appeared to be a half-assembled diorama of a Colonial kitchen. It was three-fifteen on a balmy, sweetly scented May afternoon, and I'd just arrived at her house, half a mile from my own, with perfectly pruned rosebushes lining the walkway from the street to the front door. We'd passed the living room and the den, both decorator-perfect, and ended up in the kitchen, where Janet was thawing a pot of beef stew on the stove and had the wineglasses out on the counter.

"Half a glass," I said, as she started to pour from a lovely bottle of Malbec. We'd already agreed that I would fetch the kids from Enrichment, the after-school program that Stonefield: A Learning Community offered between the hours of three and six for working parents. I would, therefore, drink responsibly. Of course, Janet had no idea that I'd helped myself to a handful of my dad's Vicodin in the car, and that there were more pills in my purse and in my pocket.

"And thanks for asking. My dad's adjusting." Sipping my wine, I told Janet about how, the day after his arrival, my father had switched from silent to belligerent, throwing things and shouting at the attendants to show him another room, that he'd reserved a suite, goddamnit, and if there wasn't a suite he at least wanted a better view. As best I could figure, he thought he was in a hotel, on a business trip. He'd unpacked, hanging his shirts and pants in the closet, and if he'd noticed the lack of ties and jackets, or that the only shoes I'd sent with him were sneakers, he hadn't said anything. Eastwood had assigned seating at meal-times, and his case manager, a young woman named Nancy Yanoff, reported that my father was eating and seemed to be enjoying the company of the other residents at his table. Meanwhile, I was scrambling to get my parents' house on the market, to finish filling out the thick sheaf of forms the long-term care required, and to figure out a long-term plan for my mom.

God bless narcotics. The pills gave me the energy and confidence to get through the day. They lulled me to sleep at night. They made it possible for me to have an uncomfortable conversation with my husband about how long my mom could stay. Dave was still being generous, still speaking to me kindly, but I sensed that his patience had a limit, and that in a month or two I'd find myself approaching it.

For now, though, he'd moved his belongings back to the master bedroom. I'd hastily ordered a dresser, two bedside tables, lamps, and an area rug for the guest room that had previously contained only a bed. Most nights I'd fall asleep before Dave did. Sometimes, if he woke me up with the bathroom light, I'd take my book and go to Ellie's bedroom, lying beside my daughter in the queen-sized bed we'd been smart to purchase, telling her that Daddy was snoring again when she woke up and was surprised to see she had company. "But all things considered, it's not too bad," I told my friend.

Janet looked at me sidewise, skepticism all over her face. "How is it going with Little Ronnie?"

"Okay, here's the shocker. She's actually functioning. She helps take care of Ellie in the afternoons." It was true that my mother still had the annoying habit of wandering down to the kitchen for breakfast, lunch, and dinner with the expectation that someone (not her) would put a hot, balanced meal on the table, and clean up afterward. She would leave her dirty clothes piled in the hamper with the unspoken assumption that they would be washed and put away, and she would announce that she had an appointment here or there instead of requesting a ride . . . but she was spending a few hours each day with Ellie. "And Ellie's actually calmed down a little. I think, in a weird way, she feels responsible for her grandmother."

Janet nodded, sipped her wine, and said, "Maybe I could rent your mother. My three need to get the memo that they're responsible for more than just wiping themselves." She made a face, flashing her crooked teeth. "And one of the boys isn't even doing that so well. I don't know which one—I buy them identical undies, and it's not really the kind of thing you want to, you know, investigate thoroughly . . ."

I smiled, imagining my friend with a pair of lab tweezers and a fingerprinting kit, gingerly tugging a pair of skidmarked Transformers underpants out of an inside-out pair of little boy's jeans.

"And did I tell you that Maya is now a vegan? And the boys won't eat vegan food—which I can't really blame them for—so I'm now cooking two meals a night? What happened?" she asked. Her cheeks were flushed, eyes narrowed, ponytail askew. "I mean, really. I was Phi Beta Kappa. I was most likely to succeed. I billed more hours than any other associate my first three years out of law school. And now I spend my days driving my kids to hockey practice and swim club and choir rehearsal, and my afternoons making lasagna with tofu cheese, and my nights folding their under-wear and checking their homework and spraying the insides of hockey skates with Lysol. I don't even know who I am anymore."

She poured wine almost to the top of her glass and took a healthy swallow. "Do you know what I think when I wake up in the morning?" Without waiting for an answer, she said, "I count how many hours there are until I can have a glass of wine. There's something wrong with me, if that's all I'm looking forward to. If I have this . . ."— she gestured, hands spread to indicate the room, the house, the neighborhood—"this life, these kids, this house, this husband, and I love him, I swear I do, but most days the only thing that's giving me any pleasure, the only thing I'm looking forward to at all is my goddamn glass of wine. That's a problem, isn't it?"

"I don't know," I said, and started reflexively straightening the stack of catalogs on the counter. Pottery Barn. J.Crew. L.L.Bean. Lands' End. Ballard Designs. Garnet Hill. Saks. Nordstrom.

Restoration Hardware. Sundance. All the same ones I got and kept in a basket in the powder room, to leaf through late at night. If Janet was counting the hours until her five o'clock drink, I was in way worse shape than she was. I wasn't waiting until five anymore. Or even noon. My days began with pills—I would wake up sad and shaky and overwhelmed and I'd need a little pop of something just to get out of bed—and I kept a steady dose of opiates in my bloodstream all day long. More and more, my mind returned to that quiz in the doctor's office, and I found myself wondering: What would happen if I tried to cut back and I couldn't?

You can stop, my mind said soothingly. *But you don't have to. Not right now.* Which sounded good . . . except what if I couldn't? What if I was really and truly addicted, just like the actresses in the tabloids, or the homeless people I avoided while they begged at the intersections and on the sidewalks of Center City? What if that was me? Late at night, with Dave snoring away and Ellie and my mother asleep down the hall, I'd lie awake, the bitterness of the pills still on my tongue and my laptop making the tops of my thighs sweat, Googling rehabs, reading articles about drugs and alcohol, taking quizzes and reading blogs and newspaper stories about mommies who drank and celebrities who'd ended up addicted to painkillers or Xanax. With my Oxy or Percocet still pulsing in my head, I would point and click my way down the tunnel as midnight slipped into the small hours of the morning.

"I think you're a great mother," I told Janet. "You're doing an amazing job. And you know this isn't going to last. You'll blink and they'll be in college."

"College," she repeated. She lifted her glass and seemed surprised to find it almost empty. "I was going to have this big life. Barry and I were supposed to have adventures. I was going to be a prosecutor, then a judge, and then maybe I'd teach law. I used to dream about that. And now . . ." Her lips curled, her face twisting into an expression of deep disgust. "Allison, I'm a *housewife*. When I go online, I'm researching cereal coupons, or trying to figure out if my kid's ADHD medicine is going to interact with his asthma stuff. The last thing I read for pleasure was *Wonder*, which was great but was written for ten-year-olds, and the only reason I even read that was because it was lying around the living room because Maya had to read it for school. I have all these clothes . . ."

As discreetly as I could, I snuck a look at the clock on my phone, wondering if my mail had been delivered yet and if the pills I'd ordered from Penny Lane had arrived. They came in regular Express Mail envelopes, but I couldn't risk Dave's intercepting one of them. I didn't want the first real conversation we had in forever to be about why I was illegally purchasing prescription medication on the Internet.

I slipped my hand into my pocket, touching my tin. At this point, I could guess just by its weight how many pills it contained. Ten, I estimated. Surely ten pills would last me until tomorrow, if they had to? Maybe I could excuse myself, tell Janet I had to make a call, and see if one of my doctors would phone in another prescription, just to tide me over.

"All these clothes," she repeated. "Skirts and suits and jackets. High heels. All that stuff, just hanging there."

"You'll wear them again," I told her. I knew Janet's plan had been to start working part-time the previous fall, when the boys started kindergarten. But then Conor had gotten his ADHD diagnosis, and Janet had spent what felt like an entire year at some doctor's or therapist's office every day after school. As soon as Conor had been stabilized with the right combination of medicine and tutoring and a psychologist to teach him cognitive behavioral strategies for managing his disorder (translation: how to keep from screaming and throwing things when he got frustrated), Dylan had started acting out, getting in fights at school, yelling at his teachers, hiding in the bathroom when recess was over. This, of course, meant therapy for him, too. Somewhere in there, Maya had stopped speaking to her mother. When Janet had described her attempts to give Maya the "your changing body" talk, and how Maya had literally thrown the helpful *Care & Keeping of You* book into the hallway so hard it had left a dent in the paint, Barry and I had laughed, Barry so hard there were tears glistening in his beard, but I could tell that Janet was heartbroken at her daughter's silent treatment.

"Five years from now you'll be running the attorney general's office, and you'll be too important to take my calls," I told her.

"Ha." It was a very bleak "Ha." I wanted to reassure her that we'd get through this time, that in three or five or eight years things would come around right and we would find ourselves again the smart, vital women we'd once been . . . but who was I to talk?

"OMG," Janet said, looking at the clock. Somehow, it was five-thirty. "Are you okay to drive? Are you sure?"

"I'm good." I'd had only a single glass of wine. At least, as far as she knew.

"Want me to come with you?"

"That's okay. I'll have the boys back here by six-fifteen."

She nodded. Then she hugged me, with her wineglass still in her hand. "You're my best friend," she said, and, briefly, rested her head on my shoulder. I gave her a squeeze, located my purse, got behind the wheel, and pulled out of Janet's driveway. My heart lurched as I heard a car honking and the word "ASSHOLE!" float down the street. *Shit,* I thought, realizing how close I'd come to backing into the side of someone's BMW. Oh, well. The other car had probably been speeding. I hoped Janet hadn't seen it as I put the car in drive and proceeded toward Stonefield, coming to a full stop at each stop sign, keeping assiduously to the speed limit. Where had that BMW even come from?

I pulled up at a red light, with my eyelids feeling as heavy as if someone had coated them with wet sand. I kept my foot on the brake and let my eyes slip shut, feeling the warmth of the pills surging through my veins, that intoxicating sense of everything being right with the universe. My head swung forward. I could feel my hair against my cheeks . . .

Someone behind me was honking. I bolted upright, opening my eyes. "Jesus, cool your jets!" I hit the gas and was jerked backward as my car leapt through the intersection. Why was everyone in such a goddamn rush? What happened to manners? I squinted into the rearview mirror, trying to make out the face behind the wheel of the car that had honked, wondering if it was anyone I knew . . . and then, in an instant, the sign for Stonefield was looming up on my right. I stomped on the brakes, hit the turn signal, and heard the squeal of rubber on the road as I made the turn, cutting off the car in my right-hand lane. My heart thudded as I hit the brakes. There were two cars in front of me, and I could see Janet's twins waiting, in their baseball caps and matching backpacks, along with Eloise, in the Lilly Pulitzer sundress she'd picked out herself. I put the car in park, grabbed the key fob, and hopped out of my seat. The heel of my shoe must have caught on the floor mat, because instead of the graceful exit I'd planned on, I tripped and went down hard on the pavement, landing on my hands and knees.

"Ow!" I yelled. My palms were stinging, dotted with beads of blood, and my pants were torn at the knee. I wondered if anyone had seen me. I looked around, swallowing hard as I spotted Mrs. Dale, one of the teachers in Ellie's class, standing at the curb with a clipboard in her hand. Just my luck. Miss Reckord, the other teacher, was a sweet-faced, dumpling-shaped twenty-five-year-old with rosy cheeks and a whispery voice. The little boys all nursed crushes on her, and the girls fought to sit on her lap at story time, where they could finger her dangly earrings. Mrs. Dale was a different story. Thin-lipped, broad-shouldered, and flat-chested, with hair the color and consistency of a Brillo pad and skin as pale as yogurt, Mrs. Dale—who had, as far as I knew, no first name that was ever used by anyone in the Stonefield community—had been bringing five-year-olds to heel for more than thirty years. Mrs. Dale was not impressed with your special little snowflake. She did not believe in affirmations or unearned compliments to boost a kid's self-esteem, or the unspoken Stonefield philosophy that every child was a winner. She believed in children keeping their hands to themselves, not running in the hallways, and coloring inside the lines. She took zero shit off of anyone, and she never, ever smiled.

I waved at her, surreptitiously sliding my bleeding palms into my pockets. "Sorry I'm late! Come on, everyone!" I opened the rear passenger side door, scooping Eloise up by her armpits and hoisting her into her seat.

Mrs. Dale was watching me. "Did you get my messages about the board meeting?"

Oof. I'd gotten several calls from the school over the past few days—maybe even the past few weeks—but I'd hit "Ignore" and let them go straight to voicemail. I was busy. I was tired. I had a job, unlike half the mothers of kids in Ellie's class. Why didn't the school ever call them?

"Sorry. I've been running around like crazy. New project . . ."

"MOMMY, I'm BLOODY!" Eloise shrieked. I looked at her and, sure enough, my bloody palm had left a red smear on her pink-and-green dress.

Mrs. Dale stepped closer. "Mrs. Weiss? Are you all right?"

"What? Oh, yeah. Just ripped my pants, no big deal. I'm such a klutz. Don't ever stand near me in a Zumba class." I followed her gaze down to my palms. Blushing, I grabbed a baby wipe from the box in the backseat and cleaned my hands, then fumbled with the buckle of the seat belt, tugging it hard against Ellie's chest.

"Ow, Mommy, that HURTS!"

"Sorry, sorry," I said. I could feel it now, the pills and the wine, surging through me with each heartbeat, singing their imperative: *Sleep. Now.* I finally clicked the buckle shut. "We'll be at Janet's in ten minutes. I'll give you a *Despicable Me* Band-Aid."

"I HATE *Despicable Me!*"

"Sure you do," I muttered. She'd loved it last week. "Dylan? Conor? You guys okay?" The boys nodded. One of them had a handheld video game. The other had an iPod, with the buds stuck in his ears. I pulled the rear door shut, turned, and felt Mrs. Dale's hand close around my hand. Around my key fob.

"Why don't you come in and have a cup of coffee?"

"Oh, that's so nice of you, but I really . . . I have to . . . Janet's got dinner on the table, and Ellie's going to freak out if I don't get her cleaned up."

"We can wash her dress in the nurse's office. We've got Band-Aids there, and snacks if the boys are hungry."

"That's very kind." I could hear my pulse thumping in my ears. "But I really have to get these guys going."

Mrs. Dale's hand stayed in place. "Have you been drinking?" she asked, stepping close, eyes narrowed, nostrils flaring, like she was trying to smell my breath.

I stiffened, feeling the flesh of my back break out in goose bumps, almost swooning in terror. *Busted.* I was busted. I'd get arrested. I'd lose my license. Dave would find out. Everyone would know.

I pulled myself up straight, trying to look and sound as sober as I could. "Janet and I had a glass of wine, but that was over an hour ago. I'm fine. Really. I swear." I said it firmly, trying to look and sound respectable and sober, hoping that Mrs. Dale would be mindful that I was, for all intents and purposes, her employer. I smoothed my hair and tried to ignore my torn pants and my bloody palms, and project a look of serenity and competence.

Mrs. Dale appeared to be unmoved. "Mrs. Weiss, I think you need to come inside."

"I'm *fine.*" I yanked at the keys, pulling them out of her hand so hard that I stumbled backward, almost falling on the sidewalk.

"Listen to me." Her voice was the commanding, imperious one I'd heard on the playground, a tone that could get a few dozen unruly kindergartners to snap to attention. "As a teacher, I am a mandated reporter. If I believe that children are in danger, I have to call the Department of—"

"What are you talking about?" My voice was almost a shout. I widened my eyes to show how completely ridiculous she was being. "You think the children are in danger?" The soft comfort of the pills was gone, vanished, evaporated, as if it had never been there. My body was on high alert, heart pounding, adrenaline whipping through my bloodstream, and I could hear my voice getting higher and louder. "I had one glass of wine." Never mind the pills I'd taken beforehand. "One. Glass. I'm fine."

"I don't know what you've had, but I can't let you drive with children in your car." She put a hand—a patronizing hand—between my shoulder blades. "Come inside. Sit down. Have coffee."

Now there were three cars behind mine. I recognized Tracy Kelly, and Quinn Gamer, and a man I didn't know, and all of them were staring. Quinn had her phone in her hand, busily texting, probably telling someone—her husband, a friend—exactly what was going on; Allison Weiss, Mrs. Vibrator in Every Purse, had shown up at Stonefield wasted.

"Mommy?"

I looked inside the car, where Ellie was buckled into her booster seat, with her thumb hooked into her mouth. Ellie hadn't sucked her thumb since she was three. "Why is everybody YELLING?"

"Okay," I said, and opened my hand. The key fob slid out from my sweaty fingers and fell onto the sidewalk with a *clink*. "Okay."

Twelve

Mrs. Dale got the kids out of the car and drove it to the teachers' lot. She left me in her classroom, then disappeared with Ellie and the boys. I hoped she was taking them back to the Enrichment room, giving them treats, letting them play with the newest toys. I took a seat at one of the munchkin-sized desks and pulled out my phone. Janet answered on the third ring.

"Allison?"

"Hey!" I said, trying to sound upbeat and untroubled, even though fingers of cold sweat were tracing the curve of my spine and I'd noticed my hands shaking as I'd punched in her number. "Just letting you know that I'm running a little late. The traffic was a mess," I lied, knowing that Janet would believe me. "Sit tight. I'll have them home as soon as I can."

"Take your time," she said.

We hung up, and I rummaged through my purse for a bottle of water. I sipped it, looking longingly at my tin, knowing how stupid it would be to take a pill now, now of all times. My heart was still beating so hard I could feel my temples pounding, and I could feel more sweat collecting there, beading above my upper lip. Then I thought, *In for a penny, in for a pound.* The pills were my normal. They'd help me calm down. They would get me through this. And if they did, I promised God and Ellie and whatever forces or spirits might have been listening, I would stop. I would.

I slid two blue pills under my tongue just as Mrs. Dale came into the room, carrying a steaming WORLD'S BEST TEACHER mug and packets of sugar and Cremora and Sweet 'N Low.

"Thanks," I said. I dumped fake cream and sugar into the cup and sipped. Mrs. Dale sat at her desk and loaded folders into a tan leather satchel. I waited for the lecture to begin. When it didn't, I started talking.

"Listen. I appreciate what you did out there. I understand that it's your job. But, like I told you, I had one glass of wine, this afternoon with Janet Mallory. You can call her if you don't believe me."

She looked at me steadily. "Were you taking anything else?"

That's when I glimpsed my loophole. My way out. The light at the end of the tunnel, shining glorious and gold. "Oh my God," I whispered, widening my eyes, letting my jaw go slack, doing everything but slapping my forehead. "My back went out over the weekend, and I'm taking . . .

God, what's it called? A muscle relaxer, and a painkiller. I totally forgot I'm not supposed to drink with them." I hung my head, my expression of shame entirely unfeigned. "Oh my God, what is wrong with me?"

Maybe I imagined it, but I thought Mrs. Dale's expression softened. So I kept going. "I'm so sorry," I whispered. "I can't believe I didn't double-check." I swallowed hard. The enormity of the situation—the trouble I could be in, the fact that I could have hurt children, mine and someone else's, or hit someone else, some stranger on the road—was covering me like a skin of ice, freezing my feet, my knees, my belly. If she reported this, I could lose my daughter. If Dave found out that I was driving under the influence . . . I shook my head, unwilling to even think about it. I couldn't let myself go there. Containment. Containment was the name of the game. "You were absolutely right to not let me drive. I'm sorry. It'll never happen again."

Mrs. Dale's expression was unreadable. Was she buying any of this? I couldn't tell.

"You were taking painkillers?" she finally asked. I started nodding almost before the last syllable was out of her mouth.

"That's right. And a muscle relaxant. My back . . ."

She looked at me for another long moment. "When my niece had a C-section," she finally said, "they gave her Percocet. Her doctor kept prescribing them for almost six months after she'd given birth, and when he cut her off, she found another doctor, a pain specialist, to write her prescriptions for Vicodin and OxyContin."

I tried not to flinch. Vicodin and Oxy. My favorites, my nearest and dearest . . . and, at that very moment, I wanted about a dozen of each. I wanted not to be there, not to have been seen by the ladies in the carpool lane, who were probably already spreading the word, not to be in that classroom that smelled like little-kid sweat and banana bread, being lectured by some old battle-ax who probably had no idea what it was like, trying to raise kids and hold a job and run a household these days.

"She took those pills for years. I believe that we all got used to it when Vicki didn't seem quite right, or when she was tired all the time. We'd ask her about what she was taking, and she'd say it was no big deal, and because she had prescriptions, because she was under a doctor's care, none of us worried. We didn't know she was borrowing pills from her friends when her prescriptions ran out, or buying them from someone she met at the gym . . . or that she'd gotten a prescription for Xanax and was trading those for her neighbor's painkillers."

"What happened?" I asked.

"What happened was, she died," Mrs. Dale said.

In the quiet, empty classroom, I heard myself gasp. "On the death certificate it said respiratory failure, but she had taken about five times more pills than she should have, and she had a few glasses of wine on top of it, and she went to sleep and she didn't wake up." She looked at me, unflinching. "Her little girl found her. It was a school morning, and my niece's husband was in the shower, and Brianna went into the bedroom and tapped her mom's shoulder." I sat there, frozen, my body prickling with goose pimples, my eyes and nose stinging with unshed tears. I could picture it—a woman about my age, in a nightgown, on her back in bed, underneath the covers. The sound of running water from the bathroom, the billow of steam and the smell of soap, and a little girl in Ariel pajamas shaking the woman's shoulder gently, then more insistently, not noticing the stiff, unyielding texture of the flesh, or how cold it was, saying *Mommy, Mommy, wake up!* And in my head, the little girl was Ellie.

I swallowed hard. Oh, God. What was I going to do? I had to stop, that was clear. But what if I couldn't? Mrs. Dale was looking at me. I wanted to explain, to tell her how this had happened, how stressful my life was, between my job and my parents and my husband and his work wife and Ellie, and how sometimes I didn't like being a mother much at all—how I liked the concept, but the reality of it was killing me. I couldn't take the tears and tantrums and endless Monopoly games, the way Ellie would wander down the stairs half a dozen times after she'd been put to bed, requesting a glass of water, a story, her nightlight turned on, her night-light turned off, how she'd bang on the door when I was in the shower, or even on the toilet, just trying to pee or put in a tampon, until I was ready to scream, to grab her by her little shoulders and shake her, shouting, *Just stay in bed, please! Just leave me alone and give me five minutes of peace!*

"Brianna was four," said Mrs. Dale.

"Four," I repeated. I imagined Ellie going to move-up day with only her daddy in the audience to cheer as she crossed over the bridge to first grade. I thought about her getting her period with no one to tell her what to do . . . or, worse, some bimbo of a stepmother who'd regard my daughter as competition. Her bat mitzvah . . . her first date . . . senior prom . . . college acceptance letters. All without a mother to encourage her and console her, to love her, no matter what.

I dropped my head. *No more,* I thought. *I can't do this anymore.* And right on the heels of that thought came, inevitably, another: *I need them.* I couldn't imagine leaving Ellie to face life without a mother . . . but I also couldn't imagine facing my life without a chemical buffer between me and Dave, me and my mother, me and the Internet, me and my feelings. How could I survive without that sweet river of calm wending its way through my body, easing me, untying knots from the soles of my feet to the top of my head? How could I make it through a day without knowing I had that reliable comfort waiting at the finish line?

I gave my head a little shake. This was stupid. So I had let things get a little out of hand. So I'd come to school a little loopy. Nobody had gotten hurt, right? And I wasn't going to die. I wasn't. I wasn't taking that much, and it was prescription medication, not heroin I was buying on the streets. It wasn't like I was some cracked-out junkie . . . or like I'd end up dead in bed with a mouthful of puke and a little girl to find me. I was smarter than that.

Except, a little voice inside me whispered, *wasn't Mrs. Dale's niece on the same stuff as you? And you're buying extra, and you're not taking it as prescribed. Not even close.* I told the voice to shut up, but it persisted. *Instead of taking one every four hours, you're taking four every one hour . . . and you're drinking on top of that.*

You need help.

No, I don't.

This can't go on.

I'm doing fine!

"I'm fine," I muttered, half to Mrs. Dale and half to myself . . . but, even as I said it, I could imagine a little girl shaking her mother's shoulder. Her mother's cold, stiff, dead shoulder.

"I'm not trying to scare you," said Mrs. Dale. "But I know what this looks like. And I know it can happen to anyone. The nicest people. The smartest people. My niece was so beautiful. You'd never look at her and think that she was a drug addict. She was just taking what the doctors gave her. Right until she died."

"I appreciate what you're saying, but that's not me. I don't have a problem." Never mind the surveys I'd taken, the questionnaires I'd filled out, the increasing number of pills I needed to get through the day. Never mind the promises—*not before nine, not before noon, not while I'm working, not when I'm with Eloise*—that I'd broken, one after another, every day, stretching back for months. "I don't. I just made a mistake today, and you were right to take my keys, and I swear, I swear on my daughter's life, that it'll never happen again." I took a gulp of lukewarm coffee and forced myself to ask, "Are you going to report me?"

After an interminable pause, Mrs. Dale shook her head.

"Thank you. I'm sorry. I promise . . . I swear to you," I repeated, "this will never happen again."

She gazed at me, and her eyes, behind her bifocals, looked kind. "There's no shame in asking for help if you need it," she said . . . and then she walked out, leaving me alone with my coffee, and my keys.

I waited until she was out the door before I shoved my hand in my purse and touched the Altoids tin, then the prescription bottles, one, two, three, four. I had pills halfway to my mouth before something inside me, the little voice of reason, rose up and demanded, *What the FUCK are you doing?*

I put the pills back. I put the cap on the bottle. I put the bottle in my purse, and laid my head on top of my folded arms . . . and then, alone in the empty classroom, I started to cry.

Thirteen

The next morning, I didn't take a single pill. I dropped Ellie off at school, treated myself to an extra-hot latte with a double shot of espresso, and then drove to Center City, pulled on oversized sunglasses and a baseball cap and slipped through the side door of the church on Pine Street I'd found online the night before. In the basement, about twenty people, most of them men, sat in folding metal chairs. Tattered posters were thumb-tacked to the walls. One read "The Twelve Steps" and the other "The Twelve Traditions." In the front of the room was a wooden desk with two more folding chairs behind it and a sculpture of the letters AA carved out of wood on top, along with a battered-looking three-ring binder and a basket. I pulled my baseball cap low, flipped my collar up, and took the seat closest to the door. The chairs began to fill, until there were almost fifty people in the room.

I looked around, dividing the attendees into categories: Aged Homeless (lots of layers of dirty clothes, and not many teeth) and Young Punks (pale, white, wormy Eminem clones in obscene T-shirts and with multiple piercings). There were old guys in Phillies jackets you'd pass on the street without a second look, and a single woman in a business suit with gold hoop earrings and leather pumps that I knew couldn't have cost less than five hundred dollars, but it was mostly a collection of people who looked nothing like me.

"This seat taken?" asked a young man—maybe a teenager—in a blue T-shirt. When I shook my head, he sat down, swiped at his nose, and gave the pimple on his chin a squeeze. "Hey," he said.

"Hey," I said back. He had a ring through his nose that made me think of Ferdinand the bull; Ferdinand, who didn't want to fight, just sit and sniff the flowers. I glanced at my phone—five minutes until this thing kicked off—and continued my appraisal. The crowd was mostly made up of men, but in the back of the room I spotted two more women, both in their fifties or sixties, looking like, as Dave's frat buddy Dan might have said, they'd been ridden hard and put away wet. One of them had unnaturally blonde hair pulled into a high ponytail that went uncomfortably with her weathered face. The other was a brunette with gaudy earrings and a phlegmy cough. The blonde wore sweatpants, the brunette, a pair of high-waisted jeans and a mock turtleneck, à la Jennifer Aniston, circa *Friends*, season one. To pass the time, I made up jobs for them. The blonde was a cashier at a gas station; the brunette waited tables at a diner. Not a hipster diner with Pabst Blue Ribbon on tap and a legitimate chef using artisanal ingredients in the kitchen, either, but a grungy place somewhere in Northeast Philadelphia, where the mashed potatoes came from a box, where truckers and cabdrivers and construction workers came to eat meatloaf and play Patsy Cline on the jukebox.

"First time?"

Oh, joy. Ferdinand was making conversation. I hoped a curt nod would appease him. It did not.

"You court-stipulated?"

I didn't know what that meant. "Excuse me?" I asked, and then yawned. For the past twenty minutes, I hadn't been able to stop yawning. My nose was running, and my eyes were watery. Allergies, I figured. Also, I felt like I was jumping out of my skin. My toes wanted to tap; my legs wanted to bounce and kick; my torso wanted to squirm. It was all I could do to hold still.

"Didja get, like, a DUI or something?"

"Oh, no. No, nothing like that." Were all the

people at this meeting here just because a judge told them they had to be?

He gave me a grin. When he smiled I saw that, in spite of the ring in his nose and the spiderweb tattooed on his neck, he was still more boy than man. Not too long ago, he'd been climbing off a school bus every afternoon, and dressing up on Halloween. Someone had kissed him when he'd fallen down, had put silver dollars under his pillow in exchange for his baby teeth, had signed his report cards and attended his parent-teacher conferences, had worried when he'd stayed out late, lying awake in the dark, waiting for the sound of his key in the front door.

An elderly man in a plaid shirt and khaki pants with a large bandage on one cheek took a seat behind the desk and rapped his knuckles on the table. "Welcome to Alcoholics Anonymous. My name is Tom, and I'm an alcoholic." At least, that was what I suspected he said. Between the way he mumbled and his thick-as-taffy Philadelphia accent, I caught maybe every third syllable.

"Hi, Tom!" the room chorused, their voices cheery, as if being an alcoholic was something awesome to celebrate.

"This is an open meeting of Alcoholics Anonymous. Anyone who wishes to attend may do so. The only requirement for membership in AA is a desire to stop drinking. I've asked a friend to read 'How It Works.' "

As Tom's friend, a rotund white-bearded man who'd introduced himself by saying "I'm Glen, and I don't drink alcohol," droned through both sides of a laminated piece of paper—something about half-measures availing us nothing, something else about suggested steps as a program of recovery—I began plotting my escape. Aside from the business-suit woman, who was probably completing a degree in therapy or social work and observing this as part of her coursework, there was no one in the room I could imagine even having a conversation with.

"Many of us exclaimed, 'What an order! I can't go through with it,' " Glen read. I shrugged my purse onto my shoulder. Who talked like that? No one I knew. "Do not be discouraged. No one among us has been able to maintain anything like perfect adherence to these principles. We are not saints. The point is that we are willing to grow along spiritual lines. We claim spiritual progress, rather than spiritual perfection. Our description of the alcoholic, the chapter to the agnostic, and our personal adventures before and after make clear three pertinent ideas. One, That we were alcoholic and could not manage our own lives."

Not me, I thought. Except for that little slipup the day before, I was managing my own life just fine. Not to mention my daughter's life, my husband's life, and my parents' lives.

"Two," Glen continued. "That probably no

human power could have relieved our alcoholism."

Wrong again. I could do this myself. I just hadn't tried. I would cut back on my own. Eighteen pills today, then sixteen pills tomorrow, and fourteen by the weekend, and ten a day by Monday . . .

"Three: That God could and would if He were sought." Everyone in the room joined in, chanting those last words: *could and would if He were sought.* At which point, I realized that I had wandered into a cult. Why hadn't anyone told me that AA was some strange turn-it-over-to-God deal? I thought it was a self-help thing, where you got together with other drunks and druggies and figured out how to solve your problem. Shows what I knew.

"Any anniversaries?" Tom asked from behind the desk, looking around the room. "Anyone here counting days?"

A young man in a blue sweatshirt and dirty work boots raised his hand. "I'm Greg, and I'm an alcoholic and an addict."

"Hi, Greg!" chorused the room.

"Today I got thirty days."

The room burst into applause. "And," Greg said on his way up to the front of the room, where Tom gave him a bear hug and what looked like a poker chip, "my parole officer says if I stay clean for ninety and I pass all my piss tests, that bitch has gotta let me see my kid."

Awesome, I thought, as the room clapped for this charming sentiment. *Greg has a kid. Greg has a parole officer. Greg just called his kid's mother a bitch.* Suddenly I needed to leave with an urgency that approached my desperate need for a pill first thing in the morning. I sidled over toward the coffee urn, thinking that I'd stay there until the group's attention was occupied, then make a break for it. Meanwhile, I pretended to be interested in the dog-eared posters framed behind smeary glass: KEEP IT SIMPLE. ONE DAY AT A TIME. THERE BUT FOR THE GRACE OF GOD.

I don't belong here, I thought. *These people aren't like me. I'm not as bad as they are; not even close. I can figure this out on my own.*

"This is a speaker meeting," said Tom. "I've asked one of my sponsees, Tyler, to speak." He pointed to his left, where a man who was maybe twenty-one, with skin the color of skim milk past its sell-by date, sat slumped in a thin, discolored T-shirt, jeans, and battered sneakers.

"Hey," he said, managing to pull himself upright. "I'm Tyler, and I'm an alcoholic and an addict."

"Hey, Tyler!"

Tyler hocked back snot and scratched his forearm. "Yeah, so. Um. Tom here's my sponsor. He's a real good guy. And he said I gotta come to a meeting and speak, so here I am. I've got . . . what is it? Fifty-seven days today."

The room applauded, with people calling out "Congratulations!" and "Way to go!" and "Keep coming back!" Tyler ducked his head modestly and delivered the next part of his speech directly into his sternum.

"I know I'm s'posed to be sharing my experience, strength, and hope, but I'm mostly gonna be sharing hope, because . . ." He gave a self-deprecating chuckle. "I don't really have much experience with this whole not-using thing."

With that, Tyler launched into his tale. Mom was an alcoholic, Dad was a heroin addict. They'd leave him alone in the house for days at a time while they were "out partyin'." Tyler had his first drink at eleven, stealing a pint of his grandfather's vodka and drinking the whole thing. "And, from then on, I guess it was just one big party." I dumped powdered creamer into a Styrofoam cup and listened. "I'd drink vodka before school, sneak a few beers during lunch, smoke a joint in the parking lot before I came home. And that was ninth grade." By tenth grade he was smoking meth; by the time he was expelled in the eleventh grade, he was sneaking out of the house in the middle of the night to hitchhike to Kensington, where he'd started to shoot heroin. Finally, his parents performed an intervention. No word on whether they'd cleaned up their own acts or were just sober enough to notice that their son was in trouble.

"They said I had to move out or go to rehab. This was after I, uh, stole my mom's engagement ring and pawned it, 'cause I was all strung out, you know, and I, like, needed to score, and I didn't care what it took. Didn't care who I hurt. That was me when I was using."

As quietly as I could, I tossed my coffee cup into the trash can and slipped out the door. *This isn't for me,* I thought. I didn't do meth, I didn't shoot heroin, and God knows I never stole anything from anyone. I didn't even smoke!

I walked briskly back to my car. Anyone who saw me would think I was a regular stay-at-home mom on her way to pick up some essential, forgotten ingredient—a dozen eggs, a cup of sugar— before her kids came home from school. Which I was, I decided. I wasn't an addict, like the people in that room. I was a working mother under an inordinate amount of stress due to her job, her marriage, and a father in crisis; a woman who had, quite naturally, turned to an available remedy to help her manage her days.

"I'm fine," I said. And then, to prove it, I bought a dozen eggs and a bag of brown sugar at the grocery store, and had fresh chocolate-chip cookies waiting when Eloise came home.

Fourteen

"Mommy!"

I blinked, rolling onto my side, running through my own internal whiteboard. Today is TUESDAY. It is five-fifteen. The next meal is DINNER, and you'd better start cooking. I heard, then saw, the doorknob of my bedroom turning back and forth.

"Mommy's resting!" I called, and closed my eyes again. I'd been working flat out from five in the morning until it was time to take Ellie to school, and then from the moment I'd gotten back home until one. I'd decided to take a nap, and, after three blue Oxys failed to do the trick, I'd chewed up two more, then shut my eyes, and it was like I'd been punched hard in the head. I hadn't just fallen asleep, I thought, trying to get my legs moving. I'd been knocked out, plunged into unconsciousness.

My phone was blinking. There were three new e-mails and a pair of texts from Sarah. *CALL ME BACK,* read the memo line. *R U okay?* read the second. *U sounded weird.*

Oh, God. I had no memory of speaking to Sarah. What had I said? What had I done? Panic surged through me. I pushed myself out of bed, pressed the phone to my ear, dialed Sarah's number, and hurried to the bathroom so I could pee and talk at the same time.

I got her voicemail. "Hey, Sarah, it's Allison. Um. Sorry if I sounded a little out of it." I wiped and flushed, feeling frantic and sick and disgusted with myself, wondering how to gracefully ask what I'd said. "Call me back—I'm fine now!"

I opened the bedroom door and almost bumped into my mother. As always, she had her face on— foundation and eyeliner and a gooey lipgloss pout. A studded black leather belt showed off her tinier-than-ever waist, and her French manicure looked just-that-afternoon fresh, but her expression was worried as she twisted her hands and looked me over. "Allison, are you okay?" she asked.

"Fine!" I edged past her, down the stairs. Had I remembered to defrost the chicken? Was there a vegetable I could cook to go with it? And—oh, God—had I said something to my mother after I'd taken all that Oxy?

"You seem . . ." She followed me down the stairs, impressively managing to keep pace with my half trot, even though I was barefoot and she was in heels. "You seem like you're not doing well."

"I'm okay!" I pulled a box of rice out of the pantry, along with a can of hearts of palm. The chicken was still half-frozen in the fridge. I put it in the microwave. "Really. Just, you know, lots of stuff with work . . . and I'm worried about Daddy." Normally, changing the subject to my father would be enough to start the waterworks, but my mother was looking at me with an unfamiliar intensity, narrowing her eyes as she studied my face.

"You know," she said, "if you needed to take a break . . . if you and Dave wanted to go away somewhere, I'd be happy to stay with Ellie."

I blinked. Was this my mother? My mother, who could barely take care of herself?

"That's really generous of you. But I'm fine. Like I said, just a little overwhelmed right now." My mind was running on its typical three tracks. There was dinner to be prepared. There was work to be considered—I'd filed my blog post, but I still had to throw some red meat to the commenters, whom I'd been neglecting. And, as always, there were the pills to count, and count again. Did I have enough? Were there more on the way? Had I sent money to my Penny Lane account?

I shook my head. Ellie and my mother both watched me as I cracked eggs, shook bread-crumbs into a bowl, set the table, and preheated the oven.

"Ellie, let's go play cards," said my mom. They filed into the living room.

Everything's cool, I told myself, vowing to apologize to Sarah in person and to be more present— or at least more awake—for Ellie. *I am fine.*

I heard the garage door creaking upward. "Daddy, Daddy, Daddy!" Ellie chanted, sprinting toward the door. I wasn't expecting Dave for dinner. Hadn't he told me that he had some dinner thing to go to, some bash one of the big unions was throwing that he needed to attend? Or had that been the night before?

"Ellie, help me set the table," I called. I could hear Dave's low voice mixing with Ellie's bright chatter, and then the two of them came into the kitchen with Ellie's feet balanced on Dave's shoes, clutching his hands and giggling as he walked.

"How was your day?" he asked.

"Fine! Busy!" I bent to check on the chicken.

"Mommy was sleeping," Ellie announced.

"Mommy was tired," I said, feeling grateful that Dave couldn't see my face. I hadn't told him about my run-in with Mrs. Dale. Ellie hadn't, either. At least not yet. I knew better than to tell her not to say anything—that, of course, would guarantee that she'd go running to Dave with the whole story, about how Mommy fell down and Mommy got her dress all bloody and Mommy got put in a time-out by a teacher. My hope was that her typical five-year-old attention span would save me, and that events from the other day would be, to Ellie, as distant as things that had happened years ago.

"Do you know Mommy snores when she sleeps?" Ellie inquired.

"I do not!" I was smiling so hard that my cheeks ached as I cracked ice cubes into a pitcher, then gave the hearts of palm a squeeze of lime juice, a drizzle of olive oil, and a sprinkling of salt.

"You do too. And you DROOL. There was a whole PUDDLE underneath your face."

"Tough day at the office," I said, and turned to get the milk out of the refrigerator. When I shut the refrigerator door, Dave and my mother were looking at each other.

"What?" I said. Neither adult answered.

"What?" I said again, trying to sound happy, trying to look happy, trying to pretend I hadn't spent the past five hours passed out in a puddle of my own saliva.

"Are you sure you're all right?" my mother finally ventured.

"I'm all right," I said. Smile still in place, voice still untroubled. Dinner in the oven. Blog post filed. At least, I thought I'd filed it. I would cut Ellie's chicken, then I'd run upstairs just to double-check. And have another pill. "Everything's good."

My mom and Dave exchanged a look. "Hey, Ellie, how about you and Grandma go out for sushi so Mommy and Daddy can talk," Dave said.

"Sushi, sushi!" chanted Ellie, grabbing my mother's hand and towing her toward the door.

"Do you need a ride?" I asked.

"We'll get a cab!" called my mother. The door swung shut behind them.

"Let's sit down in the dining room," Dave said. I felt my knees start to quiver as I followed him there. The dining room was low on my list of priorities, which meant the only furniture in it was the table and six cheap IKEA chairs. The walls were bare, covered in an unattractive greenish-blue wallpaper that I'd planned on removing as soon as I had the time and then the money.

"What is it?" I said, trying to sound casual and unconcerned.

"Sit down," Dave said.

I curled my fingers around the back of a chair. "Not until you tell me what's wrong."

He sighed. Typical Dave. He could never come right out and say something. There had to be a few moments of prefatory sighing and throat-clearing first. "You and I need to talk."

"Okay," I said slowly, buying time. The news began to register in my body. My chest felt heavy, and my knees had that airy, trembly feeling. Was he going to ask me for a divorce? My heart stopped beating as Dave reached into his work bag and pulled out a FedEx envelope. From Penny Lane. *Shit,* I thought. *Oh, shit, shit, shit.*

"What is this?" He hadn't opened it. And the return address probably said something banal about Computer Parts or eBay Services. Maybe

268

there was a chance I could talk my way out of this.

"It's a SIM card for my cell phone." I widened my eyes. "Terrifying, I know."

"You're telling me that if I open this envelope I'm not going to find drugs?"

My heart was thudding so hard I was surprised Dave couldn't hear it. "Oh, Jesus, Dave. What are you, McGruff the Crime Dog? You think I'm"—I curled my fingers into sarcastic air quotes, rolling my eyes at the very notion—"doing drugs?"

He lifted the envelope and shook it. I braced myself for the sound of rattling, praying that the package had come from one of the vendors who was liberal with the bubble wrap. No rattle. *Thank you, God.* But Dave wasn't giving up.

"Why don't you open the envelope and show me what's inside."

Maybe it was the smug look on his face, or the accusation in his tone. Whatever it was, it infuriated me. "Because I don't fucking have to!" I yelled. "Because I didn't sign up to play show and tell! Because you're my husband, not Inspector Javert!"

A wave of dizziness swept from the base of my spine to the crown of my head. There was a ringing in my ears, a high-pitched chime. My mouth was dry. My palms were icy. I wanted a pill. I needed a pill. Just the thought of them, crunching between my teeth, that familiar bitterness flooding my mouth, helped me relax the tiniest bit.

Dave continued to stare at me. I thought about that day at Stonefield, and how, a few hours ago, I'd called Sarah but had no idea what I'd said. I thought about the money I was spending, the naps I was taking, the sleepless nights, my racing heart. *This needs to stop,* said a voice in my head. *It can be over right now. This can be the end.*

"I don't—" I blurted. I made myself shut my mouth, take a seat, look him straight in the eye when I spoke. "Okay. I will tell you the truth. I have been buying stuff online. But it's prescription medication. You know I've got herniated discs."

Dave reached into his work bag. From the inside pocket he pulled out a Ziploc bag full of empty prescription bottles. He reached in again and pulled out a sheaf of papers. I squinted until I could see what they were—printouts from Penny Lane, detailing every purchase I'd made.

Closing my eyes, I turned my face toward the wall.

"I called Janet last night," Dave said into the silence. "I told her I was worried about you. I asked if she'd seen anything alarming—if you were late dropping Ellie off, or picking her up."

"I have never been late," I said. That, at least, was pretty much the truth.

"And then," he continued doggedly, "I called the school."

Oh, shit. "Dave . . ."

"Mrs. Dale called me back. She said you seemed like you were—the word she used was 'impaired'—when you came to get the kids a few days ago. She said you told her you were drinking. That you'd had a glass of wine with a prescription medication, and you'd forgotten that you weren't supposed to."

I tried to interrupt. "Dave, listen . . ."

"You were going to drive drunk with Ellie in the car!" He started yelling, his face red, a vein throbbing in the center of his forehead, tears in his eyes. "What if she died? What if you died? What the fuck is the matter with you?"

I started to cry. "I don't know. Maybe I don't like having a husband who won't even talk to me anymore. Maybe I'm sick of being the one who does everything around here."

He glared at me, unmoved by my tears. "Don't make this my fault, Allison."

"You don't know." My voice cracked on the last word. "You have no idea what it's like. Dealing with Ellie. Dealing with my parents. My work . . ."

"Maybe not," he said coolly. "Maybe I don't know. But I think there are people in the world who manage to do all of those things without becoming drug addicts."

"I am not a drug addict!" And fuck that bitch

Mrs. Dale for ratting me out. I mentally tore up the check I'd been planning to send to the Annual Giving campaign. I'd take myself shopping instead. "Okay. Obviously I shouldn't have been drinking on top of the medication. I was tired, and I made a mistake. I'm not perfect."

"You aren't yourself. I don't know any other way to say it. And everyone's noticed. Me, your mom, Ellie . . ." He reached across the table, but I pulled my hand away before he could touch me. "If you want to get some help, I'll support you as best I can."

My laugh was high and shrill. "Help? What, like rehab? You think I need to go to rehab? You think I'm Lindsay Lohan now?"

"I don't know what you need. But I know you're taking more of those pills than you should be. I'm worried about you . . . and, quite frankly, I'm worried about you taking care of Ellie."

I thought I'd been scared before, that day at Stonefield, when Mrs. Dale hadn't let me drive. I was wrong. That wasn't anything. This was real fear. This was true terror. And the best defense was a good offense. My father used to say that all the time. I drew myself up straight, grateful that I was wearing makeup, that I'd washed my hair that morning, that my clothes were clean. "Are you suggesting that I'm an unfit mother?"

Dave shook his head. "I'm saying that I'm worried about you, and I'm worried about Ellie when she's with you. You need to take this seriously, Allison. People die from what you're doing."

"Okay! So fine! I'll quit!" I made a show of extracting a bottle of Vicodin from my purse, uncapping it, and pouring the pills down the drain. I had a small secret stash, of course—a mints tin stuffed in my purse, a dozen Oxys in the bottom of my tampon box, a few Percocet in the glove compartment.

I turned on my heel and made what might have been a grand exit if my hip hadn't caught the side of the table. I stumbled, and would have fallen if I hadn't grabbed the wall. Dave was right behind me, holding my gaze, glaring at me, with no trace of goodwill or humor or love in his expression.

"I don't want to have to spy on you," he said. "But I will do whatever I have to do to keep Ellie safe."

"Ellie," I said, with all the dignity I could muster, "is perfectly safe. I would never, ever do anything to put her at risk." Except, of course, the thing I'd done a few days ago.

"If you want help, I am here for you."

I rolled my eyes. "Great. See if you can send me to the place the guy from *Friends* went. They have Pilates."

"Allison."

"I promise," I roared, before he could get off

another adult-sounding, well-meaning warning. "I promise I promise I promise." And I kept my promise all the way up the stairs, down the hall, and into the bathroom, where I fished pills out of the tampon box where I'd hidden them, and swallowed them, one, two, three.

Fifteen

I was too upset to sleep that night. I sat in the living room with my laptop, pounding out a blog post called "Husbands Just Don't Understand," while Ronnie slept in the guest bedroom and Dave snored away down the hall. I burned through work I'd been putting off, spending ninety minutes engaging with the comments section and coming up with story ideas for one of the magazines that had been e-mailing in the wake of my "vibrator in every purse" comment. Every time I felt my brain edging toward the words *Dave knows what I've been doing* or *I'm going to lose my family* or even just *I want to stop and I can't,* I would march myself into the bathroom and take another pill. By six a.m., I was wild-eyed, smelling of acrid sweat, feeling both sluggish and frantic. And, somehow, the unthinkable had happened. I was out of pills.

"Can you take Ellie to school?" I rasped through the bathroom door. Rats' teeth of panic were nibbling at my heart. Dave sounded disgustingly collected.

"Sure. No problem."

I went to the computer and logged on to Penny Lane, to make sure I hadn't placed an order and then forgotten about it. No. There was only the stuff that Dave had intercepted. Prior to that was an order for sixty pills that had arrived two days ago, and every last one of them was gone. I stared at the screen, feeling my jaw drop as I did the math. Thirty pills in less than a day and a half? That couldn't be right. Except I could remember the package arriving, and how fast I'd gotten the envelope open and transferred the pills into my mints tin, how before I'd even gotten inside the house I had four of those babies inside me.

"Fuck," I whispered. I went to the bedroom and began to go through my usual hiding places: my tampon box, the second drawer of my bedside table, the zippered pockets inside the different purses I'd used that month. There was nothing. I couldn't even find a piece of a broken pill to tide me over. Everything was gone.

I sat down on the bed, heart thumping, palms and temples greasy with cold sweat. I picked up my phone and scrolled through the names of my doctors. *Called her last week . . . called him on Monday . . . haven't called her in so long she'll probably ask questions about why I need painkillers now.*

Think, I told myself fiercely as I heard the garage door open and the car pull out of the driveway. Maybe there was stuff left in my father's medicine cabinet . . . except I knew that there wasn't. I'd cleared it all out before the Realtor had come for a final walk-through. Did my mom have anything? And did I want to risk trying to get her out of the house so I could check?

Forty minutes after Dave's departure, still in my pajama bottoms and the Wonder Woman T-shirt I'd worn while I worked, I sat on the examination table of a strip-mall clinic where a cab had dropped me off, talking to a doctor with a heavy accent and bags under his eyes.

"You hurt the back when?"

"Two years ago." I was shivering, sweating, and having a hard time keeping my legs still. My knees wanted to kick, my feet wanted to tap, my body itched all over, and my fingers wanted to dig into my skin and start clawing. *Withdrawal,* I thought bleakly. A loop of every movie I'd ever seen in which a junkie kicked his or her habit had set itself on "repeat" in my mind. I was terrified of the agony I suspected was awaiting me . . . and I was furious at myself, furious that I'd let this happen, not stayed on top of what I had and what I needed. All those weeks—months, even—of promising myself I'd cut back, just not today, when in fact my use had increased and increased, my tolerance building until I needed four, or five, or even six little blue OxyContin to feel the transporting euphoria that a single Vicodin had once given me . . . and now here I was with nothing.

"You take how much of the painkiller?"

"I don't know. A lot. Maybe ten pills a day," I lied.

"Of the thirty milligrams?"

"Yes." Ten was a good day, and Oxys weren't the only thing I was taking, but never mind. He'd give me something—I didn't even care what. Then I'd get on top of this. I'd slow my roll, start being prudent. No more pills first thing in the morning, no more pills in the middle of the night. Three or four days—a week, tops—and I'd have this under control.

"Every day, you take them?"

I nodded, launching into the story I'd already told the intake nurse. "And, like I said, I'm going to see my regular doctor, only she's out sick, and I'm leaving for vacation this afternoon, and if you could just give me maybe ten pills, just so I can get through the plane trip . . ."

He leaned back against the exam room's sink, taking me in. His name was Dr. Desgupta, and his eyes, behind heavy brown plastic frames, were not unkind.

"Every day, you're taking these pills," he said again.

I bent my head and prayed. *Please, God, just let him give me enough to get through the day and I'll stop, I'll get help, I'll do something, I swear I will.*

"And is it because the back hurts? Or is it because you need them, because you are getting sick without them?"

I didn't answer. I wrapped my arms around myself and concentrated, as hard as I could, on not throwing up. "Sick," I finally said. "I've never tried to stop, and I think . . . I mean, I'm not feeling so great already."

"There is medication. Suboxone." I lifted my head. "An opiate agonist-antagonist. It blocks your receptors, so you can't take the heroin, or the Vicodin, or the OxyContin. Whatever narcotic you were taking. But it gives you some opiate, too. Not enough so you get, you know, the high, but enough that you feel okay."

I nodded. This sounded like an acceptable solution. I could take this Suboxone stuff and stop hurting, and then take a day to sort myself out. I'd get more pills, either online or from doctors, enough so that this would never happen again. I would contact a lawyer, and a child psychologist, which Ellie would undoubtedly require. I would taper myself off the pills, maybe try more of those meetings, or get myself a therapist, or start running again. But all I wanted, at that moment, was something to take, something to swallow or smoke or snort. Something that would ease my panic, slow my heartbeat, let me feel okay again.

"Here." Dr. Desgupta had finally pulled out his prescription pad. "I will write for seven days. The medicine is a film; you dissolve it under your tongue." He ripped off the page. I snatched it out of his hand. "How long ago was last dose of OxyContin?"

I tried to remember what time it had been when I'd chewed up the last of my pills, and tried not to remember licking the inside of the jewelry box where I'd found the final two Vicodin. If you were ever wondering whether you had a problem or not, the taste of jewelry-box felt was answer enough. "Four in the morning?"

He looked at the clock, calculating. He had big brown eyes, a bald head with a few strands of black hair carefully arranged on top, and a soft, accented voice. "Take first one at noon. You should be started in the withdrawal by then. Feeling like you have the flu. Sweaty, hands shaking . . . you feel like that, you take first one."

"Thank you," I said faintly, and was up and out of the chair, the prescription in one hand and my cell phone in the other, before he could tell me goodbye.

I could remember the rest of the day only in snatches. I remembered my cab ride from the doc-in-a-box to the drive-through lane of the pharmacy. The flu, the doctor had told me . . . except this was to the flu like a pack of rabid pit bulls was to a Chihuahua. I was running with foul-smelling sweat and shaking so hard that my teeth were chattering. My skin was covered in goose pimples; whatever I'd eaten the day before churned unhappily in my belly. I remembered the pharmacist telling me that the medicine wasn't covered by my insurance without prior approval, and insisting, over and over, that I didn't care, that it didn't matter, that I'd pay out of pocket and worry about reimbursement later.

Back at home, I speed-read the instructions, then tore open one of the packets and let the yellow film dissolve into sour slime under my tongue. I locked the bedroom door and lay on my bed, where I endured six hours of the worst hell I could imagine. My entire body twitched and burned. My legs kicked and flailed uncontrol-lably. I couldn't hold still, couldn't get comfort-able. My skin felt like it was host to hundreds of thousands of fiery ants wearing boots made of poison-tipped needles. I scratched and clawed, but I couldn't make them go away. The first time I threw up, I made it to the toilet, and, from there, I managed to send my mother and Dave a text explaining that I was sick and that, between the two of them, they'd have to handle Ellie and her obligations. The second time, I made it to the sink. The third time, I couldn't even make it out of bed. I was freezing cold, so I'd tried to get under the covers, but the kicking—kicking! I was actually kicking!—had disarranged everything, had loosened the fitted sheets and the mattress cover. I writhed on the bed, trying to moan into the pillow, praying that the Suboxone would start its work, that I'd feel better, that Ellie wouldn't see or hear this.

My mother knocked at the door. "Allison? Allison, are you okay?"

"Flu," I called back, in a voice that didn't sound like mine. I'd gotten myself wrapped in a blanket and was sitting, hunched over and moaning, in the old glider chair I'd used to nurse Ellie. I was burning up, my hair glued to my cheeks in matted clumps, making high, whining noises. I moaned and rocked, moaned and rocked, as the minutes dragged by. At six o'clock I couldn't stand it any longer. I found the phone, crawled into bed, and managed to dial the clinic and tell the receptionist that it was an emergency and that I needed Dr. Desgupta.

"Yes, hello?" he answered.

I told him my name. My voice was a high, wavering whisper. I didn't sound like myself; I sounded like Ellie when she woke up sick in the middle of the night. "There's something wrong . . . I'm really sick . . ."

"You are having the nausea and the diarrhea?"

"Yes," I whispered. I was crying, on top of everything else. "I'm cold . . . I can't stop shaking . . . everything hurts . . . I feel like I'm going to die . . ."

"Twenty-four hours," he said calmly. "The Suboxone is kicking the opiates off your receptors. But in a day or two you will be well again."

A day or two? I wasn't sure I could take another twenty minutes of this agony. "I can't do this," I said. My voice was sounding less like human conversation than like a cat's yowl. "Please, you have to help me . . . I think I need to go to a hospital . . ."

"I am thinking," the doctor said calmly, "that maybe you need to be in a rehab bed." He trilled the "r" of "rehab," making it sound like something wonderful and exotic.

"No rehab," I said. "I'm not an addict. Please. I'm not. I'm just really, really sick."

"You go to one of these places, they will help you," he explained. "There is no need to stay for the twenty-eight days unless you like. But you need to be watched until you are well."

Rehab. I started crying even harder, because I suspected that he was right. Maybe I didn't need rehab, but I needed to be somewhere with nurses and doctors and medicine and machines. The pain was intolerable. I could barely speak; I couldn't keep my legs still. I actually wanted to die. Death would be an improvement over this.

The doorknob turned. Shaking and sick, I felt the weight of Ellie's body as she crawled beside me. "Mommy?" she whispered. With her tiny hands she patted my hair, then my forehead. "Mommy, do you need true love's kiss?"

I made some noise, thinking that I'd never hated myself as much as I did at that moment. Then my mother was there. "Oh my God." Somehow, she kept her voice calm as she said, "Ellie, go to your room. Let me help your mommy."

I opened my eye. "Mom." She bent down and hugged me hard. I whispered Dr. Desgupta's name, then handed her the phone, and shut my eyes again as I heard her say, "Yes, I'm Allison Weiss's mother, and she's very, very ill."

Curled on my side, I rocked and rocked. Faintly, as if I were listening through a paper tube, I could hear my mother's voice, her questions and answers. *Opiate addiction . . . Suboxone . . . Precipitated withdrawal . . . Which facility would you recommend?*

"No rehab!" I moaned, and grabbed at my mother's sleeve.

"Yes, rehab," she said, and pulled herself away. She wasn't falling apart or weeping. There were no snail tracks of mascara on her cheeks, no trembling hands or whimpered complaints about how she could not go on. It was funny, I thought. All it took for my mother to actually be a mother was a little withdrawal. "You're sick, honey.

You're sick, but I'm going to help you get better."

I shut my eyes. Later I remembered voices in the bedroom, a stethoscope against my chest, my mother's voice, then Dave's, reciting from the Penny Lane invoice a list of what I'd been taking, how many, and for how long. *We see a lot of this,* someone—a paramedic—had said. More than you'd expect. Happens to the nicest people. *The nicest people,* I thought. That was me. Then they lifted me onto a gurney, and I felt the sting of a needle in my arm, and when I opened my eyes again I was in a hospital bed, feeling as if every bone in my body had been smashed, then clumsily reset.

"Where am I? What happened?" I whispered. Dave stood there in a Blind Melon T-shirt and jeans, looking at me. I hurt all over. My body felt like a skinned knee, flayed and bloody, like a single, stinging nerve ending . . . and I was more ashamed than I had ever been in my life. I couldn't deal with this. Not now. Not until someone gave me something for the pain.

"You're in the hospital. You had something called precipitated withdrawal." Dave had come to the doorway, but had not taken a single step inside the room, like he'd committed to stopping by, but not staying, at a party whose guests he had no interest in knowing. "It's what happens when you've been taking lots of opiates for a long time, and then something kicks them off your system."

"FYI, it's not a lot of fun," I whispered. Dave didn't smile.

"There're two days left of school." Dave was doing his reasonable, just-the-facts thing, the one I recognized from telephone conversations with his editor. "Your mom and I can manage Ellie. Then she can do day camp at Stonefield."

"My mom can barely manage herself," I said.

"You need to go somewhere," he said.

"You mean rehab." Dave did not deny it. "Look," I said, into the silence. "Obviously, buying pills online was a bad idea. I know I was taking way more than I should have. I'm under a lot of stress. I've been making some bad decisions. But look, it's been . . . " I looked around for a clock, then took my best guess. "What, twenty-four hours since I had anything, right?" Without waiting for him to confirm, I plowed on. "So I should be fine. Maybe I just need some rest. Fluids. Then I can come home, and I'll be okay. I just won't take any more pills."

Could I do it? I wondered, even as I made my case. Maybe, twenty-four hours later, I'd be physically free, but I knew that if I was home alone I'd be on the computer or the phone, getting more.

You're an addict.
No I'm not.
You can't stop.
Yes I can.

And in that moment, in that bed, what I'd done, what I'd let myself become, hit me hard. I had endangered my daughter. Janet's boys. Myself. Even though no one had gotten hurt—*yet, my mind whispered; no one has gotten hurt yet*—the truth was that if I kept going this way, Ellie might grow up with an absence far worse than what I endured. She would have the same hole in her heart that I had, the same questions that tormented me—why wasn't I good enough for my own mother to love?

"It's just twenty-eight days," Dave said.

"What about my dad?" I managed. "What about Ellie?"

"Your father's in a safe place. Your mom can take care of herself, and I can take care of Eloise."

"And what if I don't go?"

Dave didn't answer. He just looked at me steadily. "I hope you'll do the right thing," he finally said. "Because I need to do whatever it takes to make sure that Ellie is safe."

Panic was blooming inside me, pushing the air out of my lungs, as I sorted out what that could mean. I imagined Dave moving out, and taking Ellie with him. I pictured my husband in his good navy blue suit, standing in front of a judge, all the evidence—the envelopes from Penny Lane, bank statements and receipts, copies of all the prescriptions I'd accumulated from all the different doctors. *Your honor, my wife is not capable of caring for a small child.* Or, worse, what if I came home from the hospital and found that the locks had been changed?

"Allison. Be reasonable." His voice was as gentle as it had been on the phone the day we'd moved my dad to Eastwood. "Is this how you want to live your life? Is this the kind of mom you want to be?"

I opened my mouth to tell him, once again, that things were all right, that they were almost entirely okay; that yes, obviously, there'd been some slips, that things had gotten out of hand, but they were by no means completely off the rails or—what was the word they kept using in that meeting?—unmanageable. My life was not unmanageable. I could manage it just fine.

But before I could say that, I thought about how I'd been spending my days. Waking up in the morning, my very first thoughts were not of my daughter or my husband, not of my job or my friends or my plans for the day, but of how many pills I had left, and whether it was enough, and how I was going to get more. The time I spent chasing them, the energy, the money, the mental resources . . . and the truth was, at that point I was barely feeling the euphoria they'd once provided. A year ago, one or two Vicodin could make me feel great. These days, four or five Oxys—the medicine they gave to cancer patients, for God's sake, cancer patients who were dying—were barely enough to get me feeling normal. Was this how I wanted to live?

But how could I leave? How could I walk away from everything—my home, my work, my father, my daughter? There was no way. I could just go home and fix this on my own. I could do better. I could get it under control, cut back, be more reasonable. Except, even as I began to outline a plan in my head, I was suspecting a different truth. My "off" switch was broken, possibly forever. Having just one pill felt about as likely as taking just one breath.

I looked up at my husband. "I suppose you've already found a place to ship me?"

He nodded. "It's in New Jersey. It's very highly rated. And my insurance will pay for twenty-eight days."

Twenty-eight days, I thought. *I could do anything for twenty-eight days.*

"Okay," I said quietly, thinking, *This has to end somehow, somewhere, and maybe this is as good an ending as any.* "Okay."

PART THREE

Checking In

Sixteen

When I was a girl, every summer my parents and I would spend a week in Avalon, at the Jersey Shore. Every summer we'd rented the same little cottage a block away from the beach and set up camp there. Now that I was a mother myself, I would have called it a relocation instead of a vacation, but back then it was like being transported to the land of fairy tales. Every day I'd swim in the ocean, and at night I'd fall asleep listening to the sound of the waves through my open window instead of the hum of our house's central air, looking at the little bedroom that was mine by the glow of moonlight on water instead of my Snow White night-light. The last night, we'd go to the boardwalk in Wildwood, gorge ourselves on sweet grilled sausages and cotton candy, play the carnival games, ride the Ferris wheel and the roller coaster.

In the mornings, we'd eat cold cereal and toast, then pack up a cooler of sodas and snacks and walk the single block between our cottage and the beach. My mother would spread out a pink-and-white-striped blanket; my father would rock the stem of our umbrella back and forth, digging it into the sand, and then swoop me into his arms and carry me, screeching with half-pretend terror, out into the waves.

Every year, I was allowed to buy a single souvenir. The summer I was eight years old, I'd saved a few dollars of tooth fairy and allowance money, augmented by the quarters I'd cadged from the sofa cushions and the dollar bills from the lint filter in the dryer. My plan was to go to the store by myself, buy a pair of Jersey Shore snow globes, and give them to my parents for Chanukah.

I waited until my mother was dozing, facedown on her beach towel, her back and legs gleaming with Hawaiian Tropic lotion, and my dad was settled into his folding chair with the *Examiner* before I took my shovel and pail as camouflage and walked down the beach, toward a spot where, beneath the disinterested gaze of a teenage babysitter, a half-dozen kids were at work making sand mermaids, with long, wavy strands of seaweed mer-hair and seashell bikinis. "Stay where we can see you," my father called as I walked off, and I told him that I would. I waited until he'd opened the Business section before double-checking to make sure I had my change purse and walking from the beach to the sidewalk, then to the corner, looking both ways before I crossed the street.

The store where we shopped every year was a high-ceilinged, barnlike room where the sunshine streamed in through skylights. It was full of bins of lacquered seashells and preserved starfish, penny candy and wrapped pieces of taffy. Behind a glass case were glossy slabs of fudge and caramel-dipped apples. Next to the cash register were racks of postcards, some featuring pretty girls in bikinis, with "See the Sights at the Jersey Shore" written underneath them. That morning, though, it was cloudy outside, and the store looked dim and empty. The cash register was abandoned; there weren't any teenage clerks in their red pinnies, restocking shelves or telling shoppers where they could find inflatable floats or swim diapers. Instead of a sparkling treasure trove, the merchandise—marked-down T-shirts, foam beer cozies, "Jersey Shore" shot glasses, skimpy beach towels—looked dingy and cheap. The postcard rack squeaked when I spun it, and I noticed a card I hadn't seen before. It had a picture of a very heavy woman in a red one-piece bathing suit not unlike my own. "The Jersey Shore's Good, but the Food Is Great!" read the words printed over the sand. I stared, not quite understanding the joke but knowing that the woman in the bathing suit was the brunt of it, and wondering under what circumstances she'd posed for the picture. Had she just been lying there, sunning herself, when a man with a camera came by and tricked her, saying, *You're so pretty, let me take your picture?* Or had she been aware the picture was going to be used for a joke? And if that was the case, why had she allowed it, knowing that people would laugh at her?

I readjusted my grasp on my change purse, gave the metal rack a final spin, and was heading off to find the snow globes when a man grabbed me by the shoulder and spun me around.

"Did you see?" he demanded. I blinked up at him. He wore a baseball shirt with the buttons open over his bare chest, cutoff denim shorts, and leather sandals. His eyes looked wild and his teeth were stained brown, and the smell of liquor coming off of him was so thick it was almost visible, like the cloud surrounding Pig-Pen in the *Peanuts* comic strip. As I stared, the man shook my shoulder again. "Did you see?"

I shook my head. I hadn't seen anything, but even if I had, I would have denied it. There was something wrong with this man; even a little kid like me could tell. I couldn't remember ever being so scared. Worse than the waves of liquor smell that rolled off him was the feeling of not-rightness. His pupils were too big; his hand was holding me way too hard. A squeak escaped my lips as tears spilled onto my cheeks. I wished I'd never come here, never snuck away from my parents. I wished they would come rescue me, right this minute. As we stood there, with his fingers still curled into the flesh of my shoulder, a woman, barefoot in a bikini top and a short denim skirt, with the kind of bleached-blonde hair my mother would have dismissed with a curled lip and the word "cheap," came around the corner. She had a red plastic shopping basket over one forearm, empty except for a canister of Pringles, and a tattoo of what looked like a heart visible above the bra cup of her swimsuit.

"You're scaring her, Kenny," the woman said, and knelt down beside me. She had a southern accent and a sweet, high voice, but she, too, smelled like booze when she breathed. "What's your name, pretty girl? You want some fudge?"

"No, thank you," I whispered, as wild-eyed Kenny repeated, in a droning whine, "She saw us."

"She didn't see a thing." The woman's eyes looked like spinning pinwheels, her pupils tiny pinpricks of black in the blue of her irises. "How about a lollipop, pretty little miss?"

"I have to go now," I whispered, and ran past them, out the door. I knew which way the beach was—there was only one street to cross, then I'd be there—but, somehow, I must have gone the wrong way, because when I stopped running I couldn't see the water, and the street was completely unfamiliar. BAR AND GRILLE, read one sign. I heard the sound of an American flag, hanging at the corner, snapping in the breeze. There were people on the street, but not tourists, not people like me and my parents, in swimsuits and sun hats, carrying coolers and portable radios and folding chairs. All I saw were a few men dressed like Kenny, men with dark glasses and bent heads and a palpable aura of strangeness, of *off-ness,* around them, going in and out of the BAR AND GRILLE. I stood on the corner in my pink rubber flip-flops and my white terry-cloth cover-up. I'd dropped my change purse at some point during my flight.

Eventually, a man in a blue bathing suit, with a coating of white zinc on his nose, found me standing on the street corner, crying. "Little girl, are you lost?" I'd told him my name and that I lived in Cherry Hill but was staying in Avalon, and he'd walked me back to the beach, just two blocks away, where I found my parents at the lifeguard station. "Where did you go?" my mother asked, her voice shaking as she scooped me into her arms. My father gave me a lecture about staying where I could see them and not ever, ever scaring my mother like that. "You know how sensitive she is," he'd said, and I'd nodded, crying wordlessly, meaning to explain that I'd wanted to go shopping, to get presents, to surprise them, but I never caught my breath enough to form the words, and they never asked where I'd gone, or why. They'd taken me back to the blanket and given me lemonade. My sobs tapered off into hiccups, and, eventually, I'd fallen asleep in the wedge of shade under our umbrella, and had to be woken up so they could walk me back to the cottage for lunch. By the afternoon, I'd all but forgotten about my adventure . . . but as I got older, I'd remembered, and I would spend hours trying to figure out what the couple, he with the baseball shirt, she with the shopping basket and the southern accent, had been doing that they'd worried I had seen. Had they robbed the place? Shoplifted a bottle? Were they paranoid because of something they'd smoked or swallowed, jumping at shadows, scaring little girls for no reason? I never knew . . . but the sense of that morning had never left me, the idea that every-thing could change with just one wrong turn. There was a parallel universe that ran alongside the normal world, and if you went through the wrong door, or turned left instead of right, ran up the street instead of down it, you could acciden-tally push the curtain aside and end up in that other place, where everything was different and everything was wrong.

That was how I felt, waking up that first morning in a single bed in a small, dingy room at Meadowcrest. "Oh, shit, not here," I'd said when Dave had pulled off the road and I'd seen the signs that read MEADOWCREST: PUTTING FAMILIES FIRST. There were at least half a dozen billboards with the same slogan along I-95 on the way from Center City to the airport, with a picture of a white guy with a superhero's jawline holding a beaming toddler in his arms. Dave and I had joked about it, wondering if the guy had been told he'd be posing for an ad for beer or Cialis, and the ribbing his buddies must have given him when he'd turned out to be the face of addiction.

Tight-lipped, without smiling, Dave had said, "They had a bed."

"I want to go to Malibu. Seriously. If I'm going to do this, I might as well do it right." I still felt awful—sick and weak and nauseous, and gutted from the shame—but I had lifted my chin, trying to look imperious with my ratty hair and my dirty clothes and Ellie's Princess Jasmine fleece blanket wrapped around my shoulders. "Take me to the place where Liza Minnelli's on the board of directors."

Dave said nothing to me as he pulled the car up to the guard's stand. "Allison Weiss. She's checking in."

"I'm checking in!" I sang, trying to remember the lyrics of the *Simpsons* rehab anthem. "No more pot or Demerol. No more drugs or alcohol! No more stinking fun at all . . . !" I glanced sideways, wondering if Dave remembered how, when we'd started dating, we'd call each other and watch *The Simpsons* together, him in his apartment, me in mine, and how we'd speculate, during commercials, about whether the severely nerdy bow-tied weather guy on the NBC station got laid nonstop.

He parked the car, took my duffel bag out of the backseat, and walked me inside, where a woman behind a receptionist's desk led us to the comfortable, well-appointed waiting room, with leather couches and baskets of hundred-calorie snack packs and a wide-screen TV.

They'd been showing *Jeopardy!* The categories were World History, English Literature, Ends in "Y," Famous Faces, and—ha—Potent Potables. Curled on the couch in my Jasmine blanket, I answered every question right. "Do I really need to be here?" I'd asked Dave.

"Yes, Allie," said Dave, sounding distant and tired. "You do." I could see wrinkles at the corners of his eyes and a few grayish patches in the beard that had grown in since that morning, and the cuff of one pant leg was tucked into his sock. How must these last few days have been for him? I wondered, before deciding it was better not to think about it.

I'd tried to tell him that I felt much better, that, clearly, I'd had some kind of bad reaction to Suboxone, but now I was fine and, as *Jeopardy!* indicated, clearheaded, that it would be all right for him to take me home, and I remembered him not-too-gently removing (*prying* might have been a better word) my fingers from his forearms and delivering me into the care of a short, bald male nurse who'd hummed Lady Gaga's "The Edge of Glory" while he'd taken my blood and medical history, before handing me a plastic pee cup and directing me to the bathroom. "Gotta pat you down," he'd said when I came out, handing me a robe and telling me to take everything off. "And we're gonna do the old squat-and-cough." I stared at him until I realized he was serious. Then, shaking my head in disbelief, I squatted. And coughed.

Once my exam was done, I'd joined Dave in a cubicle, where a young woman with doughy features and too much blue eyeliner sat behind a computer and asked me embarrassing questions. When I didn't answer, or couldn't, Dave stepped in. "I think she's been abusing painkillers for about a year," he'd said, and, "Yes, she has prescriptions, but she's also been buying things online," and, finally, most terrifyingly, "Yes, I'll pay out of pocket for what insurance doesn't cover." I'd grabbed his sleeve again and leaned close, whispering, "Dave . . ."

He'd pulled his arm away and given me a look that could only be called cold. "You need to get yourself together," he'd said. "If not for your own sake, then for Ellie's."

So here I was. I looked around, running my hands down my body. My jeans felt greasy; the waistband had slipped down my hips, the way it did when I'd worn them for too long without a wash. My clogs, resting by the side of the bed, were stained with something I didn't want to examine too closely. My T-shirt smelled bad, and there was a smear of the same offensive something on its sleeve. I had clean clothes in the duffel Dave had packed, but I'd last seen it on the other side of the receptionist's desk. "We'll just hang on to it up here until one of the staffers has time to search it, 'kay?" she'd said.

"Good morning, Meadowcrest!" a voice blared from the ceiling. I bolted upright with my heart thudding in my chest. I still felt weak, and sick, and I ached all over. I wasn't sure whether that was related to precipitated withdrawal, or how much was the result of the phenobarbital they were giving me to get me through the worst of the lingering withdrawal symptoms.

"It is now seven a.m.," said the ceiling. "Ladies, please head down to get your morning meds. Breakfast will begin at seven-thirty. Gentlemen, you'll eat at eight o'clock. Room inspections will commence at nine. Riiiiiise and shiiiine!"

I collapsed on my back. My head hit the pillow with a crackling sound. Investigation revealed that both the pillow and the mattress were thin, sad-looking affairs encased in crinkly, stained plastic. Lovely.

Swinging my feet onto the floor, I took my first good look at my room: a narrow, cell-like space with a bed, a desk, a scarred wooden wardrobe, and a tattered poster reading ONE DAY AT A TIME stuck to the wall with a scrap of Scotch tape. My duffel bag, which now had a construction-paper label bearing the words ALLISON W. and SEARCHED attached to one strap with a garbage bag twist-tie, sat on the floor beside me.

I took one shuffling step, then two, then crossed the room to the door, where a man in a khaki uniform was pushing a mop. "Excuse me," I said.

He looked at me blankly.

"Is there someone here I can talk to?"

The blank look continued.

"I'm not supposed to be here," I said, enunciating each word clearly. "I need to talk to someone so I can go home."

The man—a janitor, I guessed—shrugged and cocked his thumb toward the opposite end of the hall. There was a desk with no one behind it. A few people—teenagers, mostly—were milling in the hall, wearing pajama bottoms and slippers and sweatshirts, making quiet conversation. I stood there until they saw me. "Excuse me," I said. "Is there anyone who works here who can help me?"

"They come in at eight o'clock," said one of the shufflers in slippers. I went back to my room, where, for lack of anything better to do, I unzipped the duffel bag and inspected its contents. Dave hadn't even let me go home from the hospital long enough to pack. He was probably worried that I'd use the opportunity to run, when all I wanted to do was say goodbye to Ellie and my mom. A look in the mirror in my hospital room had convinced me to wait. If Ellie had seen me looking so sick, she'd probably have been even more worried. I hoped Dave would tell her I'd gone away on a last-minute trip to New York.

I made the bed, smoothing the thin, pilled brown comforter before I started going through the bag. There were six pairs of tennis socks, two pairs of lace panties that I had bought before Eloise's birth and not tried to squeeze myself into since, a single sports bra, a pair of jeans, two long-sleeved T-shirts, and a pair of black velvet leggings that I recognized as the bottom half of a long-ago Catwoman Halloween costume. I stopped rummaging after that. It was just too depressing. Why had Dave packed, and not Janet or even my mom? Was there anything like a toothbrush and deodorant in here? How had he managed to pack everything I'd needed that weekend when Ellie was a newborn, but get it so wrong this time?

Maybe he was scared, I thought. Five years ago, he'd been packing for a romantic retreat, a family honeymoon by the beach. This time, he'd been shipping a drug addict to rehab. Big difference.

Someone was knocking on the other side of my bathroom door. "Come in," I called. My voice was weak and croaky. A girl who didn't look much older than fourteen stuck her head into my room and looked around.

"We share the bathroom and you gotta keep it

clean and everything off the floor," she said. "Or else we'll both get demerits."

Demerits? "Okay," I said, and forced myself to stand on legs that felt as though something large and angry had been chewing on them all night long.

"I'm going to brush my teeth. Do you need to use the bathroom?"

I shook my head, although I wasn't sure what I needed, other than my pills. I cast a sideways glance at my purse. Maybe there was a stash I'd missed, or even some dust in the Altoids tin that could help.

"I'm Allison," I said.

"Hi," said the girl as she followed my gaze. "Forget it," she said. "They search everything that comes in." She had shimmering blonde hair hanging to the small of her back, a small, foxy face, pale eyes, and vivid purple bruises running up and down her bare arms.

"I'm Aubrey," she said, and tugged at the strap of her tank top. She was dressed like she was ready to go clubbing, or at least the way I imagined girls on their way to clubs would dress. Her jeans were tight enough to preclude circulation, her black boots had high heels, her top was made of some thin silvery fabric, which she had matched with silver eye shadow and, if I wasn't mistaken, false eyelashes that were also dusted with glitter.

"Listen," I said, trying not to sound as desperate as I felt. "Who do I talk to about getting out of here?"

Aubrey snickered.

"No, seriously. I think this is a mistake."

"Sure," said Aubrey, in the same indulgent tone I used to jolly Eloise out of her bad moods.

"Please. There must be, like, a counselor, or a supervisor. Someone I can talk to."

"Yeah, you'd think so," Aubrey said. "For what this place costs, there should be. But there's nobody, like, official, until lunchtime. Hey, it could be worse," she said, after seeing the look on my face. "My last place, there were, like, six girls to a room, in bunk beds. At least here you've got your own space. So why are you here?" she asked.

"Because my husband's an asshole," I said.

She smiled, then quickly pressed her lips together, covering her discolored teeth. "You better not let the RCs hear you say that," she said. "They'll say you're in denial. That until you're ready to admit you have a problem, you won't ever get better."

"What if I don't have a problem?"

She lifted her narrow shoulders in a shrug. "I dunno. Honestly, I've never seen anyone in rehab who didn't have a problem. And I've been in rehab a lot."

Yay, you, I thought.

"What were you taking?" she asked. When I

didn't answer, she said, "C'mon, you must have been taking something."

"Oh. Um. Painkillers. Prescription painkillers." The "prescription" suddenly struck me as important, a way of announcing to this girl that I wasn't scoring crack on the streets, that I might be a junkie, but I was a reputable junkie.

"Percs?" she asked, smoothing her hair. "Vics? Oxys?"

"All of the above," I said ruefully.

"Yeah. That's how I started." She looked over my shoulder, out the window, which revealed an unlovely view of a waterlogged field. "You know how it goes. One day you're snorting a Perc before history class, the next day you're down in Kensington, and some guy named D-Block is sticking a needle in your arm."

"Ah," I said. Meanwhile, I was thinking, *D-Block?* There was no D-Block in my story. Or Kensington. Or needles.

"You court-stipulated?" she asked, without much interest. She'd moved on from her hair and the window and was now checking her eye makeup in a mirror she'd pulled out of her pocket.

I shook my head.

"Did you fail a random?"

I tried to make sense of the question. "I don't know what that means."

"Like, a random drug test at work. A lot of the older ladies are here for that." She gave me a look that was not unsympathetic. "No offense."

"Oh, none taken." I wasn't sure whether her "no offense" applied to my age or to the assumption that I'd gotten in trouble at work. "No, I work for myself, so no drug tests or anything."

"Lose your license? DUI?"

I shook my head. "How about you?" I said, like we'd just been introduced at a cocktail party and she'd just tapped the conversational ball over to my side of the net. "Are you working, or in school?"

"I waitressed." It took her a minute to remember how conversation happened. "What do you do?"

"I'm a journalist," I said, which sounded like more of a real job than "blogger."

"Huh." She tugged at her hair. "Did you have to go to college for that?"

"Um. Well, I did. But I guess, technically, you don't have to. You just need to have something to say." I had to remind myself that I was here to get help for myself, not to rescue anyone else, or save all the little broken birds. *You are not coming out of here with an intern,* I told myself. I didn't plan on staying long enough to learn names, let alone collect résumés.

"Good morning, Meadowcrest!" the intercom said again. Aubrey rolled her eyes and shot her middle finger at the ceiling. "Ladies, it's about that time. Morning meds, breakfast, and inspections. Riiiise and shiiine!"

There was another knock. "Are you the new girl?" an older woman asked. She had curly white hair and wore black polyester slacks, white orthopedic sneakers with pristine laces, and a red cardigan with shiny cut-glass buttons. Reading glasses dangled from a beaded chain against her sizable bosom. She wore a gold watch, a gold wedding band, a gold cross hanging on a necklace, and another necklace with little ceramic figurines in the shapes of boys and girls, probably intended to represent her grand-children.

"Hello," she said, offering me her hand to shake. "I'm Mary. I'm an alcoholic."

Aubrey rolled her eyes. "You don't have to say that, like, everywhere you go, Mare," she said. "Only in meetings."

"I'm trying to get used to it," Mary said.

"Hi," I said, and tried to think of a polite follow-up. "So, how long have you two been here?"

"Three days," said Aubrey.

"Four for me," said Mary. "We're the new kids on the block." She looked at Aubrey anxiously. "Did I get that right? New kids on the block?"

Aubrey made a face. "Like, how should I know? They're oldies."

"Well," said Mary, looking flustered. "Do you want some help with your room?"

"Fuck," Aubrey said. I followed her gaze past

the bathroom to what must have been her bedroom, a narrow space the twin of mine. Based on its appearance, Aubrey had had a seizure in the middle of the night and flung everything she possessed to its four corners.

"I'll help," said Mary. I decided to join in, thus avoiding demerits, whatever they turned out to be. I wouldn't be staying here long, but that didn't mean I wanted to make a bad impression. Bending down, I began to gather up girl things: ninety-nine-cent nail polish, Victoria's Secret panties, a black eyeliner pencil, a paperback copy of *The Big Book of Alcoholics Anonymous*, a packet of Xeroxed pages labeled RELAPSE PREVENTION, a piece of posterboard with MY TIMELINE OF ABUSE written on top, a blouse, a pair of inside-out jeans, a single Ugg boot, and a half-empty package of peanut butter cookies.

"Do you know where we are, exactly? Like, what town?" I'd been so sick and so out of it on the ride down, I'd barely noticed exactly where we were heading.

"Buttfuck, New Jersey," Aubrey said, shoving books and papers under her bed. "I mean, I guess it's got a name, but I have no fucking clue what it's called. All rehabs are, like, in the middle of fucking nowhere. So you can't cop."

I took my armload of stuff and deposited it gently at the bottom of her freestanding wardrobe. "How many times have you done this?"

She kept her smirk in place while she answered, but her eyes looked sad. "Six."

Six rehabs. Dear Lord.

"How about you?" I asked Mary, who shook her head.

"Oh, no, dear, this is my first time in treatment. Come on," she said. "We should get in line for meds."

Aubrey wandered toward the bathroom. In my bedroom, I put on clean jeans and a T-shirt, gave my plastic pillow a fluff, and zipped up my duffel and set it in the wardrobe. Then I followed Mary out of the bedroom and into the wide, fluorescent-lit hallway. Dozens of doors just like mine ran along each side of it, amplifying the place's resemblance to a cheap motel. We walked down the hall until we arrived at the desk I'd found earlier. There were maybe two dozen women milling around, most of them dressed, a few in pajamas and robes. Many of them held white plastic binders. "What's that?" I asked, pointing to the one Mary had in her arms.

"It's the welcome packet, and the schedule. You didn't get one?"

I shook my head no. A heavy-set woman wearing khakis and a yellow short-sleeved shirt hunched behind the computer at the desk. An engraved plastic nametag announced that she was MARGO, and the words MEADOWCREST

COTTAGE were sewn in red thread onto the right side of her chest. Her desk was a poor relation to the burnished oak desk out front, with a bouquet of flowers and a dish of hard candy. This desk was made of cheap pressboard, and, instead of blossoms or treats, there was a stack of papers with the title A LETTER FROM YOUR ADDICTION.

Dear Friend, I've come to visit once again. I love to see you suffer mentally, physically, spiritually, and socially. I want to have you restless so you can never relax. I want you jumpy and nervous and anxious. I want to make you agitated and irritable so everything and everybody makes you uncomfortable. I want you to be depressed and confused so that you can't think clearly or positively. I want to make you hate everything and everybody—especially yourself. I want you to feel guilty and remorseful for the things you have done in the past that you'll never be able to let go. I want to make you angry and hateful toward the world for the way it is and the way you are. I want you to feel sorry for yourself and blame everything but your addiction for the way things are. I want you to be deceitful and untrustworthy, and to manipulate and con as many people as possible. I want to make you fearful and paranoid for no reason at all and I want you to wake up during all hours of the night screaming for me. You know you can't sleep without me; I'm even in your dreams.

"Excuse me," I said, aiming a smile at Margo. "I'm hoping I can speak to someone about leaving."

She looked up at me. "Where's your tag?"

"Tag?"

"Tag," she repeated, pointing to my chest in a way I might have found a little forward if I hadn't been such a wreck. "When you're admitted, they give you a nametag with your welcome binder and your schedule. You need to wear it at all times."

"Right. But I'm not staying. I'm not supposed to—"

She lifted her hand. "Honey, I can't even talk to you till you've got your tag on. Check your room."

"Fine." I went back to my room as more women drifted out into the hallway. Most of them appeared to be Aubrey's age, but I saw a few thirty- and fortysomethings, and some who were even older. The young girls wore tight jeans, high heels, faces full of makeup. The women my age wore looser pants, less paint, and, inevitably, Dansko clogs. The official shoe of playgrounds, operating rooms, restaurant kitchens, and rehab. "Excuse me," said a sad, frail, hunched-over woman who looked even older than Mary, as she used a walker to make her way toward the desk. I shuddered, thinking that if I were an eighty-year-old addict, I would hope my friends and my children would leave me alone to drink and drug in peace.

Sure enough, back in my cell of a room, on top of the desk, I found a beige plastic nametag clipped to a black lanyard with my name—ALLISON W.—typed on the front. Beside it was a binder and schedule. I spared my single bed a longing glance, wishing I could just go back to sleep, then looped the tag over my neck and proceeded back down the hall.

Seventeen

The scent of mass-produced food was seeping from behind the cafeteria's double doors. Even if I hadn't been so nauseous, I couldn't imagine eating anything. I felt like Persephone in the underworld—one bite, one sip, a single pomegranate seed, and I'd be stuck here forever.

I walked back to the desk and flapped my nametag at Margo, the desk drone. "I'd like to call home."

"Morning meds," she said, without looking up.

I went to the nurse's counter, stood in line for twenty minutes, swallowed what was in the little white paper cup she gave me, and then returned.

"I took my medicine," I said, showing Margo the empty cup, feeling grateful she hadn't asked to see my empty mouth, the way the nurse had. "May I please use the phone?"

"You're on a seven-day blackout," she recited without looking past my chin. "No visits, no phone calls."

"Excuse me? I don't remember agreeing to that."

Margo heaved a mighty sigh. "If you're here, then you signed a contract agreeing to follow our rules."

"May I see that contract, please?" I remembered signing my name to all kinds of things—releases for my doctor to share my medical history, releases for Meadowcrest to talk to my insurance company—but it seemed unlikely that I'd sign something promising I wouldn't call home for a week. Nor did it seem reasonable that they'd expect parents with young children to go that long between calls. Besides, could a contract be legally binding if the person who signed it was fresh out of the ER and still going through withdrawal?

Margo yawned without bothering to cover her mouth. "You can ask your counselor."

"Who is my counselor?"

"You'll be assigned one after orientation."

"When's that?"

"After breakfast."

"I'm not planning on staying for breakfast." I made myself smile and lowered my voice. "This isn't the right place for me. I just want to go home."

"You need to discuss that with your—"

Before she could say "counselor," I pointed toward the front of the building—the nice desk, the clean waiting room with its wide-screen TV and baskets of snacks, the door—and said, "What happens if I just walk out of here right now?"

That got her attention. She sat up straighter and looked at me like she was seeing me for the first time. "If you choose to sign yourself out AMA, you can leave after twenty-four hours," she recited. "We can't let you go right now. You still have detox drugs in your system. It would be a liability."

"Even if I have someone pick me up? And I go right to a hospital or something?" A hospital sounded good. I'd get a private room, and I'd bring my own bedding, of course. I pictured an IV in my arm, delivering whatever drugs would make this process more bearable. Then maybe I'd take myself to a spa for a few days. Fresh air, long hikes, nothing stronger than aspirin and iced tea. That was the ticket.

"Twenty-four hours. That's the rule."

"Okay." I could endure anything for twenty-four hours. I'd been in labor that long, having Eloise. I went back down the hall and found Mary and Aubrey waiting in line.

"Where'd you cop?" I heard a statuesque

brunette, who could have been a model except for her acne-ravaged complexion, ask a petite blonde girl in a see-through top. I didn't hear the girl's answer, but the brunette gave a squeal. "Ohmygod, no way! Who was your dealer?"

The petite girl gave a shrug. "He just said to call him Money." She must have noticed me staring, because she turned toward me, eyes narrowed. "You work here?"

"Me? No, I . . ." Now there were a few young girls staring at me.

"Booze?" asked the tall brunette.

"Pills," I said, deciding to keep it short and sweet.

"Yeah," the brunette said wistfully. "That's how I started." I was beginning to get the impression that pills were how everyone started, and that when you couldn't afford or find the pills anymore, you moved on to heroin.

"Come on," said Aubrey, as the herd of girls and women began moving down the hall. "Breakfast."

I bypassed the limp slices of French toast and greasy discs of sausage in stainless steel pans on steam tables, with jugs of flavored corn syrup masquerading as maple, and made a mug of tea. The room was chilly and cavernous, a high-school cafeteria from hell with unflattering lights, worn linoleum, and aged inspirational posters, including the inevitable kitten-on-a-branch "Hang In There!" thumbtacked to walls painted a washed-out yellow. Six long plastic-topped tables with bolted-on benches took up most of the room's space. Each one was adorned with a tiny ceramic vase of plastic flowers—someone's sad attempt at making the place look pretty. The air smelled like the ghosts of a thousand departed high-school cafeteria lunches—steamed burgers and stale French fries, cut-up iceberg lettuce birthed from a bag and served with preservative-laden croutons hard enough to crack a tooth. I sat at the end of a table, numb and aching for my pills, listening as the conversation between the tall, dark-haired girl and the petite blonde continued.

". . . parents found my works underneath my mattress and, like, hired an interventionist . . ."

"You had an intervention? That is so cool! Shit, my mom said she was taking me to the movies, and then she dropped me off here . . ."

I sipped my tea and watched the clock. I would say as little as possible for as long as I could. I'd sit through their orientation and endure the mandatory twenty-four hours. Then I'd find a supervisor, explain the situation, and get Dave or Janet or someone to come pick me up.

I didn't belong here. I wasn't like these women. I didn't have any DUIs that needed to be expunged, a judge hadn't ordered me to stay, and I hadn't flunked a drug test at work. Nobody named D-Block had ever stuck a needle in my arm, and I wasn't sure I could find Kensington even with my GPS. *Heroin,* I thought, and shuddered. These girls had done IV drugs, and probably worse things to get the drugs. All I'd done was swallow a few too many pills, all of which (except the ones I'd ordered online) had been legitimately prescribed. I didn't belong here, and all I needed to do was figure out how quickly I could leave. My daughter needed me. So did my readers. How on earth had I let Dave convince me, even for a minute, that I could just check out of all of my responsibilities to come to a place like this?

"What's your damage?" asked the girl next to me. She was in her twenties, broad-shouldered and solid, with no makeup on her pale skin and long brown hair piled on top of her head in a messy bun. She wore gray sweatpants and an Eagles jersey and a nametag that read LENA.

"Excuse me?"

"Your stuff. Your drug of choice," she explained in a flat, nasal voice, as Mary sat down across from me.

"Pills. But I don't really . . . I mean, I don't think that I'm . . ." I shut my mouth and tried again. "I'm not actually planning on staying. I don't think this is the right place for me."

The Eagles-jersey girl and Mary both gave me knowing smiles. "That's what I said," Mary told us. With her blue eyes and white curls, her rounded hips and sagging bosom, she looked like Mrs. Claus. Possibly like Mrs. Claus after a rough weekend, during which she'd discovered naughty pictures of the elves on Santa's hard drive. "I used to put my gin in a water bottle. Because that was *classy*." A Boston accent turned the word to *clah-see*. I sipped my tea as the other girls and women nodded. "So I came down here with my bottle of Dasani, thinking I had everyone fooled."

"I wasn't fooling anyone," said Lena. "I came straight from the hospital. They Narcanned me."

"Excuse me?" I asked.

"I OD'd. I almost died. They had to give me Narcan—it's a shot that, like, brings you back to life. I woke up and ripped the IVs out of my arm and, like, ran out the door. I had my stash in my bra," she said.

"Ah." *Stash in bra,* I thought. Add that to the list of things I didn't do and did not completely understand. Was *stash* different from *works?*

"But they caught me—of course." Lena used her hands when she talked, big, broad, sweeping motions. When she wasn't gesturing, she was smoothing her ponytail like a pet. "I was in jail for six weeks, and then I was on work release, but I fucked that up and got loaded, and my PO busted me . . ." PO. Work release. Jail. Gin in water bottles. Drinking before the third hour of the *Today* show. I looked around, again noting the doors, wondering what would really happen if I just got up, collected my purse and duffel bag, and walked out. Of course, I didn't know exactly where I was. That was a problem. Nor did I have any money—I remembered that they'd taken my wallet and my phone when they'd taken my bag. I rested my throbbing temples in my palms and forced myself to breathe slowly, trying to keep that jumping-out-of-my-skin feeling at bay.

A buzzer sounded. The girls and women stood, trays in hand, and marched to a stainless steel window cut into the wall. I picked up my own empty tray and got in line, depositing my silverware in a bin full of detergent, pushing my mug through the slot, from which a plastic-gloved, hair-netted dishwasher grabbed it. "Come on," said Aubrey, and I followed the crowd out the door.

Eighteen

At nine o'clock that morning, I was sitting on a couch covered in a shiny and decidedly unnatural fabric in a room called the Ladies' Lounge, and a thumb-shaped, red-faced man was yelling at me.

"All addicts are selfish," he said. He was, like the famed little teapot, short and stout. His cheap acrylic sweater was a red that matched his face. His blue slacks bunched alarmingly at his crotch, the cuffs so short they displayed his argyle socks and an expanse of hairy white shin. His tassled loafers were scuffed. On his sweater was pinned a nametag reading DARNTON. He looked at us accusingly. There were three of us in orientation: me, and Aubrey, and Mary, who'd been crying quietly since she'd walked through the door.

"All addicts are selfish," Darnton repeated, and raised his caterpillar-thick eyebrows, daring us to disagree. When no one did, he opened the blue-covered paperback in his hand and began reading. I wondered idly whether he was starting where he'd left off with the last group; whether he just worked his way right through *The Big Book*, regardless of who was listening. "The first requirement is that we be convinced that any life run on self-will can hardly be a success." I blinked. My hands hurt and were trembling. My head was still throbbing. I wanted to lie down, curled beneath a blanket, soothed and calmed by my pills.

"Why are you here?" Darnton asked Aubrey.

She shrugged. " 'Cause my parents found my works."

"Do you want to stop using?"

Another shrug. "I guess."

"You guess," Darnton repeated, his voice rich with sarcasm. Was mocking addicts really an effective way to get them to change? Before I could come to any conclusions, Darnton turned on Mary. "How about you?"

"I was drinking too much," she whispered in a quavering voice. "I did terrible things."

Darnton appeared just as interested in Mary's self-flagellation as he did in Aubrey's non-chalance. "And you?"

I forced myself to sit up straight. "I was taking painkillers."

"And you were taking painkillers because . . . ?" the thumb persisted.

"Because I was in pain," I said. Duh. Never mind that the pain was spiritual instead of physical. The thumb did not need to know that. I turned my eyes toward the wall, where two posters were hanging. STEP ONE, I read. *We admitted that we were powerless over alcohol and that our lives had become unmanageable,* then tuned back into the jerky little man lecturing us about our "character defects," hectoring us about what he kept calling "the brain disease of addiction," a disease that, he claimed, was rooted in self-centeredness.

"If anything, I was using the pills because I was trying to do too much for other people," I interrupted. "My father's got Alzheimer's, so I've been helping him and my mother. I take care of my daughter. And I write for a women's website."

Darnton's eyebrows were practically at his hairline . . . or where his hairline must have been at some point. "Oh, a writer," he said. He probably thought I was lying. Given my scratched hands, my pallor, my ratty hair and attire, my vague smell of puke—and, of course, the fact that I was in rehab—I couldn't blame him.

"Yes, I'm a writer," I said. "And my life was not unmanageable. Everyone else's life was unmanageable."

The thumb opened his book again and kept reading. "Selfishness—self-centeredness! That, we think, is the root of our trouble. Driven by a hundred forms of fear, self-delusion, self-seeking, and self-pity—"

"I volunteered," I said, hearing my voice quiver. I swallowed hard. No way was I going to cry in front of this hectoring little jerk. "I ran my house. I took care of my daughter. I took care of my parents. I helped out at my daughter's school . . ."

He lifted his eyebrows again. "Doing everything, were we?"

"So either I'm selfish or I'm a martyr?"

The man shrugged. "Your best thinking got you here. Think about that." He returned to his reading. "The alcoholic is an extreme example of self-will run riot, though he usually doesn't think so." He paused to give me a significant look.

"I'm not a 'he,' " I said. I'd been acquainted with *The Big Book* for only twenty minutes, but I could already tell that it needed a gender update.

"Above everything, we alcoholics must be rid of this selfishness. We must, or it kills us!" He set the book down and looked us over. Aubrey appeared to be asleep, and Mary was crying quietly into her hands.

"You think your life is fine," he said to me. *Better than yours,* I thought unkindly, imagining the existence that went with his outfit—a vinyl-sided house in some unremarkable suburb, a ten-year-old shoebox of a car with spent shocks, waiting for his tax refund to arrive so he could pay down the interest on his credit card. A little man with a little mind and a handful of slogans he'd repeat, no matter who was in the room with him or what their problems were.

"I bet when you go home, and you're looking at things with sober eyes, you're going to think differently." When I didn't answer, he said, "Before I got sober, I'd been building shelves in my kitchen. I thought they were beautiful. I thought I really knew what I was doing. When I came home, I saw that those shelves were a disaster. They were crooked. The cabinet doors didn't shut. I'd kicked a hole in the wall when I got frustrated."

"Sorry to hear that," I said, even though I wasn't. I couldn't have cared less about this man with his bad haircut and cheap clothes. Besides, my house looked fine. No holes in my walls, no crooked cabinets. I had Henry the handyman on speed dial.

"You were taking care of your parents," said the little man.

"My father has early-stage Alzheimer's."

Mary finally stopped crying long enough to look up. "Me, too! I mean, not me. My husband."

Darnton lifted a hand, silencing Mary. "And your daughter," the little man continued.

"My daughter. My business. My husband. My house."

"Did you ever think that you were . . ."—he hooked his fingers into scare quotes—" 'helping' all those people so you could control them?"

Suddenly I was so tired I could barely speak, and I was craving a pill so badly I could cry. How was I going to live the rest of my life, in a world overrun with idiots like this one, without the promise of any comfort at the end of the day? "I was helping them because they needed help."

"I'm selfish," said Aubrey, in a whisper. Her heavily shadowed eyelids were cast down, and she worried a cuticle as she spoke. "I stole from my parents. I stole from my grandma."

"What about you?" the man asked Mary.

"I don't think I was," she said hesitantly. "My drinking didn't get bad until after my daughter had her babies. She had triplets, because of the in vitro, so I'd drive from Maryland to Long Island once a week, and spend three days with her, and then drive down to New Jersey for the weekends to help my son. He's single, and he only sees his two on the weekends. That's why I drank, I think. I'd be so wound up after all that driving, and the kids, that I just couldn't turn myself off. So I'd have a gin and tonic—that was what my husband and I always drank, gin and tonics—and when that didn't do it, I'd have two, and then . . ." Tears spilled over the reddened rims of her eyes. "I got a DUI," she whispered. One hand wandered to the hem of her sweatshirt and tugged at it as she spoke. "I rear-ended someone with my grandbabies in the car. I wasn't planning on driving, but my son got stuck at work, and I was the only one who could get the kids. I should have said no, made up some reason why I couldn't drive them, but I was so ashamed. So ashamed," she repeated, then started to cry again.

Great, I thought. *An angry thumb, a drunk granny, and a thief.* What was wrong with this picture? The fact that I was in it.

"Excuse me," I said politely, and walked to the door.

Darnton glared at me. "Orientation's until ten-fifteen. Then you have Equine."

"Equine? Yeah, no," I said. "I need to speak to someone now." I exited the room. Margo, the woman from the breakfast hour, had been replaced by another young woman in the same outfit. This one had a mustache, faint but discernible. *The Big Book* was open on her computer keyboard. Underneath it, I could see *People* magazine—"*The Bachelor*'s Women Tell All!"

"Oh my God," I said. "I'm going to miss the Fantasy Suites."

The woman flashed a quick smile. She wore a pin, instead of a nametag on a lanyard around her neck, which read WANDA. "Yeah, sorry. No TV for you guys, just recovery-related movies."

"How will I live," I wondered, "if I don't know whether he picks Kelly S. or Kelly D.?" As I spoke, I remembered all the episodes I'd watched with Ellie snuggled on the bed beside me, a bowl of popcorn between us, her head on my shoulder as she slipped into sleep. Normal. (Sort of.) Happy. God, what had happened to take me away from that and bring me here?

The woman lowered her voice. "Can you actually tell them apart?"

"One's a hairdresser, and the other one's a former NBA dancer," I said.

"Okay, but they look exactly the same."

"All the women on that show look exactly the same." I could talk about this forever and had, in fact, written several well-received blog posts on the homogeneity of *The Bachelor*'s ladies.

"Tell you what," said the woman. "I can't sneak in a DVD. But I'll tell you who got roses."

"Deal," I said, feeling incrementally relieved that not everyone in this place was a monster. Just then, a new Meadowcrest employee cruised into view. Wanda shoved her *People* magazine out of sight, as the new woman—middle-aged, blonde hair in a bob, tired blue eyes behind wire-rimmed glasses—looked me over.

"Hi there," I said, sounding professional and polite. "Can you help me find my counselor?"

"Who is it?"

"Well, I'm hoping you can help me with that. I actually don't have a name yet. I just finished orientation." As far as I was concerned, that was true.

"Normally, you aren't assigned a counselor until your third or fourth day."

"Can I use the phone?"

"If you just came, you're on your seven-day blackout. You need to get permission to use the phone from your counselor."

"But you just told me I don't have a counselor." This conversation was beginning to feel like a tired Abbott and Costello routine.

"Then," said the woman, her voice smug, "you'll just have to be patient, won't you?"

"I don't think you understand," I said. "This is a mistake. I don't need to be in rehab. I'm not a drug addict. I was taking painkillers that were prescribed to me by a doctor. Now I'm fine, and I want to go home."

"You can sign yourself out AMA—that's 'against medical advice'—but your counselor needs to sign your paperwork."

"But I don't have a counselor!"

She stared at me for a minute. I stared right back, my feet planted firmly.

"Hold on," she finally grumbled. Bending over the telephone, she muttered something I couldn't catch. A minute later, a very large woman with lank brown hair, pale skin, and pale, bulging eyes came waddling around the corner. Her khaki pants swished with each step; her lanyard flapped and flopped against the lolloping rolls of her flesh.

"Allison? I'm Michelle. I understand that there's a problem?" Her voice was high and singsongy. She sounded a lot like Miss Katie, who taught kindergarten at Stonefield.

I followed her into a closet-sized office dominated by a desk. A fan clipped to the doorframe pushed the air around, along with the smell of microwaved pizza. The Twelve Steps hung on the wall. Michelle settled herself into her chair, which squeaked in protest. "Why don't you tell me what's going on?"

I explained it all: the heroin addicts at breakfast, the condescending little man at orientation, how I understood that I was having problems managing my medication—"but not, you know, rehab-level problems."

Michelle turned to her computer, tapped briefly on the keyboard, and then turned to stare at me with her bulgy eyes. "You were taking six hundred milligrams of OxyContin a day?"

I shrugged, trying not to squirm. "Only on really

bad days. Normally it wasn't that many," I lied.

She picked up a cheap plastic pen and tapped it against her desk. "My guess, Allison, is that the pills were a way for you to self-medicate. To remove yourself from painful situations without actually going anywhere."

It sounded reasonable, but I wouldn't let myself nod or give any other indication that she might be right.

"So I think . . ." She raised a hand, as if I'd tried to interrupt her. "No, just hear me out. I think that you really do need to be here."

"Maybe I do need help," I said. "But I don't think this is the place for me. No offense, but I think I'm here because my husband thought I'd change my mind before he got me in the car. I bet he found this place in five minutes on the Internet. I didn't leave him time for lots of research. And I think there are probably places that might be a better fit. Where the"—I searched for an institutional-sounding word—"population might be more like me."

An alarmed expression flitted across Michelle's face. It was quickly replaced by the tranquil look she'd been wearing since our conversation began. "Why do you feel that way?"

"Well, for starters, I'm old enough to be most of the other girls' mother."

"That's not true," she said. "There are quite a few women your age or older."

"I'll give you 'a few,' but not 'quite a few,' " I said. "Unless you're hiding them somewhere. Besides, these girls were doing street drugs."

"And you weren't?"

I shook my head. "No. I had prescriptions." Except for the ones I ordered online, but never mind that.

"Do you think that makes you different from the rest of the ladies here?"

I hesitated, sensing a trap. "Yes," I finally said. "I do think I'm different."

"Do you think you're better?" I didn't answer. "*I* think," said Michelle, "that what I'm hearing is your disease talking. You know, addiction is the only disease that tells you that you don't have a disease."

"I'm not sure I actually believe that addiction is a disease," said, but Michelle was on a roll.

"Your *disease* is telling you that you don't belong here. Your *disease* is saying that you didn't even have a problem, or that if you did, it wasn't that bad. Your *disease* is saying, 'I can handle this. I'll do it on my own. I can cut back. I don't need the Twelve Steps, and I definitely don't need rehab.' " I was quiet. This, of course, was exactly what I'd been thinking.

"But your best thinking is what got you here. Think about that for a minute." This, of course, was exactly what Darnton had told me. Another trite slogan, one they probably recited to every patient who was giving them trouble.

"I'd like to speak to my husband and my mom. I need to know how my daughter is doing."

"Your counselor can help you to arrange that."

"But I don't have a counselor!" I closed my mouth. I was shouting again. "Look, you don't understand," I said, and knotted my fingers together so my hands would stop shaking. "I didn't have time to make any arrangements for my daughter or my mom. My father just moved into an assisted-living facility, and my mom moved in with us."

"Well, then," said Michelle, with a simper, "it sounds like your husband will have plenty of help at home."

Under other circumstances, I would have laughed. "If my mother was a normal person, that would be true," I told her. "But my mother's basically another child. She doesn't drive, and even if she did, she doesn't know Ellie's schedule, and Ellie won't be her priority. She'll be worried about my dad." I was getting overwhelmed just thinking about the mess I'd left behind, the assignments I hadn't completed, the comments I hadn't approved, the dentist's appointment I hadn't made for Ellie, the checkup that I'd postponed for myself, the visit from the roofers that I'd never gotten around to scheduling. "I can't stay here," I told Michelle. "It's impossible.

There are too many things I need to take care of."

She nodded. "So many of us women feel like we're the ones holding up the world. Like it's all going to fall down without us."

"I can't speak for anyone else, but in my case, that's actually true," I offered. Michelle appeared not to hear.

"Acceptance is hard," she said.

I frowned. "Acceptance of what?"

"Why don't you tell me, Allison? What are you having a hard time accepting?"

I tried not to roll my eyes. "For starters, that you won't let me talk to my daughter and explain why I'm not home. I don't think that's an unreasonable request. Please," I said. Maybe it was withdrawal, the exhaustion of what my body had been through over the past few days, but I was too tired and too sad to keep arguing. "I just want to talk to someone at my home."

Michelle swiped her mouse back and forth, peered at her computer screen, and then spent a minute typing. "The head of our counseling department has an opening at noon. His name is Nicholas."

"Thank you. I appreciate your help." There. I could be reasonable, I could be polite . . . and I was feeling encouraged.

"For now, though, I need you to go join your group."

"Thank you," I said again, thinking that I was on

my way. It had taken me three hours to orchestrate even the promise of a phone call home. By day's end, I was confident I'd be able to talk my way out of here and get myself home.

Nineteen

I walked out the door and onto the sidewalk. The fresh air felt good on my face after the recirculated staleness I'd been breathing inside. I was halfway across the lawn before I heard someone yelling. "Hey," he called. "You can't walk there! Hey!"

I turned and saw a young man in khakis. "That's the men's path."

I looked around to make sure he was talking to me, then down at what seemed to be gender-neutral pavement. "Excuse me?"

"Men and women have to walk on separate paths. Yours is here." He pointed. I shrugged and started across the grass. "No!" he hollered. "You have to go back and start at the beginning! No walking across the grass!"

I stopped and stared at him. "Is this like Simon Says?"

" 'Half-measures availed us nothing!' "

"Excuse me?"

"From *The Big Book*. You can't take shortcuts."

Whatever. I went back to the door, got on the

proper path, and found Aubrey and Mary standing in the middle of a fenced-in oval, staring uneasily at a big horse with a brown coat and a sandy mane, which was ignoring them as it nibbled on a clump of grass. I waved at them, then ducked through the fence and was crossing the muddy ground when a woman in a cowboy hat held up her hand.

"I think you missed the entrance."

Shit. I sighed, went back through the fence, walked the long way around the ring, and pushed open the gate. "What's up?"

The woman in the cowboy hat didn't answer. Aubrey, whose glittery eyeshadow and high-heeled boots looked strange in the June sunshine, said, "We're supposed to put this on that." *This* was a tangle of leather straps and metal buckles. *That* was the horse.

"Why?"

"This is equine therapy," Mary explained.

"How's it supposed to help us?"

"Well, I'm not exactly sure, dear."

Aubrey handed me the straps and buckles. It was some kind of harness. At least that was my best guess. My experience with horses was limited to taking Ellie on pony rides at the zoo. "Excuse me," I asked the woman in the cowboy hat. "Can you tell me what the point of this is?"

She didn't answer. "I don't think they're allowed to talk to us," Mary said.

"This is ridiculous," I muttered. Aubrey shifted from foot to foot, rubbing her arms with her palms. "Do you have any idea what this has to do with anything?"

Aubrey shrugged, shaking her head. "Maybe it's about working as a team? Or building confidence or something? I don't know. Half the shit in rehab doesn't have anything to do with anything, and the other half's so boring you could die. Just wait till Ed McGreavey does the 'Find Your Purpose' lecture."

"You didn't like that?" Mary asked. "Oh, I've heard that it's very inspiring."

Aubrey began finger-combing her hair. "Yeah, I thought so, too, like, the first time I heard it. But after you've heard it, like, three or four times, and you've seen Big Ed cry at the exact same part . . ."

"When he talks about how his brother broke his leg when they were heli-skiing?"

"You know it."

I looked at the harness, then looked at the horse. "So we just have to get the harness on the horse somehow?"

"And," said Aubrey, "we have to be touching each other while we do it."

"Huh?"

"Like a conga line," Mary explained, and put her hands on my hips.

"Okay." With Mary holding my hips and Aubrey holding hers, we inched across the ring and approached the horse. It lifted its head and gave us the equine equivalent of a raspberry. Aubrey squealed, and Mary flinched backward.

"He's more afraid of us than we are of him," I said. I found a vaguely loop-shaped opening in the complicated mess of straps and pushed it over the horse's head. Then I tied the remaining dangling straps in a bow. "There. Done."

Mary was frowning. "That doesn't look right."

"They said it had to be on. They didn't say it had to be pretty." I pulled on the straps. The horse didn't move. I yanked harder. "Come on, you." Finally, reluctantly, the horse lifted one foot, then another.

"It's moving!" Aubrey cheered.

"We did it!" Mary cried. The stone-faced woman in the cowboy hat said nothing as she watched our progress. We were almost done with our second lap when a golf cart zipped up to the fence and a kid in khakis called my name. "Allison W.?"

I handed the reins to Mary and caught a ride in the cart, which dropped me at a single-story building that looked like it was made of wood but turned out to be covered in vinyl siding. The couch in the waiting room looked like leather, but wasn't, and the Twelve Steps framed and hung on the wall were simplified: *I Can't,* read Step One. *God Can,* said Step Two. *Let Him,* Step Three advised. *God again,* I thought, and collapsed onto the couch. The God thing was going to be a problem. I'd been raised Jewish, with a vague notion of God as a wrathful old guy with a long white beard who was big on testing and tormenting His followers: casting Adam and Eve out of the garden, punishing poor Job, drowning Egyptian soldiers. Was that God—a God I wasn't even sure I believed in—actually supposed to keep me from taking too much OxyContin? Especially when He let kindergartners get shot in their classrooms and young mothers die of cancer and millions of people suffer and die because of their skin color or religion?

There were no magazines I recognized in the waiting area, just battered copies of something called *Grapevine*, which appeared to be a cross between *True Confessions* and *MAD*, only for drunks. In the hallway outside, I saw a constant flow of people, men and women, alone and in groups, slouchy dudes with shifty eyes, pretty girls in jeans so tight I wondered if they were actually leggings with pockets painted on. Finally, a door flew open and a willowy African-American man in a linen suit smiled at me.

"Allison W.?"

I nodded, getting to my feet and breathing deeply as another wave of dizziness swept over my body.

"Come on in."

His office was by far the nicest place I'd seen at Meadowcrest. There was a plush Oriental rug on the floor. The walls were painted a pretty celery green, the carved and polished wooden desk looked like a genuine antique, and the chair behind it was leather. The obligatory copy of the Twelve Steps hung on the wall—did they buy them in bulk?—but at least his had a pretty gold-leaf frame.

Nicholas took my hand. "It's nice to meet you," he said. Maybe it was the way he actually appeared to be seeing me when he looked my way, or maybe it was that my gaydar was pinging, but Nicholas reminded me of Dr. McCarthy in Philadelphia. Dr. McCarthy, in whose office I'd taken that quiz, Dr. McCarthy, who'd asked me so kindly what I was doing to take care of myself. How different would things be if I'd told him then what was going on, or even if I'd just stopped it all right there, before I'd learned about ordering pills on the Internet?

I took the chair on the other side of his desk and looked at a picture in a silver frame. There was Nicholas and an older white guy, both of them in tuxedoes, each with one hand on the shoulder of a pretty dark-haired girl in what looked like a flower girl's dress.

He saw me looking. "Our wedding," he said.

"Is that your daughter? She's beautiful."

"My goddaughter, Gia," he said. "You've got a

little girl, right?" There was, no surprise, a folder open on his desk, with my name typed on the tab.

"Eloise," I said, feeling my heart beating, hearing her name catch in my throat.

"From the book?"

"From the book," I confirmed. *Ellie,* I thought, remembering her funny, imperious gestures, the way she would yell every fifth word, or complain that whatever I was doing was taking for HOURS, or come home crying because "everyone else in kindergarten has loosed a tooth but me."

Nicholas sat down, flipped open the first page of my folder, and ran his finger from top to bottom.

"So, painkillers."

"That's right."

"Why?"

"I beg your pardon?"

He crossed his legs, folded his hands in his lap, and looked at me steadily. "Why were you taking so many painkillers? Were you in pain?"

"I guess that's how it started. I hurt my back at the gym."

"So you were taking them for back pain?"

I shook my head. "Just . . . pain. Pain in general. Or to unwind at the end of the day. I thought it was sort of the same as having a glass of wine at night. Except I never really liked wine. And I did love pills. I loved how they made me feel."

He lifted one arched eyebrow. "Twenty pills," said Nicholas, "is more than one glass of wine."

Blushing, I said, "Well, obviously, things got a little out of hand. But not, you know, rehab-level out of hand. That's why I asked to see you. I really don't think I need to be here."

Nicholas flipped to another page in the folder. Then another one. "I had a conversation with your husband while you were in Equine," he began.

I felt as if I'd swallowed a stone, but I kept my voice calm. "Oh?"

"He was able to fill me in on a little more of what's been going on in your life."

My lungs expanded enough for me to take a deep breath. "So you know about my father being sick?" That was good news, I told myself. If he knew about my dad, and maybe even about Ellie, if he had any sense of my job, and what it was like to get torn apart in public, maybe he'd understand why pills were so seductive . . . and he'd know that someone who was managing that kind of life, keeping all those balls in the air, was clearly not someone who required this kind of facility.

"He told me about your father, yes. And the incident at your daughter's school?" His voice lifted, turning the sentence into a question.

I winced, feeling my face go pale at the memory. "That was awful. I had a glass of wine with a friend after I'd taken my medication." I congratulated myself for the use of the phrase "my medication," even though I knew the pills I took had been bought online rather than prescribed.

"I'm sure you know that David is very concerned. About your safety, and also your daughter's."

"That was a terrible day. What happened—what I did—it was awful. But I would never do anything like that again." My sinuses were burning, my eyes brimming with unshed tears. "I love my daughter. I'd never hurt her."

"Sometimes, in our addiction, we do things we'd never, ever do if we were sober." His voice was low and soothing, like the world's best yoga teacher. "David also said there was an incident with your business? The misappropriation of some funds?"

I sat up straight. How did Dave even know about that? "Th-that was a clerical error," I stammered. "I was just being careless. It was the end of a week from hell; I was trying to get my parents' financial stuff over to our accountant so they could admit him at the assisted-living place . . ." I shut my mouth. The thing with Ellie had been a mistake. The thing with the money— another mistake. The word "unmanageable" was floating around in my head with dismaying persistence. I pushed it away. I was managing. I was managing fine.

"Have any authorities been involved?" asked Nicholas. "The police? The Department of

Youth and Family Services?" I shook my head. "Teachers are mandated reporters, and normally, in a case like that, they'd be obligated to tell someone at DYFS what was going on." He gave me a serious look. "You're very lucky that no one got hurt . . . and that you still have custody of your daughter."

I felt sick as I nodded numbly, accepting the reality of how badly I'd fucked up. They could have taken Ellie away. I could have gone to jail.

"You're an intelligent woman," said Nicholas. "I think that if you're here, if you agreed to come here, even if there were extenuating circumstances, probably a part of you thinks you need to be here."

I opened my mouth to say *No way.* Then I made myself think. *An intelligent woman,* Nicholas had said. What would an intelligent woman do under these circumstances? Would she resist; would she fight; would she argue and continue to insist that she didn't have a problem and that she didn't belong? Or would she fake compliance? Would she nod and agree, march to meetings and activities with the rest of the zombies, eat the crappy cafeteria food and drink the Kool-Aid? If I did all that, if I toed the line and recited the slogans and—I glanced at the poster on Nicholas's wall—made a searching and fearless moral inventory of myself, I could probably get out of here in a week. Two weeks, tops.

"You know what?" I said. "Maybe you're right. Maybe there was a part of me that knew it was time to stop. I was concerned about how many I was taking. I was concerned that I needed to keep taking more and more to feel the same way. Then I was worried about having to take them just to feel normal, and always worrying about whether I had enough, and if I was going to run out, and which doctor I could call to get more. And I didn't . . ." I swallowed hard around the lump in my throat, letting Nicholas hear the catch in my voice. "I didn't want to be all spaced out around my daughter. She deserves a mom who's there for her."

"Had you made attempts to stop before?" Nicholas's voice was so calm, so quiet. Did learning to talk that way require special training?

I shook my head, thinking about that afternoon at Stonefield, Mrs. Dale wrestling the car keys away from me, telling me that I wasn't safe to drive my own daughter, and how I'd sworn to myself that I would quit, or at least stop taking so much. I thought about that terrible AA meeting the next morning, and how by noon that day I'd been right back in the bathroom, staring at my face in the mirror as I shook pills into my hand. In spite of my best intentions, and the very real threat of being exposed or shamed or worse, I hadn't even been able to make it halfway through one day without a pill.

Nicholas pushed a box of tissues across the desk. "What are you feeling?"

"I don't know," I said, and swiped at my face. "I'm not feeling well."

"That's completely understandable. You're still going through withdrawal."

"I feel so stupid," I blurted. "I've never been in trouble my whole life, you know? I've been successful. I'm good at my job. I have a beautiful little girl. I had everything I wanted. And now . . ."

Now I'm a drug addict. The words rose in my head. I shoved them away. I wasn't. I *wasn't.* I was just having a little problem. I was *experiencing technical difficulties,* like they said on TV.

"I'm worried about being here," I said. I figured this was exactly what someone who'd come to a place like this would say. It also happened to be the truth. "My mom is staying with us, but, really, she's not going to be much help. My husband works full-time, and I'm the only one who can write my blog posts. There's not, like, a substitute I can call in."

"You're going to be surprised at how people step up," said Nicholas.

I shook my head, brushing tears off my cheeks. I made myself take a deep, slow breath. What was the stupid slogan I'd seen on the church basement wall? "One Day at a Time." I would get through this place, one day at a time. I would fake contrition, pretend acceptance, act like I bought every bit of the Higher Power hooey, and sort out the rest of it when I was back home. I sniffled, wiped my face again, and gave Nicholas a brave look. "I don't suppose you have massages here," I said, feeling the tiredness, the sickness of withdrawal, the sadness that had colored everything gray settle inside me.

"Every other week, we have someone come in." He leaned forward to match my posture and kept his voice low. "I can't promise you it's going to rival what you'd get at Adolf Biecker." I suppressed a smile. Somehow he'd landed on my favorite Philadelphia salon, the one I never told my mother I patronized, because she operated on the assumption that anyone named Adolf was a Nazi.

"And in our common room, you'll find any number of board games." He smiled, then made a show of looking around, making sure we were alone. "You haven't lived until you've played Jenga with someone having DTs. We're talking guaranteed victory."

I smiled in spite of myself. Then I remembered my mission. "I want to make a phone call," I said. "Michelle said I needed permission from my counselor, but I don't have one yet, and I need to tell my daughter . . ." I felt the lump swelling in my throat again, remembering how I must have looked in the throes of withdrawal. "I want to tell her that I miss her, and that I'm thinking about her. I want her to know I'm okay."

"I don't think that should be a problem," he said, and scribbled something on the back of a business card. "You can use the phones behind the main desk back in Residential. And you have my permission to skip drum circle, if you're still feeling woozy."

Drum circle? "I am," I said, grateful that not everyone here was a robot who'd treat me like a junkie. "Two other things. I'm supposed to be on TV next week." I tried to sound casual, as if I were the kind of woman who was on TV so regularly that mentioning it was akin to saying that I was the snack mom for that weekend's six-and-under soccer game. The *Newsmakers on Nine* people, perhaps unsurprisingly, had asked me back, this time to talk about abstinence-only sex ed in public schools. "And my daughter's birthday party is on the fourteenth, and I can't miss it." That, I decided, would be my endgame. I'd be out of here in time for Ellie's birthday party. I would meet her at BouncyTime, where she'd asked to have her party (in hindsight, she had decided the giant slide was the most fun she'd ever had in her entire life), and then, when the party was over, I'd load the trunk of the Prius with presents and leftover pizza, and we'd drive back home.

Nicholas steepled his fingers and rested his chin on top of them. "That," he said, "might be a problem."

"I can skip the TV thing," I said, eager to show that I was a reasonable woman, able to compromise. "But I can't miss Ellie's birthday."

"Normally, twenty-eight days is twenty-eight days. It's your time to focus on yourself." When he saw the look on my face, his voice softened. "Your daughter is going to have other birthdays. She probably won't even remember you weren't at this one."

I gave him a thin smile. "You don't know my daughter."

"Well, I won't tell you we've never made exceptions." He turned to his computer, tapped at the keyboard. "It looks like you're going to be in Bernice's group. Why don't you mention it to her, see what she says."

"Okay. When will I meet her?"

"Monday."

Monday? I blinked in disbelief. Today was Thursday, and I wasn't seeing a therapist until Monday? I filed that factoid away for the letter to the director of Meadowcrest that I was already composing in my head.

"All I'd suggest is that you keep an open mind," Nicholas said. "I know you're not in the best place physically to process a lot of new information, but just listen as much as you can."

I got up, with the card in my hands . . . and then, before I could stop myself, I blurted the question that had kept me awake for months.

"What if this doesn't work? What if I can't stop?"

"Honesty, willingness, and open-mindedness," said Nicholas. "You're being honest already, telling me what's scaring you. Are you willing to try? And keep an open mind about twelve-step fellowships?"

I looked out the window—gathering clouds, trees stretching their budding branches toward the sky, shadows flickering across the grounds. Girls strolled along the path, carrying what I now knew were copies of *The Big Book*, and they didn't look like drunks and junkies, just regular people, leading ordinary lives.

Across the desk, Nicholas was still looking at me, waiting for my answer. "I don't think I believe in God," I finally said.

He smiled. "How cheesy would it sound if I told you that God believes in you?"

For what seemed like the first time since I'd landed in this dump, I smiled. "Pretty cheesy."

"For a lot of beginners, their Higher Power is the group itself—it's the other people working toward the same goal, supporting your sobriety."

I pointed out the window at a guy I'd glimpsed from the waiting room. He had pierced ears and a tattooed neck, and wore a baseball cap pulled low over his brow. His sweatshirt hung midway down his thighs, his jeans sagged off his hips, and his enormous, unlaced basketball shoes looked big as boats. "Does he get to be my Higher Power?"

Nicholas followed my finger. "Maybe not him specifically." He squeezed my shoulder. "Lunchtime," he said. "Hang in there. I know this part is hard. Just try to keep an open mind. Try to listen."

I nodded as if I was listening, as if I believed every word he'd told me, and walked back across the campus, taking care to stay on the women's path. Inside Residential, all the women were lined up again, in front of a window from which a small, plump, dark-skinned woman with bobbed black hair and big, round glasses was dispensing medications.

"Boy, did you miss all the fun," said Mary. "We had to figure out a way to get the horse to jump over a puddle."

"Fucking bullshit," Aubrey muttered. "How is leading around a horse on a rope supposed to help me not shoot dope?"

"You are a poet!" said Mary. "I bet you didn't know it!"

Aubrey snorted, then gazed down balefully at her mud-caked feet. "These fucking boots are ruined." In front of the window, a woman gulped her pills, then opened her mouth wide and waggled her tongue at the nurse.

"How desperate do you have to be," I wondered, "to convince someone to save their saliva-coated pill for you?"

"Just wait," Aubrey said. "When you've only slept for two hours a night six days in a row, you'll give anything for that pill." She banged a boot heel against the wall, sending a shower of flaked dirt onto the carpet.

"Aubrey F., that's a demerit," called the teenage boy behind the desk. I wondered what it meant, and made a mental note to find out later. Aubrey rolled her eyes and, when he turned back to the desk, shot him the finger. Mary giggled as the cafeteria doors swung open, releasing the smell of detergent and deep fryer, and we filed in for lunch.

Twenty

"So listen," said Aubrey, after we'd gathered our chicken fingers, Tater Tots, and canned corn and taken a seat at one of the long cafeteria tables. "Do you think . . ." She twirled a lock of hair around her finger.

"No," Mary said immediately. She was cutting her chicken fingers into cubes, dipping each cube into ranch dressing, and then popping them in her mouth, one after another.

"But he's in rehab, too!" Aubrey stabbed an entire chicken strip, doused it in ketchup, and held it aloft on her fork as she nibbled. "If I think he's not gonna stay sober, doesn't that mean that I'm not gonna make it, either?"

"I'm not saying you can't give him a chance,"

said Mary. "Remember what they said back in the Cold War? 'Trust but verify'?"

Aubrey dunked her chicken back into the ketchup slick. "Like I remember the Cold War."

Mary turned to me, the light glinting off her glasses as the chain swung against her bosom. "Aubrey's boyfriend is in rehab, too. She's trying to decide whether to see him again when she's done here." Over the younger woman's head, Mary mouthed the words *Bad idea.*

I looked at Aubrey's bruised arms. "This would be the guy who did that to you?"

Aubrey gave a shamefaced nod.

"Oh, Aubrey. Why would you even think of going back to someone who hurt you like that?"

She mumbled something I couldn't hear.

"What?"

She raised her head. "We've got a kid," she said defiantly. "A little boy." She flipped her white plastic binder so I could see a snapshot of a toddler centered in the plastic cover, a beaming toddler with fine blond hair and two bottom teeth and a slick of drool on his ruddy red chin.

I felt my heart clench. This child, who couldn't possibly be a day over eighteen, had a baby? She'd had a baby with a drug addict who beat her?

Mary reached for her hands across the table. "What kind of life is that for Cody?" she asked. "Do you want him to grow up thinking that men push women around? Choke them? Hit them?"

"It only happens when he's high," Aubrey protested.

"But you told us he's high all the time," Mary said.

"Well, but maybe if he goes to rehab and takes it seriously this time . . ."

"Who's got the baby now?" I asked.

"Justin's mom. That's who we were living with. Me and Justin and Cody."

A recovery coach—I'd learned that's what the khaki-clad teenagers who seemed to be running Meadowcrest were called—tapped Aubrey's shoulder. "They need you in Detox," he said. Aubrey cleared her tray. We watched her go.

"I'll pray for her," Mary said, and touched the gold cross around her neck before returning to her chicken. "Not that I'm judging," she said, "but I'm not sure Aubrey has the equipment she needs to make better choices."

Another recovery coach, a girl with elfin features and delicate, pointed ears exposed by a cropped haircut, tapped my shoulder. "Allison W.? There's a phone free, if you want to make your call."

I hurried out of the cafeteria, clutching the card Nicholas had given me, the bright, coppery taste of pennies and fear in my mouth as I dialed.

"Hi, Mom. It's Allison."

"Oh, Allie . . ." She sounded—big surprise—

353

like she was going to cry. "Hold on," she said, before the sobs could start. "Ellie's been wanting to talk to you."

I waited, sweating, my heart beating too hard, my lips creased into a smile, thinking that if I looked happy, even fake-happy, I would sound happy, too. Finally, I heard heavy breathing in my ear.

"Mommy? Daddy says you are in the HOSPITAL!"

My insides seemed to collapse at the sound of her voice, everything under my skin turning to dust. *Keep it together,* I told myself. At least "hospital" was better than "rehab," even if it wasn't as good as "business trip," which was what I'd been hoping for. "Hi, honey. I'm in a kind of hospital. It's a kind of place where mommies go to rest and get better."

"Why do you need to REST? You sleep all the TIME. You are always taking a NAP and I have to be QUIET." She paused, and then her voice was grave. "Are you sick?"

"Not sick like that time you had an earache, or when Daddy had the flu. It's a different kind of sick. So I'm just going to stay here until I'm all better and the doctors say I can come home."

"How many days?" Ellie demanded.

"I'm not sure, El. But I'm going to try very hard to be there for your party, and I'll be able to talk to you on the phone, and I can send you letters."

"Can you send me a present? Or some candy or a pop?"

I smiled. Maybe it was good that she didn't seem shattered—or, really, fazed in the slightest. Or maybe this was just her typical compensation, the way she'd try to make my father, and Hank, and now me, feel better about our screwups.

My job, I decided, was not to scare her. Let her think Mommy had some version of an earache or the flu, something that wasn't fatal and that the doctors knew how to fix.

"What dress are you wearing?" I asked.

"New Maxi." New Maxi was a pink-and-white-patterned maxi dress, not to be confused with Old Maxi, which I'd bought her at the Gap last summer. "Grandma does NOT make my dresses FIGHT. She says they're supposed to all get along. But I ask you, where's the fun in THAT?" Ellie demanded.

I smiled and made a noise somewhere between laughter and a sob, then sneezed three times in a row. "Not much fun at all, really."

"But she said we could get a pedicure. AND that I could get a JEWEL on my toes."

"Well, aren't you lucky?"

"Grandma is AWESOME," Ellie said . . . which was news to me. "And she let me have noodles for two nights!" The recovery coach tapped my shoulder and, when I looked up, pointed at her watch.

"I love you and I miss you," I said. "You are my favorite."

"I KNOW I am," she trumpeted. "I KNOW I am your favorite!"

"Is Daddy there?" I asked.

Ellie sounded indignant. "Daddy is at WORK. It's the middle of the DAYTIME."

"I will call you when I can, and I'm going to write you a letter as soon as we say goodbye. Listen to Grandma and Daddy, and eat your growing foods, and make your bed in the morning, and floss your teeth."

"I have to go now. *Sam & Cat* is on!" There was a thump, the muffled sound of voices, and then my mom was on the line.

"How . . . how are you doing?"

"As well as I can, I guess."

"Don't worry about anything. Everything here is going well."

"Really?" I'd braced myself for a litany of complaints, bracketed by *When will you be home?* and laced with plenty of implied *How could you*s, but my mother sounded . . . cheerful? Could that be?

"You just take care of yourself. Everything's under control. We've got . . . ." There was a brief pause. "Let's see, gymnastics today, is that right?"

"TUMBLING!" Ellie shouted in the background.

"And then Sadie's birthday party on Saturday, and Chloe's birthday party on Sunday . . ."

"I have presents for them in the downstairs closet."

"Yes. We found them, and we made cards. You just take care of yourself . . ." Almost imperceptibly, I heard her voice thicken. "We'll see you when we can."

"Thanks, Mom. Thanks for everything." I hung up the phone and sat there, teary-eyed and sneezing, as the recovery coach tapped my shoulder and, on the other side of the desk, a guy with tears tattooed on his cheeks shouted for Seroquel.

"You know, there's a seven-day blackout," said Miss Timex. "You won't be talking to anybody again until that's over."

I didn't answer. I'd already decided that the khaki brigade wasn't worth wasting my breath on. Nicholas would be my go-to guy.

"You need to join your group," she told me as I walked past the desk.

"Nicholas said I could lie down if I wanted."

She narrowed her eyes. "Are you not feeling well?"

"I feel awful," I said, and followed her as, sighing heavily, she walked me down the hall and unlocked the room where I'd woken up that morning.

I hung the handful of items that needed hangers

in the gouged and battered freestanding wardrobe. Then I pulled a sheet of paper from the notebook I'd been issued and wrote Ellie a note. *What do you call a grasshopper with a broken leg? Unhoppy! I love you and miss you and will see you soon.* I drew a heart, a dozen *X*'s and *O*'s, then wrote *MOM*.

After I'd emptied my duffel bag, I went through my purse. My plan had been to curl up with a novel and try to make the time go by, but my e-reader, like my wallet and phone, was gone. I marched back out to the desk.

"Nothing but recovery-related reading," said Wanda, my *People* magazine–loving friend. She looked left and right before mouthing the word *Sorry.*

"Is there a library?"

"You can buy approved reading materials in the gift shop. But it's only open on Monday, Tuesday, and Friday mornings, and I think maybe Sunday afternoons."

That figured. I remembered a *New York Times* story about rehabs from a few years ago. Most of them were private businesses, some were run by families, and all of them were for-profit . . . and the profits they turned were jaw-dropping. It wasn't enough that they were milking patients and insurance companies for upwards of a thousand dollars a day so we could eat crappy cafeteria food, sleep in rooms that made Harry Potter's under-the-staircase setup look like a Four Seasons suite, and be lectured about our selfishness by old men in polyester. We also had to pay what were undoubtedly inflated prices for recovery-related literature.

"You can read *The Big Book*," she said, and handed me a copy of a squat paperback with a dark-blue cover. No words, no title on the cover, just the embossed AA logo.

I carried it back to my room, lay on the bed, and began reading, starting at the beginning, then flipping randomly. *The Big Book* was first published in 1939, and it didn't take me long to realize that it was in desperate need of an update. The prose was windy, the sentences convoluted, the slang hopelessly dated (I snickered at a reference to "whoopee parties," whatever those were). Worse, the working assumption, in spite of a footnote stating otherwise, seemed to be that all boozers were men. There was a blog post in that, for sure; maybe a whole series of them. If the Twelve Steps were the order of the day, and they were still geared toward middle-class, middle-aged white guys, how were women (not to mention non-white people, or gay people) expected to get better?

I kept reading. From what I could tell, in order to get sober the AA way, you had to have some kind of spiritual awakening . . . or, as the gassy prose of "The Doctor's Opinion" put it, "one feels that something more than human power is needed to produce the essential psychic change." So you got sober by finding God. And if you weren't a believer? I flipped to the chapter called "We Agnostics," and found that AA preached that if you didn't believe, you were lying to yourself, "for deep down in every man, woman, and child is the fundamental idea of God. It may be obscured by calamity, by pomp, by worship of other things, but in some form or other it is always there."

So my choices were God and nothing. I shut the book, feeling frustrated. A few minutes later, Aubrey stuck her head through my doorway. "We need to go to Share."

I consulted my binder and made my way to the art therapy room. Three round tables had been pushed to the walls and two dozen folding chairs were arranged in a semicircle, with women seated in most of them. I took a seat between Mary and Aubrey.

"Good afternoon, Meadowcrest!" called the middle-aged woman sitting behind a desk at the center of the semicircle. A moderator, I figured, except she wasn't wearing khaki. Her laminated nametag hung on a pink cord, instead of a plain black one. Her name, according to her tag, was Gabrielle.

"Good afternoon!" the group called back.

"Is this anyone's first community meeting?"

After Mary looked at me pointedly, I raised my

hand. "Hi, I'm Allison." When this was met with silence, I muttered, "Pills."

"Hi, Allison!" the room chorused.

"Welcome," said Gabrielle, who then began reading from the binder. "Here at Meadowcrest, we are a community." *Just like Stonefield,* I thought. *And probably just as expensive.* "Is there any feedback?" Silence. "Responses to yesterday's kudos and callouts?" More silence. "Okay, then. Today we're going to hear from Aubrey. Aubrey, are you ready to share?"

Aubrey crossed her skinny legs, tucked stray locks of dyed hair behind her small ears, and licked her lips. "Hi, um, I'm Aubrey, and I'm an addict."

"Hi, Aubrey!"

She lifted one little hand in a half wave. "Hi. Um, okay. So I was born in Philadelphia in 1994 . . ."

Oh, God. In 1994 I'd been in college.

"My parents were both alcoholics," Aubrey continued, twirling a strand of blonde hair around one finger. "They split up when I was two, and I lived with my mom and my stepdad." She took a deep breath, pulling her knees to her chest. "I guess the first time he started abusing me, I was five. I remember he came into my bed, and at first he was just snuggling me. I liked that part. He said I was his special girl, and that he loved me more than he loved Mommy, that I was prettier, only we couldn't tell Mommy; it had to be our secret."

I started to cry as Aubrey went into the details of what happened for the first time the year she turned six, and kept happening until she was fourteen and moved out of the house and in with a boyfriend of her own, who was twenty-two and living in his parents' basement. How at first pot and vodka made the pain of what was happening go away, and how pills were even better, and how heroin was even better than that.

By the time Aubrey moved from snorting dope to shooting it, I was crying so hard it felt like something had ruptured inside me. Tears sheeted my face as her boyfriend turned abusive, as she moved in with her estranged father, who stole her money and her drugs, as she got pregnant and delivered an addicted baby when she was only seventeen.

Lurid and awful as it was, Aubrey's story turned out to be dismayingly typical as my week crawled by. During every "Share" session, twice each day, a woman would talk about how her addiction had happened. Typically, the stories involved abuse, neglect, unplanned pregnancies, dropping out of school, and running away from home. There were boyfriends who hit; there were parents who looked the other way. Instead of being the exception, rape and molestation were the rule.

My mom's new husband. My sister's boyfriend.

The babysitter (female). The big boy with the swimming pool who lived at the end of our street. I listened, crying, knowing how badly these girls had been damaged, and how pathetic my own story sounded. What would happen when it was my turn to share? Could I say that the stress of motherhood, writing blog posts, coping with a faltering marriage, and aging parents, parents who maybe weren't the greatest but had never hit me and certainly had never molested me, had driven me to pills? They'd laugh at me. I would laugh at me.

On my third day at Meadowcrest, a woman named Shannon told her story. Shannon was different from the other girls. She was older, for one thing, almost thirty as opposed to half-past teenager, and she was educated—she talked about her college graduation, and made a reference to graduate school. She'd lived in Brooklyn, had wanted to be a writer, had loved pills in college and had discovered, in the real world, that heroin was cheaper and could make her feel even better.

"Eventually, it turned me into someone I didn't recognize," Shannon told the room, in her quiet, cultured voice. "You know that part in *The Big Book* where it talks about the real alcoholic?" Shannon flipped open her own blue-covered paperback and read. " 'Here is the fellow who has been puzzling you, especially in his lack of control. He does absurd, incredible, tragic things while drinking.' Or, if you're in the rooms"—"the rooms," I'd learned, was a shorthand term for AA meetings—"you'll hear someone talking about how they paid for their seat, and 'paid' stands for 'pitiful acts of incomprehensible destruction.' "

Shannon sucked in a breath and scrubbed her hands along her thighs. "That was me. I did things that were incomprehensible. I stole from my parents. I stole from my great-aunt, who was dying. I went to visit her and stole jewelry right out of her bedroom, and medication from her bedside table."

In my folding chair, I felt my body flush, remembering the pills I'd taken from my dad. Shannon continued, her voice a monotone. "I slept with guys who could give me heroin. I sold everything I had—artwork my friends had made for me, jewelry I'd inherited—for drugs." Her lips curved into a bitter smile. "You know how they say an alcoholic will steal your wallet, but an addict will steal your wallet, then lie about it and help you look for it the next day? I can't tell you the lies I told, or the stuff I stole, or the things I did to myself in my active addiction. And you know the scariest part?" Her voice was rising. "After everything I've done, everything I've been through, I don't know if I can stop. I don't know if I want to. I'm not even sure that when I get out of here I'm not going to be right back on that corner. Because nothing ever—ever—made me feel as good as heroin did. And I'm not sure I want to live the whole rest of my life without that feeling."

The entire room seemed to sigh. I found that I was nodding in spite of myself. I looked around, waiting for a counselor who would say "One day at a time," or tell us to "play the tape" of how our pleasures had turned on us, or remind Shannon it wasn't for the rest of her life, just right now, this minute, this hour, this day, that she had friends, that there were people who loved her and wanted her to get well . . . but there were never any counselors in Share. *Nobody here but us chickies,* Mary had said when I'd asked her.

"The last time I went home, there was one navy-blue dress in my closet, and a pair of shoes. My parents had gotten rid of the rest of my stuff— my desk, my books, my clothes, all the posters I used to have on the walls. There was just that one dress. My mom told me, 'That's the dress we're going to bury you in.' "

Nobody spoke. Shannon rubbed her palms on her jeans again, then looked up. Her shoulder-length hair was in a ponytail, and if it wasn't for her pockmarked complexion and the deep circles beneath her tear-reddened eyes, you would have no way of guessing that she was a junkie. She looked like any other young woman, dressed down, like she could be a teacher or a bank teller or a web designer. Just like me. And now she was trapped. The thing that had once been a pleasure, a treat, was now a necessity, as vital as air and water. *I don't know if I can stop. I don't know if I want to.* Just like me . . . because, honestly, I wasn't sure I could stop. And I knew what all of that meant: that I wasn't just a lady who'd taken a few too many pills and developed a pesky little physical dependence. It meant I was an addict—the same as Mary and her DUI, and Aubrey and her six trips through rehab, and Marissa, who'd lost her front tooth and custody of her kid after she and her boyfriend had gotten into a fistfight over the last bag of dope.

Hello, I'm Allison, and I'm an addict.

I shook my head. It wasn't true. I wasn't an addict. I was just . . . it was only . . . Aubrey was staring at me. "You okay?" she asked. Her eyes were wide and clear, rimmed with sparkly silver liner and heavily mascara'd lashes. The bruises on her arms had started to fade. She was still way too thin, but she looked better.

"I'm fine," I whispered, even as a shudder wracked my shoulders. My skin bristled with goose bumps. My stomach lurched. I hadn't let myself think much about the future, or anything besides getting through each day, keeping my head down, not attracting attention, doing what was necessary until I could go home. All this time, I'd been telling myself I wasn't an addict, that I didn't need to be here, and that as soon as I could I'd go home and go back to my pills, only I'd be more careful. Now every question I'd been asked, every slogan they'd repeated, every phrase I'd glimpsed on a poster or heard in passing was coming at me, like dozens of poison-tipped arrows ripping through the sky. *Who is an addict?* began the chapter of the same name in the Narcotics Anonymous Basic Text. *Most of us do not have to think twice about this question. We know! Our whole life and thinking was centered in drugs in one form or another—the getting and using and finding ways and means to get more. We lived to use and used to live.*

That wasn't me, I thought, as Shannon pulled a crumpled sheet of paper out of her back pocket, a list like the one they made all of us write, a list of what we had that was good in our lives besides drugs. "My parents still love me," she read in a quivering voice that made her sound like she was twelve instead of thirty. "I can still write, I think. I'm not HIV-positive. I don't have hep C."

I shuddered. *Not me,* I thought again . . . but the words from the Basic Text wouldn't stop playing. *Very simply, an addict is a man or woman whose life is controlled by drugs. We are people in the grip of a continuing and progressive illness whose ends are always the same: jails, institutions, and death.* I shook my head, so hard that Aubrey and Mary both looked up. *No. Not me. Not me.*

Twenty-One

Rehab time, it turned out, was like dog years. Every hour felt like a day. The weekdays were bad, but Saturdays and Sundays were almost impossible. The handful of counselors went home, along with the more senior and experienced recovery coaches, leaving the youngest and greenest to tend the farm. The inmates were running the asylum, in some cases almost literally. One of the RCs casually confided that, not six months prior, she, too, had been a Meadowcrest patient.

On Saturday and Sunday, our hours were filled with busywork and bullshit activities that seemed to have nothing to do with recovery and everything to do with keeping a bunch of junkies occupied. By Sunday, I was sitting through my tenth—or was it my twelfth?—Share, so inured to the recitations of abuse, neglect, and damage that I'd started subbing in my favorite fictional characters. *Hi, my name is Daenerys Targaryen, and I'm an addict (Hi, Dany!). I guess you could say it all started when my brother married me off to Khal Drogo, a vicious Dothraki warlord, when I was just thirteen. I started drinking after my husband killed my brother by pouring molten gold on his head. For a while, it was social. I'd have a drink before dinner with my bloodriders, maybe two if we'd had a rough day, but after Mirri Maz Duur murdered my husband, it turned into an all-day-long thing . . .* After Share came Meditation, where we'd spread yoga mats on the cafeteria floor and spend forty minutes dozing to the sounds of Enya on one of the RCs' iPods, and Activity, which mostly consisted of pickup basketball games for the guys and walking around the track for the ladies, and Free Time, where we could play board games or read *The Big Book* or write letters home. I had bought a bunch of cards at the gift shop, and on Sunday had spent an hour writing notes to Ellie and to Janet. "Greetings from rehab!" I'd begun, hoping Janet would get the joke, imagining that at some unspecified point in the future, we would be able to laugh about this.

I had spent twenty minutes gnawing on my pen cap, trying to decide what I could possibly say to my mother, or to Dave. I'd finally settled on a few generic lines for both of them. *Thank you for taking care of Ellie. I'm doing much better. Miss you. See you soon.*

That left me with the rest of the afternoon to kill. I'd eaten a salad for lunch, then gone outside with Aubrey and Shannon. There was a volleyball net, but the guys had taken over the court, and we weren't allowed to use the ropes course. "Some insurance thing," Aubrey had explained as we walked around the track and she pointed out the rusted zipline and the storage shed where, two summers ago, one of the girls from the women's residential program had gotten in trouble for having sex with one of the men.

"I can't even imagine wanting to have sex in here," I said. Aubrey moaned, rolled her eyes, and launched into a familiar monologue about how bad she missed Justin and, specifically, the things Justin would do to her. "I think it's, like, closing back up," she said, and I told her I was pretty sure that was medically impossible, then sneezed, one, two, three times in a row, so hard it was almost painful. Shannon grinned at me.

"You're dope-sneezing!"

"What?"

Aubrey lowered her voice. "When you do a lot of downers, your systems all slow down. Like, were you really constipated?"

I tried to remember and couldn't.

"And probably you, like, never sneezed at all when you were on dope," Aubrey continued. "So now, you're Sneezy!"

"Good to know," I said. Already, I could hear the way living around all these young women had changed my vocabulary. *It's a clip*, they'd say when they meant it was a situation, or *It's about to go off* when trouble was starting. Aubrey and a few of her friends had started calling me A-Dub. Occasionally, I would make them laugh by saying something in my best middle-aged-white-lady vocabulary and voice, and then throw my fingers in the air and say, straight-faced, "I'm gangsta." It was like suddenly having a pack of little sisters. Drug-addicted, lying, stealing, occasionally home-less, swapping-sex-for-money little sisters, but sisters nevertheless. When I was growing up I had begged my parents for a sister, imagining a cute little Cabbage Patch Kid that lived and breathed, that I could dress up and teach to swim and ride a bike. No sibling had been forthcoming. My requests had been met with pained smiles from my mother and a strangely stern talking-to from my dad. *You're hurting your mother's feelings,* he told me in a voice that had made me cry. I had been maybe eight or nine years old. I wondered if there'd been some kind of medical issue, a reason why I was an only child that went beyond my mother's selfishness or the way raising me seemed not like a fulfillment but like an interruption.

I walked, and wondered what Ellie was doing on this sunny, sweet-scented morning. Was someone making her pancakes and letting her sprinkle chocolate chips onto each one? Was my mother reminding her to brush her teeth, because some-times she'd just put water on the toothbrush and lie? Were her friends asking where I'd gone, and did she know what to tell them?

On Monday, I finally met with my therapist. She was a middle-aged black woman who wore a jewel-toned pantsuit, sensible heels, glasses, and a highlighted bob that could have been a wig. There were six of us in Bernice's group: me, Aubrey, Shannon, Mary, Lena, and the other Oxy addict, Marissa, who had a daughter Eloise's age. Lena was gay, and flirtatious: night after night during the in-house AA or NA meetings, I'd watch the various Ashleys and Brittanys fight over who got to sit in her lap. Lena would unbraid their hair and whisper into their ears; she'd plant delicate kisses along their cheeks while the RCs pretended not to notice.

"Miz Lena," said Bernice, flipping through a clipboard. We'd already signed in, rating our moods on a scale of one to ten. We had circled the cartoon face that best represented our current emotional state, and rated the chances, on a one-to-ten scale, of using again if we were sent home that day. I answered honestly. My mood was a one. My emotional state was a frowny-face. If I went home that day, the chances that I would use were one hundred percent. Under the question "Are you experiencing any medical issues?" I wrote about my insomnia—just as Aubrey had predicted, they'd cut off my Trazodone and I was down to two hours of sleep a night. I mentioned the night sweats that soaked my shirts, my lack of appetite, and the way my hair was coming out in handfuls. I checked "yes" for anxiety and depression, "no" for a question about whether I had "kudos or callouts" for other residents. Then I remembered that whoever was reading these forms would decide whether I could attend my television appearance, and Ellie's birthday party, and that I hadn't provided the answers of a sane, sober woman happily on her way to a drug-free life. I hastily revised my responses, upgrading my mood and downgrading the chances that I'd use again, rewriting and erasing until Bernice collected the forms.

Lena yanked at the strings of her hooded sweatshirt. "Whatever they said," she began, in her low, raspy voice, "it's a total exaggeration."

Bernice raised an eyebrow. "How do you know 'they' were saying anything about you? What do you think you did wrong?"

More squirming and string-yanking. "I guess maybe I wasn't so respectful during the AA meeting last night."

I rolled my eyes. Lena had sat in the back row with an Ashley in her lap as the speaker detailed his rock bottom, which involved leaping from the twelfth-story balcony of his New York City apartment to a neighboring balcony because he was pretty sure his neighbor had left her door unlocked and he wanted to see if she had any goodies in her bathroom cabinet. "I didn't even care that I could have fallen and died," he said. "I just wanted something so bad."

Bernice turned to me. "New girl. Allison. What

are you here for?"

"Pills." I should have saved time and just put it on my nametag. ALLISON W.—PILLS.

"Huh. What'd you think of Miss Lena's performance last night?"

I sighed. I didn't want to get on Lena's bad side. From what I'd heard, she could be vindictive. She'd let a girl drop to the art therapy room floor during trust falls after the girl had ratted out one of Lena's friends for sneaking in loose cigarettes in her Bumpit.

"Come on," said Bernice. "This is a program of total honesty."

"I think Lena could have been a little more respectful."

Lena pulled her sweatshirt hood up over her head and muttered something.

"What was that?" asked Bernice. "Share with the group, please."

"I said you'd treat this like a joke, too, if you'd been through it five times."

Five times. When I'd first arrived I'd been shocked to hear numbers like that. Now it just made me sad. Repeat offenders, I had learned, were the rule, not the exception. If you were an addict, there was rehab, and if rehab didn't work, there was more rehab. Some of the rehabs were different—one girl, a Xanax addict, had been through aversion therapy, where she'd get a shock while looking at a picture of her drug of choice—but most of them were the same. They followed the Twelve Steps; they relied on a Higher Power to bring the "still sick and suffering" to sobriety; they were programs of total abstinence, which meant you could never have so much as a sip of beer or a glass of wine, even if your problem had been prescription pills or crack cocaine. If rehab didn't work, they'd send you back again . . . and I was learning that rehab hardly ever took the first time, and that most of the women had been through the process more than once.

Bernice was staring at me, her eyes sharp behind the thick lenses of her glasses. She looked like someone they'd cast as a mom in a TV commercial, the one who'd have to be convinced that the heat-and-eat spaghetti sauce was as good as what her own mother used to make. "How'd you feel, watching Miss Lena at the meeting last night? No. Scratch that. Let's back up. How do you feel about being here in general?"

I shrugged. "Fine, I guess."

The group groaned . . . then, as I watched in astonishment, everyone stood and did ten jumping jacks.

"You can't say 'fine.' Or 'good,' " Marissa explained. "Bernie thinks they're meaningless."

"Tell me how you really feel," said Bernice.

"Okay. Um. Well. I knew I needed help." After nearly a week in here, I knew that was Rehab 101.

You had to start by admitting you had a problem, or they'd badger you and break you down, pushing and pushing until you blurted the worst thing you'd ever done in the worst moment of what they insisted you call your active addiction.

"How come?" she asked, tilting her head, watching me closely. "You get a DUI? Fail a drug test?"

"No, no, nothing like that." I swallowed hard, knowing what was coming, as Bernice looked down at her notes.

"Says here you got in some trouble at your daughter's school."

"That's right." No point in lying. "I went to pick up my daughter and my friend's kids at their school, and I'd had some pills. I thought I was fine—" Aubrey nudged me, whispering, *"No 'fine's."* "Sorry. I thought I was okay to drive," I amended. "I know what I can handle, when I'm okay and when I'm not—but my friend and I had been drinking, and even though I'd only had one glass . . ."

"On top of the painkillers," Bernice said.

I nodded. "Right. Wine and painkillers. The teacher in charge of the carpool line took my keys away."

"So you signed yourself in?"

"Um." I swallowed hard, wondering, again, exactly what these people knew, and how much

I'd told them when I'd arrived. "I—my husband and I—there was . . . I guess I'd call it kind of an intervention. He found out what I was doing, and he told me I needed to get some help, and I agreed."

Bernice looked at my file again. "Walk us through exactly what happened before you came here."

I cringed at the memories—the sickness of withdrawal, the doc-in-the-box, the ill-fated Suboxone, Ellie finding me in bed, sick and covered in vomit. Ellie seeing me on my hands and knees, ass in the air, face pressed into the carpet, desperate for one more crumb of Oxy.

"Allison?" Bernice was looking at me. Her expression was not unkind. "Little secret. Whatever you did, whatever you're remembering that's making you look like you just ate a lemon, believe me. Believe me. Someone in here's done worse, or seen worse."

I shook my head. I couldn't speak. What kind of mother would let herself get so out of control, fall down so far, that her daughter would witness such a scene? I sat there, breathing, until I was able to speak again.

"My husband found out what I'd been doing. About buying the pills online," I began. I told them about the night I'd spent awake, my laptop heating my thighs, gobbling pills one after another until they were all gone. Heads nodded as I described how frantic, how terrified, how awful I'd felt, knowing I'd come to the end of my stash, with no idea how to get more. I told them about taking a cab to the doctor's office in the strip mall, where, as Bernice put it, "you found some quack to give you Suboxone." Her penciled-in eyebrows ascended. "Because replacing one drug with another is a great idea and nothing could possibly go wrong there, am I right?"

I didn't answer. I'd already figured out that Meadowcrest took a dim view of Suboxone. There were rehabs that would use other opiates to help addicts through withdrawal, but I hadn't landed at one of them.

"So here you sit."

"Here I sit," I repeated, and wondered, again, what was happening at home. How was Ellie getting to sleep each night, without me to read her three books and sing her three songs, and give the ritual spritz of monster spray? How was she getting dressed, without me to make her sundresses fight? Had Sarah posted anything on Ladiesroom explaining my absence, or had she found a substitute mom-and-marriage columnist? How was Dave managing with my mother? Was she getting to Eastwood to see my dad? Had he gotten any worse? I pictured Dave having a long lunch with his work wife, at a cozy table for two at the pub near the paper, my husband pouring out his heart as L. McIntyre listened sympathetically, nodding and making comforting noises while she mentally decorated my still-empty house, the one that would be her blank canvas once I'd been dispensed with and she'd moved in.

"What's going on with the husband?" asked Bernice. I felt my eyes widen. *Can they read our minds?*

"I think he's got a girlfriend. When I left he had a work wife. I'm thinking she probably got a promotion. But listen," I said, suddenly desperate to turn the focus from me to someone else, anyone else. "It's okay. Dave's a good dad, and he's got my mom there to help. I'm sure everything's—"

"No fine!" the room chorused. I shut my mouth. Bernice's gold bracelets glinted as she wrote in her pad.

"So are you two . . . estranged? Separated?"

"I don't know what we are," I admitted. "I can't get him to talk to me. He wouldn't do counseling."

"Did he know about the drugs?" asked Bernice.

I shook my head automatically before I remembered the envelope he'd intercepted; the receipts he'd brandished, the toneless recital in front of the girl in the cubicle the day I'd arrived, with Dave giving dismayingly accurate estimates of how much and how long. "He knew." I wiped my eyes. I'd cried more in less than a week in rehab than I had in the previous ten years of my life, and it wasn't like I had a particularly gut-wrenching story to weep over. "I don't know. We used to be in love, and then we had Ellie, and it was like we turned into just two people running a day care. He was the one who wanted us to live in the suburbs. He went out there and bought a house without my even seeing it. He was going to write a book, so he had this chunk of money. Then the book contract got canceled, and I started earning more, so I was the one picking up the slack there, but it was never part of the plan, you know? The plan was, I'd stay home with the baby, he'd be the breadwinner. Only he wasn't winning a ton of bread, and my daughter turned out to be kind of hard to deal with sometimes, and now I just feel so unhappy . . ." I buried my face in my hands. "I don't understand it. I have everything I want, everything I was supposed to want, so why am I so sad?"

"So you used." the counselor's voice was gentle.

I nodded. "Yeah."

"And did it work?"

I nodded, still with my face buried in my hands. "For a while, it felt good. It smoothed out all the rough edges. It made me feel like I could get through my days. But then I was doing so much of it, and spending so much on it, and worrying all the time about where I was going to get more. And I could have hurt my daughter." I lifted my head. My nose was running; my eyes felt red and raw. I looked at Bernice, her calm face, her kind eyes.

"Allison," she told me, "you can do this. You are going to be okay."

"Really?" I sniffled.

"Really really. If you want it. If you'll do the work. It'll probably be the hardest thing you've ever done in your life. But people do come back. I wouldn't be here if I didn't see it. I wouldn't be doing this work if I didn't see miracles every day."

I tasted the word "miracle." More God stuff. But whatever. Just waking up every morning and thinking that my life would be all right without pills, that I could manage work and my parents and Ellie . . . that would be enough.

"Allison W.?" A khaki-bot teenager stood in the doorway. "Michelle wants to see you."

"Go on," said Bernice.

"See you tomorrow?" I asked hopefully.

She shook her head. "I was gonna wait until the end of group to tell y'all, but today's my last day here."

Unhappy murmurs rippled through the circle. I sank back in my seat, stunned and angry. I finally had a therapist, a therapist I liked, and she was leaving after my first session? "Where are you going?" asked Shannon.

"I'll be doing outpatient, over in Cherry Hill." She smiled. "So I might see some of you on the other side."

"Wait," I protested. "You can't leave! I just got here!"

She gave me another smile, although this one seemed more professional than kind. Of course she couldn't let herself get attached to women she would know for only four weeks, or, in my case, forty-five minutes. "I'm sure they'll find someone great to replace me."

There didn't seem to be time to discuss it. So I shuffled down the hallway behind the recovery coach, yawning enormously. The night before, I'd dropped off at ten and woken up just after midnight, wide-awake and drenched in sweat. I'd taken a shower, put on fresh clothes, and put myself back to bed, trying to get some more sleep, but it hadn't happened. My thoughts chased one another until I was so frantic and sad that I was sobbing into my pillow, thinking about getting divorced, and what it would do to Ellie, and what single motherhood would do to me. "Can't you give me Ambien?" I'd asked the desk drone after four hours of that misery. "I have a prescription."

"Ambien? In here?" the RC on duty, the one everyone called Ninja Noreen for her habit of sneaking into bedrooms and shining her flashlight directly into their eyes during the hourly bed checks, actually snorted at the thought.

"Okay, then something that's approved for in here."

"Most alcoholics and opiate users have disrupted sleep. We don't believe in sleep aids. You're going to just have to ride this out.

Eventually, your body's clock will reset itself." They gave me melatonin, a natural sleep aid, which didn't do a thing, and a CD of ocean sounds to listen to, which was just as ineffective. I was starting to feel like I was going crazy . . . and nobody seemed to care. *Dear Ellie,* I would write in the middle of another sleepless night, with my notebook on my lap and a towel next to me to wipe away the sweat and the inevitable tears. *I miss you so much. I can't wait to see you. Are you making lots of treats with Grandma? Are you playing lots of Monopoly and Sorry?* I would write to her about baking and board games, telling her, over and over, that I missed her and I loved her, all the while wondering how this had happened, trying to find an answer to the only question that mattered: *How does a suburban lady who's pushing middle age end up in rehab? How did this happen to me?*

Twenty-Two

"I understand you have a television appearance scheduled for Thursday?" Michelle began.

"That's right." I'd made an appointment with Michelle to discuss a visit to *Newsmakers on Nine*, even though I was half hoping she would tell me I couldn't do it. I felt so exhausted and on edge that I wasn't sure I'd make any sense on the air. I also looked lousy. My skin was pale, my face felt drawn, my lips, even my eyelids, were chapped and peeling, and there were huge dark circles under my eyes and a good inch of dark roots showing at the crown of my dyed-and-highlighted head. If I'd harbored thoughts of emerging from rehab tanned and rested and ready to take on the world, those notions had quickly been dispelled. I wouldn't be all right in twenty-eight days, or six months, or even a year. On my last day of orientation they'd shown us a video called *The Brain Disease of Addiction*, from which I'd learned that I could look forward to a year to eighteen months of no sleep and mood swings and depression and generally feeling awful. How could I live through that? I was sure the video wasn't meant to discourage, but I was also sure I wasn't the only woman who came out of it thinking, *Eighteen months? That won't be happening. Sobriety's not for me.*

"Well, Allison, the team's been discussing it, and here is what we can offer." Michelle picked up a pen between two pudgy fingers. "Being out on your own would most likely be too stressful for you at this stage of your recovery." I felt myself exhale. "However, we can have a sober coach accompany you to the program."

I held up my hand. "Excuse me? A sober coach?" I thought those were jokes, invented by the tabloids and stand-up comedians.

She nodded. "Someone who can make sure there's no opportunity for a slip."

"Who would this sober coach be? And what kind of training would a sober coach have?"

Michelle's jowls flushed. "Obviously, Allison, we would send you with someone who has a lot of good clean time under her belt."

"But not a therapist," I surmised. "Look, some of the RCs are terrific, but some of them might as well be stocking shelves at Wawa for all they care. And none of them have degrees. In anything."

Michelle plowed on. "We can arrange transportation to the show and have a sober coach accompany you and then bring you back here."

"Would this cost anything extra?" I knew, from hearing other girls talk, that Meadowcrest cost a thousand dollars a day, and anything extra, from a thirty-minute massage to a family session, cost extra.

"The cost would come to . . ." She scanned the sheet of paper. "Three thousand dollars."

I stared at her, too shocked to laugh. "Are you fucking kidding me?"

"There's no need for profanity," Michelle said primly.

"Three thousand fucking dollars? Yes, there fucking is!"

Michelle gave me a smile as fake as a porn star's chest. "Why don't you think about it, Allison?"

I sighed. "I'll need to call my editor to cancel."

"Are you eligible for phone passes?"

I had no idea. "Of course I am."

Michelle scribbled out a pass.

"Just so you know," I said, "my daughter's birthday party is on Saturday. I am going to be there."

Even before I'd finished saying "birthday party," Michelle was shaking her head.

"I'm sorry, Allison, but the rules are, you need to have had at least six sessions with your counselor before you're eligible for a day pass. By this Saturday, you'll only have had three."

"But that's not my fault! You guys didn't even assign me a counselor until I'd been here almost a week!"

Michelle pursed her lips into a simper. "As you know, Allison, we've been having some staffing issues."

"Then don't you think you need to adjust the rules to reflect that? You can't require someone to have a certain number of sessions, and then have so few counselors on staff that it's impossible to hit that number. And I've done everything else!" My hands were shaking as I fumbled for the evidence. "Look, here's my time line of addiction." I pulled it out of my binder and brandished it in her face. Michelle gave it a skeptical look.

"That's it, Allison? Just one page?"

"I didn't use anything until I was in my thirties. Sorry. Late bloomer. But look . . ." I pointed at the page. "I've attended every Share and all the in-house AA meetings since I've been here. I went to a guest lecture on Sunday, and I'm volunteering in the soup kitchen on Wednesday." And wouldn't that be fun. "Listen," I said, realizing that my speeches were getting me nowhere. "It's my daughter. She's turning six. She isn't going to understand why I can't be there."

"Children are more resilient than we give them credit for. I bet your daughter will surprise you." Michelle looked pleased when she'd shot down my TV appearance. Now she looked positively delighted, as if she could barely contain her glee. I could imagine my hands wrapping around her flabby neck, my fingers sinking into the folds of flesh as I squeezed. I made myself stop, and take a breath, and refocus.

"Michelle. Please. I'm asking you as a mother. As a fellow human being. Please don't punish my daughter because I'm an addict. Please let me go to her party."

"The rules are the rules, Allison, and you didn't do what you needed to in order to get your pass."

"But you didn't give me a chance! Aren't you listening to me? Because of your staffing issues there was absolutely no way I could have met your requirements."

"I understand that I'm hearing your disease talking. I'm hearing it say, 'I want what I want, and I want it right now.' Which is how addicts live their lives. Everything has to be now, now,

now." I was shaking my head, trying to protest, but Michelle kept talking. "We think there's always going to be someone there to clean up our messes, cover for us, call the boss or the professor, make excuses."

"I never asked anyone to cover for me. I cleaned up my own messes. I never . . ." Oh, this was impossible. Didn't she understand that I wasn't one of those addicts who slept all day and got high all night? Didn't she realize that, far from making my life unmanageable, the pills were the only thing that gave me even a prayer of a shot at managing?

Michelle kept talking. "In sobriety, we don't make excuses, and we don't make other people cover for us. We live life on life's terms. We take responsibility for our own actions, and our own failures. This was your failure, Allison, and you need to own it."

Tears were spilling down my cheeks. I'd heard the phrase "seeing red" all my life but never known it was a thing that really happened. As I sat there, a red shadow had descended over my world. My heart thumped in my ears, as loud as one of those person-sized drums you see in marching bands. It took everything I had not to lunge across the desk and hit her.

"I am going to my daughter's party. I told her I'd be there, and I'm going."

"Allison—"

"No. We're done chatting. We're through."

Still shaking with rage, I got up, closed the door, went back to my room, and lay on my bed. *Okay,* I told myself. *Think.* Maybe I could sneak out the night before the party, climb out of my bedroom window and start walking. Only where? I wasn't sure where I was, how far away from Philadelphia, whether there were buses or trains. Even if I waited until daylight, I wouldn't know where to go, or even how long it would take to get there.

I rolled from side to side and wondered what Ellie was doing. When we'd bought the Haverford house, we'd made only one improvement: in Ellie's room, instead of the standard double-hung windows, I'd had the contractor install a deep, cushioned window seat with built-in bookshelves on either side. It had turned out even better than I'd hoped. The cushions were detachable, and the lid of the seat lifted up for storage. Since Ellie had been too little to read, we'd repurposed the seat as a stage, hanging gold-tassled curtains that Ellie could open with a flourish, building a ticket box out of a shoebox and construction paper and glitter. At night, Ellie's collection of Beanie Babies and stuffed bears would perform a Broad-way revue, singing everything from expurgated selections from *The Book of Mormon* and *Urinetown* to *Bye Bye Birdie* and *The Sound of Music* . . .

I sat up straight, remembering *The Sound of*

Music. Hadn't that musical featured a talent show—a show within a show—and hadn't the von Trapps used the show as cover when they made their escape?

There were talent shows in rehab. I knew that from the Sandra-Bullock-gets-sober film, *28 Days*, which they'd shown us. Could that be the answer? Suggest a show, come up with an act, convince Dave that I'd gotten a day pass . . . well. I'd figure out the specifics later, but for now, I could at least see a glimmer of possibility.

Twenty-Three

The next day at breakfast, I brought it up, as casually as I could. "You guys all know *The Sound of Music*, right?"

Blank looks from around the table. "Is it like *American Idol*?" ventured one of the Ashleys.

"No. Well, actually, you know what? There is a talent competition. See, there's this big family, and the mother has died, so the father hires a governess."

The Ashley made a face. "You can't hire a governess. They have to be elected."

"No, no, not a governor. A governess. It's a fancy way of saying babysitter. So anyhow, she takes care of the kids, and the father starts to fall in love with her . . ."

Aubrey immediately launched into a pornographic soundtrack, thrusting her hips as she sang, "Bow chicka bow-wow . . ."

"Cut it out!" I said sternly. "This is a classic!" I remembered Christopher Plummer and Julie Andrews dancing on the veranda, his arms around her tiny waist, her eyes gazing up at him like he was the God she'd failed to find in the convent. "So they fall in love, and the kids, who've never gotten more than ten minutes of their father's time, start to straighten up and fly right. There's, like, six kids, and one of them's a sixteen-year-old, and she's in love with the messenger boy . . ."

"The messenger boy!" Lena snickered. "She needs a man with a real job." She shook her head. "Ridin' around on his bus pass, probably. Fuck that shit."

"Anyhow. The Nazis organize this big talent show, and the Von Trapp Family Singers enter . . ."

"Wait, wait. That's their name? That's a terrible name."

"Well, this was a long time ago," I said. "Cut them some slack. So who's into it?"

I looked around the circle. The Ashley was peeling strips of pink polish off of her fingernails. Aubrey was scribbling in her notebook—probably a list of everything she intended to do when they let her go. We all had versions of that list. The women my age wrote about the luxuries we missed, the foods we wanted to eat, the clothes we'd neglected to pack, taking a shower in which the water would not emerge in a lukewarm trickle, reading books where every single story did not involve an identical arc of despair and recovery, or watching made-for-TV movies that did not involve some C-list actor in the grip of either DTs or a divine revelation. The young girls, as far as I could tell, all wanted drugs and sex, typically in that order, often from the same person.

I sat up straight and breathed in from my diaphragm, trying to remember back to high-school choir. "Raindrops on roses and whiskers on kittens . . . Bright copper kettles and warm woolen mittens . . . Brown paper packages tied up with strings . . ."

"These are a few of my favorite things!" sang Shannon. She was looking better than she had during Share. Her skin didn't look as dull, and her hair was shiny. "I used to watch it with my parents. It's cute!"

"It's corny," said Lena.

"But we could change it!" I said. "Like . . ." I thought for a minute. "Dealers on corners and elbows with track marks. Cop cars and dive bars and—"

"Blow jobs in state parks," said Mary, who immediately clapped her hands over her mouth and giggled.

"Silver-white Beamers, got repo'd last spring.

These are a few of my favorite things!" I sang. "When the dog bites! When the cops call! When I'm feeling sad . . . I simply remember my favorite pills, and then I won't feel so bad."

Everyone applauded. Mary frowned. "Do you think it glamorizes drug use?"

"Maybe we should do a song about how bad it is," Shannon offered. "Like, do you guys know *Avenue Q*? There's this song called 'Mix Tape.'" She straightened her shoulders and began to sing in a low, pleasant alto. "'He likes me. I think he likes me. But does he like me, like me, like I like him? Will we be friends, or something more? I think he's interested, but I'm not sure . . .'"

She thought for a minute, and then sang, "Piss test. Just failed my piss test. I didn't know I'd have one . . . but then I did! And I smoked crack. And had some beers. And now I'm sitting here . . . all full of fear!"

Lena's nose wrinkled. "I dunno. Does everything have to be, like, a musical? What about a Beyoncé video?"

"Sure," I said, even though my knowledge of Beyoncé videos was limited to the one where she pranced around in a leotard and waved her hand to flash her ring.

"And what about the girls who can't sing?" asked Mary.

"We could do skits. Like a parody of *Are You Smarter Than a Fifth Grader?*"

Aubrey looked impressed. "You know that show?"

I frowned. "Dude. I'm old, not dead." I forked my fingers, fake-gangsta-style. "I'm A-Dub, bitch!"

"I'm ancient," said Mary, who did not sound upset, as she began to sing. "Gonna take a sentimental gurney . . . Gonna set my heart at ease . . . Gonna ride that gurney down to detox . . . Hope they don't have bedbugs or fleas . . ."

"Oh, my God, we need to do one about Ed McGreavey!" I said as I joined in the other girls' applause. "Do you guys know *Les Miz*?"

"It's about French revolutionaries," said Shannon. "And there's a love triangle . . ."

"And this horrible innkeeper, who puts cat meat in the stew, and overcharges for everything, and steals from the patrons."

"Does he have fake hair?" asked the Ashley.

"Probably. He's a revolting human being who takes advantage of the needy," said Shannon.

"That's our boy," said Lena, who'd spent more time with Ed than the rest of us combined.

"Master of the house!" I sang. My voice wasn't as strong as Shannon's, but at least I could carry a tune. "Quick to catch your eye! Never wants a passerby to pass him by. Servant to the poor! Butler to the great! Hypocrite and toady and inebriate!" I set down my pen, considering. "Wow. We don't even really need to change it."

"What's an inebriate?" asked one of the girls.

"A drunk."

"Didn't Ed do meth?" asked Aubrey.

I shrugged, but Lena was nodding. "Oh, yeah. He came back here weighing eighty pounds and missing all his teeth. He shows a picture at the lecture."

"Not the one about finding your purpose?" I'd seen that already, and I was certain that if a shot of Ed weighing eighty pounds and minus teeth had been on offer, I'd have remembered it.

"No, no, he does another one. It's called 'Finding Your Bottom,' " said an Ashley.

I burst out laughing. Mary was laughing, too. "What?" Lena asked.

" 'Finding Your Bottom'?" Aubrey asked. "My grandmother always used to say that someone was so stupid he couldn't find his own ass with both hands and a flashlight."

"How did Ed find his bottom?" Shannon asked. "Where did Ed find his bottom?"

"He was in San Francisco, giving blow jobs for drug money," said Lena.

"As one does," I murmured, and thought, again, how different I was from the drunks and druggies who populated this establishment, and how every anecdote, every personal revelation, every Share, was just another argument in favor of my not being here. *Stick it out,* I told myself.

"Hey," I said. "Did you guys see the movie *Pitch Perfect?* or *Mamma Mia?* Think there's anything there? Or, wait! Here's one for Michelle: If you change your mind, I'm the first in line . . . I'm the one you'll see . . . No one gets around me!"

"Gonna make some rules to break, have you pee in my cup," sang a Xanax addict named Samantha, who'd wandered over to our table, drawn by the singing. "Gonna turn my flashlight on, gonna wake you up."

"I think," said a girl named Rebecca, who was so quiet that the most I'd heard her do was announce her name in Share, "that we should do a skit about applying to work here. Like, 'Do you have a heartbeat?' "

"Have you been to college?" asked Mary. "No? Do you know what college is?"

"This is never going to happen," said Lena.

"Why not?" I asked.

"Because!" She rolled her eyes. "Do you honestly think they're going to sit here and let us make fun of them? They're stupid, but they're not complete idiots."

"So we don't tell them," I said. "We'll just spread the word quietly. We'll tell everyone that we're holding a talent show in the cafeteria during Meditation after lunch on Saturday." And then, I thought, when the staffers inevitably got wind of what was going on and hurried to shut it down, I'd stroll out to the parking lot, cool as Captain von Trapp facing down the Nazis, and let Dave drive me to Ellie's party.

Twenty-Four

"Are you feeling all right?" my new therapist, Kirsten, asked. I nodded, even though I could barely breathe, and I hadn't been able to eat even a bite of pineapple or a single strawberry for breakfast. Three days ago, she'd asked me who to invite for my family session, the sit-down all the inmates had to endure before Meadowcrest released them from its clutches. I'd put Dave's name and my mother's on the list. "Do you want me to get in touch?" Kirsten had asked, and I'd nodded, knowing I wouldn't be able to handle it if Dave turned me down. Which he did. "He didn't say why," Kirsten reported. She was Bernice's opposite in almost every way—tall and young and white and willowy, with thin silver rings on her fingers and pencil skirts and sensible heels that were supposed to make her look grown-up but instead made her look like a teenager who was trying too hard. "Don't read too much into it. It doesn't mean he doesn't want to be involved in your treatment."

"Or my life," I'd murmured, and spent the next two nights of sleeplessness fretting that he'd have divorce papers ready for me as soon as I set foot out of Meadowcrest.

"All it means is that he can't attend today's session."

But why wouldn't he make it a priority, canceling whatever other interviews or conferences he had planned? What could be more important than helping me?

My mother had agreed to come. At the appointed hour, I'd gotten up and gotten dressed, letting Aubrey help with my hair and makeup. Shannon lent me a cashmere cardigan, and a belt to keep my jeans up—in spite of the starchy food, I'd actually lost weight, mostly because I was too distraught to eat. Mary pulled out her rosary beads and told me she'd be in chapel, praying for me, and even Lena muttered a gruff "Good luck."

I sat in a chair in Kirsten's office, legs crossed, trying not to shake visibly as the door opened and my mother, impeccable in the St. John knit suit that I recognized as the one she'd worn to her grand-niece Maddie's bat mitzvah, walked into the room. She'd gotten her hair styled and set, every trace of gray removed, and it hung in a mass of curling-iron ringlets, each one the same. She'd left it long, even after she'd turned forty, and fifty, and sixty. "Men like to see a woman take her hair down," she'd told me, even as her own hair got increasingly brittle and thin, with its shine and color coming from a bottle. Her makeup was its typical mask, the same stuff she'd probably been wearing the same way since the 1970s, liquid black eyeliner flicked up at the corner of each lid to make cat eyes, foundation blended all the way down her jawline to her neck, and her preferred Lipglass lipgloss for that lacquered, new-car finish.

But beyond the hair and makeup, there was something different—an alertness to her expression, a confidence as she moved across the room, like she knew she'd make it to the other side without requiring assistance, without bumping into anything or banging her shins on the coffee table. My whole life, my mother had been accident-prone. "Whoops," I could remember my father saying a thousand times, his hand on her elbow, guiding her away from something sharp, keeping her on her feet.

"What can I get you? Coffee? Water?" Kirsten asked.

"No, thank you," she said. From her flared nostrils, the way she held her arms tightly against her body and clutched her bag at her side, I could tell that she'd noted the smell of institutional cleaners and cheap, processed food, the RCs with their troubled complexions, the heroin girls with their piercings and tattoos. Maybe she'd even glimpsed Michelle, whose size she would regard as a personal affront. A place full of fuckups, she'd think . . . and here was her daughter among them.

"Hi, Mom." I wasn't sure if I should hug her,

and she didn't make any move toward me. "How's Ellie?"

"Oh, Ellie's wonderful. She's playing at Hank's this morning." A frown creased her glossy lips. "That boy is always sticky."

"Hank has allergies."

"I'm not sure that entirely explains it. Ellie misses you . . ." My mom's voice trailed off. My eyes filled with tears.

"Why don't you have a seat," Kirsten told my mom, giving me a significant look. "And, Allison, remember. Of course you're concerned about your daughter, but we're here to focus on you."

With that, my mother lifted her chin. "How are you?" she asked.

I shrugged. "Well, given the fact that I'm in rehab, not too bad."

She flinched at the word "rehab."

"You hadn't noticed any changes in your daughter?" Kirsten asked. "Allison seemed the same to you?"

My mother doesn't notice me at all, I thought, as she took a seat and started working the clasp of her handbag, clicking it open, then shut. That wasn't particularly charitable, or entirely true— my mother noticed me; she just noticed my father much more—but I wasn't in an especially generous or honest frame of mind. This was the most embarrassing thing I could imagine; worse than the time my mom had been called to school after I'd barfed up all those doughnuts after our birthday breakfast gone wrong, or the time they'd called her in fifth grade after my best friend, Sandy Strauss, and I got in trouble for telling the new girl, a kid whose southern accent was strange to our ears and who had the improbable name Scarlett, that we'd called in to Z-100 and won tickets to a Gofios concert and that she could come with us. Where was Scarlett now? I couldn't recall her last name, but I could remember her narrow, rabbity face, her watery blue eyes that always looked like she'd just been crying.

"Allison?" I blinked to find Kirsten and my mother both looking at me. "I asked your mother if she'd noticed any changes in your behavior over the past year."

"You have to remember that my father was diagnosed around that time. I think my mom—well, all of us, really—were focused on him."

"That doesn't mean I wasn't paying attention to you," my mother said a little sharply. She turned to Kirsten. "I did notice. Especially since I started staying with Allison and Dave. Her moods were . . . a little strange. Sometimes she'd seem sleepy . . . or cheerful, but with an edge to it. Like she could go from being so happy to crying in a minute."

"I never cried," I said.

"Allison," said Kirsten, in her professionally soothing voice, "try to just listen, okay?"

I nodded. But I couldn't believe that my mother would have the nerve to come in here and try to make it sound like I was the needy one.

Kirsten turned from me to my mother. "The way your daughter's described it, she was under a tremendous amount of stress." Kirsten bent, reading from the folder she held open in her lap. "She was working a lot, and taking care of her daughter, and helping you with your husband. He has Alzheimer's, is that correct?"

My mother nodded wordlessly. Tears slid down her cheeks. Now, I thought, we'd landed on the topic that would take up the rest of the session, the rest of the day, if that was possible. My father, comma, suffering of, and mother's subsequent agony.

"Are you surprised that Allison ended up in a place like this?" Kirsten asked.

It got so quiet I could hear the clock ticking. Then, unbelievably, my mother shook her head. "No," she said in a husky whisper. "No, I wouldn't say I was surprised."

I opened my mouth, feeling shocked. I wanted to remind her what a good girl I'd been, never skipping school, always turning in my homework, getting a job three weeks after I graduated from Franklin & Marshall, never embarrassing her, never being a burden. But it seemed the shocks were just getting started. My mother asked, "It runs in families, doesn't it?"

Kirsten nodded. "We know from research that a child who has a parent with an addiction is eight times more likely to develop substance-abuse problems him- or herself."

I braced myself. I knew what was coming from listening to the other women. Next I'd hear how my mother's father had been a secret tippler, or how Grandma Sadie had gotten strung out on Mexican diet pills. My mother bent her head, crying harder. "I never meant to hurt her," she wept. "If I could be here myself . . . if I could take this pain away . . ."

Kirsten passed my mother a box of tissues, an act that was strictly forbidden during normal therapy sessions, on the grounds that being handed a box could derail someone's epiphany. *Her issue, her tissue,* the group would chant. My mother grabbed a fistful and wiped her eyes.

"What do you mean, you never meant to hurt Allison?" Kirsten asked. When my mother didn't answer, I said, "Yeah, I'd like to know what you're talking about."

"You don't remember." Her voice was dull. "Well, maybe you wouldn't. You were just four."

"Remember what? What happened when I was four?" She clicked her purse clasp open, then shut, and I remembered—of course I knew what had happened. The Accident.

"But that didn't have anything to do with me," I

started to say. My mother, her eyes on Kirsten, started talking at the same time.

"I was in a car accident," she said. "I was drunk. And Allison was in the car with me."

My mouth dropped open. My mother kept talking.

"You had your seat belt on, but there were no car seats back then. When I . . . when the car . . ." She gulped. "I drove into a telephone pole. You broke your arm."

My body felt icy. "I don't remember any of this," I said, but something tickled at the back of my mind. A whining buzz, hands on my shoulder, a burning smell in the air, a man's voice saying, "Hold still, and you'll get a lolly when it's done."

My tongue felt thick as I tried to talk. "Did you get arrested?"

She shook her head. "Back then . . . back then it was different. But your father . . ." She buried her face in her hands. "He was so angry he took you away for a week."

I didn't remember that, either. "Where did we go?"

"Down the shore. It was the summertime. He must have rented a place, you know, that little cottage in Avalon where we'd go? It belonged to one of the partners at his firm. I never asked, I never knew for sure, but I think he went there. And when he came back, he told me . . . t-told me that if I ever hurt you again, if I ever did anything to put you in danger, that he'd leave me, and he would never come back. He would take you away and I'd never see either one of you again."

Puzzle pieces clicked into place in my mind. Keys slid into locks. Doors opened, revealing a different world behind them. "So you stopped driving."

She nodded.

"But you didn't stop drinking."

Her eyes welled up again. "I couldn't," she whispered. "I tried, so many times. I wanted to. For you. For your father. I wanted to be a good mother, and a good wife, but I . . ." She shook her head. I shut my eyes, remembering scenes from my girlhood. Being seven or eight years old, having a friend sleep over, and telling her to whisper when we got up the next morning. "My mom sleeps late." But she wasn't incapacitated. By ten o'clock most mornings, she was at the tennis court . . . and, if she sipped white wine and seltzer all afternoon, I never saw her sloppy, or tipsy, or heard her slur or saw her stumble.

"So you made sure Dad would never get mad at you again." *By acting like a little girl, a bubbleheaded teenager,* I thought but did not say, as my mother nodded again.

"And you stayed away from me."

She looked up, her eyes accusing. "You didn't need me!"

"What?" I looked at Kirsten, hoping she'd jump

in. "What little girl doesn't need her mother?"

"You were so smart," said my mom. Her voice was almost pleading. "You could do everything by yourself. You never wanted my help getting dressed, or picking out your clothes, or with your homework. You didn't want me walking you to school." She dropped her voice to a whisper. "I felt like you were ashamed of me. Like you knew what I'd done. How stupid and reckless I'd been. You didn't want anything to do with me."

I closed my eyes, trying to imagine my mother, my beautiful, distant mother, as an alcoholic, who'd kept this secret for more than thirty-five years. How circumscribed her life must have been. No car. No friends, not real ones, because who could she trust, and how could she talk honestly to anyone? No relationship with me, and a kind of desperate, clingy, please-don't-leave-me marriage, in which other people—my dad, me—did everything because she didn't trust herself to do anything. It explained so much.

"Were you ever going to tell me?"

She didn't hesitate before shaking her head. "How could I have told you that I'd almost gotten you killed? How could you ever forgive me? But now . . ." She lifted her head, looking around. "If I'd known that you were at risk I would have said something. I would have warned you. But I never thought . . ." She shook her head again, and pressed her hands together. I saw that she was trembling, and that there was a fine mist of sweat at her temples, and above her upper lip. She must have wanted a drink so badly. I wondered what it had cost her, to get herself out of bed, and dressed, and all the way out to New Jersey, alone and sober. I wondered if she had a flask in the car, or if she'd tucked one of those airport-sized bottles into her purse, and if she was counting the minutes, the seconds, until she could slip away, into the bathroom or the backseat, to unscrew the lid with slick, shaking hands, to raise the bottle to her lips and find that relief.

"You weren't like me. You were strong. You had it all figured out."

"I don't have anything figured out," I said. "And I'm not strong."

"I wonder," Kirsten said, "if you two might have that in common. The ability to put on a show, where everything looks good from the outside."

I didn't answer. Probably, even now, my mom did look fine from the outside. Her makeup was always perfect, her clothing was impeccable, and she had a mantel full of tennis trophies to prove her athletic prowess. But inside she was a wreck, a walking-around mess. Just like me. My mother raised her head. "Allison," she said, "you need to know that I have never once been impaired around your daughter."

"Did you quit?" I asked.

She bent her head. "When your dad was

diagnosed, I made myself cut back to just two glasses of wine at night," she said. "I want to help you, Allison."

"Was it hard?" I asked. Could you really go from being a full-blown alcoholic to drinking just two glasses of wine at night? Was my mom telling the truth? There was no way of knowing.

"I'll do whatever I can to help you," she said. "Only please." She was crying again, but her voice was steady. "You have to stop taking those pills. You have to try. For Ellie's sake. You can't hurt her, and you can't waste your life hiding, the way I did, pretending that things are okay, being drunk or on pills or whatever, and not being a real mother, and not really living your life." She got to her feet, crouched in front of me, and grabbed both of my hands in her icy ones. Up close, I could see what I hadn't seen, hadn't wanted to see, my whole life. It was there in the web of wrinkles around her eyes, the way her lip liner didn't strictly conform to her lips and, more than that, the faint sweet-and-sour fruity smell that exuded from her pores. I'd never given a name to that odor, any more than I'd given a name to Dave's scent, or Ellie's. People had their own smells, that was all. But now it was like I was getting blasted with it, like I'd dived headfirst into a vat of cheap white wine, in which my mother had been marinating for decades.

I'd never noticed. I'd never even guessed. Even

though the clues were all there, I had never put them together to come up with the inescapable conclusion. What was wrong with me, I wondered, as my mother squeezed my hands and held on hard. Was I just as selfish as she was, that she'd been sick and suffering, and I'd never seen?

"Promise me, Allison."

"I never want to be in a place like this again," I said. It was the most I could give her and not be lying.

"That's a start," Kirsten said.

Twenty-Five

I staggered out of the room, a minute after my mother's departure. I hadn't remembered the Accident when I was a girl, but I now felt like I'd been in one in that little room, like a bus had run me over and left me flattened on the pavement.

"Drink a lot of water," Kirsten said. "Breathe. It's a lot to take in."

I tottered along the women's path, head down lest I accidentally make eye contact with the men, and snuck a glance at the visitor's parking lot. My mother's car and driver would be waiting. She could go out into the wide world, wherever she wanted to go. Soon, I would have that freedom, too. Where would I go? What would I do?

It was a sticky June day, the drone of bumblebees and lawn mowers in the humid air that sat like a wet blanket on my limbs and my shoulders. The sun blazed in a hazy blue-gray sky, and the air itself looked thick with pollen that dimmed all the colors, making it fuzzy and faint. Somewhere there were kids splashing in swimming pools, dads underneath umbrellas, streaming the game on their phones, moms dispensing sunscreen and sandwiches and saying *Oh, won't that hit the spot* to offers of a cold beer or some white wine or a vodka-and-cranberry, tart and refreshing, just the thing for a hot summer day.

Behind the administration building I found a little garden, overgrown with weeds, the borders of the flower beds ragged, squirrels chittering in the dogwood tree, a splintery wooden bench in its center. I sat on the bench, staring numbly straight ahead. I felt like I'd been looking at one of those optical illusions. Examine it one way you'd see a beautiful young woman, the smooth lines of her chin and cheeks, the ripe curls of her hair. Then you'd blink or tilt your head and realize you were seeing a withered crone, her nose a tumorous hump, the young girl's hat really the old woman's rat's nest of hair. The world I had once known did not exist, had never existed. Instead of the Tale of the Childlike Mom, the Distant Dad, and the Love They Shared, I had, instead, to consider the Story of the Drunk Mother, the Dad Who Could Never Trust Her, and the daughter who was an endless source of worry for both of them.

Had I known? On some level, I must have at least guessed. All those afternoon naps in her bedroom with the shades drawn . . . and yet she'd emerge every morning in her tennis whites or her golf clothes to drink a little glass of orange juice (wheatgrass juice in the 1990s) and go off to her game. There was that ever-present tumbler full of wine and seltzer . . . but I never saw her take a sip of anything stronger. She smoked, but so did plenty of moms back then. She didn't drive, but that didn't seem worse than other parents' idiosyncrasies: Dorothy Feld's mother had weighed three hundred pounds until she got her stomach stapled; Kurt Dessange's dad wore a toupee that looked like it was made out of spray-painted pine needles.

"All those years," I said out loud. Years of lying, years of hiding. Years of her knowing she wasn't living right, that she wasn't the mother or the wife she could have been. Years of loneliness, because those kinds of secrets you couldn't tell, not to your own mother or sister or your very best girlfriend. *I don't love my husband. I'm having an affair. Sometimes I can't stand my children.* I could imagine saying these things, but *I'm a secret alcoholic? I drove drunk with my daughter in the car? I want to stop and can't?* Who could tell another soul things like that?

Who would react with anything other than horror?

You're only as sick as your secrets. Another little slogan I'd picked up. Not to mention that whole fearless and searching moral inventory, where you'd list all your faults and then tell someone else exactly what you'd done wrong. "That sounds horrible," I'd told Wanda at the desk, after she'd finished her whispered recap of the previous night's *Bachelor* episode. "No, no," she'd said, with a kind of crazy glow in her eye, "it's the most liberating thing you can imagine! It makes you free!"

"Free," I croaked. My mom had never been free. She'd lived her whole life under the yoke of her secrets, with a man who probably desperately wanted her to get better but didn't know how to fix her, or how to help. So what were my chances? Where did that leave me? Was it possible that I wasn't really an addict, that I could take pills, just more carefully than I'd taken them before? Or was it like everyone in here said, that the only path the pills would put me on would end in jails, institutions, and death? *Half-measures availed us nothing,* said *The Big Book. We stood at the turning point.* Well, here I was. Which way would I turn?

One afternoon on our honeymoon in Mexico, Dave and I had gone fishing. It had been one of those perfect days: not too hot, with a crisp breeze, the sun glinting off the waves' surfaces,

412

and the fish shoving one another out of the way for the privilege of swallowing our hooks. We'd caught half a dozen striped bass in just four hours on the water. Then, while we'd sat back (with beers, I remembered, and the tortas I'd bought in a little *panadería* on the street), the mate had set up a table and two twenty-gallon buckets of water near the back of the boat and expertly gutted each fish, stroking the blade down the center of their bellies and deftly sliding out their guts. I felt like that now, like someone had sliced me open and dumped out my insides, then stitched me back together and set me on my feet.

"So how'd it go?" Lena asked at lunch, which was manicotti, limp noodles and rubbery cheese in a meat sauce that made you sorry for the cows that had given up their lives to enter the food chain. Just the smell turned my stomach. I'd made myself a cup of tea and sat, shivering, in my customary spot between Aubrey and Mary.

"Are you all right?" asked Shannon.

"Clearly, she isn't," said Mary. "Just look at the poor girl!" She squeezed my shoulders. "Honey, what's wrong?"

"What did they say?" asked Aubrey. "Were you, like, molested by an uncle or something?"

"Oh, for heaven's sake," said Mary.

"Well, it happens," I heard Aubrey reply.

"Not that," I said, in a voice I barely recognized as my own. "It turns out that my mother's an

413

alcoholic." I took a breath. "It explains a lot."

"You didn't know?" asked Lena.

"I feel pretty stupid," I admitted.

"Hey," said Lena, "addicts lie."

I nodded, wondering what that said about my mother, and what it said about me. She'd lied, but I'd never noticed, never tried to figure it out. I thought of that day I'd gotten lost in Avalon when I was little, how the streets and the store and the sidewalks and the sand had all looked different, completely different, like they belonged in a world I couldn't even imagine, and how the walls between this world and that one were so thin. One slip, one misplaced foot, one secret out in the open and you'd go crashing through the boundaries and find yourself in that other, unimagined world where everything was different, where everything was wrong. I made myself drink my tea, and a glass of water, and follow the group out onto the Meadowcrest lawn, where we sat in a circle and listened to a man with a flowing gray beard and a woman young enough to be his daughter who was probably his girlfriend bang on African drums and tell us that music had the power to heal. Eventually, I opened my notebook again, flipping through pages of jokes and songs that would get me to my daughter. *Eyes on the prize,* I told myself, and bent my head and began to write.

Twenty-Six

Three days after I came up with the concept of a talent show at our table, we had more skits and songs than we could use. The entire women's campus had caught talent-show fever. Girls who hadn't been interested in anything but reconnecting with their boyfriends or their dealers were busy writing lyrics or scraping together costumes or finding props for *The Sound of Rehab*.

As we walked to Share, two girls, Amanda and Samantha, were performing a version of a Run-D.M.C. rap called "My Addiction," instead of "My Adidas." "My addiction walked through high-school doors and danced all over coliseum floors . . . spent all my dough just blowing trees . . . we made a mean team, my addiction and me." I was learning all kinds of new words and phrases. "Blowing trees," I learned, was smoking marijuana. "On my grind" meant working. "So, when I'm at my desk, writing a blog post, that means I'm on my grind?" I asked, and both Amanda and Samantha started laughing and said, "Nah, it's a little different than that," but they wouldn't tell me how.

We were almost at the art therapy room when Michelle popped her head out of her office. "Allison W., can I see you for a moment?"

I rolled my eyes, left the group, and took a seat on the opposite side of her desk. "Allison," she began, "I understand there's a talent show in the works."

I shrugged, saying nothing.

"You know," Michelle continued, "that any activities have to be approved by staff."

"Oh, sure," I said. Then I resumed my silence. Michelle stared at me for a moment. Then she reached into a folder and pulled out a script that, judging from the coffee stains, looked as if it had been retrieved from a cafeteria garbage can. " 'How do you solve a problem like an RC,' " she read, in a tuneless, cheerless voice. " 'How do you make them understand your world? How do you make them stay . . . and listen to what you'd say . . . when they look at you like you're a human—' "

"You know," I interrupted, "it really sounds much better when you sing it." I sat up straight and demonstrated. "Many a thing you know you'd like to tell them. Many a thing you'd hope they'd understand . . . Low bottoms and low IQs . . . they're low on empathy, too . . . with nary a prayer of ever getting canned." I bent my head to hide my smile. "You see?"

"Allison, I admire your team spirit. But you are not permitted to perform skits and songs that make fun of the staff members."

"Why?" I asked. "I mean, of course, assuming

that there *is* a talent show." I arranged my face into an approximation of confusion. "And why do you think I'm the one in charge?"

"Allison, I'm not going to get into that with you. What I need you to understand—"

I cut her off before she could finish. "What I need you to understand is that, to misquote Alexander Haig, I'm not in charge here. I've got nothing to do with anything. I'm just some poor, stupid pill-head who can't figure out how many sessions with her therapist it takes to get a day pass."

Michelle narrowed her eyes, causing them to practically vanish into her doughy face. "Let me ask you something, Allison. Do you want to get better?"

"Better than what?" I muttered. *Better than you?* I thought. I was pretty sure I'd achieved that particular goal already.

"Think about it," she suggested in a sugary-sweet tone, and sent me off to Share, where I listened to a thirty-eight-year-old mother of two named Dice describe her descent from high-school cheerleader to crackhead. She'd arrived at Meadowcrest after her parents told her they could no longer care for her boys (twelve and nine), and would be putting them in foster care unless she got her act together.

I would never, I thought, as Dice described leaving her boys home alone or, worse, with strangers while she wandered the streets to cop. Her hands, with the nails bitten short and bloody, trembled as she worked to extract pictures of her sons from underneath the plastic lining of her binder. "That's Dominic Junior, my little Nicky, and that's Christopher. He eats so much I can't even believe it. Like, mixin' bowls full of cereal, gallons of milk . . . I tell him we should just get a cow, let him suck on that, 'stead of using all our money on milk . . ."

Had she ever been like me and Janet, with a husband and a house, a car in the garage and money in the bank? Had she ever had a chance at that kind of life?

"Allison?"

I glanced up. Gabrielle, she of the pink lanyard and officious-bank-lady look, was staring at me. So, I noticed, were the rest of the eighteen girls and women in the circle. "Allison, are you ready to share?"

"Um." I closed my notebook, then drummed my fingertips on its cover. I had known this day was coming, but, of course, they never told you exactly when it would be your turn. I sat up straight, remembering how every Share began. "Well. Let's see. I was born in New Jersey, in 1974. I think I tried liquor for the first time at someone's bat mitzvah, when I was twelve or thirteen. We were sneaking glasses off the grown-ups' table. I had maybe a sip, and I hated the way it tasted, and that was that until I was sixteen. Um." I tilted my body back in my chair, looked up at the ceiling and noticed, without surprise, that it was stained. Everything in this place was worn and dirty, frayed and patched, like we didn't deserve anything better. "I got drunk at a party when I was sixteen. Vodka and peach schnapps, which was a thing back then. I hated the way it made me feel, and I didn't drink again until college . . . and even then, it was, like, a beer. Or maybe I'd have a few puffs of a joint."

"You're kidding," said a new girl whose name I didn't know. I could have gotten defensive, but instead, I just shrugged.

"Yeah, I know it sounds ridiculous, but it's the truth. I didn't like booze, I didn't like pot, and I didn't really try anything else because there wasn't much else around . . . oh, wait, I did do mushrooms one time, but they made me puke, so forget that." I shuddered. "I hate throwing up."

"Don't do heroin," said Lena, and everyone else laughed.

"So, flash forward, I'm thirty-four, I'm married, I have a kid, I throw my back out at my gym, and my doctor gives me Vicodin." I breathed, remembering. "And it was like that scene in *The Wizard of Oz* where everything goes from black-and-white to color. It was like that was the way the world was meant to feel." I could feel my body reacting to the memory, the blood rising to the

419

surface of my skin, my heartbeat quickening. "I was calm, I was happy, I felt like I could get more things accomplished. I started writing these blog posts, and they really took off. The pills made me brave enough to write with all those people reading. They made me patient enough to put up with my daughter, who is gorgeous and smart but can be a handful. They made me who I was supposed to be. I know that's not what I'm supposed to say in here," I said, before anyone could chide me for romanticizing my use or failing to "play the tape," "but I also know that we're supposed to be honest. And that's the God's honest truth. I loved the way I felt when I was on pills."

"So what happened?" Gabrielle prompted.

I sighed. "I just started taking too many of them. More pills, different kinds, stronger medications, and then, eventually, I wasn't taking them to feel good, I was taking them just to feel normal. I was napping all the time, and I was impatient with my daughter. I wasn't myself. I took money from a petty cash account at work and moved it into my personal account. It wasn't exactly embezzlement, but it wasn't exactly something I was supposed to be doing. And . . ." Here came the hard part. "I tried to drive while I was impaired. One of the teachers saw what was going on and took my keys away. Then my husband found out what was going on and . . ." I shrugged. By now, my look of contrition was so well-rehearsed that it felt almost natural on my face. "Here I am. Just another sick person trying to get better."

For a minute, there was silence, as the ladies contemplated my boring, bare-bones, drama-free tale. Everyone had something better—an overdose, an arrest, an intervention full of tears and accusations. The previous week one of the women, a fifth-grade teacher who'd also bought pills online, had talked about being blackmailed. The person she bought from spent an afternoon on Google, figured out where she worked and to whom she was married, and then e-mailed her to say that if she didn't pay first five hundred, then a thousand, then three thousand dollars, he'd tell her husband and her boss—and maybe even the local paper—just what she'd been up to. It had gone on for months. Linda had drained her savings account and dipped into her twelve-year-old daughter's college fund before trying to kill herself. Luckily, it hadn't worked, and now she was here . . . and as for the guy who'd tortured her, Linda said with a sad smile that her counselor had helped her fill out a form on the DEA's website. "I have no idea if they caught him," she'd said. "Probably he's still out there, shaking down other housewives."

I remembered feeling almost dizzy with relief that nothing like that had ever happened to me.

Now, with dozens of puzzled and accusatory faces staring at me, I almost wished something more catastrophic had landed me at Meadowcrest.

"That's it?" an Ashley or a Brittany murmured. I wondered if I should have talked about learning that my mom was an alcoholic . . . but where could I have fit that in?

"Hey, look, I'm sorry I don't have some big, dramatic story about almost dying, or almost killing someone, or getting in a car crash . . ."

"It's not that." I'd expected Gabrielle to be the one to push me for more details, more emotion, just more in general, but instead it was shiny-haired, tiny-voiced Aubrey, all scrunched up in the seat on my left, who was calling me out. "It's like you're telling your story, only it sounds like it happened to someone else." She squirmed as I looked at her, but she didn't back down. "Were you sad about it? When it was happening?"

"Of course I was sad!" I snapped. "God. Do you think I'd be here if I wasn't sad?"

"But you don't sound sad." Now one of the Brittanys had taken up the attack, only she didn't sound angry as much as puzzled. "You just sound, like, okay, this happened, then that happened, and then I started taking Percocet, and then I started taking Oxy . . ."

I wanted to say that progression was a central part of every other girl's story—first the booze, then the pills, then the powder, then the needle. So why was I being criticized for giving a version of the same tale everyone told?

"What about when your daughter would want you to play with her, and you'd tell her to go away?" Finally, Mary had decided to join the conversation. "How do you feel about that?"

"I feel incredibly ashamed. I hate myself for not being there for her." I mustered up all the sincerity I could—the hurt look, the shaky voice, the defeated posture acknowledging I'd committed the ultimate female transgression, the Sin of Bad Motherhood. "I feel awful about what I did. That's why I'm here. So I won't ever have to do those things again."

This announcement was met with unexpected silence. Aubrey fidgeted in her seat; an Amber retied her shoelaces. Gabrielle flipped to a fresh page in her notebook. Finally, she said, "I guess maybe Allison's story sounds different to us because she wasn't using for very long." She looked at me. "What was it, six months?"

"About that." Six months was as long as I'd been buying pills online. My actual abuse—or, if not abuse, the length of time my use had been problematic—was closer to two years.

"For most of us, there was that big wake-up call," Mary continued. "I got a DUI. Aubrey got arrested. People lost their relationships, or had their kids taken away. But just because Allison's got a high bottom . . ."

"Thank you," I murmured. High bottom. Was there a lovelier phrase in the English language?

"It doesn't mean she didn't have a bottom. Or that she's not in trouble. Or that she doesn't need our help."

"Thank you," I said again. As the next Share began—this one from a twenty-eight-year-old heroin addict from New Mexico who'd come to New Jersey as part of some kind of rehab exchange program—I returned my attention to the new lyrics to "One Day More." "One more day, then I'm in rehab . . . Gonna get drunk off my ass . . . I'll buy ev'ry pill and take it . . . plus Champagne and speed and grass." Would Melanie be able to pull off the role of Liesl, the besotted sixteen-going-on-seventeen-year-old, who we'd decided would be in love with crystal meth instead of Rolfe the Nazi messenger boy? I looked around the circle, realizing that I'd never know. If everything went the way I'd planned, I'd be in the car with Dave when the first song began. I felt a surprising amount of regret, as I looked at Mary, and Aubrey, and Shannon, and realized I'd never hear how their stories turned out. *Ellie,* I told myself sternly. Ellie was the one who mattered.

That night they turned the phones on, so that the women who were off the seven-day blackout could have their regular twice-a-week ten-minute phone call home. "Where am I picking you up?" asked Dave, who'd swallowed my story about having a day pass without a single question.

"You can just wait in the parking lot. I think I remember what the car looks like."

I waited for a laugh that did not come. "When do you need to be back?" He sounded like he was scheduling a dentist's appointment, not a reunion with his wife.

"Eight." Actually, I wasn't planning on coming back at all. I would attend Ellie's party, then ask Dave to take me for an early dinner, during which I would convince him that I'd gotten everything I could out of my rehab experience and was ready to come home. "Is Ellie excited?"

"She is. She and your mom have been making cupcakes, and paper chains."

"Paper chains?" I hadn't heard of such a thing since I was Ellie's age myself, and, certainly, they hadn't been a feature of any of the birthday parties I'd attended with her.

"Yup. We decided to have the party here instead of BouncyTime. It's always too loud there. She gets overwhelmed. And, after Jayden's party . . ." He let his voice trail off, too polite to remind me of the disaster Jayden's party had become.

"Okay," I said slowly. I was surprised that nobody had asked me, or even told me, before making this change, but my main concern was that the party was a success, and that Ellie was happy. "So did you hire a magician? That petting zoo that Chloe had? And what about favors?" Lately, the trend was for kids to burn CDs of their own party-music mixes, and hand them out in the goody bags.

"I think there's just going to be games."

"Games?" I wondered if he meant something like laser tag.

"Party games. Charades, and pin-the-tail-on-the-donkey. Like that. Your mother's really the one running the show, and it sounds like it's under control."

Charades? Paper chains and homemade cupcakes? I wasn't sure anything was under control . . . but I tried to sound cheerful as I said, "See you Saturday."

This will work, I told myself as I got ready for bed that night. As always, I was thinking of Ellie. What had she done that day? What dress had she worn? Had she eaten her dinner, or snuck it into the toilet, the way I'd caught her doing the week before I left? Were there kids she knew at the Stonefield camp? Did she like the counselors? How was my mother handling life without my dad? And what about Dave?

I couldn't bring myself to ask him the big questions: *Do you still love me? What do you tell yourself about why I'm in here? Will we still be married when I'm out?*

I refused to let myself think about it. Instead, I brushed my teeth, put on what I knew would be the first of at least two sets of pajamas (I was still waking up at midnight, or one in the morning, having completely sweated through the first pair), and, feeling clumsy and strange, got down on my knees.

"Are you there, God?" I began. "It's me, Allison. Thank you for the beautiful sunshine today. Thank you for the inspiration about the talent show. Thank you . . ." At this part, my voice got clogged with tears. "Thank you for keeping Ellie safe. For not letting me hurt her. Thank you for another day of not using." That last part struck me as completely ridiculous—how could I possibly use, even if I wanted to, in a place like this? I said it anyhow. Then I worked myself back upright, stretched, and climbed into bed.

At ten o'clock, the lights went out. For a moment, I lay in the darkness. Then Aubrey called, from the other bedroom, "Good night, Allison."

"Good night, Aubrey," I called back.

"Good night, Mary," Shannon said.

"Good night, Shannon," said Mary.

"Good night, Ashley."

"Which one?"

Giggles, then, "Ashley C."

"Good night, Marissa."

I remembered what Nicholas had told me, about how sometimes beginners substituted the group for God.

"Good night, Ashley D."

"Good night, Lena."

Could you call this love, or a Higher Power? All of us working toward the same goal, helping one another as best we could? *Something that's bigger than you, and something that's kind and forgiving,* I'd heard one of the meeting leaders say. *That's all your Higher Power has to be.* So could this be it?

I wasn't sure. I shut my eyes, rolled onto my side, and slipped into what had become my standard two hours' worth of sleep, followed by five hours of lying awake, sweating and crying in my narrow bed, waiting for the flashlight's glare to shine through the slit of a window, wondering how I'd gotten here and what my life would be like when I got out.

Twenty-Seven

By Saturday morning, you would have thought the ladies of Meadowcrest were getting ready for a wedding . . . or an actual Broadway debut. Lena was on her bedroom floor, attempting to press a pair of pants with a curling iron. Aubrey was humming scales in the bathroom, Mary was practicing "Sentimental Gurney" in the hall, and the girls I'd dubbed the Greek Chorus were singing "Dope that's so slammin' it makes your heart flutter . . . Dealers on corners and needles in gutters . . . Wax-paper Baggies all tied up with strings . . . These were a few of my favorite things." Knowing I'd be heading home, I got Aubrey to help with my hair and makeup. She plucked my eyebrows, smoothed on concealer, and used mascara to cover my gray hairs. "Thanks for doing this," she said, unwinding the Velcro curlers she'd used. "Of all the times I've been in rehab, this was the most fun." I was so touched that for one wild instant I thought about staying —directing the talent show, seeing how it all turned out. Then I thought of Ellie, gave Aubrey a hug, and said, "I'm glad I met you."

At ten o'clock, while some poor woman who'd driven in from the Pine Barrens attempted to share her experience, strength, and hope, we passed and re-passed scripts from hand to hand, making corrections, adding new jokes. By the time the announcement blared, "Ladies, please proceed to the cafeteria for afternoon Meditation," I was trembling with nerves. Sure enough, instead of the typical single, bored RC, there was Michelle . . . and Kirsten . . . and Jean and Phil, two counselors I didn't know. A half-dozen RCs were lined up by the door . . . and at the head of the line stood none other than my pal Ed McGreavey, noted heli-skier and locator of lost bottoms.

"Good morning!" he said pleasantly as we filed into the room. "Ladies," he said, as the women stared at him, then at me. "I understand you've got a performance in the works. I want to tell you, personally, how happy it makes me to see this kind of motivation!" So that was his strategy, I thought. If you can't beat 'em, join 'em . . . and act like it was your good idea all along. "We're looking forward to hearing what you've got."

I smiled as, behind me, Amanda and Samantha got into position. "Ladies and gentlemen!" I said, nodding at Ed and at the pimply RC who'd hollered at me about walking on the wrong path. "Welcome to the inaugural, one-time-only, debut performance of *The Sound of Rehab*."

Behind Amanda and Samantha, the rest of the women lined up in a half circle. Aubrey stepped to the front of the circle, twirling and twirling, before she opened her mouth and, in a very credible Julie Andrews–ish manner, began to sing, "The hills are alive . . . with the sounds of rehab . . . with songs drunks have sung . . . for a hundred years!"

I slipped to the door. "Be right back," I whipered to Mary. I was sorry to miss it, I thought as I hurried to my room, grabbed my purse, strolled past the empty desk, pushed through the double doors, and found Dave in the parking lot, behind the wheel of the Prius, right where he said he would be.

He looked at me with suspicion as I practically skipped into the passenger's seat. "Go, go, go!" I hollered, pounding the dashboard.

"You okay?"

"I'm great! It just feels so good to be getting out of here!" I could barely breathe, or hear anything, because of the thunder of my heartbeat in my ears as we pulled past the security guard's hut, but no one said a word. The gate lifted, and we were on the road, driving toward Philadelphia. Free.

"Tell me everything," I said, adjusting the seat, and then the music, looking around for coffee or candy or anything at all from the outside world.

Dave's voice was terse, his words careful. "Ellie's been doing fine. She seems to like camp, and her swimming's gotten much better. And your mother's really stepped up to the plate. She's been driving Ellie to camp in the mornings—"

"Wait. Driving? My mom?" I felt my throat start to close again, remembering her promise, that she'd never be impaired around my daughter.

"She went out and renewed her license. Passed the test on her first try."

"Wow," I said, wondering why she hadn't told me. Dave drove us along an unfamiliar two-lane road, past a farm stand selling sweet corn and tomatoes, and a small white church. "How long's the ride home?"

"Maybe half an hour."

"That's all?"

"You don't remember?" His tone betrayed little curiosity. Dave looked good, lean and broad-shouldered as ever in his worn jeans and dark-blue collared shirt. He smelled good, too, freshly showered, the bracing scent of Dial soap filling the car.

"I wasn't in great shape at the time." I stared at him, willing him to take his eyes off the road, even for just a second, and spare me a look. When he didn't, I began talking. "Dave. I know we haven't really discussed things, and we probably won't have much of a chance today, but I want you to know how sorry I am about everything."

For a long moment, he didn't answer. "Let's just focus on Ellie," he finally said, in that maddening, almost robotic tone.

"Can't you tell me anything? Give me a hint? Because, you know, if I'm going to be single, there's a trainer who comes to Meadowcrest once a week. I gotta start working on my fitness if I'm going to be back on the market."

I saw the corners of his eyes crinkle in what wasn't quite a smile, but was at least a sign that I could still amuse him. "I made mistakes, too," he said. "I knew there was something going on for a while, and I didn't try to find out what. It was just easier to let things go."

"No, no, it wasn't your fault. It was me. I thought I could handle everything . . . that the pills were helping me handle everything . . ." I reached over the gearshift for his free hand, and he let me take it, and hold it, until we left the highway. We sat in silence until Dave parked in front of our garage.

"Mommy, Mommy, MOMMY!" Ellie shrieked

once we were inside, racing into my arms, almost knocking the wind out of me. She wore a party dress with a purple sash and crinolines, her hair in a neat French braid, her feet in lace-cuffed socks and Mary Janes.

"Hi, baby girl." Oh, God, she'd gotten so much bigger. I lifted her up, burying my face in the crook of her neck, inhaling the scent of her skin. "I missed you, oh, so much."

"Why did you have to LEAVE?" She wriggled out of my arms, planted her hands on her hips, and scowled at me.

"Because I needed to get some help. Sometimes mommies need a time-out."

"Hmph." Ellie looked as if she'd heard these lines before. "Well, you're all better now, right?"

"She's getting better," said Dave. "Mommy can spend the day with you, and then I need to take her back."

Ellie's eyes filled with tears. "Why do you have to go BACK? You aren't even SICK. You look FINE."

"Remember what we talked about, Ellie?" And here was my mother. I blinked at Casual Ronnie; my mother without her lipgloss, without foundation and mascara, with her hair—I could barely believe it—pulled back in a ponytail, dressed in jeans (jeans!), with an apron (another item I'd never seen or imagined her to possess) wrapped around her waist. A pair of sneakers on her feet, where I'd only ever seen high heels or jeweled sandals, her fingernails clipped short, filed, no polish. "The doctors are taking good care of your mom, and she'll be home as soon as she's ready."

"But there is nothing WRONG with her!"

"Ellie," said Dave, "why don't you go count the apples and make sure there's enough for everyone to get one?"

Ellie gave us a darkly suspicious look before stomping off toward the dining room. "We're bobbing for apples," she called over her shoulder.

"Isn't that more of a Halloween thing?" I looked around, with a feeling of dread gathering in the pit of my stomach. There was an old-school portrait of a donkey taped to the dining-room wall, along with a metal bin full of water with a bowl full of apples beside it.

"I thought we'd play party games," my mother said.

"Party games," I repeated. It didn't sound like an awful idea, and maybe it wasn't, unless you knew that these days, in our neighborhood, a typical six-year-old's birthday party might include an outing to the local bowling alley, where the lanes were equipped with bumpers and at least some of the snacks would be gluten-free, or a scavenger hunt at the Franklin Institute in Philadelphia, followed by a make-your-own-sundae bar.

I followed Ellie into the dining room and found

her sitting in the corner with an apple in her hand. "Hey, El," I said, and began to sing. " 'I did not live until today . . . how can I live when we are parted?' "

" 'Tomorrow you'll be worlds away,' " she sang, eyes wide, one hand over her heart, teenage Cosette falling in love. " 'And yet with you my world has started.' "

" 'One more day out on my own,' " I sang. " 'One more day with him not caring.' " I tried not to look at Dave, who was standing in the kitchen with his back to me as Ellie sang, " 'I was born to be with you!' " She stretched out her arms and I lifted her up, holding her against me, singing, " 'What a life I might have known.' " I tickled her ribs and she wrapped her arms around my neck, cheeks pink, a picture of delight. " 'But he never saw me there.' " I peeked over her head. Dave was watching us—maybe, I hoped, preparing to launch into the Valjean/Javert section—but before he could start a car pulled up the driveway and Hank emerged from the backseat.

"MY PARTY FRIENDS ARE HERE!" Ellie shrieked, vaulting out of my arms and hitting the ground at a sprint. I got one last whiff of her scent, a final instance of the sweetness of her skin against mine. Then she was gone.

"Happy birthday, Ellie," Hank said shyly, wiping his nose and handing my daughter an enormous, elaborately wrapped box with pink-

and-white-striped wrapping paper and pink-and-silver ribbons.

"Wow," I said as Mrs. Hank smiled indulgently at her son. She wore dark glasses, skinny jeans, and a silky sleeveless top. "Looks like someone blew his allowance."

"He's in love," Mrs. Hank affirmed, leaning over to offer her smooth cheek for the pro forma air kiss. "Meanwhile, you! You look amazing!" She eyed me up and down. I tried not to flinch under her scrutiny and wondered exactly what she was seeing. I had Aubrey's work in my favor, but my clothing options weren't great. I was wearing the best of the limited choices Dave had given me, which meant jeans that were too loose and a T-shirt that was too casual to look right underneath Shannon's cardigan. The good news was that I'd been taking every yoga class Meadowcrest offered, plus walking around the track with Shannon and Aubrey. That, and the sunshine, and the water I'd been drinking, and the absence of drugs meant that my skin was tanned and clear, and my eyes were bright.

"Amazing," Mrs. Hank repeated. I wished I could remember her first name. It was Carol, or Kara, something in that family. We'd had coffee together, and chatted at PTA meetings, with most of our conversations revolving around Hank's allergies and Ellie's sensitivities. "Are you doing a cleanse?"

"Something like that," I said.

"Allison?"

My mom called me into the kitchen, where she stood with a tray of cupcakes in her hands. Homemade. Oh, dear. Ellie had probably told her cupcakes but had failed to tell her to get them at Sweet Sue's. Their cupcakes were incredible, dense and rich, topped with swirls of icing in flavors you could never hope to duplicate at home, dulce de leche and salted caramel and panna cotta. My mother had baked treats that I bet came from a box, with frosting I was certain came from a can. I wondered how that conversation had gone, with Ellie telling my mom about the bakery and my mother somehow convincing her that baking from scratch would be better and more fun.

"Can you help me with the punch?" my mom asked.

Punch. I didn't say a word as I poured ginger ale over a block of melting sherbet in the cut-crystal punch bowl Dave and I had gotten for our wedding and, if I remembered right, had never used. My mother's transformation was astonishing. She was exuding the kind of quiet confidence I couldn't remember from my own childhood, when she'd been either brisk and brittle, rushing me out of rooms, or as giggly and giddy as a young girl, waiting for my father to come home.

"This is some affair," I said, as she arranged the cupcakes next to the punch bowl.

"Ellie and I planned it together. She helped me bake the cupcakes, and we went online and found all the party games. We downloaded the donkey!" My mother seemed very pleased with her achievement.

"That's great!" For a minute, I wanted to tell her about the talent show, and I felt a pang of unhappiness as I realized it was probably over by now.

"How are you feeling?" My mother's eyes were on the cupcakes as she waited for my answer.

"Physically, I'm okay. Mentally . . ." I sighed. I couldn't think of how to explain what I was feeling. Most days, I barely knew myself.

Mrs. Hank came breezing into the kitchen, along with a few other mothers whose names, thankfully, I knew. Holly Harper was Amelia's mom, and Susan van der Meer belonged with Sadie. "How can we help?"

My mom picked up Mason jars filled with marshmallows and penny candy and carried them into the dining room. Mrs. Hank turned to me with a conspiratorial look on her face. "Listen," she said, "we promise we won't tell a soul." I felt the muscles in my torso clench. Somebody knew. Somebody knew, someone had found out, someone had told, and now all the moms knew exactly what was wrong with me . . . and they wanted details.

"But here's the thing," Mrs. Hank continued.

"My high-school reunion's coming up, and Holly's got an—"

"Anniversary," said Holly. "And it was Jeff's big idea to go back to Hawaii. He's got this picture of me from twenty years ago in a bikini, and then he went online and actually found the goddamn thing on eBay—I should have known he was up to something when he asked what size I wore, and of course I lied, because, seriously, like I'm going to tell him the truth?"

Laughter all around. I laughed, too, and wondered how fast they'd grab their little darlings and dash out of my house if I told them what I'd been lying to my husband about.

"Just tell us," Carol/Kara whispered. "If it's a trainer . . . or one of the food-delivery things . . ."

"Oh, guys, really. I wish it was some big secret. But I just haven't been that hungry lately."

There was a beat of incredulous silence while the three of them just stared at me. Holly Harper started laughing first, and then the other two joined in.

"Oh! Good one!" said Kara/Carol. She mimed wiping tears from the smooth skin beneath her eyes. "Okay, seriously. Is it a juice fast?"

I opened my mouth to provide another jokey denial, and for a single terrifying instant I was sure that what would tumble from my lips would be the truth, the tale of what had really happened, possibly in the rhyming lyrics of one of the talent-

439

show songs: *Vicodin, and lots of them! OxyContin, pots of them! Chewing pills up by the peck . . . Allison was bound to wreck!*

"Allison?" My knees trembled in relief as Janet came into the room, a wrapped gift box in her hands. By the time she crossed the kitchen she'd assessed the situation, setting down her gift and grabbing me in a hug. "How are you?"

"She's thin," said Susan van der Meer, in a tone just short of accusatory.

Janet kept one arm around me as she turned to face my interrogators. "Her dad's been sick," she said. "Allison and her mom had to move him into assisted living a few weeks ago."

I saw surprise on their faces, heard sympathetic murmurs. "Oh, I'm so sorry," said Susan, and Holly said, "Isn't it the worst? We went through it last year, after Jeff's mom had an aneurysm."

"Excuse me for a minute," I said. I made myself breathe until the dizziness went away, then led Janet up the stairs and down the hall to my bedroom. She closed the door behind us, then looked me up and down.

"Okay, you look . . ."

"Thin!" I said, and started making some shrill noises that approximated laughter. "I'm thin, can you believe it! What's my secret? Do you think I should tell them, or would they just fall over dead from the shock?" I sank down on the bed and put my face in my hands. "I went rogue," I confessed.

"Wait, what?" Janet ducked into my bathroom. I heard drawers and cabinets opening and closing. A minute later, she came out with her hands filled with concealer, brushes, my flat iron, and a comb.

"I don't actually have a day pass. They told me I couldn't go. It was some big red-tape night-mare. I was supposed to have a certain number of sessions with my counselor, only they didn't even assign me a counselor until I'd been there almost a week, and then she left, and they weren't going to let me leave . . ."

"Okay. Deep breath. You made it. You're here now. Want some water?"

Downstairs, I could hear the door opening, and my mother, suddenly transformed into the gracious lady of the manor, greeting Ellie's other grand-mother, Doreen. If I'd stayed at Meadowcrest, if I'd gone to the talent show, then to Circle and to Share, the party would have gone off without a hitch. I wasn't indispensable. I wasn't even sure Ellie would have missed me.

"We should go downstairs."

"Here. Wait." Gently, Janet dabbed a sponge dipped in foundation on my cheeks and chin. She tapped powder onto a brush and swiped lipstick onto my lips, either undoing or redoing Aubrey's work. "When are you getting out?"

As I started to explain the logistics, there was a knock on the door.

"Allison?" called Dave. "We're going to get started."

All through the afternoon, through the games, through the cupcakes and ice cream and the inevitable gluten-free versions that the allergic and intolerant kids' mothers had sent, I felt like a fake, like this was a show someone else had written, and I'd been assigned the role of wife and mother. And, louder and louder, like something out of an Edgar Allan Poe short story, I could hear a voice whispering, *Pills*. While I negotiated the rest of the night with Dave, assuring him that I was free until eight o'clock, pleading with him to take me to Han Dynasty for dinner "so I can eat something that tastes like something" before he sent me back, I thought, *Pills*. Handing out the goody bags, packed with candy necklaces my mom and Ellie had strung and handwritten notes that read "Thank You for Coming to My Party," I thought, *Pills, pills, where am I going to find pills?*

The plan, which Dave reluctantly agreed to, was to drive Ellie to Hank's house for dinner with Hank's family. My mom would get a break, Dave would take me out for Chinese food, we'd have our talk, and then, depending on how the talk went, either he'd drive me back to Meadowcrest or I'd convince him that I could come home.

By the time Dave, Ellie, and I got to Hank's house, I could almost taste the familiar, delectable bitterness on my tongue. I got out of the car as soon as it stopped, led Ellie inside, and asked Mrs. Hank—her name, I finally remembered, was not Kara or Carol but Danielle—if I could borrow a tampon. She waved toward her staircase. "Master bathroom. Everything's in the cabinet under the sink."

Up in the bathroom, I locked the door, put a tampon in my pocket, then opened the medicine cabinet above the sink. Beside the half-used bottles of antibiotics and Advil and Tylenol PM, there were Percocet, five and ten milligrams, both with refills, and an unopened, unexpired bottle of thirty-milligram OxyContin, prescribed for Hank's father.

"Mommy!" I heard Ellie yell from downstairs.

"Hang on!" I called back, and began opening the bottles, shaking a few pills into my palms, stashing them in the pockets of my jeans.

"Mommy?" Ellie sounded like she was right outside the bathroom door. For once, she wasn't yelling.

"Just—" *Hang on,* I was about to say, when I caught sight of myself in the mirror. My eyes were enormous and frantic. My face was pale, except for two blotches of red high on my cheeks. I looked like a thief, like a junkie, like Brittany B., who'd come to Meadowcrest from jail after she and her boyfriend had robbed the local Rite-Aid . . . and all I could think of, all that

I wanted, was for Eloise to go away, to go to Hank's room or the playroom or the basement or the backyard, anywhere that I could have five minutes and get myself a little peace.

What happens if you get caught? a voice in my head whispered. It seemed like a crazy thought—there had to be dozens of bottles in here, all of them (I'd checked) with refills on the labels. No way would Mrs. Hank miss a few pills, if I selected judiciously. There'd be more than enough to carry me through rehab, if I decided to return, or through my first few days home.

And then what? my mind persisted. Then I'd have to go back to my old rounds, my old sources, days of counting pills, worrying and wondering if I had enough . . . and, if I didn't, how I'd get more.

"Mommy?" Ellie sounded like she was crying. "I am sorry if I am a bother."

"What?" I sank down to the floor, my ear pressed against the door, a bottle of Percocet still in my hand.

"If that's why you went away. Because I am a bother."

It felt like a knife in my heart. "Oh, El. Oh, honey, no. You're not a bother to me. I love you! I'll . . . just give me a minute, I'll be out in a minute, and we can talk, I'll explain about every-thing . . ."

I put the first pill under my tongue and got that first blast of bitterness. Then it hit me. This was it:

the moment they talked about in those stupid AA handouts and alluded to with those mealy-mouthed slogans, delivered with an earnestness suggesting they had been freshly minted in that moment. *Half-measures availed us nothing. We stood at the turning point. One is too many and a thousand is never enough.* It didn't matter that my turning point didn't involve turning a trick in the back of a car, or looting my parents' retirement fund, or sticking a needle in my arm. This was it. My hand in a stranger's medicine cabinet, my little girl on the other side of a locked door, needing a mother who only wanted her to go away. *Congratulations, Allison Rose Weiss. You've finally made it all the way down.*

I spat the pill out into my hand, then flushed it down the toilet. I put the pills back in the bottles. I put the bottles back in the cabinet. I sprayed about half a bottle's worth of air freshener, in case it turned out Mrs. Hank had a suspicious mind.

Outside the door, Ellie was standing with her hands in her pockets, pale-faced, in her pretty party dress, the one we'd picked out online the month before, with her sitting on my lap and me scrolling through the pages, still struggling with her "th" sound, her little finger pointing, "I will have lis one, and lat one, and lis one," and me saying, "No, honey, just pick your favorite," and her turning to me, eyes brimming, saying, "But they are ALL OF THEM MY FAVORITE."

I bent down and lifted her in my arms.

"Do you need to take a nap now?" she asked. "I will be quiet."

If anyone ever asked me what it felt like the instant my heart broke, I would tell them how I felt, hearing that.

"No. No nap. I'm okay." And I was. At least physically. Sure, I wanted the pills so bad that I was shaking. I could still taste that delectable bitterness in the back of my throat, could already feel the phantom calm and comfort as my shoulders unclenched and my heartbeat slowed, but I could get through it, minute by minute, second by second, if I had to. Even though I suspected I would remember that bliss, and crave it, for the rest of my life.

I took Ellie downstairs to play with Hank. Dave was in the kitchen, talking about the Eagles' dubious fortunes with Mr. Hank. "Honey, can I talk to you for a minute?"

I took him by the forearm, walked him out to the driveway, and told him the truth, watching my words register on his face—his wrinkled forehead, his mouth slowly falling open. "You did what?" Before I could start to explain my talent-show exit strategy again, he said, "No. You know what? Never mind." His hand was on his phone. I turned away, my eyes brimming. I wanted to ask if I got any credit for honesty, if it meant any-thing to him that I'd told the truth, however belatedly . . . but, before I could ask, he was connected to Meadowcrest.

"Yes . . . no, I don't know who I need to speak with . . . I thought my wife had a day pass, but now she's telling me she didn't . . . Allison W. . . . Yes, I'll hold."

While he was holding, I went back into the Hanks' house. Ellie was engrossed in a game of Wii bowling. "I'll be home soon," I whispered. She barely spared me a hug. Mrs. Hank—Danielle—was in the kitchen. "Thanks for taking her," I said. "I wonder if you could be extra nice to her for the next little while . . ."

"Are you going away again?" Danielle asked. She wasn't my friend, but, at that moment, I wished she was.

"Yes. I actually . . ." *I'm going back to rehab,* I almost said. It was right there, the words lined up all in a row, but I wasn't sure if that was oversharing, or asking for sympathy where I didn't deserve any. "A work thing," I finally concluded.

"Well, don't worry. Your mother's a rock star. And Ellie is always welcome here."

I thanked her. Dave was already behind the wheel when I got back outside. "Are they letting me come back?" I whispered.

He backed out of the driveway. "At first someone named Michelle wanted me to call a facility in Mississippi that treats dual-diagnosis

447

patients. That's when you're an addict with mental illness."

I gave a mirthless giggle. "Does Michelle know I'm Jewish? I might be crazy, but there's no way I'm going to Mississippi."

"Eventually, they said you could come back. No guarantees about staying. Someone named Nicholas is going to be waiting for you."

Nicholas. I shut my eyes. Then I made myself open them again. "Do you want to talk about . . . anything?"

I could see his knuckles, tight on the wheel, the jut of his jaw as he ground his back teeth. "Honestly? Right now, no. I don't." We drove for a minute, me sitting there clutching my purse handles hard, Dave's face set, until he burst out, "When are you going to stop lying?"

"Now," I said immediately. "I'm done with . . . with that. With all of it. I don't want to be that kind of person. Or that kind of mom, or that kind of wife."

Dave said nothing. I didn't expect a response. I'd been honest, but, of course, what else would a liar say, except *I'm done with lying* and *I'm done with using* and *I don't want to be that way anymore?* It was classic I-got-busted talk . . . and part of accepting life on life's terms, the way they told us we had to, meant living with the knowledge that maybe he'd never be able to trust me again.

I sat in silence, the way I had during my first trip to Meadowcrest. Dave pulled up in front of the main building and sat there, the car in park, the engine still running. I'd had half an hour to think of what to say, but all I could manage was "Thank you for the ride." I got out of the car, walked past the nice-desk receptionist, back beyond the RESIDENTS ONLY PAST THIS POINT sign, to the shabby hallway with its smell of cafeteria food and disinfectant. I left my purse in my empty bedroom, looped my nametag around my neck, and took the women's path to Nicholas's office, where, as promised, he was waiting for me.

"Allison W.," he said. His voice was so kind.

I sat in front of his desk and bent my head. Then I said the words I'd already said, in Group and Share and the AA meetings, where I'd sat off to the side and scribbled lyrics in my notebook. "I think I'm really in trouble," I whispered. "I think I'm an addict. I need help."

"Okay," he said. His hand on my shoulder was gentle. "The good news is, you've come to the right place."

PART FOUR

The Promises

Twenty-Eight

"How about these clementines?" The clerk at the Whole Foods on South Street—a white guy of maybe twenty with mild blue eyes, a wide, untroubled brow, and dreadlocks down to his waist—gave me a gentle, *Namaste* kind of smile. He spoke softly and slowly, with great deliberation. It was maddening. This guy wouldn't have lasted a day in the suburbs, but in Center City, where the Whole Foods was next to a yoga studio, infuriating slowness was the rule. "Should we leave them in the box? Or take them out of the box and put the fruit in a bag?"

"Fruit in a bag, please." I was only buying a dozen things—a turkey breast to grill for dinner, the miniature oranges that Ellie loved in her school lunches, a twenty-dollar maple-scented candle that was way too expensive but that I'd found impossible to resist—but I could already tell that I was going to be checking out for a while. *Use it as a chance to practice patience,* Bernice's voice said in my head. When I'd left Meadowcrest, I'd joined Bernice's outpatient group, and her voice had taken up residence in my brain. I tried not to sigh, and actually managed a smile as the clerk first rummaged in his drawer, then patted down his pockets, and finally called over a manager, who called over a second manager, who located a pair of scissors to snip through the netting.

"Oh, dear. It looks like a few of these are moldy," said the clerk as the miniature oranges tumbled from their wooden crate into a plastic bag.

"Mommy, I do not want MOLDY CLEMEN-TINES," Ellie announced.

"Do you want to get another box?" the clerk asked. Behind me, the woman with the Phil&Teds stroller and the black woolen peacoat gave a small but audible groan. *Send her peace.* That wasn't Bernice; that was the voice of my new yoga instructor, Loyal. *Peace,* I thought. Old Allison would have scoffed at the dopey sayings, at the idea that the checkout line at the super-market offered a chance to practice anything at all (not to mention at the notion of someone named Loyal). New Allison took advice wherever she could get it—at meetings, from magazines, from Oprah's Super Soul Sundays, and from Celestial Seasonings tea bags.

"That's okay," I told the clerk. "How about just separate out the moldy ones? You can toss those, and we'll take the good ones home."

He looked at me, concern furrowing his brow. "Are you sure? You can just go get another box. It's no trouble at all."

"It's fine."

"Ooookay." Clearly, it might have been fine for me, but it was deeply troubling for him. "Now, how about the turkey? Would you like that in a separate bag?"

"Please." I held up the shopping bags I'd brought. The clerk blinked, like he'd never seen or imagined such a thing.

"So . . . use that one?"

"Oh my God," murmured the woman in the peacoat. Ellie, meanwhile, had crouched down, the better to inspect the beeswax lip balms.

"Mommy, is this MAKEUP?"

"Kind of. Not exactly."

"Well, can I HAVE it?"

"No, honey, we have stuff like that at home. You can use what we've got. We'll shop the closet!"

"But that will have your SPITTY STUFF ALL OVER IT!"

I squatted down, feeling my body protest. My hips creaked; my back twinged. I'd done an hour of hot yoga that morning and had a run planned for tomorrow. *How'd you do it?* they asked in AA and NA meetings, when you went up front to collect your chip—for your first twenty-four hours of sobriety, then for thirty days, sixty days, ninety days, six months, nine months, a year, and on from there. *One day at a time* was the rote answer, the line you had to say, but each time I'd collected a chip I'd made sure to say that exercise was part of my recovery. It was a chance to get completely out of my head, forty minutes when all I could do was take the next step, find the next pose, manage the next inhalation. No matter how crappy or sad I felt, how locked in my own head, in my own unhappy run of thoughts, I would force myself up and out of bed, into the clothes I'd laid out the night before, and I would make myself go through my paces like I was swallowing a dose of some noxious medicine that I knew it was critical to get down.

Some mornings Ellie would join me for a walk down Pine Street, all the way to the Delaware River, or we'd do workout routines in the basement of the row house where I'd rented an apartment back in Philadelphia. Dave had found his own place, just a few blocks away. He'd kept the fancy treadmill; I'd found one on Craigslist, along with hand weights and a step bench. Together, Ellie and I had downloaded free fitness videos, and gotten various ten-, fifteen-, and twenty-minute workouts from magazines. We would do jump squats and mountain climbers. We'd lunge our way back and forth across the basement, and do planks and push-ups, V-sits and donkey kicks, all while playing word games. I'd start with a letter of the alphabet; Ellie would give me a classmate at her new public school whose name began with that letter . . . and then, typically, a rundown as to why she didn't like that particular kid. ("D is for Dylan, who is nice sometimes but would not let me have the window seat on the bus when we went to the art museum.")

In the grocery store, I looked Ellie in the eye. "Ellie. Remember how we talked about using a respectful inside voice?"

She pursed her lips. "Yes, except I wanted a COOKIE and you said NO COOKIE."

"I said no cookie until after dinner."

"And now I want lipstick and you are saying NO and ALL YOU EVER SAY IS NO."

"Oh, honey." I held my arms open. After a minute, Ellie let me hug her. "I know things feel hard sometimes. But there's good stuff, too."

"Ma'am?"

I straightened up. The clerk was holding my maple candle and the jug of on-sale moisturizer I'd selected. "Do you want your non-food items in a separate bag?"

"Sure," I said, and gave him a smile.

"You," said the peacoat woman, "are a saint."

I smiled at her. "Believe me, I'm not." She was maybe five years younger than I was, her hair bundled in a careless ponytail at the nape of her neck, a diamond sparkling on her left hand. I wondered, as I always did when I met strangers these days, whether she was one of them or one of us; one of the earthlings, who could take or leave a glass of wine, or a joint, or a Vicodin or an Oxy; or one of the Martians, for whom, as the Basic Text said, *one was too many and a thousand was never enough*. You never can tell, Bernice said, and, from the people in my group, I knew it was true—pass any one of them on the street, and you'd have no idea that they were drunks and druggies. Well, maybe you'd guess about Brian, who had the word THUG tattooed on the fingers of his right hand, and LIFE on the fingers of his left. But you'd never guess about Jeannie, a lawyer, who came to meetings in smart suits and leather boots, and who'd lost her license after blacking out and plowing her car into a statue of George Washington on New Year's Day. Gregory looked like your run-of-the-mill fabulous gay guy, in his gorgeous made-to-measure shirts and hand-sewn shoes. Maybe you'd think that he liked to party on weekends, but you'd never imagine that he'd done three years in prison for drug trafficking. I wondered how I looked—to the clerk, now ringing up my yogurt in slow motion, to the young mother behind me, pushing her stroller back and forth in angry little jerks. Probably no different from the rest of the earthlings, with my hair in a bun, in my workout pants and zippered black sweatshirt. I still wore my wedding ring, and Dave still wore his. We'd never discussed it, which meant I didn't know whether I was wearing the platinum band out of hope or nostalgia or just so creepy guys in the dairy aisle wouldn't ask me for help in picking out heavy cream.

"Ma'am?" After what felt like another five

minutes' worth of wrangling—debit or credit? Cash back? Tens or twenties?—I gave Ellie the little bag with the candle and the moisturizer and slung the bigger one over my shoulder, along with my purse, and the two of us walked onto South Street. I'd drop her off with Dave, then go to the five-thirty meeting of what had become my home group, the AA meeting I attended every week. He'd grill the turkey, I'd make rice and asparagus to go with it when I got back, and the three of us would share dinner together before Ellie and I went home.

No big changes for the first year was what they told us at Meadowcrest, but Dave and I had had to downsize, moving to modest apartments in the city and putting the big house on the market, especially after it became clear that my job, at least for the first little while, would be staying sober, with blogging a very distant second. I had struggled with it mightily, complaining to Bernice that there was no box on the tax return that read "not taking pills."

"I hate that this is what I do," I told her and the other seven members of my outpatient group, the one I attended four mornings a week, two hours at a time. I was desperate for my world to return to the way it had been before I'd gone to rehab, before I'd started with the pills. "I want my life back. Does anyone else get that?" Fabulous Gregory had nodded. Brian had grunted. Jeannie had shrugged and said that her pre-sobriety life hadn't been all that great.

"Tell us what you mean," Bernice prompted.

"I mean," I said, "I wake up. I take Ellie to school. I get some exercise. I come here for two hours. I go to AA meetings for another hour or two, and I don't take pills, and I don't take pills, and I don't take pills." I raised my hands, empty palms held open to the ceiling. "And that's it. God, can you imagine if I had a college reunion coming up? 'What are you up to these days, Allison?' 'Well, I don't take pills.' 'And . . . that's it?' 'Yeah, it's pretty much a full-time gig.' "

"Why you so worried 'bout what other people gonna think?" Bernice could switch in and out of ghetto vernacular—or what she referred to as "the colorful patois of my youth"—with ease. When she was talking to me, she'd alternate between her brassiest round-the-way tones and her most overeducated and multisyllabic. "You really worried about what the tax man's gonna think? Or some made-up person at some college reunion you don't even have coming up?"

"I don't know," I muttered. "I just feel useless."

"Useless," said Bernice, "is better than using. And if you use . . ."

"You die," the group chanted. I hung my head. I still wasn't entirely convinced this was true, but I'd heard it enough, and seen enough evidence, to at least be open to the possibility. There would be no one more pill or just one drink for me. That way lay madness . . . or jails, institutions, and death, as the Basic Text liked to say.

The night of Ellie's birthday party, when I'd gone back to Meadowcrest, I was humbled. More than that, I was scared. In that moment, in the bathroom, I'd seen a version of my life unfolding, a path where I faked and glad-handed my way through the rest of the twenty-eight days, and then went home and picked up my addiction right where I'd put it down. Soon, of course, the pills would get too expensive, and, probably, I'd be making less money, assuming I'd be able to work at all. Maybe it would take years, maybe just months, but, eventually, I would do what all the women I'd met had done, and trade the pricy Vicodin and Percocet and Oxy for heroin, which gave you twice the high at a quarter of the cost. I pictured myself dropping Ellie off at Stonefield in the morning, then driving my Prius to the Badlands, where even a straight white lady like me could buy whatever she wanted. *Philadelphia Magazine* had done a special report on the city's ten worst drug corners and, of course, I had firsthand recommendations from the various Ashleys and Brittanys. And maybe I'd get away with it, for a little while. Or maybe I'd get into a car accident with a thousand dollars' worth of H stuffed in my bra, like one of the Meadowcrest girls. Or I'd get arrested, dragged off to jail, and left to kick on a concrete floor with nothing but Tylenol 3, like an Amber had told us all about.

Dave would divorce me—that part, of course, was nonnegotiable. Worse, I would lose Ellie. In a few years' time . . . well. *You know how they say you never see any baby pigeons?* I remembered Lena asking in group one day. *You know what else you never see's an old lady heroin addict. Or,* Shannon had added, *one with kids.*

Back in my room, my *Big Book* was still open on my desk and my clothes were still in the dresser. "Ohmygod, where *were* you?" Aubrey demanded as she stormed into my bedroom, followed by Lena, who was still wearing the mascara mustache she'd donned to appear in our play. "We were so worried," said Mary. She twisted her eyeglass chain. "The RCs wouldn't tell us anything, but they were all on their walkie-talkies, and they made us all sit in the lounge and watch *28 Days* again. They thought you ran away!"

"I did," I confessed. Sitting cross-legged on my bed, the expectant faces of the women who'd become my friends around me, I couldn't remember ever feeling so scared. Admitting you had a problem was the first step—everyone knew that—but admitting you had a problem also left you open to the possibility that maybe you couldn't fix it. "I got Dave to pick me up, and I went to Ellie's birthday party, and we dropped her off at her friend's house, and I was in the bathroom, and I looked in the medicine cabinet, and I was thinking, *Please let there be something in here,* and then . . ." Shannon took my hand in hers.

"What is wrong with me?" I cried. "What's wrong with me that I can be at my daughter's birthday party, having a perfectly nice time, and the only thing I can think about is where am I going to get pills?"

Lena made a face. Mary patted my shoulder. But it was little Aubrey who spoke up. "What's wrong with you is what's wrong with all of us," she said. "We're sick people . . ."

". . . getting better," the room chorused.

Nicholas wanted me to stay at Meadowcrest for ninety days. Horrified at the thought of being away from Ellie for so long, I'd bargained him down to sixty. I threw myself into the work, the meetings, the lectures, the role-playing assignments, the making of posters, the writing of book reports, knowing that I was safe at Meadowcrest. I couldn't get pills, even if I wanted them. The world would be a different story.

A week before my discharge, Dave came to a family session. I was so nervous that I hadn't been able to eat anything the day before. "What's the worst thing that could happen?" Kirsten asked me, but I couldn't bring myself to tell her. The worst thing was that he'd show up with papers, or a lawyer's name; that he'd tell me he didn't know if he'd ever be able to trust me again and that he didn't want to stay married. I'd gone into the meeting prepared for that, so it was actually a relief when Dave sat there, stone-faced, and ran down the list of my lies, my failings, my fuckups and betrayals—the money I'd blown on pills, the way I'd put my job, my health, and my safety at risk, and worst of all, the way I'd put Ellie in danger. "It's the lying," he'd said, in a soft, toneless voice. "That's what I can't get over. She had this whole secret life. I don't even know who she is anymore."

I didn't even try to defend myself, to point out the ways he'd let me down and made it hard to tell him the truth about how I was feeling. I'd been warned about what was known in the AA rooms as cross-talk. I couldn't argue, or bring up L. McIntyre, or talk about how he used marathon training as an excuse to literally run away from his wife and his daughter. I couldn't do anything but sit there and stare at my hands and try not to cry when Kirsten asked if he thought our marriage was irreparably damaged and listen to him sigh and then, slowly, say, "I don't know."

After sixty days, most of the women who'd been there when I arrived had gone. Mary had left early, after her husband developed a bladder infection and her kids couldn't manage it—and him—without her. Aubrey's insurance had cut her off after twenty-eight days. When her parents and her boyfriend all declined to come get her, Meadowcrest had gotten her a bus ticket back to Center City. Lena and Marissa and Shannon had all gone and been replaced by a fresh crop of Ashleys and Brittanys and Ambers and Caitlyns. Addicts, it seemed, were a renewable resource. The world made more of us every day.

By nine o'clock on my discharge day, I was standing in the reception room with my bags neatly packed. By noon, I was in a meeting in a church on Pine Street. *Hi, my name is Allison, and I'm an addict. Hi, Allison, welcome,* the room chorused back. At three, I was in Bernice's office in Cherry Hill. Technically, it was an intake evaluation, during which she'd determine whether I was an appropriate addition to her intensive outpatient group, the just-out-of-rehab folks whose therapists had determined they were ready to live in the world again. "One thing we gon' do right this minute," she'd said, and spun her big push-button telephone around on her desk until it faced me. While she watched, I called every one of my doctors who'd ever prescribed me anything stronger than an aspirin, and told them what had happened and where I'd been.

Some of them had been brusque and businesslike about it. Dr. Andi had practically been in tears. "Oh, God, Allison. Was this my fault? Was this going on and I didn't see it?"

"Don't blame yourself," I told her as Bernice listened on speakerphone. "I was playing you. I was good at it, too. Just . . . if I ever call you in the middle of the night and tell you I'm in agony . . ."

"Nothing!" said Dr. Andi, laughing. "Not even a hot water bottle!"

"Now go and do the next right thing," Bernice told me. I'd left her office feeling rattled and dazed. No more pills. Not unless I went back online or I found new doctors, convinced them I was in trouble, got them to give me what I needed . . . I shook my head, raised my shoulders, and quickened my pace along the street. No more. That part of my life was over. I had a daughter who needed me, I had a life to live, and I was determined to be clearheaded for all of it.

My determination lasted exactly twenty-three days. Looking back, I was trying to do too much, too fast, to have it all be normal again. Then, at ten o'clock one night, after a day of outpatient therapy and meetings and Monopoly with Ellie, I found myself thinking, *Would just one glass of wine be so bad?* Just a glass of red, like a million other women were probably sipping at that very moment, a little something to ease me, to calm me, to send me off to sleep?

I had the glass in one hand and the bottle— leftover Manischewitz from some Passover seder—in the other. Even though I'd never been a drinker, I could taste the kosher wine, sweet as syrup on my tongue, warming me, calming me as it went down.

I don't know where I found the strength—if that's what it was—to put down the bottle and pick up what people in meetings called the thousand-pound telephone. I called Sheila, a big, tall home health aide from my IOP group who'd been addicted to crack and who called me, and all the other women in the group who were under the age of fifty, baby girl. "SheilaIwanttodrink," I blurted before I'd even said "hello," or my name.

"Who this?" she asked, laughing. "Which white girl calling me 'bout wanting a drank?" *Drank* was how she said it, and the delicious silliness of it made me laugh.

"It's Allison. The Jewish one."

"Ooh, Allison, with that pretty little baby, callin' me 'bout wanting to drink. You're not even a drinker, right?"

"No," I said. "Pills. But you can't buy them on the corner."

"Not in your neighborhood, I guess," she said, and cackled. "So what you want," she said, suddenly serious, "that glass of wine or your baby? Because you know it is never just one glass of wine. Not for us. And you know where it ends, right?"

"I know," I said. I was gripping the phone tight, tight, tight. Tears were coursing down my cheeks. They'd told us that in rehab, and in group: we had given up the right to drink or take drugs like normal people. No Champagne toasts at weddings, no Vicodin after we had our teeth pulled. And what did we get in return for that sacrifice? Our lives back. Not just returned, but improved. Bernice closed every session with the Promises: "If we are painstaking about this phase of our development, we will be amazed before we are halfway through. We are going to know a new freedom and a new happiness. We will not regret the past nor wish to shut the door on it. We will comprehend the word 'serenity' and we will know peace. No matter how far down the scale we have gone, we will see how our experience can benefit others. That feeling of uselessness and self-pity will disappear. We will lose interest in selfish things and gain interest in our fellows. Self-seeking will slip away. Our whole attitude and outlook upon life will change. Fear of people and of economic insecurity will leave us. We will intuitively know how to handle situations which used to baffle us. We will suddenly realize that God is doing for us what we could not do for ourselves."

To me, it sounded like bullshit . . . maybe because I was still clinging, hard, to the notion that my life had been pretty much okay, or that I'd pulled out of my tailspin before things had gotten really bad. I didn't want better; I just wanted what I'd had before it all got so crazy, before we moved to Haverford, back when it had been the three of us in the row house in Center City. This was a point about which Bernice and I disagreed. "Don't you quit before the miracle happens," she would tell me. "I want you to experience everything this program has to offer. There's a new life out there for you, and it's better than any life you could ever have imagined. I want you to have that new life."

"Okay," I would tell her, and she'd tell me to keep doing the next right thing, and the next right thing, and the next right thing after that, and that "God" stood for Good Orderly Direction and "Fear" stood for Face Everything and Recover. All those silly sayings, those stupid platitudes, the ones I'd scoffed and rolled my eyes at. Now I wrote them down, I memorized them, I printed them out in pretty fonts and stuck them on my computer monitor, on my bathroom mirror, on my refrigerator door, and recited them to myself while I waited in supermarket lines.

In the mornings, before I put on my exercise clothes, I rolled out of bed, onto my knees, and prayed, even though I felt stupid, like an imposter, like someone acting out the idea of prayer instead of actually doing it. *Dear God,* I would think. After months and months of hearing the phrase "God of our understanding," of listening to people refer to "my Higher Power, whom I choose to call Goddess," or "Nature," I still couldn't come up with any image of God except the old tried-and-true: an ancient dude with a long white beard and a stern look on his face. *Thank you for helping me stay sober another day. Thank you for not letting me hurt Ellie, or myself, or anyone else, while I was using.* I'd run down my list, thanking God for central air-conditioning when it was hot out and my space heater when it was cold, for a favorite sweater, a comfortable pair of boots, a peaceful few minutes with my daughter.

I thanked God for my mother, who'd moved into a posh fifty-five-and-over community near Eastwood, near my dad. She'd taken up bridge, and found new friends for golf and tennis, and she came into the city two, sometimes three days a week, to spend afternoons with Ellie and give me time to go to my appointments and my meetings. I thanked God for my dad, who still, sometimes, knew who I was when I brought Ellie to visit him every other week. "Proud of you," he would tell me, and I wasn't sure what he thought he was proud of me for. Did he know I'd been in rehab, or why? Did he remember anything about how I'd become an accidental writer? Did he know that I was married and a mom? Or, in his head, was I still eighteen, with my acceptance letter from Franklin & Marshall in my hand, telling him about my big plans for my future?

I thanked God for Janet, who drove to Center City once a week to have lunch with me. I'd regale her with funny stories from my AA and NA meetings. Janet especially liked to hear about Leonard, who'd begin his recitations by thanking God "for keeping me out of the titty bars for another day." "What happens if he goes back?" she'd asked, and I'd told her how shamefaced Leonard looked when he'd stood up and said, "Well, they got me again!" We'd split a dessert and talk about our kids, our parents, and whether sex addiction was really a thing. "I love you," she would say, her face solemn, and she'd hug me at the end of every visit. Once, she'd cried, telling me that she thought she should have noticed, should have seen that I was in trouble, should have done something. I told her it was my problem and my job to solve it. "Just be my friend," I said. "That's what I need most." I thanked God that L. McIntyre was, like Dave had insisted, just a friend. "Maybe it could have been something more," he'd told me over dinner after my third week home. "But what kind of jerk cheats on his wife while she's in rehab?"

Thank God for Dave, I thought . . . and, last, I would thank God for what was, blasphemous as it sounded, the best development of my new, sober life, a small black-and-white dog named Bingo.

We'd gotten her in September, my first month back from rehab. Ellie and I had driven from Philadelphia down to Baltimore through a gorgeous fall afternoon, the sky a brilliant blue, smelling of leaves and wood smoke and, faintly, of the coming cold. Our first stop had been Target, where we'd bought everything we would need—a leash and harness made of pink nylon, a compromise between the faux-leather and rhine-stone rig Ellie had fallen in love with and the plain red I preferred. We had plastic food and water dishes, a carrying crate, a ten-pound sack of dog food, a fluffy round brown-and-pink polka-dotted dog bed, a chewy toy, a squeaky toy, and the Cesar Millan video that Janet, who'd adopted three different rescue dogs, had recommended.

"Can the puppy sleep in my room?" asked Ellie.

"Fine with me," I said. Ellie had been asking for a dog ever since she'd read *Fancy Nancy and the Posh Puppy*. Of course, she'd lobbied for a teacup poodle, but had been surprisingly amenable when I'd explained that there were many dogs who needed homes, and it would be better to adopt one of them. Together, we'd spent a half hour each night online, reading about breeds, watching videos of pups, getting a season pass on TiVo for *Too Cute*. Ellie had been keeping the tantrums to a minimum, and doing her chores—making her bed and clearing her dishes and helping me make her lunches and load the dishwasher—without complaint.

"One eleven, one thirteen . . . here we go!" The house was a yellow cape, with a front yard dotted with little piles of dog poop. As we pulled into the driveway, the front door opened, and a teenage girl came out with a small white dog with black spots on a leash. The dog had a finely molded face, a whiskered snout, and a long tail that curled at its tip. One of her ears stood up straight; the other one flopped like a book page you'd turned down to mark your place.

"BINGO!" yelled Ellie, and she was out of the car almost before it had stopped rolling. She raced across the lawn, fell to her knees a few feet away from the dog, then, as instructed, held out her hand for it to sniff. The dog, who'd seemed alarmed by Ellie's charge, sniffed her hand, then wagged its tail, sat calmly, and allowed Ellie to pet it.

"She is so CUTE!" Ellie said to the girl, who looked amused at Ellie's antics. I walked over, shook her hand, and signed the papers while Ellie crooned at the puppy. She was a young adult dog, her Internet profile had said, somewhere between three and five years old. She had shown up pregnant at a shelter. They'd found her a foster family, where she'd given birth, and all five of the puppies were quickly adopted. "Now we just need to find a place for Mom," said the website, and that, of course, had made me want to drive straight to Baltimore and bring the sad-eyed little dog home. She was, according to the website, some kind of terrier mix, a solid fifteen pounds, spayed, friendly, good with kids, and with all of her shots.

"I wish we could tell you more about her," said the teenager, who had a brown ponytail and a metallic smile. "She was a good mom when the pups were here."

"I'm sure we'll figure it out," I'd said. On the application, which had struck me as astonishingly detailed, there'd been a question about whether I had ever been arrested or in jail. Nothing about rehab or addiction, but still, I wondered if I would have answered those questions honestly . . . and, if I had, whether they would have turned me down. It was crazy: Who needed a pet more than a sick person trying to get better? Who would take better care of a dog than someone trying to demonstrate to the world that she was, indeed, worthy of its trust again?

Ellie and I walked Bingo around the block, Bingo trotting briskly, Ellie clutching the leash with two hands. "Say goodbye," Ellie instructed the dog. Bingo was docile as I scooped her up and placed her in her crate, even as Ellie begged me to let the dog ride in her lap. She didn't make a sound the entire ride home. Once we were back in Philadelphia, we walked her around the neighborhood, letting her sniff the trees and hydrants. She ignored other dogs, hiding, trembling, behind my legs when they got close enough to try to sniff her. "She is SHY," said Ellie, who didn't seem to mind, as long as Bingo let her put the little tinsel collar she'd crafted around her neck, and hold the leash while they walked.

"Do you think we should try to find a better name for her?" I asked.

Ellie considered as we approached our front door. Finally, she shook her head. "I think she is a Bingo," she decided, and I told Ellie that I thought she was right.

At home, Bingo sniffed her dish full of kibble, had a few laps of water, then wormed underneath my bed, in spite of Ellie's importuning and threats to drag her out into the open. "Let's just leave her be." Ellie had gotten into her pajamas, and we read *Squids Will Be Squids* and *A Big Guy Took My Ball* before I kissed her good night and tucked her into her bed. As tempting as it was to let Ellie sleep with me every night, I'd heard enough lectures about boundaries to know that I needed to put them in place (plus, she hadn't had an accident in months, but I didn't want to take chances with my new mattress). She was my daughter, not my friend, or my comfort, or my confidante . . . and so, as much as I would have liked the feeling of another warm body in my bed, or the sweet smile she wore when she woke up (in the handful of seconds before remembering that the world and most of the people in it displeased her), I made sure she at least began each night in her own room.

So it was just me in the bedroom when Bingo inched her way out from underneath the bed and peered up at me. Her tail drooped. Her expression seemed despondent. I wondered if she missed her pups, or if she even remembered she'd had them—I knew so little about dogs!

"What is it?" I asked, putting down *A Woman's Guide to the Twelve Steps*.

Silence.

"Do you want to go out?" I guessed.

Nothing. I took her downstairs, clipped her to her leash, walked her down the steps, and stood at the edge of the sidewalk while she did her business. Upstairs, instead of going back underneath the bed, she stood at the edge and looked at me.

"Oh, okay," I said, and patted the mattress. Before the second word was out of my mouth, Bingo had hopped nimbly onto the bed and was settling down against me, folding herself into the space behind my bent knees as I lay curled up on my side.

"You're going to sleep there?" No answer. I pulled the comforter up over both of us and closed my eyes. *Thank you, God, for Bingo. Thank you for Ellie. Thank you for such beautiful weather. Thank you for helping me not take pills today.* It wasn't much of a prayer, but it was the best I could do.

Each year since we'd moved to Haverford, I'd hosted a Chanukah Happening (on the invitations,

I'd spell it Chappening). Dozens of kids, parents, colleagues, and relatives and friends would fill our house, some bearing gifts for Ellie, or boxes of chocolates, or, more likely, bottles of wine. I would serve roast chickens, a giant green salad, and a table full of desserts the guests had brought. In the living room, kids would spin dreidels, and guests would be participating in the latke cook-off in the kitchen. We'd have straight potato pan-cakes, sweet-potato latkes, latkes with zucchini and shreds of carrots, latkes made with flour or potato starch or, once, tapioca. Barry would contribute *sufganiyot,* the sweet filled doughnuts that were also traditional Chanukah fare, and, for weeks, the kitchen would smell like a deep fryer and my hair and skin would feel lightly coated with grease.

There would be beer and wine at those parties . . . and, as the crowd got bigger and the preparations more elaborate, I'd taken more and more pills to get myself through it, to deal with the tension of whether Dave was helping me or even talking to me, pills to cope with my mom, who would show up with an eight-pound brisket and demand the use of an oven.

This year, my Chanukah Happening was limited to four people: me and Ellie, Dave and my mom. And Bingo, of course, who sat on the floor, eyes bright, tail wagging, watching the proceedings avidly, hoping that someone would drop something. Dave, I noticed, would discreetly slip her scraps, which meant that Bingo followed him around like a balloon that had been tethered to his ankle.

"Good girl," he'd say, sneaking Bingo a bit of chicken skin, then tipping his chair back and sighing. I had radically reduced the guest list, but I'd kept the menu the same: roast chicken stuffed with herbs and lemon and garlic, a salad dressed with pomegranate-seed vinaigrette, potato latkes, and a store-bought dessert—cream puffs from Whole Foods and chocolate sauce that Ellie and I had made together.

"She has a JAUNTY WALK," said Ellie, imitating Bingo's brisk stride down the street. "And at night she sleeps CURLED IN A CRULLER in Mommy's bed."

"I bet Mom likes that," he said. His eyes didn't meet mine. *I would like you better,* I thought at him.

"Hey, El, let's show Daddy how we clear the table."

"Daddy knows that I can do that." She pouted, but she got up and carefully, using two hands, carried every plate and platter from the table to the sink.

We played Sorry! after dinner—oh, irony! I tried to breathe through my discomfort, the restlessness, tried to sit with my feelings, like Bernice advised, and ignore the questions running laps in my brain. *Will he stay? Or at least come and kiss me? Does he love me a little? Is there anything left at all?*

Dave stayed as I coaxed Ellie into, then out of, her tub, combing and braiding her hair, getting her into her pajamas and reading her *This Is Not My Hat.* After I closed her bedroom door, Bingo bounded down the hallway to assume her position, curled on top of my pillow. Her tail thumped against the comforter as she watched us with her bright brown eyes.

"B-I-N-G-O," Dave sang. We were in the narrow hallway, practically touching. "You seem well." He reached out, took a strand of my hair between his fingers, and tucked it, tenderly, behind my ear. Then his body was right up against mine, his chest warm and firm, shoulders solid in my hands. "I know they said no changes for the first year, but we've both done this a bunch of times already . . ."

I laughed, walking backward, as he maneuvered me onto the bed . . . and, later, I cried when, with my head on his chest and our bare legs entwined, he got choked up as he said, "Allison, there was never anybody else. It was always only you."

"I promise . . ." I started to say. I wanted to promise him that I'd never hurt him again, never go off the rails, never give him cause to worry again . . . but those were promises I couldn't make. One minute, one hour, one day at a time.

"I never stopped loving you," I said . . . and that was the absolute truth.

We didn't move back in together. Part of me wanted it desperately, and part of me worried that we were disrupting Ellie's stable environment— some mornings Dave was in bed with me, some mornings he was at his own place, and some nights Ellie stayed there with him—but she seemed to be thriving, to be growing out of the awful yelling and stubbornness.

As for Dave and me, I often thought that we were, as coaches and sportswriters liked to say, in a rebuilding year. Not married, exactly, but not un-married. It was almost as though we were courting each other again, slowly revealing our-selves to each other. My mom or our sitter, Katrina, would come for the night, and we'd go to a concert, or out to dinner, or we'd take Bingo to the dog park where, on warm spring nights, they showed old movies, projecting the picture against a bedsheet strung between two pine trees.

"Ellie's getting big," Dave said on one of those nights. I'd been looking at the picnics other people had packed: fried chicken and biscuits and canned peaches; egg-salad sandwiches on thick-sliced whole-wheat bread; chunks of pineapple and strawberries in a fruit salad . . . and wine. Beer. Sweating thermoses of cocktails, lemon drops and Pimm's cups.

"She is," I had agreed. Every day she looked a

little taller, her hair longer, or she'd bust out some new bit of vocabulary or surprisingly apt observation about the world. Sometimes at night she'd cry that her legs hurt. *Growing pains,* Dr. McCarthy had told us.

Sometimes I felt like I was having them, too. It made me think of something else I'd heard in a meeting, about how Alcoholics Anonymous can help people with their feelings. "And it's true," the speaker had said. He had a jovial grin underneath his walrus mustache. "I feel anger better, I feel sadness better, I feel disappointment better . . ."

Life on life's terms. It was an absolute bitch. There was no more tuning out or glossing over, no more using opiates as spackle to fill in the cracks and broken bits. It was all there, raw and unlovely: the little sighs and groans Dave made, seemingly without hearing them, when he ate his cereal or made the bed; the way Ellie had to be reminded, sometimes more than twice, to flush the toilet after she used it; the glistening ovals of mucus that lined the city sidewalk. Some nights, I missed my father and regretted my mother's half-assed, mostly absent-minded parenting, and there was no pill to help with it. Some nights I couldn't sleep . . . so I would lie in my bed, alone or with Dave, and stare up into the darkness and try not to beat myself up. *We will not regret the past, nor wish to shut the door on it,* The Big Book said . . . so I would try to be grateful that I'd stopped

481

when I had instead of berating myself for letting things get as bad as they'd gotten. I had learned what I'd needed to learn, and I knew now that I was, however flawed and imperfect, however broken, undeniably a grown-up.

Then, one day, my cell phone rang, and I heard a familiar voice on the other end.

"It's a blast from your past!" said the voice, before dissolving into sniffles.

"Aubrey!" I hadn't heard from her since she'd left Meadowcrest. Mary and I e-mailed, and Shannon and I met for coffee once a month. Lena and Marissa had both disappeared, whether back into addiction or into new lives in recovery, I couldn't guess. I worried about them sometimes, but Aubrey was the one I worried about most. I'd text or call her every so often, but I had never heard back. A dozen times I'd started to type her name into Google, and a dozen times I'd made myself stop. *If she wants me to know how she's doing, she'll get in touch. Otherwise it's snooping,* I decided. Now, here she was, her voice quivering, and me clutching the phone, realizing only in that moment that I'd half believed she was dead.

"How are you?"

"I'm . . ." She gave her familiar little laugh. "I'm not so good, actually."

By now, I knew what questions to ask. Better

still, I knew how to just be quiet and listen. "What's going on?"

"I've been using for . . . oh, God, months now. I was doing good at first. Then Justin started coming around his mom's house, where I was staying with Cody . . ."

I turned away so that Ellie, engrossed in an episode of *Sam & Cat*, wouldn't see my face. Justin. The fucking no-good boyfriend.

"And, you know, he made it sound like it was going to be all different this time. Like we'd keep it under control. And I thought I could, you know, because I'd been clean for a while." She started to cry. I got the rest of the story in disjointed bursts—she'd gotten kicked out of her boyfriend's parents' house, then her mother had taken Cody and refused to let Aubrey see him until she got clean. She described couch-surfing, spending two weeks in a shelter, and then, finally, asked the question I knew was coming: "Can I crash with you for a little while?" Her voice was tiny, barely a whisper. "I could help out . . . babysit . . . I'm good with kids . . . I wouldn't ask, except I don't have anywhere else to go."

Oh, Aubrey, I thought. Aubrey, who was still more or less a kid herself. *Boundaries,* I told myself, even though I wanted nothing more than to tell her to come, to tell her that the trundle bed had fresh sheets, that Ellie would be delighted to meet her, that I would help her get well. Except I couldn't. I knew my own limits, knew how close I was to my own relapse. "I can't do that," I said. "But I can take you to a meeting. I can hook you up with Bernice. I can help you find a place to stay."

"You sound good," she said. Was she high? I couldn't tell. "I'm glad. I knew you'd do good when you got out of there."

"Aubrey, listen to me. There's a five-thirty meeting today at Fourth and Pine. That's my home group. They're really nice. They'd love to meet you. You come there, and I will meet you, and I'm going to call Bernice, and we'll find you a place."

"Ooo-kay." Definitely slurry.

"Five-thirty. Fourth and Pine." I made her say it back to me twice. Then I hung up the phone, and texted her the address, just to be sure, and started pacing, watching the door, waiting for my mother to show up for her regular Tuesday visit. Normally she was there at five at the latest, and I'd have time to grab a coffee if I wanted one before the meeting began, but that night, of course, she was running late.

"Mommy, stop WALKING," said Ellie . . . and then, in an unprecedented move, she actually turned the TV off without being asked or prompted, and looked at me. "What are you so WORRYING about?"

"I'm not worrying," I said automatically.

"Then why are you WALKING and WALK-ING?" She looked at me carefully, eyes narrowed, hair gathered in a ponytail that hung halfway down her back, pants displaying a good inch of her ankles. I'd need to go shopping again.

"I guess maybe I am a little worried." I sat down by the window, and Bingo sprang into my lap, wriggling around until her belly was exposed for a scratch. When Ronnie finally strolled into view I grabbed my bag and half trotted past Ellie.

"There's someone—a girl I knew from rehab . . ." I looked at the clock on the cable box. "I'll explain when I'm back, but I've got to go . . ."

I hurried around the corner, my keys in my hand, my purse over my shoulder, a dollar in my pocket for when they passed the basket around, my phone tucked into my bra, set on vibrate, so I'd feel it if Aubrey texted back. It was a gorgeous late afternoon, the clear, sunny sky and brilliant leaves all promising new beginnings, fresh starts. A young woman carrying a paper parasol walked with her Boston terrier on a red leash. An older couple on bicycles passed me. I watched them riding away and thought about all the normal people in the world, just going around, doing their business, living their lives, buying food and cooking meals, watching TV shows and movies, fighting and falling in love, without even the thought of a drink or a drug to make the good times even better and the bad times less awful.

Don't be like me, my mother had told me, when I'd gotten out. *Don't waste your life hiding.* But still, even with so many of the rewards of sobriety making themselves known, it was hard not to crave oblivion and numbness, a pill that could keep my feelings safely at bay. Sometimes, I wondered how I'd gotten started with the drugs . . . and sometimes I wondered why everyone in the world wasn't taking them, and how I'd found the strength, somehow, to resist, even just for that day.

There was a coffee shop around the corner from where the AA meetings were held. I stuck my head in, looking for Aubrey, recognizing people at a few of the tables: the fiftyish man in a plaid shirt and glasses who'd talked about dealing with both addiction and mental illness; the woman with a buzz cut and black army boots who'd described passing out in the SEPTA station and lying on the concrete, watching rats running up and down the tracks until the cops bundled her into a cruiser; the man who dressed like a cowboy and kept his long gray hair in a ponytail tied with a rawhide loop and talked endlessly about his girlfriend who'd redecorated while he'd been in rehab, and the contractor who had unscrewed the chandelier from his dining room and stolen it, and how he was going to get that chandelier back. Sometimes I went to meetings willingly, knowing that they helped, and some nights the only thing keeping me from staying home on the couch was the promise of a chandelier update or the latest installment in the long-running saga of Leonard vs. the Titty Bars.

"What can I get for you?" asked the barista, a man who couldn't have been older than twenty-five, with thick black eyebrows and an easy smile.

I ordered an iced mocha and checked my phone again. When they called my name, I wrapped a brown paper napkin around the plastic cup. It was five-twenty. I walked around the corner to the church. In the basement with scuffed white walls and hardwood floors, fifty chairs were set up, with a group of people settling into the front rows. Once, early on, I'd made the mistake of trying to sit in the back, and the others from Bernice's group had almost collapsed laughing. *Denial Aisle! Relapse Row!* they'd shouted, as Sheila had ushered me front and center.

No Aubrey yet, but I could see Johnette and Martin, and both Brians from my group. Gregory was there, fussing with the crease of his jeans, and Alice sat next to him, with a tote bag full of knitting in her lap. "We saved you a seat," said Sheila, and tapped the empty metal chair that stood in the center of the front row. I held my cup, feeling the cool of it against my palm, and I took my place among them.

Acknowledgments

I am grateful to have the support of the hands-down absolute best agent and editor in the business. Joanna Pulcini and Greer Hendricks have held my hand, helped me up, offered praise and constructive criticism, and have always been willing to listen and to read yet another draft. I'm the luckiest writer in the world to have these two women as colleagues and friends.

Judith Curr, publisher of Atria Books, and Carolyn Reidy, CEO and president of Simon & Schuster, are powerhouses and role models, and I'm lucky to work with them, as well as the team at Atria: Lisa Sciambra, Ben Lee, Lisa Keim, Hillary Tisman, Elisa Shokoff, LeeAnna Woodcock, and Kitt Reckord.

Anna Dorfman and Jeanne Lee keep my books looking good. Copyeditor extraordinaire Nancy Inglis saves me from myself at least once per page and forgives me all my sins, which include regularly confusing "like" and "as" and still not knowing when you spell out numbers versus when you just type the digits.

At Simon & Schuster UK, I'm grateful for the support of Suzanne Baboneau, Ian Chapman, and Jo Dickinson.

Nobody in the PR world does it better than

Marcy Engelman, and I am so glad to have her in my corner, along with Emily Gambir and Bernice Marzan. Jessica Bartolo and her team at Greater Talent Network make my speaking engagements delightful.

Special thanks to Greer's assistant, Sarah Cantin, and Joanna's assistant Josephine Hill for their patience, enthusiasm, and attention to detail.

Thanks and love to the home team—my fantastic assistant Meghan Burnett, whose unflappable calm and unfailing good humor make my work life a joy. Terri Gottlieb cares for my girls, runs the kitchen, tends to the garden, and lets me head off to work with confidence that my daughters will be happy and my house will be standing when I return. Adam Bonin's love and support goes above and beyond—he is a wonderful father and a great friend. Susan Abrams is the best BFF anyone could ever hope for. Lucy and Phoebe—you are my heart's delight, and every day I am proud to be your mother.

Bill—you are my happy ending.

Finally, to everyone who visits my Facebook page, comes to one of my readings, indulges my tweets about *The Bachelor*, and waits patiently for my next book, my deepest thanks. None of this would be possible without you.

About the Author

JENNIFER WEINER is the author of eleven books, including *Good in Bed*, *In Her Shoes*, which was made into a major motion picture, and *The Next Best Thing*. She lives with her family in Philadelphia. To learn more, visit her website at www.jennifer weiner.com.

Authors.SimonandSchuster.com/Jennifer-Weiner
JenniferWeiner.com
Facebook.com/JenniferWeiner

Permissions Acknowledgments